Succession

Volume three
The Sandstone Trilogy

Succession

Michael Beashel

ISBN: 978 0 6480569 28
ISBN *Unbound Justice*: 978 0 6480569 04
ISBN *Unshackled*: 978 0 6480569 11

Typeset by Midland Typesetters, Maryborough VIC Australia

Printed and distributed by Ingram Spark
Lightning Source Australia Pty Ltd,
Unit A1/A3 7 Janine Street,
Scoresby VIC 3179
Australia

Cover by Mark Thacker, Big Cat Design

The Sandstone Trilogy

Three novels, *Unbound Justice*, *Unshackled* and *Succession*, span 37 years of Sydney life in the second half of the nineteenth century. They follow the fortunes of John Leary, who in 1850 leaves his rural home in Ireland and sails as an assisted immigrant to New South Wales.

His trade is carpentry but his ambition is boundless. By hard work, talent and opportunism he manages to create his own construction company, never ceasing the struggle to become the biggest and the best. The building industry becomes a metaphor for his chosen city, with its mixture of squalor and grandeur, of corruption and high ideals.

The Sandstone Trilogy is a historical drama with a rich cast of compelling characters. It is also a family saga, in which love, revenge and tragedy all come to influence the Learys' destiny.

'An engrossing saga of class, commerce and dynastic struggle. Michael Beashel displays a thorough craftsmanship born of his own life on construction sites, and one perfectly suited to portraying the dog-eat-dog bullishness of one of Sydney's most remarkable eras.'

Alasdair McGregor, author of *A forger's progress: The life of Francis Greenway* and *Grand Obsessions: The life and work of Walter Burley Griffin and Marion Mahony Griffin.*

Principal Characters

The Leary Family
John Leary
Catherine Leary (née Ryan), his wife
Richard Leary, John's son by his deceased first wife, Clarissa
Brendan Leary, John's son by Catherine
Mary Leary, John's daughter by Catherine
Agatha Leary, John's daughter by Catherine
Gerry Gleeson, John's uncle

The McGuire Family
Christine McGuire, John's mother-in-law

The Bucknell Family
Bill Bucknell, John Leary's business competitor
Constance Bucknell, his wife

The Connaire Family
Sean Connaire
Veronica (Vonnie), his wife
Anne, their youngest daughter

The Carson Family
May, wife of Bert Carson
Julie Carson, her daughter
Billy Carson, her son

Leary's Employees
Ross Gibbs, coachman
Rob Jenkins, sub-foreman
Mrs Mansfield, John Leary's secretary
Tom Prentice, chief estimator
David Sullivan, general foreman

Leary's Competitors
Bucknells
Branagan and Sons
Dennings

Architect
William Turner of Turner and Harrington

St Peters Brick Company
Brian Murphy, manager

Workers' Advocate
Rory O'Connor

Chapter One

At seven-thirty on a summer evening in 1885, John Leary entered his study, closed the doors behind him and adjusted the gaslight. Opening his briefcase, he withdrew some documents and a sealed envelope. He placed the documents in front of him but put the envelope to the far right of his desk, away from the other papers, as if it would infect them.

He drew open the curtains, warm from the February sun, and looked across Blackburn Cove. Even after twenty-nine years of living here, the view still impressed him. As did the fact that this house on Wolseley Road, Point Piper, was now valuable. And so was his time, therefore he allocated this part of the day, before dinner, to complete any unfinished business. Today, like any Monday, had been busy.

Sitting down, he addressed the top document, which listed his worth. He noticed that his accountant had not included John's recent purchase of an extra thousand shares of the wool brokers, Goldsborough Mort. Picking up his pen, he made a note in the margin and placed the document next to the envelope. The words on the outside—'Confidential Investigation'—glared at him. He looked at the study doors as if sensing someone was about to walk in, then pushed the envelope out of sight beside his desk lamp.

Forcing himself to forget the envelope, he leafed through the rest of his papers. *Damn.* He'd left his plans for the alterations of his company's Annandale premises at his office; the envelope had distracted him when he'd been packing his briefcase to leave. He would have liked to work on those plans now, keen to use his drafting skills. He'd have to make a trip to Annandale in the morning. He picked up the next report, the latest inventory from his plant yard. Soon he was immersed in analysing the need to sell, buy or lease his construction equipment.

The study doors opened.

'Dinner is ready, dear.' Catherine Leary came in and stood beside the desk. His wife was always elegant, even at the end of the day. She was tall and lithe with intelligent eyes, a long fine nose and a generous mouth. Her light blonde hair, streaked with grey, was pinned in a fashionable bun. 'You look worried.'

John forced a smile. Catherine was a good wife but she could not help him solve the issue within the envelope. 'Just tired.'

'Well, you're not the young gun you once were.' John was about to react when she smiled. 'You must think again about delegating some of your responsibility.'

He smiled with her. 'I will Catherine, I will.' He collected his papers and the envelope and placed them back in his briefcase. Tomorrow the contents of that envelope would be faced—tomorrow.

He accompanied Catherine across the foyer and into the dining room. At the table, his two daughters were seated side by side, facing his two sons. Taking his place at the head of the table, John placed his napkin on his lap and took a sip of iced water from a Waterford glass. Catherine sat opposite him. The room was pleasant: the steam-driven overhead fans, set just below the twelve-foot high ceilings, tempered the evening's humidity.

'What's got you in such a good mood, Richard?' Agatha said to her half-brother. 'Won a packet at Randwick?'

'I wish,' he replied. 'No, I've just employed a cook-cum-servant. I wouldn't survive till next year if I had to live on what I call meals. Though I doubt I'd be missed.'

Agatha grinned. 'You would be missed, especially by some women.'

Richard grinned back at her.

Yes, a few women would miss him, John thought. Richard was of average height but solidly built and his wavy, dark-blond hair, inherited from his deceased mother, Clarissa, attracted the girls.

Agatha, his youngest child, a tall twenty-year-old with fair skin acceptably freckled, a well-developed figure and straight brunette hair, was someone who gave as good as she got. Richard seemed to always enjoy their banter.

John smiled at Catherine. 'Where are Christine and Uncle Gerry?'

'They're resting,' Catherine said. 'They're both a bit unwell.'

As they were in their mid-seventies, John didn't doubt that. 'We will say grace.' He glanced at Richard as they recited the words. His son, who would turn thirty this December, was not pious and didn't believe the words he mouthed. He attended Mass, but John surmised that he did so only to keep his father happy or for business contacts.

John and Catherine were devout Catholics, as was their son, Brendan. However, their eldest daughter, Mary, sitting beside Agatha, unfortunately seemed to share Richard's lack of interest in religion. She was tall and slim like her mother, and was deliberate and matter-of-fact in manner. Her straight, dark-blond hair and clear skin set off big, ocean-blue eyes that, like Catherine's, looked straight at you.

When grace was finished, Mary asked Richard if he enjoyed living in Glebe.

Richard smiled at his stepsister. 'It's all right.' He popped a piece of lamb into his mouth. 'Mmm, very tender. I do miss home cooking.'

'I'd like to think there were more attractions at Point Piper than Cook's food,' Catherine said.

'There are,' Richard said, 'and one that I miss is you.'

Catherine paused with her cutlery and smiled at him. 'That's a lovely thing to say.'

'I mean it,' Richard said.

'That is very thoughtful of you, Richard,' John said, 'and you'll be welcomed back any time!'

'Thank you, Father.'

It had been June of 1859 when Catherine had come into Richard's life, and the then three-year-old boy had latched onto her like a sling on a crane hook. Stella, Richard's nanny, had been the former maid to John's first wife, Clarissa, and she had been very close to the boy. Catherine had been adept in respecting Richard's relationship with Stella, and instinctive in not provoking rivalries. When Richard was ten years old, Stella had left the Learys to look after her sick parents and over the years they had kept in correspondence. John smiled at Catherine. In every way but one, she had been a mother to his boy.

John said to her, 'We both have you to thank, my dear, for taking us on in the early days.'

'And I was glad to do it,' Catherine said. 'Now, more roast, anyone?'

As his family helped themselves to more of the meal, John thought about his past. Catherine had been twenty when he'd first seen her at a ball. Despite his numbness over his wife's death nearly two years previously, he had wanted to know the young milliner further. He was attracted by the similarity in their looks and the fact that both Clarissa and Catherine liked business. The way Catherine had eased herself into Richard's life and his liking of her also made John feel closer to her. Catherine knew many of his circle of business friends and enjoyed conversing with them. Indeed, her deceased father had been a wool broker and had known John's father-in-law, the now departed David McGuire.

'I'll see Uncle after dinner,' Brendan said, 'and find out how he is.'

'That's nice, dear,' Catherine smiled. 'Ask him if he needs anything, or if there's anything we can do.'

'I shall.'

John wasn't surprised that Brendan would check on his great-uncle. There had been a special connection between the two of them ever since Brendan was born. At nearly twenty-three, he was a sensitive lad. This was an odd trait for someone in the building game but, according to site gossip, his tall and slim son was more than adept in the sweat-raising and gut-breaking world of construction.

'Will we use the new carriage for the ball this Saturday, dear?' Catherine said. 'I'd like to, and it's more secure.'

'Of course, the Brougham's locks are impressive. Can't have your cloak stolen like it was from the old carriage.'

After the meal, Catherine and Agatha and Mary excused themselves and left the table. Brendan followed suit. Richard stood up and was about to leave when John spoke to him.

'I'll see you at the office in the morning, with your grandmother. There's something we have to talk about.'

'Till tomorrow then,' Richard replied.

Next morning, Ross Gibbs, John's driver, a tall, broad-shouldered, uniformed man, had the regular carriage outside, waiting for him.

It was six o'clock and John was leaving the house before anyone else was up. 'Pleasant start to the day, Gibbs.'

'It is, sir,' Gibbs replied as he opened the carriage door. 'George Street?'

'No, Annandale, thank you.'

John stepped in, glad that he had a fine, comfortable carriage to take his six-foot-three-inch frame.

Pushing aside a copy of the *Sydney Morning Herald*, with its somewhat overpowering ink smell, he went to open his briefcase and paused. No, he couldn't solve that problem while on the move. For once, he indulged himself and settled back to look out the window.

New South Head Road linked the town to the expanding eastern suburbs and it gave a good view of the harbour, whose waterway was a natural transport corridor. John could see laden ships coming into the harbour while other ships, full of wheat from the colony's harvest or wool from its fat merinos, were heading out on their way back to England. John's business was not in land but in building—building the stores to pack the wool, warehouses to stock the imports, houses to shelter the growing population, banks to hold the money and churches for his clients to seek absolution. And building had brought him wealth, particularly now, five years into a construction boom that had followed a sharp recession. It was ... yes, thirty-five years, my God, since he'd come to the colony as a twenty-year-old Irish carpenter and now his company, Leary's Contracting, was one of the biggest contractors in town.

John was conscious, however, that the baton needed passing and Richard must be ready for that day. But not yet! The prospect of having nothing to do but sit in the sun and get fat only made him cranky. Bloody hell, no—not yet!

His sons worked for the company and were coming on. Educated at Sydney Grammar School, the young men could have had professional careers—Brendan in the arts and Richard in engineering—but they both knew their future lay within Leary's Contracting and had done their apprenticeships in carpentry and joinery. How would they cope in tough times? Richard could handle it. Richard was his own person and he could make Leary's even bigger. Brendan was different. He had his own ideas and a stubborn streak as thick as a hawser.

John picked up the newspaper and started reading. An article on refrigerating meat for export absorbed him. When he next looked out, the carriage was heading down Johnston Street in Annandale, where the lamp posts still shone with dew. Many people had asked him why he'd chosen Annandale for his company's main facilities. When he'd bought the buildings cheaply many years ago, they had been a distance from town but now they were close to most of his sites, which was an advantage.

He looked at his watch after he alighted. Seven o'clock on the dot. Good.

'Be ready at eight-thirty to take me to town,' he said to Gibbs.

'Yes, sir.'

John went into the building and up to his office. Sitting at his desk he found his jottings on the alterations that he'd wanted the night before, and removed a scale rule from his briefcase, together with his other papers. The whinny of a horse distracted him and he swivelled his chair and looked out. A milk cart was making the last of its deliveries, its Drysdales snorting steam, their heads high as they clopped along enjoying their lighter load. The pattern was unchanged each day: the milko got his product, calculated the quantities, set his price and delivered the goods, just as it should be. The milko was in control.

John wasn't. Clarissa's mother, Christine McGuire, who now lived with them, owned just over half of his company and every day for the past twenty-eight years he'd had to endure the situation. He scratched a faded scar over his left eye and grinned wickedly. Maybe Christine wouldn't wake tomorrow and his son Richard would inherit her shares. He glanced at his wall clock. The milko was late.

John turned in his chair and looked at his jottings of Leary's current facilities. The building at Annandale housed offices on the first floor for himself, Richard, the foremen and a meeting room. The ground floor comprised space for estimating, administration, purchasing, stores and a kitchen. A yard adjoined this for machinery, construction plant and spare materials for repairs to hoists and cranes. Annandale was adequate for now but he was planning for bigger things. He started sketching up ideas for renovations and additions, then, with ruler and set square, drafted the plans, his palm sticking to the paper in the humidity.

At eight twenty-five he slipped back into his suit jacket, grabbed his papers and popped them into his briefcase. Opening his wall cupboard he looked in the mirror to check his eyes—not bad, just a little bloodshot around their blue irises. He quickly went downstairs and outside to where Gibbs was waiting and stepped into his carriage.

'George Street now, sir?' Gibbs asked.

'Yes, please.' John popped a sweet into his mouth to take away the taste of tobacco and looked out of the carriage. Hmm, Johnston Street was becoming a fashionable area; he should get his property valued. Seventeen years ago, when he'd set up shop here, there wasn't a house within half a mile in any direction. Now there were mansions being built along the street.

The carriage turned into Parramatta Road, his broad shoulder pressing against its frame as it did so. Riffling in his briefcase he removed the document he needed—tenders. He relished bidding for work. Smiling, he scratched his cropped grey hair. He passed the Sydney University buildings and concentrated on his work.

The roof hatch opened. 'Sir, abattoirs coming up.'

John pulled up the window just before the stench entered the carriage and continued to read his report. When the roof hatch was reopened, the blood stink from Ultimo was fading, only to be replaced with the smell of smoke from Sydney's Central Station. He slipped the window down as his carriage entered the 'bullock trail' of George Street. There was a shout and two men ran past his window. The carriage soldiered on through potholes and dust, past public houses, small shops, forges and stores. As it pulled past Hay Street he sensed a change in the hum of carts, trams and people. Individual shouts, random at first, had become a roar. Odd.

'Gibbs?'

'It's weird, sir. Like some sort of riot.'

John stuck his head out as Gibbs lashed the horses up Brick-field Hill to Liverpool Street. A newspaper flyer caught his eye: 'GORDON MURDERED.'

Three men were running from shop to shop, yelling, 'Avenge the general! Kill the heathen!' More men joined them, chanting the mantra, and they formed a small crowd. Some banged on his carriage, but John kept calm. Their anger was not directed at him but at the war in the Sudan, in which the head of the British forces, General Gordon, had obviously just been killed.

Lumbering drunks rose from their lethargy to cheer on the madness. Curious tenants leaned out of their small upper-floor windows. Police stood by, watching the crowd, reluctant to do anything. John ignored them all and viewed the buildings. Every shop awning and veranda south of the Town Hall challenged his sense of symmetry and order. They were constructed to little plan and no line, at all angles and displaying every style of feature, a jumble of rambling, disjointed forms. He never got used to it.

Sitting back, he thought about the new hotel. Just a whisper here and comment there but it was rumoured that it would be the biggest in Sydney. It fuelled his thoughts and he was determined he would win the tender. He'd build it and by doing so would consolidate his company's name. He had to. There were some up-and-coming builders snapping at his heels, second stringers no doubt, but threatening the top three contractors in Sydney, of which Leary's was one. These upstarts undercut his costs and were marking their turf aggressively. If he didn't win the big pub, he'd be pushed aside. He couldn't have that.

Stopping at Leary's George Street offices, he alighted just as the crowd, now two hundred strong, rumbled up Market Street to Hyde Park, their noise challenging the sound of the nine chimes of the Post Office clock. Tucking his briefcase under his arm, he entered his building. Simmonds, his orders clerk, stood at the bottom of the stairs and John nodded to him as he went into the meeting room where he would confront the thief who'd stolen his money.

Christine McGuire, was already there: he could smell her familiar perfume. Five years earlier, at the age of seventy, she had asked John if she could live with his family and he had agreed. Her original house, three doors down from his in Wolseley Road, which he had built, was leased out.

When he entered the meeting room and greeted her she was seated, reading papers. When they had Leary's shareholder meetings, she always insisted on coming in to the George Street office. She and John were joint major owners and Richard held just nine per cent of the shares. Richard was also Construction Manager and controlled Leary's nine sites with a tight pair of reins. John was used to feeling that his son had the goods: he exercised random supervision of work, called his foremen to account and pestered clients for their payments. Leary's workers respected Richard and did what he told them to do. That was the way to run a company, lean and hard. But when Richard arrived for today's meeting, John needed to tackle him about something very important and extremely disturbing.

A tram turned from George into King Street and the screech of its wheels blended with John's polite question to Christine. 'Are you feeling better?'

Christine looked at him, her blue eyes still sharp. 'Thank you John, I am. My doctor has given me the all-clear from my congestion. Heavens, listen to what's happening on the streets! General Gordon is a great loss. Disgraceful affair'.

'Indeed,' he said. 'Let's hope Britain can send in more troops.'

She was a tough lady, and she never made it easy for John to get his own way in his own company. He looked from Christine to the meeting papers in front of him: business first, or would he wait for Richard and tackle his problematical son the moment he walked in? John removed his glasses from their case and started to clean them. There was no breeze coming through the window; you could almost see the February moisture in the room. He looked up as Richard strode in.

'Good morning, Father, Grandmother.' Richard closed the door, sat down and poured himself a glass of water from the decanter on the table.

Christine smiled and John nodded to him.

Time to face it. John touched the sealed envelope beside him, the one he dreaded. The one that held the truth about Richard's latest activities. 'I bring this meeting to order.'

There was a knock on the door.

'Come in,' John said irritably.

Brendan entered, took the chair next to the open window and wiped his face with a handkerchief.

'Brendan,' John said, 'this is a private shareholders' meeting.'

'Well, I'm here about something that's not private at all. There's plenty of talk in the company and it needs to be addressed. I want to know what you're going to do about the money that's just been stolen from Leary's Contracting.'

John had been dreading this confrontation ever since he'd received the crucial envelope the day before. In a way it was a relief that Brendan was opening the subject first. 'Very well, let's talk about it now. We can get it over with before the meeting.'

Christine McGuire's brows knitted. 'What's this about stolen money?'

Richard said boldly, 'I don't see what the fuss is about. So I helped myself to a few pounds. This is a family company! I don't call that theft.'

'Oh yes it is,' John said. 'Embezzlement is theft, whoever commits it. Richard, this is serious. You're marked as a thief before the people who work for you and the people we deal with, and that's something that will stick.'

Richard glanced at Brendan. 'How come the whole of Leary's knows about this? Have you been telling tales?'

'No need,' Brendan said calmly. 'You boasted to a friend the other day that you settled a gambling debt with Leary's money, and you were overheard.'

'The word got to me,' John put in, 'and I had our accountant check your processing of client payments.' He fixed his bitter gaze on Richard. 'He told me yesterday that you've filched eighty pounds by fiddling the books. How do you think that makes me feel? The evidence is in this envelope'—he tapped it with his finger—'and I haven't yet had the stomach to open it.'

Richard shrugged. 'Eighty pounds? It's hardly a fortune.'

Brendan said in the same quiet tone, 'It would keep a carpenter in wages for six months.'

Richard shook his head and gave Brendan a superior grin.

'This is not amusing!' John picked up the envelope, ripped it open and pulled out a sheet of paper. 'Here,' he said, and thrust it at Richard.

Richard took the page and read it.

'It gives evidence that you're a thief!' John's anger boiled. 'What have you got to say?'

Brendan leaned forward and said, 'Richard, why don't you just face up to what you've done and explain?'

Richard ruffled Brendan's curly hair. 'What do you say is the right thing to do, half-brother? Pay it back?'

Brendan looked him in the eye. 'Of course! And stop your gambling.'

Christine intervened. 'I'm shocked, Richard! I really am. I know you like the cards, and that's your affair. But if you can't fund your own gambling, don't do it! As for taking money from the company … why not ask your father for a loan? Gambling, and stealing to pay your debts—it's monstrous.'

Richard smiled again. 'Gambling's not a crime, Grandmother. It's a pastime.'

'But theft is a crime and we expect you to pay for it,' she said pointing a finger at him. 'We'll garnishee your salary. But only this once. Don't ever try it again.'

Upset at having to scold her grandson, Christine suddenly turned her attention to the younger, Brendan. She wrinkled her nose. 'What are you wearing, Brendan? Why have you come here in workman's clothes?'

'I came straight from the site, Grandmother.'

John said, 'Does Henderson know you're here?' Unlike Richard, Brendan was still working his way up at Leary's, and he was currently sub-foreman on an Annandale site under foreman Peter Henderson.

'He does, and I've arranged to work Saturday afternoon to make up the hours.'

'Time you got back there,' John said.

Christine said, 'Was it necessary to come here like this, Brendan?'

Brendan stood up. 'Eighty pounds is a hell of a lot of money to be taken from the company.'

'It's not your money,' Christine said.

'No, it's Leary's,' Brendan replied, 'and unless Richard is stopped, I'm telling you, he'll keep on abusing your trust.'

John had to end this. 'Richard, I want your promise it won't happen again.'

Richard turned and sighed. 'Why?'

John's blood raced. 'Don't come that line with me, son. You may be thirty—'

'In December, Father.'

'But no one takes that tone with me. You hear me?'

Richard looked at him. 'I hear you, Father.'

'You will now swear this was the first and last time, Richard. All right?'

Richard held his hands up. 'All right Father. All right.'

'Good,' John said, not taking his eyes off his firstborn. 'Brendan, go. The site needs you.'

'Will you be in Annandale this afternoon, Father?' Brendan asked.

'No, I'm staying in town.'

'Can I see you here at three, then?' Brendan said.

'Yes. What's it about?'

Brendan hesitated and glanced at Richard. 'My future.'

Richard smiled. 'That shouldn't take long.'

Brendan ignored him and left the room. Richard sat back, reading the papers. Hide as thick as a labourer's boot, John mused. Steals eighty pounds and he just sits there.

'Some tea, John?' Christine asked as she took up the silver pot.

'Thank you.' John watched her pour. He saw Clarissa in her just then, and felt a sadness. He still missed his first wife.

After Clarissa died, it had taken him two and a half years to fall in love again. Catherine was the daughter of wool broker William Ryan and his wife, Constance. Both Catherine's parents had passed away but she was close to her brother Donald, an unmarried partner in a law firm. She was a good woman, who had given him three children: Brendan, Mary and Agatha. In many ways, he was a lucky man.

'Father?' Richard said, rousing him from his reverie.

'Let's get on with the meeting,' John said. 'The first agenda item is the employees' annual pay rise. You know my position. Three per cent is all I'm recommending. Vote?'

'Let me read it again,' Christine said looking down. 'Dear me, it's lengthy. Truly, John, you could make this more simple.'

'I can give you a simple explanation if you like.'

'No, I'll read it,' she said. 'It's not *me* who's simple.'

'Very good.' She was in command, as always. John waited for her to make up her mind, knowing that Richard would probably agree with his grandmother. Richard, with money gifted from her, had recently purchased Sean Connaire's nine per cent share of Leary's stock. Sean and John had worked together in the early days and Sean had been John's first partner in the business. He was semi-retired now, he mentored some of the workers and did the odd general foreman's job for Leary's when needed. Sean was a modest man, and a valued long-term friend from whom John had often sought counsel. John held forty per cent of Leary's stock and he'd laboured under Christine's fifty-one per cent control for years. Unfortunately, once he became a shareholder, Richard had invariably voted with her. They had the edge if they disagreed with John.

John glanced at the portrait on the wall of David McGuire, Christine's deceased husband, a successful businessman and John's backer in the building company he'd established in 1852. David had loved John as the son he'd never had and John had taken advantage of that. John had wanted total control and had persuaded David to sell his own fifty-one per cent shareholding in Leary's to a silent partner of John's choice.

'Agreed,' Christine said, interrupting his thoughts.

'Seconded,' Richard said.

John sipped his tea, then made a note of their decision. 'Read the next item, please,' he said. 'It explains an offer from the Commercial Bank of Sydney to deposit our funds at their new escrow rates.'

'I've read it,' Richard said.

'Well,' Christine said, 'you can both wait for me. It's in three pages and I want to study it all.'

John knew she would; she liked the detail. She liked to dig and reassure herself. That's what had brought him undone and he felt the guilt again at how he'd manipulated David. Christine had been suspicious of the new Leary silent shareholder who'd bought David's majority share. *I underestimated her shrewdness.* He still found it impressive that she'd discovered that it was Beth Blackett. John's guilt turned to sadness. Beth had befriended him before he'd been engaged to Clarissa. They'd met again a couple of years after his marriage to Clarissa. Beth had her own capital from her father's lucrative Ballarat gold claim and wanted a secure investment and a guaranteed dividend, nothing more. Trusting John, she'd bought David's share and had become the silent fifty-one per cent partner with no control of the Leary's business. Beth had always loved John and before long John and she had embarked on an affair. Christine had found out about it and forced Beth to sell the shares to her and end the affair with her son-in-law on pain of being exposed.

Christine had told Clarissa about John's infidelity and sadly, shortly after learning this, Clarissa died unexpectedly from cancer.

Christine had told John she'd never forgive him for his unfaithfulness, and by maintaining her fifty-one per cent shareholding she held the power over him. He had to admit, though, her anger at him had mellowed over the years.

'Do you agree, Grandmother?'

Christine turned to Richard. 'What's that, dear?'

'The rates at the Commercial Bank. They're competitive. I think we should deposit some funds there.'

Christine glanced at John.

'The Bank of New South Wales is my choice,' John said. 'We should stick with the bank we have. Let's vote.'

'The Commercial Bank,' they both said together. John's mouth opened and Christine flushed. *She's enjoying, this, she bloody is.* But his irritation didn't last, replaced by a grudging respect. She was at an exceptional age now and wouldn't be around for much longer.

'Well, that's it,' John said. 'Any other business?'

'Nothing from me,' Richard said standing up.

'I'd say not, son! You've done quite enough.'

Richard seemed to ignore his remark. 'I'll stay in town today. I meet my suppliers on Tuesdays.'

Christine opened her arms. 'Come and give your grandmother a hug.'

Richard wrapped his arms around her. 'I'll see you soon.'

'And stop the cards,' she admonished. 'It'll do you no good. How are your digs at Glebe? Do you miss home, and me?'

He nodded his head. 'Always, dear.'

'Good day, Christine,' John said as he left the room and went upstairs to his office. He stopped outside his door and barked at his orders clerk who sat nearby, 'Simmonds. I want those orders done before three and I'll have no excuses.'

The nervous-looking clerk followed John in and sat opposite him. 'Yes, Mr Leary.'

John glanced at appointments for the next week and said, 'Right, job reports. Give them here.' He took the pile and sorted through them. It was a mixed bag of construction and all had jobs that had commenced from the middle to the end of the previous year. It was better in building to have the projects staggered where they had, ideally, a running series of start dates. That would make better use of the people Leary's employed. Most of his projects would end close to each other, putting pressure on his men to manage their completion successfully.

It was an impressive list. Ten terraces in Trafalgar Street, Stanmore; eight in Moncur Street, Woollahra and six in Forbes Street, Darlinghurst. An 18,000-square-feet wool store in Darling Harbour for Robert Richardson was a prominent project and now into the sixth month of a two-year build. Other warehouses half that size were under construction in Foveaux Street, Surry Hills, Chippendale and Sydenham. 'Where are the others?' John said.

'Sorry, sir, here they are. The bank building in Enmore, and the bond store extension at Campbell's Cove.'

'That's it. I'll check them now.'

'Yes, Mr Leary.'

John grinned at his clerk. 'Take an early mark after three,' he said. 'How's that mother of yours?' Simmonds looked down and mumbled something. *I frighten the poor bastard, I do.* 'Off you go,' John said. He would love to get his old secretary, Mrs Dawes, back, but she had retired. He'd have to find someone to share Simmonds's load, and soon. He wasn't coping with administering nine projects under construction.

His clerk paused before he left the office. 'Mr Leary?'

'What is it?'

'You need to see Mr Spencer, the ironmonger, in half an hour. It's about his order.'

'I'll see him in the meeting room,' John said, and he riffled through his papers. 'Here, take this. They're my plans for the

Annandale office alterations. Take it and give it to the chief estimator tomorrow morning.'

'Very well, Mr Leary.'

After John finished his business with the ironmonger, he had a meal brought to him: a nice piece of beef and some French claret. He was working in his office when the clock chimed three.

'Mr Brendan to see you, Mr Leary,' Simmonds said.

'Send him in.' Now, what did Brendan want again? Ah, yes, his future. He would make it quick. He leaned back in his chair as his son entered and stood before him. 'Hello, son. What is it?' Brendan remained silent. 'Come on, out with it.'

'I want to be a foreman, Father. There's a vacancy.'

A thunderclap overhead made John jump. He thought about materials and what water could do to them. 'Is your site prepared?' he asked, leaning forward in his chair.

His son looked surprised. 'For what?'

John gestured towards the window. 'For the rain!'

Brendan paused. 'We have the timber under cover, the cement protected—'

'Pumps?'

'One in the basement, Father and one on standby.'

'Good,' John said, leaning back again in the chair. 'So you want a promotion?'

'Yes,' Brendan said.

'I need a foreman at Moncur Street. You want it?'

'I do.'

John took his time before responding, knowing what he'd say next would be hard for the boy. 'Leary's needs strong men to lead it, Brendan. Do you think you're the right man for the job?'

John hoped his son would see this as a subtle insult and take offence—prove himself strong, in fact. But Brendan's reply was calm and reasonable.

'For three years I've been a sub-foreman, Father. All the foremen I've worked for will back me, including Peter Henderson.'

John said, 'Look, it's well known that you run your leading hand, carpenters and labourers competently. But I've heard other chatter: you want to pamper our workers.'

'Not pamper, Father, just look after them.'

'Well, you're not going to be a foreman,' John said.

'I'm twenty-two! You started at that age!'

John had, but he was a different person from Brendan. 'Age has something to do with it, but there's more to it than age.'

Brendan folded his arms. 'What?'

'I have my reasons. Now, your site needs you. You can go.'

Brendan stayed where he was. 'I deserve an explanation.'

John paused. 'You may not like it.'

'I'm not tough enough?'

That was it, right from his own mouth. 'No.'

Brendan paused. 'But Richard gets a rails run, doesn't he?'

'Richard's the Construction Manager,' John said. 'Don't try and compare yourself with him. He'll lead this company one day. He has the experience.'

'And don't I know it.'

John thought that response a little smart. 'You have a problem with your brother being above you?'

Brendan looked at him, then shook his head.

'Be assertive,' John said. 'Get yourself above the details and for God's sake, don't pity the bloody workers. Do that and I'll reconsider.'

'Bullying is not a sign of strength, Father.'

'Bulldust.'

Brendan leaned over his father's desk. 'You never give me half the recognition you give Richard. But I can make money for you. Leary's is a business first and a building company second. I love to build, but you have to make a profit when you do.'

This is better. 'Go on.'

'Right. Speak to Henderson; he'll tell you. You'll believe him.'

'Believe what?' John said.

'I saved Leary's twenty pounds on a timber order last week. Peter Henderson was going to give it to our usual supplier and I found another one. The quality's the same and we got it for twenty pounds less.'

John's interest increased. 'If that's the case, then good. I'm talking to him tomorrow. I'll check it out.'

'That proves something. It shows I've got a head for making us a quid.'

Fair point, John conceded. 'It shows you're thrifty and want to make money. It doesn't prove to me you're a good builder or ready for more responsibility as a foreman.'

'Thanks, Father. Thanks for nothing,' Brendan said, before he turned and left.

Brendan a foreman? Perhaps, but he'd need to change his attitude. If that happened, John would think about it.

John went to see Richard in his office. His first-born had his faults and John admitted that sometimes he was blind to them, but Richard knew building. 'Brendan came to see me.'

'To talk about his future?'

'He wants a promotion,' John said.

'He's a fussy sub-foreman, Father, but as for leading a big team, I can't see it.'

John shrugged. 'He's got a brain and he's good with his hands. He's turned out some fine furniture in his spare time.'

'What did you offer?'

'Nothing, for now. I've got another hour's work, then I'm off to find out about the new pub. We'll continue this discussion at another time.'

It was early evening but still steamy when John alighted from a cab at the Australian Club in Macquarie Street. He walked up the steps, opened the door and was confronted by a full-height steel grill and timber cage in the foyer. *What the hell?*

Suddenly the cage doors parted and a uniformed man appeared. 'Going upstairs sir?'

John hesitated then stepped into the cage. The door closed with a clang and the car jolted its way upwards, accompanied by a smell of oil. He'd heard about the new lifts that had been installed in Farmer's department store in George Street; obviously the Australian Club was following suit. Before he knew it, the lift car stopped with a jerk.

'This is your floor, sir.'

'Thank you,' John said as he stepped out onto the solid surface of the familiar first-floor foyer. Going into the dining room, he had his dinner but saw no one there who could tell him anything about the new hotel. Disappointed, he was leaving the dining room when he spotted Harold Watson, a partner at the Bank of New South Wales. Perfect timing.

Seeing him, Watson stopped and said to John, 'I say, Mr Leary, have you been for a ride in the new lift?'

'Yes, Mr Watson, and I'm impressed.'

'Well, don't be. The beastly thing has broken down more times this week than it's been used. I won't get into the contraption. It's ready to fall apart.'

John smiled at the banker. Unless something had no risk, bankers weren't interested. But he had to glean some things tonight, so he was on his best behaviour. 'Have you had dinner?'

'I have, and I was going to have a port in the bar. If you join me, I would value that.'

'Gladly,' John said, and followed the banker into the club bar. It was filled with distinguished men dressed in sombre colours. It was a pity that fashion had taken a step back with the death of the Prince Consort. One would have thought by now that something bright and lively would have been acceptable, but alas, no. Wearing bright clothes was still frowned upon, so people put their ostentation into their buildings. John smiled. *The more ostentatious the building, the more profit for him. Let's keep on wearing dull clothes if it means more money for Leary's.*

The two men settled into leather chairs in a quiet corner.

The banker opened the conversation, 'Did you put in a bid for the Customs House extensions?'

'No, and I'm glad I didn't. I've heard Dennings have done their shirt over it.'

The banker sipped his port then said, 'I heard that, too. You have the touch, Mr Leary, to keep out of projects that could turn bad. You did do your bit on the Town Hall though.'

'Years of experience. Sometimes I still get caught out, but I'm right most of the time.'

The banker smiled at him. 'Have you given any more thoughts to those escrow interest rates we discussed?'

The port lost its flavour in John's mouth. This was the prickly bit. He'd been planning his reply to the banker on the way to the club and he'd come to a decision. 'If you could give me another half a per cent, Mr Watson, then I'll leave my funds with you.'

'Can't do that. The Commercial's offered you more, I presume?'

'They have and I feel I should accept it.'

The banker raised his eyes. 'Too bad. It's good that we have the luxury of the management of all your funds, so a small loss to us is acceptable.'

'I'm encouraged you think so,' John said. 'There will be other opportunities. I'm after the big projects. The biggest hotel in Sydney is being planned, I hear.' John helped himself to more port. He knew on good authority that the Bank of New South Wales was financing the project.

'I've heard the same. Few details are forthcoming, though.'

Liar. John was convinced Harold Watson knew all about it.

The banker shifted in his chair as if he had a burr in his pants. John had unsettled him.

John said. 'So if you're not financing it, who would be?'

The banker looked up. 'I say, the chap I'm waiting for is here. You must excuse me, Mr Leary, but I have another appointment. Please don't make yourself a stranger at the bank.'

John swallowed his irritation. 'Goodnight, Mr Watson, until next time.'

Harold Watson departed and John shook his head in annoyance. Damn, he needed more information on the big job, and quickly.

Brendan finished his meal and looked at his mother. It was just the two of them left at the dinner table.

She smiled at him. 'You always have a good appetite.'

'I know. Where was Father tonight?'

'He's dining in town at the Australian Club. Something to do with work.'

Brendan was silent, remembering the run-in with his father that afternoon.

'You do like your job at Leary's?' his mother said.

'I do, Mother, but I'd like more responsibility.'

'Have you spoken to your father about that?'

'This afternoon, and it did no good.'

Catherine nodded. 'He can be hard. But do persevere,' she said, smiling encouragingly. 'I'll see what I can do. You're capable, my son. I know little of the industry but I do know character and you have a good one.'

Brendan stood up and smiled at her. 'You have to say that. You're my mother.'

'I know,' she said, 'but you do. And you must consider Richard, who's very competent, from what your father tells me. He's a determined man. So work out how best to win him to your ways.'

Brendan's mother had a solid relationship with Richard, her stepson, and Brendan knew she had a strong affection for them both. How would she view the rise of Richard and Brendan within

Leary's? Would she prefer one son over the other? Brendan didn't think so. Richard's affections towards her were genuine and so were his own.

'I shall,' he said. 'Will you excuse me? I want to talk to my great-uncle. He may be able to devise a strategy.'

'That's a good idea. Go on, my dear.'

Gerry was not in his room and Brendan searched the rest of the house. His great-uncle had lived with them since his dear wife Moira passed away in 1879. It had knocked the stuffing out of the man, as Moira had been a loving and caring woman. Gerry's health had suffered as a result of his grief and he'd sold their houses in Redfern and Moira's in Elizabeth Street, gifted money to orphanages and asked if he could live out his years with his nephew. John had gladly agreed.

Brendan went outside to look for him. The din of cicadas filled the Learys' rear garden and a harbour breeze lifted the scent of the gum leaves. His thoughts turned to the girl who'd caused him to act in a way that was out of character. It had been the other day and he'd been walking past McIntyre's on Newtown Road when she walked out in front of him. Her beauty and the way the breeze had moved the folds of her dress had caught Brendan's attention. He found himself following her and when she got on the tram, he had, too. He managed to get a seat behind her, but couldn't think of anything to say to her. He didn't follow her when she got off; it didn't seem right. But she had been in his thoughts ever since. He wondered what her name was. A cough disturbed his thoughts and he squinted into the dim light. 'Uncle, is that you?'

'Over here.'

Brendan sat beside the elderly big man and poured himself a drink from a pitcher on the little garden table where Gerry sat. 'You should be inside.'

'I prefer the fresh air,' Gerry said.

'You still don't sound well,' Brendan said in a concerned tone.

'It's this stinking cold that I can't shake,' Gerry Gleeson said, before a coughing fit overtook him. 'So, how was your day?' he asked when he'd recovered. 'Did you go to the meeting?'

'I did, and all Richard got was a slap on the wrist.'

'I told you that would happen,' Gerry said.

'But he stole money, Uncle!'

'That's not the problem, boy. It's the gambling that's the worry. Anyway, cop it sweet.'

Easy to say. But his great-uncle was right.

From an early age, Brendan had found a friend in Gerry, his own father being too busy with the business. Gerry had always had time for him, was always encouraging and ready to listen. Brendan knew he could talk to him about anything and he'd come to trust and rely on his advice. Indeed, Gerry had given time to Richard as well, up until Richard was twelve or thirteen. Brendan remembered when he was five years old, he'd asked his great-uncle why he spent less time with the adolescent Richard. His uncle had replied that Richard was his own man now, confident and able to fend for himself. Brendan had noticed that Richard was courteous to Gerry but obviously didn't want his advice. Judging by the fights Richard got into at school, Brendan knew what Gerry meant. Richard was at home in the rough and tumble of schoolyard scrapes and came out on top most times.

It was different with Gerry and himself. There was a bond there, a strong one.

'Now, let's move inside,' Gerry said. 'It's getting damp out here.'

Brendan helped the big man stand and placed his walking stick in his gnarled hand. The pair remained silent as they made their way to the workshop. At full stretch, his great-uncle was still an intimidating sight. He must've been a terror as a stonemason all those years ago. Gerry's past was a little vague and he seldom spoke about how he came to the colony as a convict stonemason in 1828. He'd been Gerry Riordan then. After getting his ticket-of-leave, he'd changed his name to Gleeson. It wasn't till the 1850s, when John Leary had started to make a name for himself and his company, that Gerry discovered that John was the son of his sister Maeve, who had married Richard Leary. Gerry had introduced himself to John and he'd been a member of the family ever since.

They entered a partitioned space in the stables. 'Cushion, please,' Gerry said. 'I'm not too proud to ask. Something for my skinny bones.' Brendan did the honours and sat his great-uncle down. He lit a lamp and their shadows flickered on the walls.

'If you're going to have a crack at your half-brother,' Gerry said, 'and I recommend you do, don't compete on his terms. He's got different rules. I'm not saying that the man is wrong, although I don't agree with his morals: all those fillies he plays with.'

Brendan was shocked. 'But he's getting married soon.'

Gerry coughed again. 'He is and I hope that hobbles him.'

Brendan didn't want to hear any more. During his own apprenticeship, he had copped the crude language men used on sites, and had seen how some men bent the rules to get ahead. Foremen had given him little quarter and he had given himself even less, wanting to do the best job at the first attempt and in the quickest time. His bosses had laughed. This was the building industry, rife with conflict and time pressures. They'd said perfection wasn't possible, but he'd persevered and risen from apprentice to carpenter to leading hand and was now a sub-foreman.

'So, how should I compete with Richard?'

Gerry tapped his forearm. 'You have to choose which ring to box in and choose it wisely.'

'He has to curb his gambling and stop his thieving. That's all I want.'

'Richard sees you as a competitor for running Leary's.' Brendan looked surprised. 'No, let me continue,' Gerry said as Brendan opened his mouth to speak. 'You have to be aware of Richard's intentions.'

'Which are?'

'To make money, pure and simple.'

'That's the goal of any business.'

Gerry leaned closer to his grand-nephew. 'Too true, but Richard sees only the here and now. You see the future and how you can shape it. Your half-brother doesn't concern himself with how men work: he doesn't see that they need to be led, not beaten into submission. Now, I'll ask you a question.'

'Yes?' Brendan said, standing up and going over to the machinery bench where his bookcase lay unfinished. He had rearranged the shelves four times and he wasn't satisfied with it. 'Go on, Uncle.'

'Do you want to run Leary's Contracting?'

Brendan hadn't really given serious thought to this before now. He was still young and had much to learn. 'Richard's next in line,' he said.

'That's a fact. But you don't have to accept it. Could you lead Leary's? Your father has to step down sometime and what if it's sooner than you think?'

'I think I could, in time, but Father's got to give me a chance or I'll never get there.'

'You asked for the promotion? Henderson's job, foreman?'

Brendan looked at him. 'I did and he knocked me back.'

Gerry slapped his thigh. 'Well? What are you going to do about it?'

Brendan leaned on the bench. 'I'm going to ask him again, that's what I'm going to do. I'm going to be a foreman, uncle.'

'Good, now back off on the sympathy for the workers.'

Brendan knew what was coming. 'Some of our workers live in squalor. Most struggle—'

'Not all of them and most of them aren't bitching about it.'

'We're driving them too hard.'

'Brendan. You have a soft heart but don't let that affect your head. Be fair, but be firm. You'll get more respect that way. Agreed?'

His great-uncle had a point. 'I'll think about it.'

'I'm going to bed,' Gerry said and pointed to the bookshelf, smiling. 'Don't work too late.' Gerry shuffled out while Brendan turned to his task.

Four equal-sized rectangular pieces of Queensland maple leaned against his bench. They had all been measured twice and sawn to the dimensions he wanted and yet for some reason they didn't fit into the bookcase's end frames that he'd already assembled. Brendan grabbed a rag and wiped the dust from his bench. After checking each shelf, he took two clamps and pressed all the shelves together with each shelf separated by thin pieces of timber so as not to bruise the finished surfaces. He inspected his stack from all sides.

All the edges were square. Good. He set the edge of the upright square at random points against the stack: no gaps there and all shelves were flush, also good. Now he did the same process with the two end frames. Then he found it, just a hint of a bow in one of them. Brendan smiled. Unclamping the pair he took the offending frame and started work on it. *Lead Leary's? Yes, he certainly could.*

Chapter Two

JOHN SAT BACK IN THE CARRIAGE, ADMIRING ITS FEATURES. THE Brougham was luxurious. He was proud that they'd be seen in it on this Saturday night at the ball, where there'd be at least two people who could help him find out about his prized project. Since Tuesday and meeting Harold Watson at the Australian Club, he'd found out nothing.

'I'd love to have worn my diamonds,' Catherine said as she adjusted her silver bracelet, 'but it's still not acceptable. I hope the Queen ends the mourning period soon so we can again dress as we are meant to for functions like this. However, it should be a convivial evening.'

'You still look captivating, my dear,' he said.

'Thank you.'

They pulled up at the William and College Street intersection to let another carriage pass. 'The first Governor's Ball of the year usually is a cracker,' John said. He heard voices and stuck his head out the window. His instincts had been right and he was glad they'd brought the stronger carriage. There was no disguising the gang, here to make its mark on this warm evening. Their distinctive colouring and clothes showed them to be larrikins. One of them grabbed the reins of John's horses.

Gibbs yelled at them, 'Go away, you lot. Get away.'

When Catherine moved to the window to see what the fuss was about, the larrikins' leader, the 'King', a thin-faced man with a hooked nose, wearing a fancy vest with glass buttons, white shirt, paper collar and pointy shoes, grinned and winked at her.

'Hello, beautiful,' the man said.

Catherine blushed and sat back.

'Get away!' John said.

The man laughed at him and John became angry. Before he could do anything, though, the carriage took off and he fell backwards onto his seat. At the same time he heard the King yelping as Gibbs's whip flicked his face.

'You f—ing bastard!' the King cried out. 'You'll keep.'

Catherine gasped.

John shook his head. 'Sorry about that. This scum rules the streets. They're after easy pickings. The police are useless in trying to control them.'

The carriage continued along College Street and down Macquarie Street to the entrance of Government House.

'It's smelly here,' Catherine said, pressing a lavender-scented handkerchief to her face.

'Sydney's sewage in all its glory. We're nearly there. The air should be clearer soon.'

The guests milled around the entrance of Government House and the gaslight lit their flushed faces. John felt proud that as a wealthy contractor he was invited to these balls. He wasn't quite at the level of the graziers and sheep cockies but he was accepted nevertheless.

Governor Loftus smiled as the Learys were presented to him. Moving on, John recognised Henry Parkes, who was next in line to shake the Governor's hand. As Catherine and John headed to the ballroom, Catherine suddenly gave a little cry. When John turned to see what was wrong she shook her head and pushed him forward. 'What is it?'

'Oh, the evil man,' she said. 'He pinched me. He actually pinched me. Well, there you are, his reputation did precede him.' John turned to go back but Catherine restrained him. 'It's not worth it. Leave it, please, John.'

The guests behind him forced John to keep moving. He'd get to Parkes later. What a start to the evening: first, bailed up by larrikins, then his wife assaulted by the old lecher not ten minutes later. He said, 'Well, let's try and have a good time.'

They entered the ballroom, a blaze of light and heat where most people were dancing, but some were in groups, drinking and laughing. They made their salutations, including greeting Catherine's brother Donald Ryan and his partner, and soon Catherine's dance card was full.

John spotted his prey: Watson from the Bank of New South Wales stood near an open window, and not thirty feet away from him was James Barnet, a leading architect. Both must be prodded for details of the new hotel. He excused himself from his brother-in-law and was making his way towards Barnet when a flash of olive skin and long dark hair caught his attention. A couple were dancing in his direction. It was Bill Bucknell, John's arch-rival, and his wife. Her sleeveless navy silk dress highlighted her voluptuous décolletage, and her jet-black hair, set in Josephine curls over her forehead, set off her fine features. John had met her once before, some time ago, and he'd been attracted to her. He kept staring as the couple melted into the crowd on the dance floor where Catherine, her head held high, was dancing and smiling at people she knew. She enjoyed these evenings and John was proud of her, but the dark-haired beauty had distracted him—again.

He was on his course to Barnet when he felt a hand on his arm.

'Evening, Mr Leary.' Suddenly, Bill Bucknell was grinning at him. Standing beside his short, red-faced, double-chinned competitor, was the tall, dark-haired beauty. Bucknell turned to his partner. 'You know Constance,' he said.

'Good evening, Mr Leary,' she said, holding out her hand.

Late thirties, a trace of an accent, exquisite. 'Good evening, Mrs Bucknell,' John replied, taking her hand. Although covered with an over-the-elbow, fine kid glove, it was warm and pulsing. He was reluctant to let it go.

'Where have you been hiding her, Mr Bucknell?' John said.

Constance smiled, her even white teeth complementing her full lips. She met John's gaze. 'I have been in Europe for the past year.' She smiled again at her husband. 'I'm glad to be home.'

'Where's your wife?' Bucknell asked him.

'Dancing. You must have passed her when you were on the dance floor.'

'Ah yes,' Bucknell glanced at the crowded floor. 'I can see her.' He reached for two glasses of champagne from a waiter.

'Catherine delights in music and dance,' John said and smiled, keeping an eye on Barnet. 'At school, she was something of a paradox because her friends called her bookish, and she was, it seems, but she takes to dance like a bricklayer to good mortar.'

'You going to the Farringtons' dinner party Saturday night?' Bucknell asked. 'We are.'

The Farringtons were a stuffy bunch and John had decided not to go, but after seeing Constance he changed his mind—plus he also had to find out if Bill Bucknell had heard anything about the hotel. 'We shall be there.'

'Excellent,' Bucknell replied. 'Come, my dear.' Bucknell took his wife's hand and they moved off. Constance smiled at John, who watched them walk away before he set sail again for Barnet.

Catherine appeared at his side. 'Are you enjoying yourself?'

John turned to her, a little annoyed. 'I am. Indeed, I am.'

'Why the frown?'

John smiled. Barnet the architect would have to wait. 'It's nothing.'

'Good,' she said, 'because my card has a vacancy and I'd like to dance with my husband.' He nodded, waited for the beat and waltzed her to the centre of the floor. She raised one eyebrow. 'Have you met anybody interesting tonight?'

'No, just the usual.'

Catherine smiled. 'I wouldn't call a woman of *that* beauty "usual".'

'You've been spying.' John smiled. 'Well, if you must know, she's Bill Bucknell's wife, Constance.'

Catherine spotted the Bucknells dancing. 'She has beautiful skin,' she said, 'and that hair.' Catherine's hair was pulled back at the sides and worn in a low knot.

'I've been thinking about Saturday week, the Farringtons' dinner party.'

'I thought you didn't like them.'

'Bucknell will be there.'

'Ah, now I know why you're going.'

John feigned surprise. 'What? No! Oh, *she'll* be there, but more importantly I have to find out from Bucknell whether he knows anything about the new hotel.'

'Can't you see Mr Bucknell during the day? Why ruin a good dinner party talking about work?'

The music came to an end. 'Let's have a rest. This heat is ener-vating.' John took her aside and said, 'I have to know about this project. It's going to be the biggest in Sydney and I aim to build it. We don't have to stay at the Farringtons' long.'

She smiled. 'Naturally, you want to speak business only. Not ogle another man's wife, just because she's beautiful.'

'I have my beauty,' he said, 'and I'm looking at her.'

Catherine blushed. 'Then I stand corrected.' She glanced behind John. 'Here is my next partner. Excuse me, dear.'

'Of course.' John looked around. Barnet was not in sight. He could be outside. 'I need to get some fresh air.' John bowed to her and walked to an exit. On the way he spotted Henry Parkes coming towards him carrying a drink. 'Mr Parkes,' he said. 'Good evening.'

Parkes nodded to John and continued walking. John stepped in front of him. 'Touch my wife again and you'll answer to me.'

Parkes frowned, then smiled. 'Ah yes, your wife is an attractive, handsome woman. No harm done.'

'Bulldust.' John prodded a finger into Parkes's vast middle. 'You've been warned. Keep your hands off her.' Parkes sniffed and John made way for him before heading to the terrace. That wouldn't stop the man but John felt better and lit a cigar.

Lights on the harbour twinkled and steam ferries tooted as they passed each other. There were a few people around but Barnet wasn't one of them. *Bugger.* He spotted Harold Watson near the window and made his way back to the ball. The bank partner must tell him something. Yes, Leary's had other projects, but this majestic new job was the prize and winning it would position Leary's as the number one contractor in Sydney. He remembered the hotels he'd built, the first one down at Day Street: Cochrane's. It was a bigger pub now—three storeys of stone—but in 1851, in brick with corrugated roofing, it had been a treasure to see.

The expansion of the railways meant big hotels. The steam engines brought wealthy country people to town and this created a big demand for accommodation, and now there were better ways to build big jobs. Four-feet-thick brick foundation walls were a start but it was in the repetition of the building's elements, the wall panels and windows, the column sections and beams, where savings could be gained. He had to convince the architects to keep the components simple and to a standard size, so that construction could be quicker and easier.

Catherine waved to him from the entrance steps. He'd dance with her but he'd see Watson first. It looked like 1885 would be a good year and the future beyond that looked even better.

The ten o'clock Mass at St Mary's Cathedral was packed. Agatha and Mary sat between John and Catherine, but Brendan wasn't here. Catherine knew where he was and glanced at John, who would be angry if he knew. She was irritated that her son was not here because she wanted to reacquaint him with someone. The priest had just finished the consecration, and she looked at the crucifix suspended above the altar. She pressed her eyes shut and made peace with God.

Mary sneezed.

'God bless you,' Catherine whispered. 'Here's a hanky.' She stood to take communion. 'Come on.' The girls and she filed down the aisle with John bringing up the rear. The floury taste of the Host melted in her mouth and she closed her eyes and concentrated. She returned to her pew with hands clasped and said her prayers.

After the service, the family made their way outside, where friends came up and greeted them. Catherine looked out for and saw Sean Connaire and his wife, Vonnie, a strapping woman in her fifties who was Catherine's friend, and their daughter, Anne. Anne had been a late arrival in the family, pleasantly surprising them. Catherine often thanked the Lord for Sean who, now in his sixties, had been John's long-term friend as well as original partner in the business. Sean's thirty-six-year-old son, Declan, was working at Leary's and lived with his wife, Brigit, and his young family on the north side of the harbour.

Brendan should have been here. He should marry and Anne was just the girl. The Connaires were not wealthy but Catherine had known twenty-year-old Anne from a baby. She was not unattractive and was quiet and gentle. The mothers had talked at times about a possible match between their children. Catherine wanted to ignite the friendship to romance and, if not that, then something close to it.

Sean and Vonnie turned to her and Sean took off his hat. 'Morning, Catherine,' he said as he buttoned up his jacket. 'It's nippy for the first day of autumn.'

'It is that. And how is Frances and her family?'

'I had a letter last week and they are all well, thank you,' Vonnie replied. Frances was Sean and Vonnie's eldest daughter and she lived in Melbourne with her husband and family.

'And Sister Mary Immaculata?'

'Bonny, Catherine,' Sean said. He had a soft spot for their daughter, Joan, whom they adopted in 1848. 'She's now novice mistress.'

'Ah, she'll make them toe the line,' Vonnie said with a smile.

'No doubt she will,' Catherine said. 'And how will you spend the rest of day, Sean?'

'He'll tend to the garden,' Vonnie replied. 'He's always there on the Lord's day, whatever the weather.' She looked behind the Leary's. 'Where's Brendan?'

'He isn't here. I think he went to Church Hill.' She was lying, and didn't like doing that. John was about to speak and she had to act. 'And how are you, Anne?'

Anne broke off her conversation with Agatha. 'Very well, thank you, Mrs Leary.'

'You are quite the young lady now.'

'Isn't it getting close to your wedding anniversary?' Sean asked.

'Good memory, Sean,' John said. 'It's on the twenty-sixth of May.'

'Twenty-five years. Best wishes for more good years ahead for both of you.'

'Thank you, Sean,' Catherine said. 'We must have you over. I know Brendan would like to see Anne again.' This wasn't quite the truth but Anne blushed and that was good. 'I'll write and let you know, Vonnie. Sometime soon, I hope.'

She nodded goodbye and took John's arm.

Mary tapped her arm and said, 'Could we go to Circular Quay on the way home? There's a shop down there that sells grand flavoured ices.'

Catherine smiled and walked down the steps. 'It's not on the way but we could. You wouldn't think you were nearly twenty-one years of age, the way you carry on, still fancying treats like an eleven-year-old.'

'But mother, they are delicious, they really are.'

'But today?' Catherine queried. 'It's so cold. Oh, all right. But we'll take an ice bucket from the shop and you can have it after your dinner.'

Mary smiled. 'Thank you.'

'Come on,' John said, 'everyone into the carriage.' He rubbed his temple. 'I'm looking forward to that roast lamb. Gibbs, Circular Quay first.'

When they were settled in their seats, Catherine turned to John. 'Did you talk to Bill Bucknell about that hotel last night?'

'I did. He pleaded ignorance but I think he knows something.'

John rubbed his head again and looked out the window. She knew he was desperate to get this project and he needed it; needed it to feed his sense of self, which was his strength and his weakness. She left him to his thoughts. Sean's kind words about their forth-coming anniversary made her smile. Twenty-five years! How quickly the time had flown by. Looking at her husband now, she thought back to the first time she had met him.

She had been twenty and working as a milliner at Madame La Roche in Pitt Street, between Hunter and King Streets, and she lived with her parents and brother Donald, in Bayswater Road, Potts Point. Her father was a wool broker and it was at the Wool Growers Ball in June 1859 that she first met Maureen Forde and her brother John Leary. They were introduced by Ian McCreadie, who was a wool broker like her father, William Ryan. Catherine had been instantly attracted to the tall young man who was still grieving for his dead wife.

Catherine suspected that it had been Maureen who'd played matchmaker between herself and John. In July of that year Maureen had invited Catherine and John to their house for after-noon tea and they had met again in town on another occasion. It had been a slow build from friendship to affection to love. Right up until her engagement to John, she'd had the feeling that Clarissa was still very much in his thoughts. Perhaps it might have been the similarities between herself and Clarissa that had initially attracted him, plus the fact that both women liked commerce and were somewhat similar in the face. The last thing she wanted, though, was to be a replacement for Clarissa. But thankfully, John had not mentioned Clarissa too many times during their engagement and she'd had an instinct that their union would work. Looking at him now in middle age, and considering what they'd achieved in love together, she knew that it had.

Catherine missed Maureen and hoped that her and her family's extended stay in Dublin would soon be over and she'd return to Sydney.

On the way back home from Circular Quay, John's head throbbed; the night before they hadn't left the Farringtons' until two o'clock in the morning. He could stand the pain if he'd found out something about the big pub. But he'd found out nothing, again. It had been the same story all week—nothing. What he had enjoyed last night, though, was flirting with Constance Bucknell.

They'd sat side by side at the dinner table and he'd sensed a mutual attraction as they enjoyed an easy conversation. The innocent brush of hands, the press of her breast on his forearm as she'd leaned over to touch a lily in a vase, the smile and the feigned shyness when he'd talked about a recent marriage scandal—all added a touch of excitement. He sensed she'd felt it too. It was disappointing when she had to depart with the ladies for tea, leaving the gentlemen to talk. He looked forward to seeing her again.

Catherine smiled at him. 'Does your head still hurt?'

'It's a bit better, thank you.'

'Why didn't Brendan come to Mass this morning?' Agatha asked.

'A question I was going to ask myself,' John said.

'He told me he's ... got work on,' Catherine said.

John caught her eye. *'What?'*

'He had to go to Campbell's warehouse to try to sort out a problem with a worker.'

'He's *where?'*

'I don't know the particulars,' she said.

John winced. 'Catherine, what did he say?'

'It was something to do with a sick foreman. I think Brendan's gone to see if he's all right.'

'The boy should have been at Mass,' John growled. What was his son doing, showing concern for a workman, and on the Sabbath? 'I won't have him missing a sacrament.'

'I'm sure it's for a good reason, dear. Let's not upset ourselves now.'

John sniffed. 'I'll talk to him.'

'Brendan has ability and ambition, and the way he cares for other people should be commended,' Catherine said before turning away.

Another stab of pain in his head stopped John responding. Catherine thrust her chin forward. She was shielding her son. He'd have to sort out Brendan.

The bond-store extension at Campbell's Cove was in order and the progress satisfactory. Brendan sat inside on a sawhorse opposite the site's foreman.

'It's not like I'm shirking, Mr Brendan,' Alan Clancy said. 'I've been sick like, and the doctor says, well you know, take it easy, and don't work too hard.' Clancy buttoned the top of his jacket and shivered.

'Wait.' Brendan went and forced the door back into place against the southerly wind. The man should be home, not out in this weather. Clancy was forty-five, a thirty-year Leary's veteran. Brendan had checked his record. Most of the Leary's old hands called him 'Mr Brendan' and he rated that as a compliment. Though still a sub-foreman, Brendan experienced respect most of the time from the longer-term employees, some of whom were many years senior to him. He must be doing something right, he thought.

'I know you're not shirking it, Alan. You've been ill for days and here you are on the Sabbath, working. When did you last see the doctor?'

'Saw the doctor last week, Mr Brendan. Yes, it was because … because the missus was crook as well. Yeah, that's right, Tuesday.' He coughed. 'This bark won't go away.'

'You should be home, man. Why are you here anyway?'

Clancy waved a hand at his makeshift desk cluttered with paperwork, orders and plans. 'Gotta catch up on all this. It won't do it by itself, no it won't, Mr Brendan. The lads don't know what to do. All them's interested in is whacking the nails in and collecting their ten shillings a day.'

'You go home now,' Brendan said, standing up.

'But, there's too much to do here. I got work to finish. Greaves my sub-foreman is just promoted from leading hand. I—'

'Go through all this with me,' Brendan said. 'Then you can leave.'

'But, can you let me do that?'

Brendan as a sub-foreman didn't have the authority to give a foreman the time off. But he would and take the consequences. The man was ill, for goodness sake. 'It'll be all right, believe me.'

Clancy scratched his chin and hesitated. 'I don't know. I don't want to get you into trouble.'

'It's settled. Come on, show me the files.'

For the next twenty minutes they worked together and Brendan understood what needed to be done. 'Have you got a ride to your house?' Brendan asked. The foreman shook his head. Brendan reached into his pocket and offered some coins. 'Get a cab.'

'No you won't, Mr Brendan. I won't have a bar of that. I'll get the tram.' Clancy touched his forehead. 'Thank you very much. I won't forget this, you hear?'

'Get home, Alan. Get into bed with a hot lemon drink. I don't want to see you until Wednesday.'

'But Mr Brendan—'

'Wednesday, and not a day earlier. Now, be off with you.'

Clancy touched his forehead and went to the door, opened it then looked back. 'Beg pardon, but there's something I've heard and I thought I should warn you about it.'

'What is it?'

'They say … well, some of the lads are saying that Mr Richard has stolen some money from the company.' Clancy looked down.

Brendan hated lying but decided to protect Richard. 'It's all rumour, Alan.'

The foreman smiled touched his hat again and left.

Brendan watched him go. So the whispers were still about. Richard was a fool. Brendan sighed and turned to the paperwork, signing the orders and checking the last two weeks' payroll sheets. Not satisfied with the summary points on the daily foreman's diary, he rewrote it in more detail to make it more understandable for Greaves. He pulled out his fob watch and looked at the time. He'd missed Mass, damn. He tidied up and locked all the external doors. On the way home he considered his future. Leary's Contracting was a fair employer. But there was restlessness in the construction industry linked to what was happening in Great Britain. New migrants had told stories of men who were banding together to protect their rights by forming associations.

He sympathised with the workers who toiled from dawn to dusk for an average wage with nothing to show for it at the end of their working lives. Well, so much for the workers, he needed to confront his continuing challenge, how to compete with his half-brother. And sooner than that—how to be a foreman.

In his digs in Glebe, Richard opened his eyes to the bleak sunlight; his head was sore from the late Saturday-night drinks. His tongue stuck to the roof of his mouth, a musky smell tickled his nose and something trapped his left arm. He focused on a tousled mass of brunette hair and lifted the bed sheet to see a naked bottom resting against him. He lowered the sheet and his thoughts drifted to the previous day. He had been on the town with two friends in the afternoon. They'd gone from hotel to hotel and had ended up gambling till early evening.

Richard had at first not wanted to play but his friends had been insistent and he'd weakened. During one hand, Richard had thought about his gambling and the theft of the eighty pounds. He was bothered, not so much by the loss of salary that he'd incur paying back the amount, but by the rumours that had circulated at Leary's about him. Men were odd like that. They accepted the gambling, but not the theft. And during that game he'd thought about not gambling ever again. Could he stop? Yes he thought he could, but was that the alcohol talking? He had shivered and realised that he might not be able to put aside something that gave him such a thrill. He'd pulled himself together and concentrated on his strategy.

After his last game for that evening, he'd seen Gillian again, a store assistant who worked at Lassetter's, a large hardware company where Richard frequently went for supplies. They'd had dinner at Skinners Family Hotel on the corner of Hunter Street, just up from where she worked in George Street. He'd had more to drink at Skinners and they had ended up back at his rooms in Glebe.

Richard eased his trapped arm, lay back and examined his rooms. They needed painting. What time was it? He grabbed his watch from the bedside table and brought it into focus— ten o'clock. No cook on the premises, as it was his day off, but that was all right. He got out of bed, naked, and went into the bathroom to wash his face, then returned to the bedroom.

He crept back into bed, lay down and stroked Gillian's neck. She moved and forced her eyes open. He kissed her.

'You don't waste much time, do you?' she murmured. 'Keep that up.'

He continued caressing her and her breathing became audible. 'Come here,' he said.

She supported herself on her arms above him. Her lower body rubbed against him. 'You like that, don't you?'

'Keep quiet,' Richard said and slid into her and they settled into a rhythm. After a minute he had to concentrate on something else, trying to delay the orgasm that would soon overwhelm him. He went through the remaining works that needed to be done on the Surry Hills warehouse, breaking them down into tasks and their resources. But his brother interrupted his thoughts. Brendan, yes, a good man and a good employee, but an idealist.

Brendan had been a quiet one, growing up. Even as youngsters, they'd fought. Richard had been jealous that Brendan took Catherine's attention away from him when that love had once only been directed at him. At games and mucking around, Brendan had not wanted to take risks and Richard had scorned him for his lack of pluck. Seven years was a big gap in ages and their relationship was not close. Still, Brendan was a bright lad, happy in his own company, getting satisfaction from within himself rather than from his fellows. But now he wanted a promotion to foreman and that showed ambition, which was worrying. He couldn't have his half-brother eclipse him.

Gillian's thighs were pressing against him, and he gave into pleasure again. Her face was flushed and her eyes were closed. She flexed her arms, her mouth opened and her eyelids flickered as she, too, gave herself over to pleasure.

'You have made me indecent, Richard Leary,' she said a little later as she lay down, resting her head on his chest. 'I hate wanting you and wanting this.'

'No one's forcing you,' he said and smiled.

'I know. That makes it worse.' She pecked his nose and got off the bed and went to the bathroom. He felt fortunate that he had indoor plumbing. The girls loved it.

Back to Brendan. His half-brother would need watching. He wasn't a threat to him, but Brendan did have the skills and with enough experience he would go far. How many jobs had Brendan worked on? Richard ticked them off, one at a time.

Gillian returned and, opening his wardrobe, took out a silk dressing gown and put it on. It was too large for her five-foot-two-inch height, but she wrapped it around herself, and tied a double knot in the cord. He smiled to himself. She was eager in bed but as soon as the act was finished she became the good girl. She certainly *looked* good, darker and perkier than Victoria Hughes, his fiancée of six months.

'Do you want some breakfast?' she said.

'Just toast and tea, thanks,' he replied. 'Use the gas ring for both. There's a set of tongs next to the stove.'

Gillian went down the stairs and Richard thought about Victoria, a good Catholic girl. Her father was wealthy and she had the right connections for his future. But Victoria was strict about sex. It had taken him four months just to get to kiss her and when he did, she made little moans but went no further. He remembered her blushing face when he had pleaded with her for more favours, but she hadn't budged.

'Where's the marmalade?' Gillian's voice came up the stairwell.

'Top cupboard, left-hand side.'

It would be different when they were married; then Victoria would let herself enjoy all the delights of the marital bed. Gillian had been the third girl he'd had since this time last year, and it was time to move her on. Today was the second time Gillian had stayed over and soon she would want him to declare himself. Couldn't have that.

She came in and placed the breakfast tray, laden with toast and a teapot and teacups, on the bed. Richard grabbed some toast and she poured the tea and sat on the bed next to him.

She said, 'What are we going to do for the rest of the morning? I have to get home by one.'

'Your parents still think you're staying with your friend?'

Gillian looked down. 'Betty's place isn't far from here. I'll call on her anyway.' She looked back at him. 'Well? What are we going to do?'

He would've liked to go sailing with her but he had to see Victoria that afternoon. Still, he had the rest of the morning and he wanted to make the most of the company. They talked about the previous night's dinner and finished their tea.

Gillian wiped away crumbs from her mouth and Richard looked at her, wanting her again. 'Mr Leary,' she said, 'if you think I'm coming back to bed with you, you have another think coming.'

Richard pushed the tray aside and clasped both her hands. He drew her towards him and he kissed her. 'Nice marmalade,' he said. 'Come here, you.'

Gillian wrestled with him. 'Oh, no you don't.'

Richard found her mouth again. She responded and the dressing gown rode up.

She murmured in his ear as his hand slipped up her thigh. 'You wretch.'

A half an hour later, Gillian dressed and kissed him. 'Goodbye Richard.' she paused. 'Will I see you again?'

Richard knew he should say no, but her smile swayed him. One more time then. 'Of course,' he said. 'I'll see you out.'

After seeing her to his front door, he washed and dressed then headed to Darling Point.

Joseph Hughes, sitting in his panelled drawing room, looked up at his visitor. 'She's out the back, Richard, in the rotunda. She's looking forward to seeing you.' Then paused before saying, 'It's been a few days.'

'Thank you, Mr Hughes,' Richard said, sensing his prospective father-in-law's irritation. He obviously hadn't been frequenting the Yarranabbee Road house enough recently. 'Will I see you later?'

Hughes placed his newspaper down. 'No, I have an engagement with Eileen and Kieran.'

'I trust they are both in good health?'

'Indeed, Richard. Kieran says that he'll call on you for a drink after work next week.'

'I'll hold your son to that. Give my respects to Mrs Hughes. Good day, sir.'

Richard made his way down the hallway towards the rear of the house. Sunlight, hidden for half the day, now streamed through the house's rear entrance on this hot Sunday afternoon. On each side of the paved path, a rainbow showed in the mist of the fixed hose that was spraying water on the freshly-mown lawn.

Victoria stood up in the rotunda and waved. 'Over here, dear.'

He came up to her, smiling. Her blonde hair and tanned skin always enthralled him. Must be Nordic blood in her family somewhere. She was tall but still shorter than him and he liked that. Victoria wore a lemon-coloured gown with a cutaway overskirt over her white skirt: a nice combination. Leading her into the shade of the rotunda he held her and she kissed him. He wanted the kiss to continue but she broke away.

'It's been too long,' she said. 'What have you been doing? Leary's Contracting, no doubt.'

Richard sat on one of the sandstone benches and took off his jacket. 'It has been a while,' he said and smiled. 'I've been busy. The jobs are taking much of my time—'

'Even on the weekends,' she pouted, 'every hour of every Saturday and Sunday?'

Richard took her hand again. 'Every hour away from you, my dear, is an hour that I've wasted.'

Victoria's pout turned to a smile again. 'Your silver tongue saves you,' she said, sitting beside him. 'Anyway, there's a big party coming up in a month and you must be on your best behaviour. From your look, you've forgotten already. Oh, Richard, I told you the last time we were together. You remember, Alexandra's twenty-first birthday party. It's going to be *the* event in Sydney and just about everybody who's *anybody* will be there.'

Richard had forgotten. It would be an awful bore but if he must go, he would. Richard kissed her again. Her eyes closed and her mouth opened, her tongue came shyly out to meet his as his hand pressed her breast.

She moved her mouth near his ear and murmured, 'You really want to go?'

'Yes.' He found her lips again and he caressed her breast, the stiffness of her basque not helping.

She eased him away and held his hands down by his sides. 'No,' she said. 'This is wrong. We have to wait till we're married.'

'But—'

'There are no buts, Richard. I enjoy it, but it's a sin. I'll have to go to confession now and tell the priest.' Richard looked at her flushed face: he wasn't going to win this afternoon. 'Speaking of weddings,' Victoria said, 'we discussed dates last time. Have you forgotten?'

What was the date again? He should know.

She seemed to read his thoughts. 'You do remember, don't you?'

'Yes, yes, of course I do.' Richard concentrated. 'It's in September or October, right?'

'Yes. Now, which month do you want?'

'I'll tell you down by the water. Come on, there'll be a breeze there.'

She followed him down the path that threaded through native trees and exotic flora. The bees hummed and the magpies chortled above the lawn, which rolled down just shy of the water's edge. It was so still, not a leaf moved. As he walked another ten feet the rising cool of the harbour with its salty tang touched his cheek. The effect was immediate.

'Oh, that's better,' she said. 'It is nicer here.'

Some clever gardener had imbedded a stone bench in the right position to take advantage of the beautiful views and the summer breeze. He sat and absorbed the scene, his hand running over the fine grains of the sandstone bench. 'What month would you prefer?' he said.

'September. October weather can be quirky. It can rain one day, be scorching hot the day after, and a freezing cold day after that. What do you think?'

'I agree,' he said. 'September.'

She joined him on the bench and took his hand. 'You do want to marry me, don't you?'

He looked at the worry groove just above her nose. 'Of course,' he said as convincingly as possible.

Victoria stroked his cheek. 'I love you, Richard. Please see me more often.'

Richard kissed her cheek. 'I love you, too.'

She laid her head on his shoulder and her hair fell over her face. As he brushed it away, he felt overwhelmed by love for her and a powerful need to protect her. He was a bit surprised by the strength of his feelings for Victoria, but they were feelings he liked, very much. He hugged her close to him, and she snuggled up to him, neither wanting to separate.

Delia, the maid, opened the linen-press window to the fresh harbour air. 'After you've chosen the clothes that need to go, ma'am,' she said, 'will I take the bundle to the church? Father was so pleased with your offer. Can I give you a hand?'

'No, thank you,' Catherine said. 'I'll manage. I can get Gibbs to deliver them, if you like.'

'They'll be right with me, ma'am. It's Tuesday and I have time. I've got the Farringtons' bundle as well.'

Mention of the Farringtons reminded Catherine of the previous Saturday night and Constance Bucknell's flirtatious behaviour towards John. She would sort that out later this morning.

'It's still musty in here,' Delia said. 'I'll go and get some more camphor.'

The breeze cooled Catherine's face, taking her thoughts away from the dinner party. It would be nice just to stay and enjoy the sensation, but she had a job to do. She turned and looked at four shelves stacked with old clothes. Stretching to the top shelf, she ran her hand down a number of garments, and selected a woollen jacket and folded it. It seemed just a short time ago when Brendan had worn it. But looking at it, Catherine realised it must have been four years ago or maybe longer. No, he'd been eighteen and she had bought it for his birthday. That's right; he'd worn it at that meeting of iron workers to which she'd accompanied him, much to Brendan's astonishment. In her time as a milliner she had visited the factories where common bonnets and hats had been made. It had appalled her seeing how the women were treated in those places and that vision had stayed with her throughout her life. At that meeting with Brendan she remembered standing up in the group and saying something about women and how they weren't regarded as equal to men workers in factories. Brendan had pulled at her sleeve to sit down, amid howls of protest, and she hadn't wanted to, but she had. She didn't know why she'd done it but it felt good when she'd told them all the truth.

She paused with the jacket. It wouldn't fit Brendan now that he was nearly twenty-three and she placed it on the shelf to go. At his age, Brendan should be married to a suitable girl. Brendan had to meet Anne Connaire. She had to find a way to do that. Her son needed to settle down. He was good looking, hardworking, kind and generous. From her associations with the factories and on her visits there she'd seen how some working girls had brazenly offered themselves to the young factory owners who were serving their time in the businesses. On one occasion, she'd interrupted such a couple kissing in a corridor. No, she didn't want some dollymop to snare her Brendan.

A pair of coarse wool trousers was the next garment she selected. As she did, a piece of paper fell out and she picked it up. She read it and laughed. It was a list of groceries in Mary's neat handwriting. Why in the trousers? Yes, of course, her daughter had gone through an odd stage just a year ago, when she liked wearing Brendan's hand-me-downs. The garment went on the pile and she recognised a pullover that had to go. Agatha had worn it to death at school. Catherine sighed while folding it. Agatha had shown the most promise in the classics and Catherine had wanted her to pursue more studies. There would come a time, she knew, when women would need an education and be equal to men.

Her own talent as a milliner had been noticed by Madame La Roche, who had instructed her in couture millinery, both design and hat making. It seemed Catherine had a talent for this and she loved the work, but found a greater challenge in wanting to know about the finances of the business and why some shops did well and others failed. It was astounding to her that, even at Madame's, there was less interest in maintaining a good cash flow and healthy profitability compared to having the best couture and keeping clients happy. Over the last ten years she had voluntarily advised a number of millinery salons on how to improve their fabric selection and their administration. Now her children were demanding less of her time, she would consider expanding that time, just a little, in doing what she liked to do best: helping women to succeed in an industry she loved.

She looked down at the garment in her hands. Alas, Agatha had decided to be like her friends, just waiting to be courted. Catherine placed the pullover on the top of the pile.

The hall clock struck eight times. She'd best get cracking if Delia was to get a decent pile of clothes to take to those less fortunate, and she needed time to get ready for an appointment in town.

Catherine looked out the tea-room window at the passing parade and glanced at the clock suspended from the glass roof of the Royal Arcade. It was five minutes before ten. She felt she looked good. Her princess-line gown, trimmed with ruched panels and ruffles, was stylish; it might be last year's fashion but that was all right with Catherine.

She was wondering if she was doing the right thing. After all, Mr Bucknell was John's competitor and would fight him to build the biggest hotel Sydney had seen. But Catherine had a point to make; if she offended her guest, so be it. A waiter hovered and she turned to him. 'I'm expecting someone,' she said.

He bowed and said, 'That's perfectly all right, madam. I'll leave you till then.' A shadow crossed the window in front of her. Her guest was dressed in a cream-coloured outfit with a fitted bodice with a low point. The front of the skirt, just above the ankles, was of the same colour and the cutaway was looped at the back. Very chic, Catherine mused.

Constance Bucknell sat beside her. 'Good morning, Mrs Leary,' she said and smiled. 'I hope you haven't been waiting long?'

Even in daylight, her guest's complexion was flawless. Men would be attracted to the dark-haired, full-lipped beauty, with her big almond eyes and high cheekbones.

'No, I haven't,' Catherine replied. 'How are you?'

'Very well. Have you ordered?'

Before Catherine could answer, the waiter appeared and took their order.

Constance looked around the room. 'It's nice isn't it? I hear they're planning another one of these in King Street.'

'They should, given the patronage this place is getting. I had to book.'

'Really? For a Tuesday?'

Catherine decided to come to the point. 'I hope you won't think me rude in what I'm about to say.'

'About what?' Constance asked, smiling.

'My husband. He has a gift and a weakness. He talks to women easily and is attentive to their needs—that's the gift. His weakness is in his tendency to flirt.'

'You think I took advantage of that?'

Catherine suspected she had. Most women would have welcomed the attention. 'I saw as much,' she said. 'But I want to let you know that he does that all the time.' Now she was stretching the truth.

'I found his attentions flattering, Mrs Leary. That was all. You see in Spain the men show their manhood by that kind of behaviour. They exaggerate and carry on.' She smiled. 'Women expect it.'

She's confident as well as beautiful. 'How charming and how interesting.' Catherine should've suspected Mrs Bucknell's Spanish lineage, given her colouring and features. 'John and I have a good marriage,' she said.

'I compliment you on that. And you have beautiful children. Your sons, especially.' Her eyes flashed. 'They are handsome.'

'Thank you.'

'Europeans have wider views about faithfulness in marriage. When people stray, discretion is the key.' This was new ground for Catherine. Affairs happened, often long-standing ones, but she did not approve of them. Did Constance approve? Was she sending a message? 'But let me assure you,' Constance continued, 'I have no interest in your husband.'

Direct as well. Catherine liked that. *Thank God.* 'I'm heartened. I appreciate your assurance. Now, can we end this on a good note?'

'By all means. I like frankness too, Mrs Leary. So please don't take offence when I tell you that I find the English are a little reserved in expressing what they mean. I am glad to know you are different, and speak your mind.'

Catherine smiled. 'Thank you. My lineage is Irish, but I take your point.'

Their teas arrived and the waiter poured for them.

Constance sipped. 'Ah, this is something English that I like!'

'But the owner here is Chinese.'

'Yes, but drinking tea in this manner is purely English,' Constance said, putting down her cup and dabbing a napkin to her lips. 'Your husband told me he is my husband's competitor. That makes you and me the wives of competitors.' She smiled. 'Does that make you my rival?'

Catherine smiled at the witticism. 'I hope not. But you talk about the English as if they were strangers to you.'

'I'm proud of my Spanish heritage, Mrs Leary, though my parents came here with little but fine breeding. Oh, it sounds like I'm talking about horses, doesn't it?'

Catherine laughed and felt herself relax. 'Tell me about your past.'

Constance felt the weight of the tea pot. 'How much time do you have?'

'I need to return to the house by one this afternoon.'

'Good,' Constance said, 'then we'd better order more tea.'

As Catherine farewelled Constance, she glanced at the clock. She still had time for some shopping before getting a cab home. Crossing George Street, she lifted her dress clear of the puddles and breathed through her mouth to avoid smelling the stench of the gutter, then entered the markets opposite. Half an hour later, happy with her purchases, she emerged and made her way to the cab stop near Market Street. Arriving there, she found barriers had been placed around it because the road was being repaired.

'Now what?' she said to herself. King Street was the next stop but she remembered another, closer, in York Street. Going back on her tracks she entered the markets once again and walked through a rear alley. The darkness blinded her for an instant and she trod carefully over slippery cabbage leaves, their smell mixing with the staleness of the trapped air. Nearing the end of the alley, a man stepped in front of her. The glass buttons caught her eye first, triggering a memory, then his face.

'Well, hello, beautiful. We meet again.' It was the King, the man who had held up their carriage on the night of the ball. Fear coursed through her as she tried to step around him. He placed a hand around her waist. 'Not so fast,' he said. 'We haven't been introduced.'

'Get away!'

'Now, is that polite?' he said and smirked. Catherine looked around. 'No, there's no one here, darlin'. We're alone.' He snatched at her handbag, causing her to drop her shopping. She slapped his face.

'Not good,' he said.

Catherine heard a swish of air, then pain for an instant, then she lost consciousness.

John was in his Annandale office. The morning sun was streaming through the window onto the scattered papers on his desk.

'I've told the men,' Richard said sitting beside him, 'to keep their eyes and ears open if they hear anything about it.'

'Good.'

'So Bill Bucknell knows nothing?'

'At Farringtons' last Saturday night,' John said, 'he mumbled that he'd heard a rumour about it, but nought else.'

'He might know the architect who's designing it,' Richard said.

'He might.' The architectural profession was a tight bunch and someone must know something. It was going to be the biggest hotel in Sydney, for goodness sake. If Bucknell had foreknowledge, he'd be in front, able to plan and get suppliers onside. 'Who's first?' John asked.

'Judd.'

'Bring him in, please.' Richard left the office and John racked his brain for other ideas. If his competitors wouldn't tell him, he'd interrogate his staff. They could've picked up something, any titbit would help. It was time for their monthly reports anyway, so he would prod. His office manager came in with Richard and they both sat down.

'Alf,' John said, 'I've read your report.'

Judd looked at his notes. 'We're down on staff, Mr Leary, with three absent from illness.'

'Three people sick? That's not good. Get to their homes tonight. If they aren't bailed up with pneumonia, I'll want to know why.'

Judd's Adam's apple bounced. 'Yes, Mr Leary.'

'And I didn't see the latest gas bill. If it's high like the last one, find out why and take steps to cut down our use. We'll look at it again next month. That's all for you, but just one thing. Have you heard anything about a big new job in town? A big hotel?'

Judd frowned. 'No, Mr Leary.'

'Thank you. You've got work, then. I won't keep you.'

Judd left and the next man came in: John Gibson, Leary's chief buyer, who sat down in the still warm chair. John smiled to himself—the hot seat.

'How's that bulk cement order?'

'Done, Mr Leary.'

'Good, and the timber situation? Is hardwood still scarce?'

Gibson pressed his lips together. 'South Coast is, but North Coast, there's plenty.'

John pointed a finger across the desk at his chief buyer. 'I'll not have that rubbish on my sites. It'll twist and warp just looking at it.' John paused. 'It's your job to get the best price. Don't accept the millers' excuses. Get the facts, man. When were you last down south?'

'Ah ... the end of January.'

'It's the third of March now. Get down there again. Just bring me back an order that saves me money. Stay there till you do. Your offsider can take over. From now on, Mr Richard, as Construction Manager, will do all the major ordering. His foremen will have the responsibility to buy for their sites. But the big stuff like bulk timber, cement, iron girders and the like, you'll buy. What's news on the big pub?'

'What big pub?'

John grinned. 'Don't worry. Off you go.'

Two down. Tom Prentice, his chief estimator, whom John had snaffled from a competitor, was next.

'Let's hear from you, Tom. Your notes told me a few things but what are the jobs we *need* to look at?'

Prentice looked straight at him. This was more like it, a man who faced him square. Estimators were essential; they had to measure all the materials and labour that went into a building job, cost them and—better—win the job.

'Two jobs, Mr Leary, not big but profitable. The first is the bank's new warehouse at Newtown.'

'Who have you got pricing it?'

'Declan.'

'Good,' John said. Sean's son had been a good foreman and had a keen interest in costing. He'd been an estimator now for three years. 'What's the margin?'

'Twelve per cent.'

'Will it take twenty?'

'No. We won't win it with that.'

John held Tom's look. He was either a good bluffer or he told the truth. John was satisfied that Tom was genuine. He had a soft spot for estimators. They had to know what they were doing or Leary's would run out of work.

'The other job?' Richard asked. 'The Petersham Memorial Hall?'

'Twenty per cent. Gives us about £300 profit after overheads have been deducted.'

'Good,' John said, clasping his hands.

Tom collected his papers and was preparing to leave.

'Stay, Tom. What's the news about the big hotel? Have you heard anything? I spoke to a bank partner and Bucknell, but they let nothing slip.'

There was a knock on the office door and Mrs Mansfield, John's new secretary, entered. 'A note for Mr Richard, sir.'

Richard took the note and read it. 'Mike Finnegan is outside and wants to see us. It's important, he says.'

'Send him in, Mrs Mansfield, please,' John said.

Mike Finnegan, a foreman, walked in, took off his hat and stood behind Tom Prentice.

'Well, Mike?' Richard asked.

'Brendan told me this morning, Mr Leary, that he'd heard somethin' at the brickworks—'

'St Peters?' John asked.

'Yeah, something about a bloody great brick order.' Finnegan paused. 'But it sounds so high.'

'Out with it,' John said.

'Three million bricks all up. They're not being made yet but they're trying to get the clay.'

'Can't be, Mike,' Richard said. 'For one job? Three million? You sure Brendan heard right?'

'That's what he said. Could even be more.'

'No,' John said. 'That's three years' supply for the whole town!'

Tom Prentice shook his head. 'Impossible.'

'I believe Mr Brendan, boss,' Finnegan said. 'He's never wrong about figures and such.'

John thought for a bit then said, 'Three million bricks.' It might be the new hotel. It had to be. How big was that?' He did some rough sums. Seven thousand common bricks needed to build each hotel room, say twenty rooms per floor plus back rooms: that would be ...

'Fifteen floors high!' Richard said.

'Plus the basements and facing bricks on the outside,' John said. 'It's a big bastard. Nothing like that's ever been built in Sydney, nothing.'

'It'll be hard to price,' Tom said, 'a job like that. Jesus, you can't cost it like an ordinary one.'

'You're right,' John said. 'Now, first off we need proof of the number of bricks.'

'I've got a friend who's a supervisor there,' Richard said. 'I'll find out.'

'Good,' John said. 'Thanks, Mike. You can go.' He turned to the others. 'If it's the pub, how are we going to win it? Richard? Any ideas?'

Richard smiled as Finnegan closed the door behind him. 'Submit the lowest price with the quickest time to build.'

That was one way, but price and time were not the only components of a winning bid. John needed ideas: maybe Brendan should be here? After all, he'd been on the spot to hear the brickworks' news. And others were needed. 'David Sullivan: he has to be in on this.'

'He's our best general foreman,' Richard said. 'The wool store he's running's got over a year left to go. But he couldn't lead a huge project like that, surely?'

John hadn't decided who would run the giant project. As Construction Manager, Richard was favoured, but John didn't want his son and heir tied up full-time on one long-term job. Their other projects would suffer from his lack of attention.

Richard sensed John's indecision. 'You want him to lead?' he said.

'Just get him in next time we meet,' John said. 'We have to verify what project needs three million bricks.' Richard didn't seem convinced. John went on the offensive. 'Now Richard, take notes. Let's try and guess what we might need in the bid. Start at the bottom ...'

'It'll be a deep hole. We'll need steam-powered shovels to save us time.' His son was right: hand digging was slow and on an excavation of that size they'd need hundreds of navvies. Steam shovels were the go. 'And we'll need drays,' Richard added. 'Big brutes to cart the excavated spoil away.'

'Tom,' John said. 'Got that?'

Tom threw his hands up. 'But there are no powered shovels in Sydney, I'm pretty sure.'

'London,' Richard said. 'That's where we'll get them. I've got some information in my office. You can send them a telegram.'

'Right,' Tom said. 'If we could get a lead on grabbing those machines, we'd be ahead of our competitors.'

'We have to request a contract for their lease,' added Richard.

'Lease?' John asked.

'We don't want to own them,' Richard said. 'We just need them to do the basement.' Richard poured himself a glass of water from a corner table and drank it. 'Now, the spoil,' he paused. 'We've got a site in Canterbury, haven't we Father?'

'We do, near the railway station. Why?'

Richard grinned. 'We can dump the basement spoil there. It'll save us money.'

'It will,' Tom said. 'We won't have to pay someone to fill their land.'

'Cranes,' Richard said. 'They'll have to be Bolton's.'

'And don't forget the elevators,' John said. 'They'll be Otis specials.'

Then they discussed labour and riggers and bricklayers. Eventually John brought the conversation to a halt. 'That's it for now. We'll meet next Tuesday, same time but in your office, Richard. I've got plans to extend the meeting room. I want answers to the things we've discussed. You're in charge. Get notes of this meeting, but keep mum. What we're talking about here, nobody's even thinking about.'

When they had gone, John spent the rest of the day completing his review of projects in hand. Placing his notes to be typed in his out-tray, he put his jacket on, left his office and turned to his secretary. 'I'm off for home, Mrs Mansfield,' he said and smiled. 'How are you settling in?'

'Very well, thank you, sir,' she replied.

'Good. If you need any help, just ask. I'll see you tomorrow.' John closed his office door and made his way down the corridor to the exit, where a policeman stood in his path.

The policeman removed his helmet. 'Are you Mr Leary?'

'I am.'

'I'm Sergeant Maddison, sir. You're to come to Sydney Hospital.'

'Hospital? Why?'

'It's Mrs Leary, she's had an accident, sir. I've got a wagon at the front. I can take you now.'

John took Catherine's hand. It was cold and clammy. She lay still, with bandages wrapped around the top of her head.

'She was found unconscious,' the doctor said, 'and she's been like that ever since. Her pulse and other signs are normal.'

John's eyes didn't leave his wife. They had found her at the markets, lying on rotting leaves. The detritus might have caused her fall, but her purse was there and it was empty. She must have had some money in the purse, to get a cab home. He asked in anguish, 'She will regain consciousness?'

The doctor hesitated. 'It's more than probable. Best she rests at the moment. I'll leave you. I have my rounds.'

The doctor's footsteps faded. This morning, Catherine had been a smiling, happy woman; now here she was, unmoving and pale. John sat on a chair and squeezed her hand again, as if his warmth could excite her blood to make her wake. Maybe the market person who found her had taken the money? Possible, but unlikely. He wouldn't have called the police if that had been the case. He'd have just taken the money and run. It must have been someone else. John closed his eyes and prayed.

A chair moved at his side and Brendan removed his hat and sat down. He looked at his mother in deep concern. 'How is she?'

'The doctor says she's just ... unconscious.'

'How did this happen?'

'The policeman said that a market person found her slumped on the ground. That person called the—'

60

'I know, Sergeant Madison told me when he came to site. She fell, you think?'

'I don't know. She might have.'

Brendan placed a hand on his mother's arm.

'She might have been attacked and her money stolen,' John said and his anxiety mounted. 'I can't make her wake up.'

Brendan stretched out his hand to him and then withdrew it. 'Father, she's in the best of care.'

John clasped his hands and sought control. He mustn't break down. 'Thank God someone found her in time.' A chill went through him.

'Father, she will come out of this.'

John looked at his son, whose face was now calm. 'Of course she will.'

'She will.'

They both sat still while the shadows lengthened over her bed.

Chapter Three

His working week finished, Brendan was on his way to Princes Street. When he got there, he saw that it was a typical Rocks street: full of run-down tenements and overcrowded footpaths, where urchins grabbed your legs and wriggling fingers found their way into your pockets. His builder's eye could see that although most of the houses needed work, they had good bones.

He wanted to find the girl. All week he'd been thinking of her and today was the day. McIntyre's factory manager had been evasive at first in talking about one of his workers, but for Brendan's five shillings he'd swapped her name and address.

Brendan thought of his mother. It was Saturday and she'd been unconscious since Tuesday when she'd fallen—or had she been attacked? Twice he'd spent time with her and he would again later today.

He found the house he wanted. A tired assembly of iron and peeling plaster held together by memories and Sydney's haze. An open front door beckoned and Brendan hesitated. Should he make this call? After all, he didn't know the girl. What if she didn't want to see him? *Oh well, here goes.*

He searched the worn veranda floorboards, careful where he trod.

'What you want, mister?' a voice said.

Brendan looked at the scrunched up face of a boy who was probably ten or eleven, but had the eyes of a youth who'd seen more on the tough streets around him than Brendan ever would in his lifetime. Hands on hips, the boy guarded the front door. 'Is Miss Carson at home?' Brendan asked.

The boy sniffed and wiped his nose. 'No.'

'She lives here, doesn't she?'

A middle-aged woman appeared behind the boy. She ran a hand through her greying hair and studied Brendan's modest but well-cut garb. 'I'm May Carson,' she said. 'What do you want? You after Julie?'

The boy rushed past Brendan and joined a group of his mates gathered at the front fence to gawk at the well-dressed stranger.

'Yes, I am,' Brendan said, removing his hat.

'Well, she ain't here,' Mrs Carson said. 'It's her Saturday off and she's down the fishos.'

'Where's that?'

'Told you he's a toff,' cried a young voice behind Brendan. 'Don't know nothin', he don't.'

'Shut up Billy!' cried the woman. 'Who are you?'

'Brendan Leary, Mrs Carson. If you could show me the way to the fishmongers I'd—'

'Hear that?' screamed Billy, 'Mongers he says.'

Mrs Carson ran at the group. 'Get away, you lot,' she said and turned to Brendan. 'Sorry about that. Why do you want to see Julie?'

Brendan hesitated. He hadn't thought of a reason and just telling Mrs Carson that he wanted to *see* her daughter sounded daft. 'I . . . have a message for her.'

'From McIntyre's?'

'Yes.' Brendan was blushing now, the lie difficult for him.

May Carson paused and Brendan was about to turn away, embarrassed.

'Go down Windmill Street and into Pottinger, right at the end,' she said. 'You'll see her.' Mrs Carson smiled showing three teeth. 'If the pong don't knock you, the seagulls will peck your hat. If she's comin' home she'll come that way.'

Brendan touched his forehead. 'Thank you, Mrs Carson.' He turned around to see that the gang of boys had gone.

He set off the short distance to Argyle Street and turned left. The smell hit him and Brendan held his breath and stepped over the drain. How people lived here, he didn't know. 'Be off now,' Brendan said, smiling as two little ones tried to jump him. 'I've nothing for you.' But he flung a coin to one and then it was on. It was as if he'd thrown a piece of meat to stray dogs and when he walked on the language would have blistered paint from a wall.

The sun was strong and he perspired in his jacket. Noises from carts, barking dogs and yells filled the street. People stood in doorways and groups of women nattered to each other. When he walked by them they stopped talking and stared at him, making him feel self-conscious.

Julie Carson. He'd seen her again outside McIntyre's, the corrugated iron and brick, garment-making factory where she worked. A man had seen Brendan watching her there and Brendan had felt embarrassed as if she was his prey. There was something about her.

'Steady, mate,' cried a voice and Brendan stepped back onto the footpath as a wagon just missed him.

It was her stance and the way she walked that attracted him: a proud carriage that belied her background. Proud, that's what it was, all right. And she looked under twenty. Brendan shook his head as the pungent smell of rotting fish filled his nostrils. He'd reached Pottinger Street but there was no sign of Julie. He stopped at the corner store, disappointed, and turned to go home when she came out of the store with a bundle under her arm. She was licking a lollypop.

She glanced at him and kept walking. She was tall, about five-feet-five maybe, with her brunette hair tied in a ponytail. He seemed glued to the footpath, unable to move. She was walking away. He went after her. 'Miss Carson?

She turned, took Brendan in with just one look, then resumed walking. 'That's me.'

Brendan followed and stopped with her at the corner to let a fish-factory wagon pass, seagulls attacking its load.

'Pooh! Puts you off fish, don't it,' Julie said and smiled. 'What do you want?' she asked, licking her sweet. 'You're not from here, are ya?' Her clear skin and hazel eyes excited him. She crossed the road and Brendan followed, noticing again the way she walked. She stopped and turned. 'You're not the law, are you?'

Brendan gaped. Why would she say that? Perhaps she was in trouble. 'No, I'm not. But if I was, would that be a problem for you?'

'No. And you're not a copper,' she said and flung her stick into a bin. 'I was teasing.'

He took off his hat. 'I'm Brendan Leary.'

'Are you now? And who's he?' Julie replied, walking away.

Brendan kept up with her. This wasn't going well. He had run out of ideas of how to get her attention. 'You see, Miss Carson, I've seen you at the factory—where you work—and I wonder if you'd go out with me.'

Julie didn't reply until she turned the corner into Princes Street. She stopped again and looked at him. 'Been spying, have ya? That's not nice. Didn't teach you that in your public school, did they?'

Brendan looked down. 'I'm sorry. I didn't mean any harm. It's just ...'

He looked up to see her grinning. 'All right, you're not a slasher, so what do you want again?'

They were nearly at her home and Brendan spied a bunch of boys running towards them, led by the keeper of Julie's front door. *Champion.* Just when he was making progress.

'Here he is!' Billy yelled. 'The toff.'

Julie sprang in front of Brendan with one hand on her hip and her feet planted ready to face the posse. 'Stop there, Billy, and say nothing.'

Billy picked his nose and looked at his gang. 'He's your fella.'

Julie's face remained calm. 'Have you cut the firewood for Ma?'

Billy sniffed. 'There's plenty in the box,' he said, grinning at Brendan and opening his mouth to speak.

'Well, cut some more,' Julie said. 'Now, off you go, and here, take this fish home.'

Billy looked from his sister to Brendan, grabbed the parcel and ran off. Julie followed him.

Brendan followed her. 'Miss Carson?'

Julie turned to face him, annoyed. 'Mr Leary,' she said, 'don't spy on me no more. Now go away. You don't belong here.'

Brendan's shoulders slumped. 'All right, I won't harass you but I would like to see you again. Maybe a walk in the Botanic Gardens on a Sunday … this coming Sunday.'

Julie sighed and looked him up and down. Brendan counted the seconds. She had to say yes. All his hopes were pinned on her next words.

'I don't know. Look Mr Leary, I'm not a moll.'

Brendan was shocked. 'Dear me, no, of course not. I'd just like to talk and walk with you. That's all.'

'That would be a change.' She glanced at her home, then back to him. 'Where again?'

'The Botanic Gardens.'

'Just you?'

'Of course.'

She pursed her lips. 'I suppose it'd be all right.' .

Brendan closed his eyes for an instant. *That was close.* Next time they met he'd have a better plan. He said, 'Next Sunday at two, then, outside the Macquarie Street entrance?'

Julie walked off. 'See you then, Mr Leary.'

Brendan waited till Julie closed her front door then punched one hand with glee.

He set off and caught the crowded tram at Circular Quay back to Oxford Street. Squeezed between an overweight matron and another woman, he didn't care, because he'd spoken to Julie and he would be seeing her again. He was happy.

His good humour vanished as he thought of his mother in hospital but also what she'd think of Julie. His mother had tried to steer Brendan towards some suitable girls—as his mother called them. The factory seamstress would not be suitable, but then Catherine Leary had been a milliner and, as a boy, he'd been with her to visit places similar to where Julie worked. His mother had always talked nicely to the women workers. But he couldn't see his mother accepting him going out with one. Still, it was early days. Julie might not even turn up next Sunday and he should be with his mother now.

It was worrying, the way she lay there, so still, her breathing the only sign of life. He thanked God for work: it kept him busy. He thought about it now, to make the tram ride pass.

His father had found out about the big hotel, probably from Mike Finnegan. Brendan had told the foreman about that massive brick order and his father had drawn the conclusion that so many bricks must be for the new project. Brendan wondered what had happened after that. If the brickworks' information was about that job then the hotel was as big as rumoured, and if Leary's won it, it could bankrupt them if they weren't careful.

A bell clanged. 'Liverpool Street,' the conductor called out. Brendan jumped off the omnibus and made his way across Hyde Park. Most of the builders in Sydney were cash-poor but they managed, though a few had gone under. The ones that went under all had one thing in common—they'd had one big job that had gone wrong. Now his father might be going the same way. Chasing the biggest job because it offered the bigger profit—or was he doing it out of vanity? His father loved being in the limelight and winning jobs and he wanted to be the most prominent builder in Sydney. Brendan had to do something to make sure Leary's wouldn't get into trouble. Richard had to be warned. But he must know about the risks, surely? Brendan crossed College Street.

He would have to get involved in the planning of the new hotel, but as a sub-foreman, how could he? And what had his father said? *Stop fussing about detail.* That was all well and good, but quality had to be there in every project and all costs had to be challenged.

Brendan stopped and a man behind him ran into him. 'Sorry,' Brendan said.

What if he could become the boss of Leary's, as his great-uncle had suggested? Could he make the big decisions? Brendan started walking again. The answer was simple: yes, he could.

Turning into the hospital, he prepared himself. His mother needed him, he knew. She needed him to be strong and to pray for her. Of that he was certain.

The bells of St Mary's Cathedral chimed out eight times but John was not in church for Sunday Mass. His children were there, praying for their mother, while he was sitting in Sydney Hospital beside his wife, who was still unconscious. The bandages were gone and her scalp was healing but she hadn't regained consciousness. It was now five days since the accident. John feared she'd always be like this. Not another wife dying ... please God, no. He wished Maureen was here, as she would have helped him, now, but his sister was in Ireland with her family for an extended stay. And to think, just last Saturday night he'd thought about a dalliance with Constance Bucknell!

If Catherine died, he'd at least have his children and they were a part of her. She'd been beside him, giving him love and support, for the last twenty-five years. No, she couldn't die.

Just a ward away from where he sat was the wife of David Sullivan, his general foreman. She had been unconscious for three years. John shut his eyes and prayed for strength. Then he remembered something David had let slip after he'd had a few drinks one day: that he'd speak out loud to his comatose wife. A doctor had told him that unconscious patients could hear. John thought about that and looked around. There was nobody else in Catherine's ward. John would give it a go.

'My darling,' he said, 'I don't know if you can hear me. It's all very strange but if you can ... I want you to help me.' He shook his head. *This is daft.* But he continued. 'Find a way. I have my faith but it's being challenged.' John took her hand again. 'Please try.'

John closed his eyes. Their wedding day, with friends and family laughing and drinking, came into his vision, but that day for him was still clouded by his grief over Clarissa's passing. Catherine had understood and her empathy had made him love her more. He remembered her coming over and whispering to him, 'I'll be with you always.'

For the first time since her accident, his neck muscles relaxed. Opening his eyes, he saw that Catherine had not moved. But what had caused that reaction in him: a message from her? No, that was too simple ... but he did feel better.

'How is she, Father?' Brendan asked as he sat down next to him. 'Mary and Agatha said that she looked paler yesterday.'

His son's clear voice focussed John's thoughts. 'You've missed Mass.'

'No, it's ten past nine. No change?'

'No, no change, son.'

The last of the dinner plates were cleared away. Just Brendan and his father were still at the dinner table and the meal had been subdued without his mother's cheerful presence. On Monday nights his father worked in his study. It was time to act. 'Father,' Brendan said, 'may I talk with you?'

John pushed back his chair. 'Is it important?'

'It is.'

'Well then, better come to the study.'

Brendan followed him and closed the doors after him.

His father sat down, lit a cigar and threw the match into an ashtray. 'What do you want to talk about?'

Brendan glanced at the model ship that his father was building in his spare time. It would be three-masted, but the hull was only half completed. Mother's condition would be on his father's mind. Nearly a week now and no change in her. Maybe right now was not a good time for him to say what he wanted, but then it might never be the right time. 'My promotion. I deserve it, Father.'

His father rested his head on the back of his chair. Cigar smoke clouded his gaze but Brendan wouldn't look away. 'Deserve?' John said.

'I've done the yards, Father, and I will do the job. You have to give me a go.'

'Perhaps, and that reminds me. That business with Clancy. You missed Mass, and for what? You had no authority to give that man time off. You're a sub-foreman only. Men have to work for their wages. And if they bludge, I'll sack them.'

Brendan was just about to defend Clancy but he knew this wasn't the time. He decided to be conciliatory. 'Very well, I shouldn't have given Clancy time off.'

'No you shouldn't have.'

'Do I get the promotion?'

John stiffened. 'Don't push me, Brendan.' His father put down his cigar. 'I still have a fear you won't make it.' Brendan flinched and nearly turned away. But no. He would stand here. He would stay until he got what he reckoned he deserved. 'But I'll give you a go,' his father said, surprising him. 'Enmore, you can have Enmore. Take on that bank job for six months, finish it on time and to budget and we'll talk again. That do you?'

Yes, it was a chance, even though Enmore was poison. The bank was a good client and Leary's had 'bought' the project, pricing it so

70

low that no competitor could win it. It would have a halfpenny of profit in it, if that.

His father reached for a folder and held it out to him. 'Here's the project's latest report.'

Brendan took the file and didn't complain. 'That'll do me.'

'It won't be easy, you know.'

Was that a hint of a smile on his father's face? No. 'Nothing worthwhile ever is,' Brendan said.

His father did smile now. 'That's something I live by.'

'Thank you, Father.'

'Oh, don't thank me. You may regret it. But I'm curious how you'll work out.' His father looked at him. 'No, better than that—I want you to succeed. Leary's needs strong men.' John reached for another file and got to work.

Brendan left him and went into the kitchen, put the kettle on and pondered his new challenge. What had he got himself into? He leaned against the kitchen counter. His father, curiously, wanted him to succeed, which was good. But he couldn't have given him a harder project. It had little margin and just one lazy supplier, who might claim higher costs, might wipe out that margin in a heartbeat. It also had a difficult acting foreman. But on Enmore, he'd prove himself to his father and no one was going to take that from him.

Mary came into the kitchen and stopped when she saw him. 'You're deep in thought,' she said. 'About Mother?'

'No, for once, no.'

'She'll be back with us soon. Making a cuppa?'

Brendan admired Mary's optimism. 'Yeah, want one?'

'Yes, please. Have you got time to talk?' Mary asked, sitting down.

Brendan opened and closed some cupboards. Mary stood up. 'Sit down,' she said, 'I'll do it.'

'The cook must have moved the tea,' Brendan said, admitting defeat.

Mary got to work in a no-nonsense style. Every movement was deliberate: the way her fingers pressed against doors and how she balanced things.

She sat down with two mugs and clasped her hands. 'Something up? I saw you meeting with Father.'

'Just about my future.'

Mary's brown eyes lit up. 'Men are lucky. I'd love to be on site.'

Brendan laughed but Mary wasn't smiling. 'You're joking,' he said. 'You?'

Her brows furrowed. 'Why shouldn't women be allowed on site? They have brains. Can add up and measure. Remember, Richard's mother worked in her father's business. And Mother was a milliner who knows her pounds and pennies.' She got up, made the tea and brought the pot to the table.

Mary had a temper and could wrestle like a man. He decided to change tack. 'What do you want to talk about?'

Mary pouted. 'Father won't let me go away for the weekend. Henri's got a place—'

'Henri?'

'Henrietta Flemming, a girl I know. Henri for short. Anyway, Father won't let me go.' She rolled her eyes. 'He thinks I'm not old enough.' She reached and squeezed his arm. Brendan jerked at the force. 'Sorry,' she said, tossing her long hair. 'I'm angry. I'm twenty-one this year, God's nightie!'

'Don't swear,' he said, smiling. He did love his sister. 'Henri's a mate?'

'She is, close,' Mary said and poured their teas. 'She thinks women should do everything a man does.'

'God forbid,' he said. Mary had few friends, and no beaux. At twenty she should be hitched. But that didn't seem to worry her as much as it did their mother. 'So, what do you want me to do?'

'Speak to Father of course, tonight if you can.'

Brendan raised his eyes. 'What would Mother think?'

Mary's shoulders drooped as she sipped her tea. 'Before the

accident—' Mary said, then paused, her eyes filling with tears. Brendan squeezed her hand. Mary cleared her throat. 'Before the accident, she said no.' Mary sat up straight. 'And I'm not going anywhere out of town till I know Mother's better.' She brightened up. 'Don't fuss Father, now. There'll be another time.'

Brendan thought about his tense talk in the study and was glad his sister wasn't in a hurry. He picked up his mug and said, 'I'll pick the time to ask him.'

Mary reached over and kissed him on the cheek. 'You're good, Brendan. Oh, I overheard Richard telling father he was going to the St Peters Brick Company tomorrow. I'd love to see bricks being made.'

'I might take you one day,' he said and smiled. Richard was going to the brickworks to find out about the new pub. *That's what I should have done.*

Foreman Mike Finnegan might have it squared away but Richard wanted to be sure—he had to see the first roof truss on the Surry Hills warehouse erected without mishap. After tethering his horse, he entered the site gate in Foveaux Street. Mike Finnegan and some workers were standing in a group at the base of a crane with its blackened stack coughing smoke, smudging the 'Bolton' brand name fixed to its jib. As he got closer the men turned to look at him. One had a smirk on his face. Richard suddenly felt guilty about the £80 embezzlement, as if the worker was going to accuse him of it. Perhaps he'd better try to avoid the cards, at least for a while. The previous night's loss at poker still hurt. He owed ten pounds and would have to go to the loan sharks for the cash.

Mike took off his hat and pointed to the truss connected to the crane. 'She'll bust the slings.'

Richard looked at the massive triangular-shaped hardwood truss and scanned its joints and connections. 'If there's a bolt out of place, it will.'

'That truss is built right,' Mike said. 'I checked it, but it'll still fail with that load.'

'It won't,' Richard said and smiled.

'Boss, I hauled one like this pup last year and the slings snapped like a twig.'

'Not on one of my sites it didn't and not with a Bolton crane.'

The workers gathered round the load. The smell of their sweat mingled with the smell of smoke and grease from the crane. 'You men have work to do,' Richard said. 'Those walls need bracing and there're windows to make.' Richard glanced at the foreman.

'You heard the boss,' Mike said. 'Get on with it.' The men went back to their tasks.

Richard stepped up to the foreman. 'You should know your loads, Mike. I gave you the tables last month.'

His foreman used his hat to block the sun as he peered up to the top of the crane's jib. 'Don't need a bunch of numbers to tell me this dog won't hunt. Just look at the tension.'

The slings attached to the truss were as taut as steel bands. The choke hitches were in place and the crane hook sat directly above the truss, as it should.

'They'll hold,' Richard said. But the bolts? The bolts that would connect the truss to the top of the brick walls. It would be too late to get them right when the truss was in the air. Better that it was done now. Richard looked where they should be and spotted them. 'Are the bolts ready?'

'Yeah.'

'Level and plumb?'

Mike nodded.

'How did you check them?'

'With a theodolite,' his foreman replied.

'And are they within the architect's specified tolerance?'

'Yeah, boss, but for the thickness of a cigarette paper.'

'Good enough,' Richard said satisfied. 'Now, get yourself up there and help the carpenters.'

Mike climbed the ladder that was leaning against the twenty-foot-high external brick wall and joined the carpenter who was already on top. Directly opposite them, across the eighty feet of open-span warehouse, sat another carpenter on top of the other external wall.

Mike gave two short whistles, the crane belched smoke and the hardwood truss, eighty feet long and as tall as Richard, gave a little bounce. The load rose and Richard glanced around the site and smiled. All eyes were on the rising truss but he wasn't worried. The crane would not fail. Cranes were special to him. From an early age he'd been fascinated by the ease with which gears, pulleys and ropes made slight work of the heaviest loads. He'd read all there was on all types of cranes, and had good contacts with crane suppliers, especially Bolton's. Foot by foot the truss climbed and a series of even taps sounding from the stretched slings told Richard all was well. Then the space between the taps lengthened and he knew the slings were reaching their limit, but they'd hold. He felt that thrill he always got when man and machine combined to create something practical. This truss was the first of twenty that would support the roof and protect the future goods underneath.

A sharp whistle and the truss stopped level with the waiting carpenters. All taps ceased and the slings were at their maximum stress. The truss slewed and one chippy gripped its bottom frame and brought it to him. His partner opposite did the same with the other end and they seated the truss on its bolts.

Mike watched as the carpenters secured the truss, then climbed down the ladder. 'You're lucky boss.'

'Luck be damned,' Richard said, grinning. 'Come into the shed and I'll show you the weight tables. That load had a margin to spare. Mike, memorise those tables, know them like you know a good beer. That's your job, not mine.'

'How's Mrs Leary?'

Richard paused before replying, 'My stepmother is still unconscious, I'm afraid, but thank you.'

Finnegan opened the site shed door and the two men went inside. 'The boys said to give Mr Leary their best wishes,' Finnegan said as he closed the door.

'Thank you again.'

Mike seemed to hesitate and looked nervous. 'There's talk around, boss. About you. Now, don't take my head off but it's about the disappearance of £80 and you've been named. I want to be able to tell the lads it's not true.'

Richard felt cold though the shed was warm. He felt very foolish. Mike was a brave man to front him with this. Richard forced a smile. 'Just a shortfall, Mike. I'm paying it back.'

Mike squinted for a second as if he didn't believe him but he recovered. 'Just what I thought. Thanks for that.'

Richard wanted to change the conversation. 'Now show me the weight tables and I'll explain them again, and after that let's look at the new drains. I want to run water down them myself to test them. Come on, I've got half an hour before I'm due at St Peters.'

The fumes disgorging from the Brick Company's smokestacks stung Richard's eyes. He brought a handkerchief to his face to protect them. He didn't like word of his theft circulating. And they knew about his gambling, too. Some of his workmates had seen him in action at the cards, both when he'd lost and when he'd won big, so he had a reputation. Some of the men would have already linked his gambling with the theft and that wasn't good. He hoped Mike would spread the word that it wasn't a theft but a shortfall.

By contrast, this visit to the brickworks was his opportunity to shine. Brendan had heard about the massive number of bricks and that had been verified by Richard's friend who worked here. This morning Richard would get the credit for finding out more about the new hotel. He blinked in the heat and went into the Brick Company's office: its interior was cool and dim like a church.

A thin-lipped man looked up from his seat. 'Yes sir?'

'Is Mr Murphy in?' Richard said.

'He is. Who are you, sir?'

'Richard Leary, I have an appointment.'

'Please wait here.'

There were pictures on the walls. One showed the raising of the tallest chimney in the southern hemisphere; another, a daguerreotype of the whole St Peters Brick Company's workforce bunched in front of the main gates, hundreds of them. A strong smell of cologne made him turn around.

'Richard, it's good to see you. It's been, what, three months?' Brian Murphy's fat face broke into a grin and Richard shook his hand. 'Come this way.'

Richard followed him into an office where the brick maker dropped into a chair and squeezed his large stomach against a desk stacked with paper. 'Place is a madhouse.'

'Business that good?'

Murphy pursed his lips. 'Plenty of orders, plenty, but costs ... they're rising faster than a politician's wage. We'll struggle this year, we will.'

'Knowing you, Brian, you'll always make a quid. What's your best price for commons?'

Murphy grinned again and slapped the desk. 'That's what I like about you, Richard. Tells it like it is. Common bricks? Can't make them cheaper than fourteen shillings a thousand. Got a batch you can have now. Bring your wagon?' Richard smiled. 'No? Well, what brings you here? Our rep Johnson does your traps, takes all Leary's orders. Good man, Johnson.'

'I needed to see you. I want some information.'

Murphy sat back. 'Always happy to help Leary's. How's your father these days? Don't see much of him.'

Richard had to be careful. This would take finesse. 'Father still keeps his hand in.'

'Excellent.'

'How's life at the top?'

'Can't complain, Mr Leary. More salary, that's for sure.'

Good. 'The big new pub?'

Murphy frowned. 'Which pub?'

Richard acted innocent. 'Why, the one everyone's talking about.'

Murphy opened his hands. 'The Imperial?'

Got its name. Good. 'The Imperial Hotel, just the biggest project in town.'

'Indeed,' Murphy said and smiled.

'Who's the architect?'

The brick maker lost his smile. 'I'd like to tell you, Richard. I would, but I can't. I'm sworn to secrecy.'

'But you know the job.'

'I do, my friend. I do.'

'Then tell me about it.'

Murphy tapped the side of his nose. 'What I know is valuable.'

'I'm sure. So what do you know?'

Murphy grinned again. In the closed office his face was sweating. 'Richard, you know me. Charity is for mugs. Everything has its price.'

Richard made his move. 'I've got a proposition. Leary's need special bricks for our bank project. One hundred thousand blues.'

Murphy whistled. 'Tough. Dark clay's scarce. I dunno where I can ...'

Richard folded his arms. 'I'm willing to pay top price for the bricks—within reason.'

Murphy closed one eye. 'You'll let me name my own price?'

'I'm not going to pay just anything, Brian, but I've got to make it worth your while.'

Murphy scribbled some numbers. 'What would you say to £1 per thousand?'

This was a high price but not extortionate and within the project's budget. 'Delivered to Enmore?'

Murphy shook his head. 'You're a hard man. All right, delivered for a quid a thousand.'

'Done. Now tell me what you know.'

Hurried footsteps outside his office distracted John and he looked up as Mrs Mansfield stood in the open doorway.

'Mr Leary,' she said. 'It's the hospital. Your wife has regained consciousness.'

John grabbed his hat. 'Get Gibbs.'

'He's waiting outside.'

John ran from his office, his heart racing. *Dear God, it's happened.* He held on as Gibbs drove the carriage down Johnston Street. *Hurry, hurry.*

Home beat a hospital ward hands down and John was pleased Catherine was back in her familiar surroundings. It would speed her recovery, he was certain of that. Just two days ago, she had had a restless trip in the ambulance back to Point Piper, but here she was in their bedroom and sleeping.

She opened her eyes. 'It's not a dream?'

'No. You're home in your own bed and it's a beautiful evening.'

'I still can't believe that I was unconscious for so long.'

'Yes. It's Thursday the twelfth of March. You fell on the ... third. You were unconscious for eight days. We were very worried, but you're home now and we're going to look after you so that you are soon back to your old self.' John stroked her hand.

The fragrance of the lilies in a vase on the bedside table was pleasant and added to the happy atmosphere. Catherine's fingers felt the satin hem of her blanket. 'When I woke in the ward, it seemed I'd just had a normal night's sleep.'

'For you, maybe, but not for us.'

'I wish I could remember what happened just before the accident. But the last thing I remember was walking down that dark alley.'

Christine's head peeped around the door. 'Good, you're awake. Care for some more company?'

'Of course,' Catherine said. 'But you shouldn't be bothering about me.'

John positioned a chair beside the bed for his mother-in-law.

'Don't fuss,' Christine said coming to the bedside. 'I'll manage.' She eased herself into the chair and smiled at Catherine. 'How's your head?'

'Still a little sore.'

'Well, it's God's blessing that we've got you back.'

'It's pleasant to be so missed, Christine. Thank you. But it'll be a while before I can get up.'

John smiled again. 'And a bit longer till you can dance.'

'I know,' Catherine said and sighed.

'When you were in hospital,' Christine said, 'I thought about Clarissa. I didn't want to go back to that time again.'

John looked at his mother-in-law and felt for her. Clarissa had been in his thoughts too.

'You must miss her still,' Catherine said.

'Like any mother misses her children. They shouldn't die before you do.' She stared at her hands. 'I miss her bright smile and vivaciousness.' She was silent for a time.

'Don't upset yourself, Christine,' John said.

Christine blinked some tears away and looked at Catherine. 'Anyway, enough of me; you're here and that's important. Brendan was the one who held out the most hope. He was not having any rot about you leaving us.'

'A good boy,' Catherine said.

'Richard kept it in, though. But I know my grandson. He was worried and John here, well, what can I say? He rarely left your side. He loves you so much.'

John raised his eyebrows in surprise. It was rare for Christine to compliment him.

'Try to sleep, dear,' he said. 'We'll go. I have to see Richard in a few moments.'

'John,' Catherine said, 'could you do me a favour?'

'Surely.'

'Could you call Delia? There are a few friends I need to tell that I'm all right. The Connaires especially.'

'I'll get her, but don't exert yourself. Come Christine, I'll help you down the stairs. Unless you want to go to your room?'

'You go ahead,' his mother-in-law said. 'I've got plenty of time.'

Christine made her way towards the stairs at her own pace. It had been a near thing with Catherine and she had been quite distressed about her accident. When John had shown interest in the twenty-year-old milliner all those years ago, Christine had been relieved. Not for the fact that he'd possibly found love again but that it raised him out of his depression after Clarissa's death. At that time, he had been a man who'd lost his way: he wasn't interested in the business and though he tried to spend time with Richard, he left most of the care to Stella, their maid and Richard's nanny. Christine helped out where she could but she was busy keeping Leary's afloat with the help of Sean Connaire. She had missed Clarissa dreadfully, too, but John's grief had been tinged with the guilt of his affair with Beth Blackett. Catherine had been patient and understanding and eventually she had succeeded in winning John's love. Christine knew that Clarissa would always have a place in John's heart, but was pleased to see her son-in-law happy and interested in life and his business again. And John had been faithful to Catherine and that, over the years, had worn away the distrust Christine had felt towards her son-in-law over his affair.

Catherine had created a loving home for John and Richard, and Brendan, Mary and Agatha when they came along. She had been warm and welcoming to Christine and to Gerry and now they all lived happily together in the big Point Piper house. She'd never expected it, but in Catherine, Christine had found another daughter to love.

Nearing the study she heard conversation through its open doors. Seating herself in a chair just outside, she listened to Richard talking with his father.

'I'm sure Turner and Harrington are the architects,' Richard said.

'But Turners are not a top practice,' John replied.

'I know that, but I'm certain, nonetheless.'

'Who told you?'

'Murphy at St Peters.'

'Let's set up a meeting soon,' John said. 'The rest of what you've told me sounds about right. The Imperial Hotel, eh? Good work, son. Yes, and you should smile. It'll give us a start, but we'll need to move fast. Oh, another thing, I've given Brendan the Enmore Bank job as foreman.'

'Are you sure?'

'I am. He'll either sink or swim and I'm hoping for the latter.'

'It's your decision, Father. It could satisfy him, I suppose. I'll check on him.'

Good boy, thought Christine—smart move.

'Do that,' John said.

Christine had always seen Richard as John's replacement when he decided to step down, but she knew that Gerry favoured Brendan. Brendan was young, but he was a quick learner and was steadily proving himself a possible contender. She smiled. Yes, it might be a contest of wills—interesting.

Christine moved away towards the stairs, smiling. Richard had done well. Brendan had found out about the big brick order for this new project but Richard had got the name of the job and its architects. The score between the sons—one all.

It was just after two o'clock and Brendan stood outside the Botanic Gardens, his coat collar buttoned up to keep out the chill southerly whipping up Macquarie Street. It was early autumn, but it felt more like winter, and by winter he'd have to have his project in shape. Brendan folded a copy of *The Bulletin* and slid it into his back trouser pocket. There was an article on the building unions in Great Britain that he would read later.

His week had not gone well. His sub-foreman Dougherty hadn't been happy about Brendan taking charge; Brendan suspected Dougherty had wanted the promotion for himself. The Enmore job had more problems than a dog with one leg and he wondered where he'd start. The bank's representative, Donald Dawkins, was a nosey man and wanted everything done to painstaking and unrealistic rules. The project was in poor shape and Brendan was thinking over the work that needed to be done to get it right.

But his thoughts about work vanished when he spotted Julie Carson crossing Macquarie Street. She was dressed in a crinoline skirt with bustle. Her light green bonnet matched the blouse worn under a coarse wool jacket.

'I didn't think you'd turn up,' she said, coming up to him.

'And why not?'

'Well, you could've changed your mind. I wouldn't have been upset.'

Brendan was taken aback by her abruptness and indifference. 'No, I wanted to come, and here I am.'

'I don't know why.'

Again Brendan was surprised. The few girls he knew, like Anne Connaire, were shy and only spoke when he asked them a question and then they only said a few words in reply. 'I don't want to argue, all right? I'm here because I wanted to be here.'

She grinned. 'Good. Now, what do you want to do? I can't stay long. Ma needs me home by three.'

This was better. 'We could just stroll and talk.'

'Lead on, then.'

Brendan walked beside her as they entered the Gardens. There were couples like them, and a few families as well, sitting on the grass. They walked without speaking for a while. 'Tell me about your work at McIntyre's,' Brendan eventually said.

She bent down to smell some lavender. 'It's not much of a job but the wages are good.' She stood up. 'The girls you know wouldn't work, would they?'

'No ... they don't,' Brendan admitted.

'Well I do. I have to. And the wages help my mum.'

'You make garments?'

'Dresses, uniforms. The work is noisy, the hours long and the bosses get familiar. Anything else you'd like to know?'

Brendan blushed. 'But that's wrong.'

'What?' she smiled. 'The long hours or the wandering hands?'

Brendan had to change the subject. Miss Carson was very forward. 'You sew?'

'On a machine. It's hot and cramped. But we're better off than Surry Hills. Those girls there work fourteen-hour days.'

Brendan remembered his visit with his mother to such a place. They stopped at a chestnut vendor. 'Would you like some?'

Her face brightened. 'Yes, please.'

Brendan paid the vendor and took two paper bags, grateful for the warmth from the heated nuts. He gave one bag to her. 'Let's sit here, out of the wind. So what do you do on the weekends?'

'Work on Saturdays up to twelve, then help Ma, or go on picnics.' She smiled and popped a chestnut in her mouth. 'See young men who follow me.' Julie looked at him, her eyes twinkling.

'Are you always this direct?'

'Mr Leary—'

'Call me Brendan, please.'

'I don't know you well enough yet, Mr Leary.'

Brendan opened his collar, despite the chill; he was nervous, and uncomfortable with the way the conversation was going. 'Are you always this confronting?'

'What's that mean?'

'Well, you say things forcefully.'

She closed the bag of chestnuts. 'Can I take these home to Ma and Billy?'

'Of course you can.'

She looked down. 'I speak the way I do because that's me. My life is simple and it's hard.' She looked back at him. 'You wouldn't know how we struggle, because your family has money.'

'We do, but I work hard as well.'

'At what?' Julie said as she pushed the bag into her jacket pocket.

'I'm a foreman on a building site.'

'So you're like a carpenter?'

'Yes, in fact I trained as a carpenter. But now I have a team to look after.'

She stood up and Brendan did likewise. 'What time is it?' she said. Brendan pulled out his watch and flipped open its gold lid. Miss Carson stroked it with a gloved finger. 'That's beautiful,' she said and looked closer. 'A quarter to three. I have to go, Mr Leary.' She put out her hand. 'I've enjoyed the talk and thank you for the chestnuts.'

Brendan held her hand. He had to ask. 'I'd like to go out with you.'

She slipped her hand from his. 'Why?'

'Does there have to be a reason?'

She smiled. 'You made your mind up, just talking to me. No reason, then?'

'I just want to ... know you.'

She hesitated. 'Come on. Walk me to the gates.' They set off, saying nothing until they reached the entrance where she stopped. She said. 'If I said yes, would you tell your family?'

Brendan hesitated just for two seconds, but it was enough.

'See, you wouldn't,' she said. 'Your mother would be angry.'

She was right there. Mother wasn't a snob, yet he felt there would be difficulties. 'I'd still like to see you again.'

'You would, would you?' she said and looked at him. 'There are girls I work with, Mr Leary, who would do anything to go out with you. You've got money, I can tell, you're a gent and you're single.' She gave him a frank stare again. 'You are, aren't you ... single?'

'I am.'

'But those girls would take you for a merry ride and make you pay.' She put out her hand again. 'I won't do that. Goodbye, Mr Leary.'

Brendan held her hand again, her grip firm and confident. 'And if I happen to meet you again?'

Julie removed her hand and did up her jacket. She glanced to his side and looked surprised.

Brendan turned around. There was a man walking by and looking at them. Nearby was a couple, talking. No one else.

'If I met you again,' Julie said, 'I'd say hello to you. But if you've any sense, you won't meet me. We're just too different. Goodbye.'

Brendan watched her walk away. Something or someone had thrown her at that moment. No matter. He wouldn't be put off. He would see her again.

Chapter Four

JOHN STOOD NEAR THE FRONT DOOR OF LEARY'S AT ANNANDALE, waiting for Richard. It was mid-March and he was itching to get to the architects.

'Who are we meeting, again?' Richard said, joining him.

'Tompkins.'

'I know him. He's a junior. If we aren't meeting William Turner, a principal, it's a waste of time.'

Richard was right. 'Well, it's a start,' John said, getting into his carriage, followed by Richard. 'I can't find anyone who knows Turner, and the other partner, Harrington, has retired.'

The overhead hatch opened. 'George Street, Gibbs,' John said, 'near Bridge Street.'

John suspected his competitors might have met the senior partner and could even now be examining early plans of the hotel. He was angry and needed a head to kick. 'What's happened to that brick order for Enmore?'

'I got it.'

'At the right price?'

'Yes, Father.'

'Good, because we need to get costs down. If the Imperial Hotel is going to be as big as rumoured, we can't build it like we do now.' Huge buildings would change construction dramatically. 'It'll be a two-year project, at least. Two years—that's unheard of for a hotel. If we aren't organised, it could easily blow out to three or four years and bankrupt us.' He was certain his competitors knew the pitfalls as well.

'All I know is things have to be kept simple,' Richard said. 'The architects control the builder, they supervise the construction and are the client's agents.'

'We can do nothing about that. The architects can still have their Gothic revival patterns, columns, gargoyles and pilasters but the building blocks, the bricks, ironwork, timbers and other things that will make up this big brute of a hotel, will need our attention.' John started to estimate the planning of a building over ten storeys high. He was still deep in thought when the carriage passed the Town Hall.

'Brendan and I went to Alexandria last week,' Richard said. 'A firm called Edwards is producing metal ceiling panels by the hundreds. It'll save time and money on the Enmore site.'

'That's the thinking you'll need on the Imperial Hotel.'

'I'm ahead of you, Father. We're planning to get our door-opening supports mass-produced in steel. It will save us from having to frame up each individual doorway in timber and save us one thousand hours of labour on site.'

'Good. Good.'

The carriage stopped outside a building in George Street. Once inside, John and Richard ascended the stairs to the first-floor offices of Turner and Harrington, Architects.

A clerk rose to meet them as they entered the foyer. 'May I help you?'

'John and Richard Leary to see Mr Tompkins.'

'Please have a seat,' the man said.

They sat down and after two minutes, John was tapping his boot on the floor. *Keep calm.*

'Mr Leary?'

A young man in a three-piece suit stood in front of them, smiling. Great start, John thought—a wet-faced urchin. 'Mr Tompkins?' John said.

'It is.'

'How are you, Jack?' Richard asked. 'Remember me from the Dodds job?'

'I do, Richard. Please come this way.'

They followed Tompkins into a small office and sat down. Tompkins closed the door after them, cutting off the ammonia smell from a nearby plan printer. 'How can I help you, gentlemen?'

'We're here to find out about the Imperial Hotel,' John said.

Tompkins gave an oily smile. 'That project is confidential.'

John sighed. 'Please tell us about it. We *are* a leading builder.'

Tompkins paused. 'We know you are and I'll tell you what I can. We have been commissioned—'

'Who by?'

'A group of private investors, Mr Leary.'

John smiled. 'But you won't tell us who?'

Tompkins spread his hands. 'Unfortunately I can't. It's going to be the most magnificent building in Sydney, the grandest hotel so far.'

John wasn't interested in the owners, not yet anyway. But he needed to keep this youth talking.

'At this point we are doing preliminary drawings,' Tompkins said.

An untruth, John thought. If St Peters Brick Company knew, then advanced plans must have already been drawn.

'How big is it?' Richard asked.

'It will be the largest hotel in Sydney.'

'We mean, how many floors?' asked John.

Tompkins' eyes lit up. 'Taller than the planned Australia Hotel.'

That was mooted to be ten floors at least. 'So how many storeys exactly?' John asked again.

Tompkins sat back and folded his arms. 'We can't say yet.'

Another lie. This clerk knew the height.

Richard leaned forward. 'Jack, Leary's wants to tender. How soon can we get the package of bid documents?'

Good question. Tompkins would have to answer it one way or another.

Tompkins smiled again. 'That's not for me to say. It's only the nineteenth of March and there's some time yet. I'll ask the senior partners. I can say that Leary's are a reputable company and are likely to be considered to tender.'

John hesitated before standing up. Of course they'd be asked to tender. But what if they weren't? Another bloody problem. Here they were assuming they'd get a crack. He stood up and said, 'We'll wait. Perhaps you can arrange for Mr Turner to come and talk to us now.'

The oily smile appeared again. 'Unfortunately, Mr Turner is at another engagement.'

Convenient. This boy knew nothing. John would talk to the butcher, not the block. 'Thank you for your time. Come Richard.'

In the street, John eased himself into the carriage. 'Waste of a morning.' He tapped on the carriage roof hatch. 'The office, please, Gibbs.'

'I can prod him,' Richard said. 'I know where he drinks.'

'Don't bother. I'll get to Turner. I have to, and we have to be on that tender list. The other tenderers—whoever they are, and I'm sure Bucknells is among them—they'll have a lead.' John sensed Leary's was behind and hated it. Was he losing his touch? This wasn't like him. There had to be another way to get an advantage. The Council, of course! John thumped his thigh. 'Sydney City Council,' he said. 'It has to give the Imperial Hotel its approval, the planning consent. Who do we know there? Think.'

Richard pursed his lips. 'Some inspectors, that's about all.'

'I know Frank Burgess. He's senior there. I'll see him. He'll tell me what he knows.'

Richard cleared his throat. 'But what about Turner? How are you going to get to him?'

John's excitement waned. Yes, the architect was still the key. 'I don't know. Any ideas?'

'No.'

John needed to find a way to the elusive Turner. On the way to Annandale he racked his brain for some ideas.

The carriage stopped outside their office. No one had ever given him any help with his business in the past, he thought. Suddenly he realised he was wrong: someone had helped him, helped him a lot—his father-in-law, David McGuire. The businessman knew little of building but had taken a calculated risk on backing him, a young, brash and ambitious carpenter. John had never got around to thanking David for his belief in him, before David had died.

In his Point Piper study, John read again the letter from the Sydney City Council. It was typical of Burgess, not giving him a direct answer about the Imperial Hotel investors. All Burgess had said was that due to the project's significance, all details would be withheld until the tenderers were known.

Turning off his gas lamp, he made his way to the bedroom. It was nearly three weeks since he and Richard had met with the Turner representative and he was still only getting bits of information. A poor show.

Catherine was already in bed when he came in. 'Dear?' she said.

'Hmm.'

'How's your model boat going?'

'It's a ship dear, the *Emily*. The hull is finished.'

'Good. That's the ship you came out on?'

'Yes.'

Catherine paused. 'I've been meaning to speak to you about Brendan.'

John had guessed as much. 'You just concentrate on getting better. Don't worry about your son.'

'I'm a mother. I'll always worry.'

'What seems to be bothering you?'

She leaned up on one elbow. 'Brendan's not happy. I've noticed a change these last two months.'

'He's all right. New job, that's all. Promotion does that and ... he asked for it.'

'I know he did. He's ambitious. But there's more to it.'

'A woman?'

There was another pause. John sensed she hadn't thought of that. 'Brendan needs a nice girl to settle down. Anne Connaire is ideal but that's not what's concerning me. John ... he so wants to be a part of the company.'

'He is.'

'You know what I mean.'

'Catherine, you understand business but you've never been involved in Leary's. You've always preferred to keep out of it. Richard has the goods and in time he will replace me. Brendan is on trial and from what I've heard he's got his work cut out. I'll give him his due, he's not complaining about it.'

'Richard is competent and you support him. I'm just asking you to do the same for Brendan. If you could open your mind to him a little more, you'd see he has a lot to offer.'

John pulled the covers up. 'I'll think about it. Now go to sleep, you need your rest.'

With two sons from different mothers, he would always face challenges. Catherine was now championing Brendan, which was natural, but she also had a close relationship, even a loving one, with Richard, so she would have ambitions for both his sons. John was due to see his uncle in the morning; he'd bet London to a brick that their conversation would be about Brendan, too.

John turned the page of his desk calendar to 7 April and prepared himself for his visitor. It was always the same, a slight feeling of self-consciousness mixed with guilt. His uncle, his mother's brother, had struggled in the colony where John had prospered with luck and guile. Convicted of murder in Cork in 1828, Gerry had been transported to New South Wales. After some years he'd earned his ticket-of-leave, and had received a conditional pardon when new evidence came to light. He had worked as a master stonemason on a number of buildings in Sydney and was well respected for his skill.

Gerry had been employed at Leary's as a stonemason and had stopped work fifteen years ago when he must have been sixty-three. He and Moira had enjoyed some good years in retirement until she'd died from a heart attack six years ago. John had looked after him since then, at Point Piper.

Familiar heavy footsteps sounded outside John's office. 'Come in, Uncle.'

Gerry entered the office and eased himself into a chair, the effort showing on his face.

'I could have seen you at the house,' John said, 'and saved you the trouble.'

His uncle waved a dismissive hand. 'I needed to get out and I like the trip to town, even in this weather.' He paused and smiled. 'Moira loved town.'

'She did,' John admitted.

'Point Piper is like a morgue during the day, and that's a little too close for comfort.'

Right, John thought. 'What's on your mind?'

'Two things. The first is Richard. You know he's gambling again?'

John sat back, shocked. This was not what he needed to hear. 'What do you know?'

Gerry scratched his cheek. 'He's betting big and he's losing big.'

'How did you find out? I told Richard to stop!'

'Rupert Jenkins told me,' Gerry said, 'and he got it first-hand.'

'Jenkins?' John said surprised. 'He's dead, surely!' John hadn't seen his old boss for many years.

Gerry grinned. 'He dodders around but his mind's still as sharp as a chisel. He says hello.'

'Jenkins was always straight with me,' John said, very worried now. 'If this is true about Richard, it's not good.'

'Too true. What matters is, your son's got to be fronted.'

Indeed. Richard was doing the planning for the Imperial Hotel and that was what John wanted of him. But Richard had not stopped gambling like he'd promised. Maybe he'd just stopped thieving from Leary's. 'I'll talk to him. I'm seeing him this morning.'

'You had better, nephew. When a gambler needs money he doesn't care where he gets it. He'll steal it and won't blink an eyelid.'

'That's a bit harsh.'

Gerry coughed. 'It's not harsh. He took eighty quid before.'

'Christine told you?'

'No, Brendan,' Gerry said. 'And the word's out around the sites. It's not good for your boy.'

No, it wouldn't be. Richard was a leader and leaders had to be trusted. 'I said I'd speak with him, Uncle. The second thing you wanted to talk about?'

His uncle held John's look. 'Brendan.'

John thought as much. The two were as thick together as a wool bale. 'Go on.'

'I need some water.'

John raised his voice. 'Mrs Mansfield, could you get Mr Gleeson a glass of water, please?'

John waited until the drink came and Gerry sipped as rain swished against the window. It was stuffy in the office.

Gerry placed the glass down with a shaky hand. 'Better. Now, tell me your plan for the Imperial Hotel.'

John was surprised at the change of subject. 'We have yet to win it!'

'So you do. But how will you build it? Right now you're ignoring the one man who can help.' Gerry's piercing eyes bore into him.

John stared at his uncle. 'You don't mean Brendan, surely?'

Gerry smiled. 'Yes, Brendan.'

John sat back and folded his arms. 'On that job? No.'

'I thought you'd say that.' Gerry said. 'Look, one: Brendan's got ability and plans things. Two: he's got control of that bastard job you flung him ... the bank one, and he has Dougherty's measure. That takes leadership and what is Brendan, twenty-three?'

'In August.'

Gerry leaned forward and jabbed a finger at John. 'How and when did *you* start?'

Heat filled John's face. His uncle knew that it had been David McGuire who had given him a big leg-up after he had come to the colony. 'We've got ten jobs going now,' John said. 'Four with new foremen. I can't afford someone like Brendan whose mind is set on perfection and whose heart pines for the workers.'

'Perfection?' Gerry said.

'Where do I start?' John said. 'All right, try this. The last ware-house we did in Blackwattle, Brendan ripped out five box-framed windows and got them replaced.'

'Go on.'

'That group of terraces in Glebe. Brendan rejected the first wagon-load of bricks. Said they weren't sized properly. Cost me plenty. Want more examples?'

Gerry smiled. 'He's your son all right.' John was startled at that answer. 'Rupert Jenkins told me how, when you worked on Cochrane's Pub in Day Street, you were a stickler for setting out and accuracy. Timber flooring structures and roof structures that wouldn't be seen to the naked eye. To the young Leary it had to be done just right. Oh yes it did.'

John ran a hand through his hair. He'd forgotten about that.

'And,' Gerry said, 'what about the wool store in Market Street for McCreadies? Jenkins told me that you disputed the set-out of the columns with a surveyor, for goodness sake. Do ya want me to list more?'

John was not on solid ground and perhaps his son was pedantic, but surely worse than he himself had ever been. 'All right. Brendan's like me, in that way.'

Gerry looked at him. 'Brendan's got the brains, nephew, the brains, and he can control men. Something Leary's needs in big dumps.'

'So he's handling Enmore well, is he? Fine, but it's early days.'

'It's going well, and if you don't believe me, talk to Sean.'

'I will,' John said, 'but one improved job doesn't mean Brendan has got the goods.'

'Nephew, it proves he's having a go.'

'Maybe. But I need more than that. I need a leader. Have you heard about his ideas on men, his mollycoddling? It's ridiculous.' John pressed his hands against the sides of his chair, concentrating on the pressure his fingers exerted on the smooth metal. 'I won't be here for ever and I want Leary's in good steady hands when I go.'

'And you'd hand this company to a gambler? Richard would go through Leary's cash like a bandsaw through softwood.'

John bristled. 'Richard would never threaten Leary's, never.'

Gerry pursed his lips. 'Are you sure of that?'

John went to reply and hesitated. No, Richard would see sense. Rupert Jenkins was probably exaggerating Richard's gambling. It was just gossip.

Gerry tapped the desk with his finger. 'Richard's got guts and he's got character but those virtues are being corroded by his weakness. I'm not judging him, John—I'm saying he needs help. Now, Brendan's not a leader ... yet, but he needs a bigger challenge.'

John had to bring this to a close. 'Brendan's an idealist and wants a perfect world. It's not.'

Gerry smiled. 'He's a thinker and he's sensitive, I grant you. But the lad's got vision too. And he's doing the hard yards. The men respect him, they do.'

John admitted that. He'd heard some things, the odd comment passed around Leary's, that stopped him sometimes. Flint-hard foremen and labourers, not known for speaking much, had praised Brendan. But it was too soon to promote him. 'I won't risk Leary's profit with him as a leader.'

Gerry forced himself up. 'But you'll give him a place on the Imperial Hotel, won't you?'

'We've got to win it first.' He didn't tell his uncle that Leary's still had to even get on the tender list.

'You didn't answer my question.' As he walked from the office, Gerry said, 'Give him more responsibility or Leary's will be the lesser for it.'

John looked at the empty doorway. Brendan must have the old man on a string. But then Gerry was no fool and he loved the boy. Then his mind turned Richard's bloody gambling! His uncle was right on one thing. Gambling was a curse and Richard needed a serve.

Now was the best time. John was three minutes late for his board meeting and, as he headed downstairs to the meeting room, Richard was in his sights.

Meanwhile Richard was worried. He was sitting in the meeting room and glancing at the board papers in front of him, trying to find an item in them that would distract him, but his mind drifted back to his gambling. It was as if his pleasure in the playing was now secondary; his gambling was now an all-encompassing part of his life. He didn't know how that had happened. Had it got worse after the theft? Yes, partly, but he also felt tormented that more people, especially his family and his dear grandmother, knew about it. He started to feel hot and he knew the reason. Whenever he thought about stopping or even trying to stop, he got nervous, as if part of his body was being taken from him.

His father came into the room and he was glad for the distraction. 'This weather's giving us problems,' Richard blurted out.

'Rain,' John said looking out the window. 'The builder's curse. Four of our jobs are still open to the skies and only minimal works

97

are happening.' His father paused and looked at him. 'So, you've been gambling again.'

Richard was startled. How did he know? 'Nothing of import, Father. Why? Who's been talking?'

'Apart from the site talk—'

God, why can't they leave it alone? 'Who's talking?' Richard's face became red. 'Name them.'

'You've every right to be angry. But it should be anger at yourself.'

No, Richard thought. This was about *defending* himself.

'It's out there Richard,' his father continued, 'and that's all you need to know. I've heard it from someone I trust, and I know you've been betting big. That's a worry, son. Where are you getting the money? Stealing from us again?'

Richard looked at him coldly. 'No, Father.'

'I want it stopped.'

Richard looked down. It was the second time he'd heard the ultimatum. Stop. Gamble no more. It was like a judge's sentence. 'I've heard comments about the money I took and that's hurt, but I've not taken any more. Look, Father, I'm over twenty-one and it's my life.'

'Gambling has no winners, Richard. You might get lucky once in a while, but you'll lose in the end.'

Deep inside he knew that to be the truth, but what did truth have to do with it? He relished the world of the round table, loved the feel of the cards, the challenge of the choice of suit. 'It's under control,' he said, hoping his voice was steady, but it didn't sound convincing. 'Don't worry.'

'I'm your father, Richard. So tell me, could you stop gambling if you wanted to?'

Richard looked out the window. He couldn't face his father with an answer he knew to be untrue. 'Yes.'

'Good. Then stop for a month and see if you miss it. A month, Richard—I mean it. If you manage that, you can stay off gambling.

If you don't, you need help and we'll talk about it again. Until then I want to hear no more.'

And Richard wanted to hear no more also. He needed a distraction and found it. 'Consider it done, Father. Anyway, I have news. We can meet Turner.'

'What?'

Richard smiled. 'I have a wedding rehearsal at Turner's home in York Street on the fifteenth of May. His daughter is one of Victoria's bridesmaids. We will meet him there.'

'Excellent.' His father seemed charged with excitement.

The meeting door opened and Christine sidled into the room, gripping her cane with determination. She sat near John, removed a pair of spectacles from her bag and peered at the shareholder papers in front of her. A scent of camphor settled over the room.

John got up and closed the door. 'We'll be as quick as we can,' he said. 'The papers are before you. Any questions?' He waited for comments but none came. 'There are no apologies and I'd like to move that the previous minutes be accepted.'

'Moved,' Richard said.

'Seconded,' Christine said.

'Carried,' John said.

'Construction report's next,' John said. 'Richard, are we sure of the estimate on this George Street bank job?'

'It's a lean price, Mr Prentice says, and I agree. Giles is the architect for the Commercial Bank. We're hopeful.'

John looked at his report. 'We lodge it next week, yes, and Raftery's the foreman?'

'Correct,' Richard replied.

'Very good.'

'Speaking of banks,' Christine said. 'Brendan's been given the Enmore project?'

John glanced at Richard. 'He's under scrutiny.'

'I'll keep him in line, dear,' Richard said. 'Your project's protected.'

Christine nodded. 'I'm sure he'll succeed.'

'Resolved to accept the construction report,' John said.

They all agreed and John collected his documents. Richard was already standing.

'Is there any other business?' John said.

Christine looked at him. 'Yes. I've been considering getting rid of my shares.'

John looked up. *No, she didn't say that!* 'Sorry?'

'I'm only thinking about it. But there's a possibility I might sell them.'

John had to think. *She wants to sell her fifty-one per cent!*

Richard placed a hand on his grandmother's sleeve. 'Now, what's this all about, dear?'

'At my age, I find I'm very tired.'

'But you're not old!' he said.

'I am, Richard, if you haven't noticed, and sometimes the business feels like something of a burden to me. Now, what can I do to change that?'

'What do you think, Father?'

John counted to five in his excitement. 'This is sudden. Why now?'

She opened her hands. 'Why not now? Share papers are a poor coffin liner.'

'Dear!' Richard exclaimed.

'Richard, come my age you'll not fear death or its trappings. You almost ... welcome it at times. But I'm not ill, don't worry. I'd just like my life to be simpler and more comfortable.'

'Have you thought whom you'll sell to?' Richard said. 'It has to be the family, surely?'

'Who knows? I haven't got that far. All I know is that I've come to a point where I don't want any further concern about Leary's Contracting. You don't need an old lady like me any longer. I'd like to bow gracefully out.'

John couldn't believe it. He looked out the window where a flag draped, soaked and heavy, against its pole and a paper box skimmed along the overflowing George Street gutter. A newspaper on the table glared back at him. John focused on the date: 7 April 1885. This was real, not a dream. Had Christine really given no thought to who would buy the shares? If she sold them outside the company—dear God!

Christine smiled at him. 'Don't worry, John. I'll not sell to a competitor.'

'That's something.' He felt astonished and confused. Odd. He should be jubilant and planning to grab them.

'I'd like them,' Richard said.

'I'm sure you would,' Christine said and smiled. 'And it's possible I might give them to you.'

This was moving too fast, John thought. 'When would you release your shares?'

'Help me up, Richard,' Christine said. 'These blessed chairs are too low to the floor. We should get new ones.'

Richard assisted his grandmother and she leaned on his elbow. 'Maybe I'm just being silly and maybe tomorrow I'll feel different, who knows?' She dabbed her face with her hanky.

John stood to farewell her and observed her carefully, seeing her with new eyes. She had just confessed she was feeling her age. Her mobility was worsening and the stairs here and at home must be tiring her. Had he shown her enough care and consideration in the last months? If he had, he'd know more about her problems and wishes and he would have heard her doubts about the shares already!

'I wish I'd known this was troubling you, Christine. Let's talk about it at home. Don't come to a hasty decision—do what's right for you.'

'Don't worry, John,' she said with a spark in her eye. 'I might sell or give them away ... *might*, mind you, but to whom? Ah, there's the puzzle.' She headed towards the door. 'Just to know you'll be thinking about it gives me a thrill.'

'Christine,' John said, 'you might not believe me, but hear this.' She stopped and turned. 'Those shares are important to me, but so is your welfare and happiness.' Did he mean that? Yes, he did. 'My family comes before everything. I realised it when I sat beside Catherine in the hospital. I'd have given all I could to make her wake up. I would have sold my house and everything I had to bring her back.'

'But what about now, John? Catherine's alive. You feel a little different now, surely. Can you say you'd put us all before your obsession with Leary's?'

John thought about it. 'Yes.'

'You mean that?'

'I do.'

She looked at him for a long time. 'Yes, I think you do. That makes me glad, son-in-law, very glad.'

'And speaking of your comfort,' John said, 'there's something I've been meaning to mention to you about the house. I'm going to add another bedroom at Point Piper, so we can accommodate more guests. We thought we could house them all upstairs if we make use of your room as well. Would you be satisfied with a new ground-floor room? We can build it to your exact requirements.'

Christine thought for a moment. 'And save my trundling up and down stairs!' She smiled at him and he suspected that she knew he didn't really need her first-floor room for guests—he was saving her pride. She said with a hint of humour, 'The ground floor will suit me very well, thank you. Richard, dear, help me to my carriage.'

John was relieved that Christine was well-disposed towards him, and that he'd been able to show her consideration. But would he have thought about doing this a year or two ago? No, if he was honest. What should he do about her shares? It made sense to try to obtain them from her, because it was simpler if he had total control of his company, but it wasn't *essential*. Things were going well and this would continue if she decided to hold onto her investment. If she really believed in him, and it appeared she did, then he might get her shares anyway, as a gift or inheritance. Or Richard might get them and that was just as good—or was it?

John contemplated the picture of Richard owning sixty per cent of the company. If Richard could steal £80 without flinching, what might he do with majority control of Leary's cash? Then again, perhaps he was capable of reforming. A little while ago he had shown embarrassment at hearing the site talk about embezzlement. Would that alone steel his resolve and make him get control of his gambling? John hoped so.

In the Enmore bank-site office, Brendan studied the drawing detailing the type of plaster cornice for the bank manager's residence on the first floor. The overall building-project work was half completed and now they would start the building finishes.

The plan's title block showed the bank's logo, which featured a wattle, and that flower reminded him of Julie and their time in the Botanical Gardens. Here it was 27 April and it'd been six weeks since he'd seen her. He wanted to see her again. Next week Anne Connaire was coming with her family for afternoon tea and his mother had been hinting Brendan should get more interested in her, but Julie was the one he was attracted to.

He looked up from his plan as Mike Dougherty came alongside him. His sub-foreman smelt of whisky and Brendan pushed the window open to the breeze. 'The basement will need airing,' Brendan said. 'It's been flooded for two days.'

Dougherty scowled and sat on a stool. 'I know that. It's done.' His eyes were red-rimmed and his left hand shook. He shoved it into his pocket when he saw Brendan looking at it. 'I want Jenkins sacked.'

Rob Jenkins again. He was Rupert Jenkins's grandson and a good builder. Dougherty kept harping about Jenkins not doing his job. Brendan had spoken to his leading hand who, once prompted, had told him it was Dougherty who wasn't doing basic site supervision and Jenkins had to do it for him. 'Jenkins is capable,' Brendan said.

'He's not. He's got to go,' Dougherty said. He stood up and folded his arms. 'Either you sack him or I'll leave.'

This was an ultimatum Brendan was not prepared for. He needed to sort this out. 'Not that easy, Mike.'

'Don't bullshit me, Leary. Yes or no. I know him better than you. Been running sites a long time.'

A direct sting at him! Dougherty hadn't accepted Brendan being put in charge here; he'd thought he would get it instead. Brendan needed the man a little longer—but did he? Maybe a clean break was the way to go. Brendan stood up and looked his foreman in the eyes. 'I won't sack Jenkins.'

Dougherty moved closer but Brendan stood his ground. 'You're green as a foreman, Leary, and Jenkins is fooling you. I'm the one who gets things done, not some smart-arsed carpenter who doesn't know shit from clay.'

'I'm not sacking him.'

Mike's face reddened. 'You know nothing, either. You're sweet on Jenkins and you've got it in for me.'

'Mike, you're a good sub-foreman and you could be better.' Now he had to say it. 'But you have a drinking problem.'

Mike clenched his fists. 'I bloody don't.'

'If you cut down on the grog,' Brendan continued, 'you'd be useful to me. But not like you are now.'

Mike's face reddened further. 'Leary, if you weren't a boss, I'd deck you.' His jaw clenched. 'I'm thinkin' about it.'

Brendan tried to keep calm but a tremor in his leg threatened to unnerve him. Keep still and think. Throw a straight left, and block with your right. His great-uncle's boxing lessons came back to him. He was ready.

Dougherty's eye twitched. 'Your call, then. I'm out of here. Send my pay home.'

He turned and left, paused outside and re-entered the office. 'And your site will be stuffed and don't think I'll cop a job in the plant yard. Yeah, I've heard the talk. You can stick your yard where the sun doesn't shine.'

Brendan got control, sat down and watched him walk away.

Outside, Rob Jenkins was coming towards the site shed and Dougherty stopped and said something to him, prodded the leading hand's chest, then moved on.

Jenkins came up to the open doorway. 'What's up, boss? Mike's in a huff.'

Brendan had a problem now. 'Sit down, Rob. He is, and he's not coming back.' Jenkins sat down, his eyes wide. He looked at Brendan and said nothing. 'It's you and me for the time being, mate. You up to it?'

Rob looked out the window and seemed to be thinking. Brendan liked that about him. He hadn't asked the details of Dougherty's departure but might have guessed. Jenkins looked back at him. 'I am. The clerk of works is going to be a problem, just for a bit.'

Brendan sounded more confident than he felt but he had to show calmness to his troops. 'Yeah, Dawkins is coming here at the end of April, that's just three days away. He'll be full-time and have the bank's authority to order us around.' Brendan needed to take the worried look off Jenkins's face. 'Kerry, the shop fitter, came good with those counters but I've seen a few things that need fixing up.' Brendan turned the page of his notebook. 'Go and tell the team before knock-off that ...' Brendan paused. 'Tell them Dougherty's off crook for the time being and you're in charge as acting sub-foreman and get them working overtime till further notice. We'll talk when you get back.'

Rob stood up and hesitated. 'Right. I'll say something, though. Just one remark. Don't get shirty.'

'Go on.'

'We're about the same age, so I'm not trying to say I'm more experienced than you. But I do have a bit of advice. Get the quality you want on the job here, sure, but ease up on the perfection. It's not possible.'

Brendan bristled. 'Don't *you* give me grief too, Rob!'

'You let me say it, so I told you.' He went to leave.

'Wait,' Brendan said. 'I did, and I'll think about it. Fair enough?'
Rob nodded. 'Fair enough.'

'Well, don't just stand there. Get going and tell the others what they need to do.'

Rob grinned and left, and Brendan started writing. Sites were like families. Everyone knew when things weren't good and the foreman had a lot to do with influencing that. Brendan would be busy with Dougherty gone, but that's what he liked. Now to work out a plan to get the bank back on side. *Sean—now there's someone who could help me do just that.*

John was sitting next to Sean Connaire in his dray on the way to the Enmore site. It was time to see if Brendan had delivered the goods and turned this job around. On the way there, Sean had given him more background on Brendan's progress and although still sceptical, he was starting to believe his former partner's opinion. Sean was a valued Leary's resource; he knew the building industry like a priest knows his missal. Now, at nearly sixty-four years of age, Sean acted as a mentor, counsellor and general building instructor and he was very happy in the role. He relished not having any direct responsibility for sites but was always keen to offer his gilt-edged advice when and where needed.

When they were nearly there, John remembered the letter Mrs Mansfield had given him on the way out of the office. He brought it out from his jacket and smiled as he read it. He'd heard the gossip last week but the letter dated the previous day, 13 May, confirmed it. 'We've won the George Street bank job. Another project to add to the list.'

Sean applied the brake to the dray. 'That's grand. Who will you put on it to lead?'

'Raftery's the man.'

'Good as any. Wait, while I'll collect my bag from the back.'

'Do you want a hand?'

Sean grinned. 'No, thank you, sir.'

John pocketed the letter, alighted and stood at the site gate waiting for Sean. 'I think this is going to be a waste of time.'

'Are you still quibbling? I thought we agreed in the dray,' Sean said, jabbing a finger at John's middle, 'that we're here at Enmore for you to see what your lad's done in the last two months. Now, if you don't want to stay, then don't waste my time.'

No one at Leary's spoke to him that way but Sean was different. He'd seen John in many lights in the past, some of them dim. 'All right, all right. I'm here aren't I? Let's look around. Have all the men left?'

'It's all clear. It's after four.'

John looked at Sean's bag. 'What's that you're carrying?'

'Don't you worry about that.'

'What I'm *not* going to worry about is Brendan. He hasn't the makings of a leader that I want.'

'I'll show you what he's done, John. Keep your powder dry till then.'

John wasn't convinced. 'Lead on, then.'

Sean unlocked the site gate, then the bank's front door, and entered. John followed. Sean placed his bag at the foot of the staircase. 'Upstairs first, bank manager's residence.'

John varied his steps as he ascended the staircase, noting there were no squeaks, a good sign of quality. 'Smart move on the banister.'

Sean nodded. Someone had wrapped carpet offcuts around it to protect it.

At the top, John examined the completed structure of the residence. He could see that Brendan had planned this well. 'I did a job like this once and left the residence to the last. I paid the price. The project went overtime.'

Sean walked over and ran his hand down the brick walls. 'Joints are aligned.' He looked down. 'And the floor is even. That's not Dougherty's doing. It's Jenkins's.'

Jenkins's name reminded John of his old boss and the news he'd had from Jenkins about Richard. 'Did you know Richard's taken up gambling again?'

Sean paused, then said, 'I've heard the rumours. Have you talked to him about it?'

'I have and he's going to stop it.'

They left the rooms and went back downstairs to the ground floor banking chamber.

'It might not be easy for him. It could be like the drink, with me,' Sean said. 'You have to keep on top of it every day of your life.'

'You think my son has an addiction?'

'Maybe.' Sean gestured to their surroundings. 'Let's keep our eyes on this. John, it's the cleanliness here that impresses me.'

John had to agree. Most sites were dirty, right up until they were handed over to their clients. It was a rough rule of thumb that an untidy site was a site likely in trouble. Brendan's Enmore project site wasn't untidy; you could eat your dinner off its floor. 'What do the others say?'

'I asked Rob Jenkins straight out,' Sean said as he collected his bag. 'He was quiet for a bit then I told him whatever he said to me would stay with me, like.'

John stopped. 'You're telling *me*, Sean!'

'That's different. Well then, he gave Brendan a lot of praise. He added that his boss wanted everything perfect, but Brendan was trying to put a priority on being practical.'

'That'd be a change!' John said. 'But is it true? A worker will always praise his boss, Sean, to protect his job. It mightn't mean anything.'

'Sure, but I spoke to a brickie I know who worked here. He had no axe to grind and he's going to give it away soon. John, he said he's never been on a site that was so well organised. The floors were clean before he started, the set-out marks on the floor were on the money, the bricks were always stacked ready for work and the cement never ran out. He said Brendan took a personal interest in his trade. There.'

To John, that sounded like commitment. If Brendan took the trouble to plan this site with so much care, then that boded well for the future. 'But he's still a little green, Sean. Come on.'

'He hasn't Richard's time in the game for sure, but,' Sean pointed to the timber framework, 'he got the counters for this ordered with a nifty sleight of hand. The shopfitter couldn't fool him with shoddy timber and he knows his waterproofing. He had Peter Giles the architect own up that he'd specified the wrong putty and Brendan told me that Giles has written papers on waterproofing for the Institute of Architects. Can you believe that? If I were you, I'd stick Brendan on George Street.'

'One step at a time, my friend.'

'Well, Brendan gave Giles a lesson in putties. I've been keeping my eye on your son. He's getting the gist of this game. Architects and suppliers are nodding their heads at him.'

John ended up at the front doors of the bank and scanned the ground floor. There was a big bin with rubbish in it. John went to it and peered inside. 'Very few offcuts.'

'Less wastage.'

'It looks that way.' Materials were piled neatly and in order ready for the next day's work, window frames stacked and protected and the whole place secured from break-ins.

Sean smiled at him.

'What are you grinning about?' John said.

'You know. I don't have to tell you. Brendan is a top foreman. It's in everything you see.'

'It looks that way, and it's good. But can he stand up to people, Sean? Can he sack a person and sleep that night? That's what I want to know.'

'He sacked Dougherty, just a fortnight ago.'

John looked sceptical. 'No, Richard told me Dougherty resigned.'

'I spoke to Dougherty,' Sean said. 'I can sniff an alcoholic with a hound's scent and I know when he lies.'

As a reformed alcoholic, Sean would know. 'What did Dougherty tell you?'

'All rot about how he'd been let down and so on but he came clean that Brendan had fronted him and that had surprised him.' Sean put his bag down. 'Brendan sacked him all right and he reckoned Brendan would have had a go at him.'

'No! Not Brendan, Sean.'

'Yes, Brendan, John, and Dougherty is no slouch. I've seen him fight.'

It was hard to believe. Brendan, his naive and altruistic son, taking on a knuckle man? A one off ... maybe, but Sean looked convinced. Sean knew men, but there was another test. 'The books?' John said.

Sean opened the bag at his feet. 'I checked them this morning at the office.' Sean pulled up a sawhorse and wiped it down with a clean rag. 'Put on your glasses and read. It's all good, there's profit in the job and all trades have been paid up to today, the fourteenth of May. I've got a call of nature. Take your time.'

John grinned, took the books of account, sat down on the sawhorse and read. He was so absorbed that he didn't hear Sean come back until he was standing near him.

'Above board, aren't they?' Sean said.

John gave the books back to Sean and put his glasses away. 'They are indeed.'

'I'll drop them back at the office tomorrow before work starts. Let's lock up and be off. Have you got time to shout your old partner a drink?'

John smiled. 'I have.' They walked out into the semi-darkness of the late autumn evening and John was deep in thought. Brendan had excelled himself on the site's quality, managed the sacking of a drunken foreman and made a tidy profit. John had thought his son would fail but from his site inspection this afternoon Brendan had achieved the opposite.

'Surprised, aren't you,' Sean said walking beside him.

'That's only half of it.' He thought about what Sean had said. Brendan not only had the site under control but he had the measure of the architects too. He hoped that he himself would get the measure of William Turner at their meeting tomorrow.

The next day, John and Richard entered William Turner's warm York Street study. 'Thank you for seeing us,' John said and smiled.

Turner directed them to two chairs and said. 'You're fortunate that I'm home today. Look here, Mr Leary, this is highly unusual, you coming to my house. I don't want it construed as favouritism.'

John controlled his temper. Typical up-nosed architect, thinking builders are a nasty bunch. Still, he had to get a lead.

Turner lit a cigar, not offering them one. 'My daughter's involved in your son's wedding. Bridesmaid or something.'

'Felicity is the chief bridesmaid,' Richard said. 'They just had a rehearsal in your drawing room.'

Turner ignored him. 'Now, here's what I can tell you. The other tenderers will know the same shortly.'

John clenched his fist on his thigh. Good. They *were* on the list. Now John wouldn't leave this study till he had it all.

Turner glanced out at the wild weather. 'The preliminary design's done. Sixteen floors—'

'Sixteen?' John said. 'That's a step up from the Australia Hotel!'

'The Australia Hotel is having difficulties attracting investors but the Imperial Hotel will be built in sixteen floors, yes. We're still working on the structure but it can be done. The elevation drawings are completed and finishes agreed.'

Leave the hard bits to last. The key to winning this job was to save money on the structure. Most architects concentrated on what looked good to the naked eye.

John knew there was real money to be made in the bricks, steel and mortar. 'We need a set of plans.'

'No doubt, but they're not ready. We want Leary's on the tender list, but you aren't getting any favours. There's a tight group of good contractors—'

'Including Bucknells,' John said. Turner's eyes flashed at him. That hit a nerve, it seemed.

'I can't tell you, but they are all good firms.' Turner pulled a bit of tobacco from his mouth. 'It's the fifteenth of May now. By the end of June we'll be out to tender. That's it. Now, if you'll excuse me, I've got to go to Forest Lodge.'

'Good,' John said. 'We'll take you. We're going that way.'

Turner hesitated. 'No need. My driver's waiting and I have to go to Randwick first.' John sensed Turner was being evasive. The architect stood up but John remained seated and looked at Richard.

'Just a couple of things,' Richard said.

Turner looked at both of them. 'I do have to leave.'

Richard ignored him. 'Where's the site?'

'Clarence Street, corner with Margaret, now—'

'When do you want the hotel opened?' John said.

Turner started walking towards his study door. 'As soon as possible, but no later than the end of July '87.'

'And the rooms, how many?' Richard said.

Turner stopped and opened the door. 'You'll see on the plans. Now, I'll see you gentlemen out.'

'On what basis did you select the tenderers?' John asked. 'Size? Turnover?'

'Mr Leary,' Turner said, looking at John and holding the door open, 'You have to go.'

In the carriage below, John shook the rainwater from his coat as he settled on the seat. 'We found out little.' He raised his voice. 'Annandale, Gibbs!'

'Turner's a toad,' Richard said.

'He's a what?'

'A toad, Father. He favours Bucknells, I know.'

'How?'

112

'At the school reunion the other week they were pissing up together like old mates.'

'But they're not Sydney Grammar old boys.'

'No,' Richard replied, 'but they're on the school's Board of Governors.'

It all fitted. 'Of course, that's why Bucknell was so bloody close-mouthed at the Farringtons' dinner party. He's got a march and making the most of it.' John slapped his thigh, 'And that banker Watson's an old Grammarian too.'

The carriage skidded on the wet roads while John concentrated on what he had to do. He'd be damned if he'd just 'play the game': do the estimate and submit a conforming bid. That was for mugs and gentlemen. Smart people made their own money and their own luck.

'I'll get the plans,' Richard said.

John was angry at himself. 'How? Steal them?'

'Nothing so blatant. Some of Turner's young guns were at the reunion.'

'Not that wet one we met? Simmonds?'

'That was Tompkins. No. One was in my class, a rascal then and now. He's struggling for cash and gambling's his weakness.'

'Like yours?'

Richard shook his head. 'I'm trying, Father. The month is over.'

'And?'

'I don't feel the urge, and better, I've got a reputation to repair.'

John had to believe him. 'Good on you, then. Don't play cards with him. Just pay him for the plans or get their tracings, whatever, but be careful.'

'I'm always that,' Richard said and smiled.

They sat back as their carriage continued to Annandale. It was a start. They'd have something to work on.

'I should get a price any day from those equipment suppliers in London,' Richard said. 'They've already said they're keen to lease us the steam shovels and pumps we'll need.'

'What about the cranes?'

'Derrick cranes, especially stiff-legged ones, are in short supply. Bolton's are favoured to get two but we may need three.'

The carriage stopped at their offices. Richard got out and John grabbed his sleeve. 'Well done, son.'

'I haven't got the plans yet.'

'You will. I'm meeting Mr Burgess next week. The Council might give us more information now that the tenderers are nearly named.'

Richard pushed open the front door. 'Good. I've got the rest of the day looking at the planning on the Imperial Hotel. I may have some ideas for you. Perhaps I could go over them after dinner tonight?'

'Not tonight. Keep those for our meeting in a fortnight.'

Richard left him and went into his office. John paused at Mrs Mansfield's desk.

'Yes, sir?' she said.

John looked at her. 'Nothing, just bring me a cup of tea, thanks, and a chocolate biscuit.' John went into his office. Tonight he had a meeting with Christine and his uncle—about Christine's shares, he assumed. Good.

Chapter Five

JOHN SHUT THE SLIDING DOORS BEHIND HIM AND WALKED INTO HIS Point Piper drawing room. Christine was sitting on the sofa, reading the *Herald*. Tonight he might be able to persuade her to sell him her shares.

His mother-in-law put the newspaper down and said, 'Good evening, John. Gerry will be along shortly.'

'And why are we meeting?'

'Richard's gambling, John. That's why we're here. It's still going on.'

John was taken aback. Had Richard lied about stopping?

'Gerry and I have discussed it,' continued Christine, 'and we wondered how long it would take you to talk to us. You didn't, so we acted.' She stared at the rug and gripped her cane.

'Very good,' John replied, now angry at the news he'd heard. He went to the drinks trolley and poured some Bushmills into two Waterford glasses.

'Am I late?' Gerry said, ambling in from the foyer.

'No,' John replied, handing him a glass. 'Come and sit down.' John sat opposite Christine, holding the whisky in his lap, the rich aroma pleasant. Gerry eased himself down into an armchair.

Christine pointed her cane at Gerry. 'Both of us have had relatives who gambled and they ended up badly, cut off from their families.'

John sipped his whisky and turned to his uncle, raising his eyebrows.

Gerry nodded. 'My brother gambled.'

'And my father,' Christine said. 'But let's talk about Richard. I'm not saying he can't control himself but what evidence do we have that he can? We can't just sit back and do nothing.'

John looked at the fire and said, 'Richard told me he's trying to stop. Maybe he is. He said he'd given it up for a month.' He saw Christine glance at Gerry. 'What are you two hatching?'

Christine pointed to the doors connecting the drawing room with the foyer. 'Close those too, will you John? This is between us and I want no eavesdroppers.'

John did as she asked, then picked his glass up and stood by the fireplace.

'You remember I said that I wanted to get rid of my shares?' she said. 'Well, I've decided what I'm going to do.'

'I thought we were here to discuss Richard's problem, not your shares.'

Christine felt her knee and winced. 'We are, John, and if you're patient, we shall suggest a way of solving both. Bear with us.'

'Sorry. Go on.'

She looked at him. 'I've kept my shares to have control over you and to control Leary's. I was content knowing I held that ace.' John bowed his head to her in ironical acknowledgement. 'But over time you've paid your dues. I'll grant you that. Clarissa loved you, ever since she first saw you on board the *Emily* on our journey to New South Wales. You two weren't meant to mix, because you were in steerage; do you remember, John?' Christine sighed. 'I was never happy that you became man and wife. But you did, and she loved you until she died, though I didn't think you deserved her. But times change and so can people. Catherine is a good woman and you have treated her well.'

116

'You have, John,' Gerry said. John glanced at his uncle. 'I mean it.'

'I haven't forgotten what you did while you were married to my daughter,' Christine said, 'but I've forgiven you. Because of your devotion to Catherine over these many years, I'm making this proposition.' She cleared her throat. 'A drink of water, please, John.' She waited till he filled a glass from the decanter and placed it beside her. She grasped the glass, drank some and put it down. 'I'm going to gift my fifty-one per cent share to your two sons, in equal portions.'

John paused and refilled his glass. Gerry leaned over for a refill and John did the honours. 'That's commendable,' John said.

'Commendable, maybe; necessary, yes. I'm getting on, John, and it's time I made this move. But there's a condition.' Christine sat back, her breathing laboured.

'Are you all right?' John asked, concerned.

'You tell him, Gerry, I need to rest.'

'Christine wants both the boys to earn their shares,' Gerry said. 'Richard is to give up the cards. He needs help even if he thinks he doesn't, because it's a hard habit to shake. Christine and I know people around town who suffer from Richard's problem.' Gerry smiled at the look of amazement on John's face. 'Yes, and you'd be surprised who they are; they include one judge and a top police-man.' Gerry finished his whisky. 'Over the years, Christine and I have been able to help gamblers, because of our experience with the gamblers in our families.'

'I've never seen you do that,' John said. 'Never.'

'All very discreet,' Gerry said. 'The priests came to us and we helped the poor souls. We've stopped now because of our age but those reformed gamblers have said they'll help a fellow sufferer—Richard.'

'But are you sure Richard's got an addiction?' John asked.

'We can't be sure, John,' Christine said. 'But we really believe that talking to other reformed gamblers might help him.'

117

'Now, as for Brendan,' Gerry continued. 'To deserve his shares he'll need to prove himself at Leary's. To do that, he'll need greater challenges. Sean told me you saw the bank job and that you were impressed.' John nodded. 'Well, give him more responsibility, a bigger role on the Imperial Hotel—'

'We have to win it yet,' John said.

Gerry waved his hand. 'If not that, another big project. If he gets through that with flying colours and if you agree, then he'll get his shares.'

'Richard already has nine per cent of shareholding in Leary's. Your gift would present him with more shares than Brendan— that's not equitable.'

'No,' Christine said, 'and there's the risk that in the meantime Richard may dispose of his shares to obtain funds. Therefore I've taken advice from our lawyer on the Company's by-laws. The situation can be changed as long as two shareholders agree.'

'Agree to what?' John asked.

'Agree to place Richard's existing nine per cent share into a trust,' Christine said. 'That way he can't sell it to get money.'

This was going too fast. 'I don't think we need to go that far.'

'John,' Christine said, 'you underestimate what gamblers are capable of. When they're short of cash, they'll do anything.' She tapped her cane on the floor for emphasis. 'That's what we have to do. He *must* live on his salary and *not* get into debt. Gerry, do you have the paper?'

Gerry pulled out a document from his pocket and placed it on the table between them.

John put his glasses on and read it. He looked up at them both. 'It's dated the fifteenth of May ... that's today.'

'We came prepared,' Christine said. 'Give it here John and I'll sign, then you can.'

In under an hour, the shares he had always coveted had moved around like chips on a gaming table. He wasn't the recipient but he accepted the outcome and was ready to think through the consequences.

Freezing Richard's shares would cause trouble. John would have to contain that somehow. Then there was Brendan to consider. How would he react if in the end Richard got more shares than him? But then again, at present, Richard did have nine per cent more than Brendan and his younger son lived with that. John began to see the sense of it all. He glanced at his relatives. Old and fading they might be, but what they had just done was shrewd and clever. He smiled as he signed.

'Don't get too happy, son-in-law,' Christine said. 'Richard's going to cry like a scalded cat when he hears what we've done. I love him but I have to do this ... for his sake. I'm certain he's got a problem and we'll have to watch him.' She glanced at Gerry. 'And we're going to have to convince him to see the people who can help him.'

A log in the fire fell on the base of the grate, sending a shower of sparks up the chimney. They all stared at it in silence.

Brendan was anxious to get away from the site for the day. Fortunately, the bank's representative, employed by them to ensure a quality build, was just about done with his inspection.

'Is there anything else you have picked up for our attention?' Brendan asked.

'Nothing of significance, Mr Leary.'

'Then, Mr Dawkins, I bid you good afternoon,' Brendan said. 'Thank you for your patience.'

The bank's clerk of works looked hard at him. 'Patients are for hospitals, Mr Leary. My job is to make sure this bank is built to the utmost standards and you have delivered that, although from a rocky start. Keep up the good work. Good afternoon.'

Dawkins turned and walked down Enmore Road to his horse. Brendan watched him go, closed the site gate for another day and hailed a cab. 'Newtown Road at the Parramatta Road end.'

He was going to try to see Julie Carson again. The afternoon tea with Anne Connaire and her family some three weeks ago had not changed his mind. Anne was a nice girl but Julie continued to attract him.

The cab started to go down Newtown Road and Brendan concentrated on his site. The Bank was content with the progress and quality, more than content: very satisfied. Donald Dawkins had been a hard nut, sceptical of builders and their tricks, but Brendan had given the clerk of works confidence in Leary's standard of work, attention to detail and sense of urgency. Dawkins was now a convert and just this afternoon he'd told Brendan that, in his end of May report, in just six days' time, he would recommend to the bank to request Brendan be Leary's nominated foreman for all their suburban branch offices. Yes, Leary's still had to tender but it was a good turnaround for the project.

He looked out at the paddocks surrounding the university buildings. 'Anywhere here, driver.'

He paid the fare and set off, hoping to see Julie, when he saw her walking out of the McIntyre building. She saw him at the same time. She brought a hand to her hair to control it in the wind. 'Mr Leary,' she said. 'Are you waiting for someone?'

'I was, Miss Carson. Are you going home?'

'So, who are you waiting for?'

Brendan just smiled at her. The McIntyre's sign glared down at him.

She said, 'I told you at the Gardens, Mr Leary, not to see me. Now I'm going to tell you again.' She set off down Newtown Road and Brendan came up alongside her and walked with her.

'I've thought about it since our meeting in the Botanic Gardens, Miss Carson. You think we cannot be friends? You think because of who I am, you can't get to know me?'

She stopped and said, 'I don't want to think about you. It can't work.' She set off again and he walked beside her in silence. She stopped at Parramatta Road and crossed it. Brendan followed her and stood beside her on the other side. She looked at him. 'I take the next tram,' she said. 'Goodbye.'

Julie got on board and Brendan followed. A spare space beckoned and Julie sat down. Brendan sat beside her and was glad that they had to squeeze close. She didn't speak as the tram turned into Broadway; she seemed oblivious to him. They remained silent until the tram reached Bathurst Street. He was happy just to sit beside her.

'You don't listen, do you?' she said.

'What about?'

'Keeping away from me.'

'I don't want to keep away.'

She flushed. 'But you must.'

'I must?'

She closed her eyes and looked down. 'You must ... oh, you know.'

'What do you mean, Miss Carson?'

She looked at him. 'Mr Leary, if you have to talk to me, call me Julie.'

This was encouraging, if unusual. The tram became crowded as it continued its journey down George Street. When it stopped at Margaret Street, he looked up and thought about the new Imperial Hotel site on the corner of Clarence and Margaret Streets.

'I get off next stop,' she said.

'I will, too.'

She touched him, just a tap on his knee. 'Why?' she said, her mouth was set tight again.

'I left my horse at Campbell's Warehouse. I have to get out there.'

As their stop neared, Julie got up and ducked between some passengers. Brendan alighted with her and started walking up George Street North. 'When can I see you again?'

Julie shook her head. 'I don't know. Look ... we're different.'

'You are quick! Yes, I'm a man and you're a girl.'

Julie didn't smile. 'You know what I mean.'

Brendan stopped to allow a woman with her baby to cross in front of him. 'Look, let's meet a few times. If it doesn't work, we'll know, won't we?'

'I know *now* it won't.'

'You're not even going to give it a try?'

Julie was silent for a moment. 'I say to you, Mr Leary—'

'Brendan.'

She hesitated. 'I say to you … *Mr Leary*, remember this day and when you don't get what you want, you'll think back on what I've said.'

'Get what I want?' Brendan thought about what she meant, then he understood. *My God to … to be intimate with her.* He swallowed. This was all moving too quickly. 'I don't give up.'

Julie shook her head. 'You're like a dog with a bone.' She stood there not saying anything and Brendan waited. 'All right,' she said. He was winning this round, he sensed it. 'I go to ten o'clock Mass at St Pats, but this Sunday, I'm going to St Mary's for a change.' Julie put out her hand. 'Goodbye, Mr Leary. I have to get some flour for Ma,' she said, pointing to a shop. 'Just in here.'

Brendan glanced at the shop. 'I'll see you Sunday, then.'

Julie turned and went into the shop and Brendan walked up to Campbell's, where he collected his horse. All right, he would get to know Julie but he'd take things slowly.

Later, Julie set off home along George Street North, carrying two pounds of flour. He was keen, her new rich friend, and that was the point. He was *rich* and rich men only expected one thing from girls like her, and she wasn't going to give him that. It was too precious. Her pal Sandra Norris was not married and in the pudding club, her baby nearly due. Julie wondered what it would be like to be with a man. Sandra had said it had been painful and short, not romantic and nice.

Brendan was handsome, though, and she'd been excited when she'd seen him outside McIntyre's. She'd not expected to see him again; it had been ten weeks since their walk in the Botanic Gardens. But any friendship was doomed. At the fishos, she'd seen him as just a young man who was not drunk, was not bad looking and could string more than three words together. She'd seen enough of him since to see he was polite and respectful. However, a stroll in the Gardens was not a proposal of marriage. Her warnings had been justified, then and now.

Walking up Argyle Street, she buttoned her jacket. The Gardens walk had been enjoyable. Brendan liked her, she thought, and he was considerate and generous, without asking a reward. The men she knew wanted a kiss if they'd given her something as simple as a cheap ribbon. That reminded her of Aiden, who was in New-castle on a job; a good man who worked as a boilermaker two doors from McIntyre's. They sometimes went home together, as he lived near her, in Gloucester Street. Aiden had seen them in the Gardens together that Sunday afternoon. That puzzled her and she had asked him the following Monday why he hadn't come up to them. Aiden had said that he'd seen her with a gent and kept away. Aiden liked her and she liked him as a friend. He was even a possible husband.

Brendan Leary wanted to meet her again and she'd made it hard for him, not because she hadn't thought about it, but because she knew it could only end in a break up.

Julie opened her front gate. Brendan would leave her in time because she wouldn't give him her body. But at least that wouldn't be an issue at Sunday Mass! She grinned and closed the gate. She would see him again ... maybe just one more time. If it didn't work, which she knew would happen, she might give Aiden a closer look.

John brought Catherine's hand to his lips and kissed it. 'Happy Anniversary, my darling.'

Catherine clasped his hands in hers and squeezed. They'd just finished an intimate dinner in a private room at their favourite restaurant in town, and were talking over the light of a single candle. 'Twenty-five years,' she said. 'I still can't believe it.'

'For me,' John said, 'it's gone quickly. There have been some rocky trails that you've helped me through. I will be forever grateful.'

She looked at him and smiled. Long ago, at the beginning of their relationship, he'd been almost a stranger. Yes, she knew that he loved her but it was as if there was a slight sense of obligation attached to his affection, and that worried her. Clarissa had still held a significant place in his heart and she'd had to work hard to make him realise that Clarissa would not be forgotten and he could make room in his heart for both of them. She did succeed, but it had been a struggle in those early years. The good thing to come from her patience was that John had been even more caring and affectionate towards her.

'I have a present for you,' he said and brought out a velvet-covered box.

Opening the gift, she found a solid silver bangle, its weight impressive and its design simple and elegant. 'How lovely! Thank you, my dear.' She moved closer to him and they kissed. She smiled as they broke away. 'I've had a wonderful night so far and I don't want it to end.' She stroked his hand. 'Let's go.' She gave him a mischievous look. 'I have a present for you at home, too.'

John smiled at her and got the attention of the waiter. 'Our bill, please.'

Brendan was sitting beside his great-uncle in St Marys, while his mother and father and sisters sat in the pew behind them. Ten pews in front of him, Julie Carson sat between her mother and her brother, Billy. Brendan closed his eyes and prayed. The Mass ended and he waited with Gerry. Julie passed them with her family but he couldn't catch her eye. 'Uncle,' he said, 'could you go back to Point Piper with Father?'

'Saw you eyeing off the good-looking one,' Gerry said. Clasping Brendan's arm, he said, 'You go boy, I'll be right.'

'Thanks,' Brendan said. The two of them headed towards the door to wait for the rest of the family. When Catherine and his sisters arrived, Brendan said, 'Mother, I'm seeing a ... friend and will get home on my own.'

'That's all right,' she said. 'We can wait for you.'

Brendan hesitated. Julie and her family might get a cab. It was a fair hike to Princes Street but he hoped they would walk home.

'Your father is talking to a supplier,' his mother said, 'and I've got to talk to the priest about a charity drive. So don't be long.'

Brendan had to go. 'Please don't wait. I'll see you at home.'

She paused. 'Very well, but don't be late for Sunday dinner.'

'I won't.'

He ran outside. The last day of May had a chill in it. He looked around and spied Julie walking with her family down Macquarie Street. Brendan ran after them, his hurried steps alerting Billy, who looked around.

'It's him,' Billy said.

Julie turned at the sound of her brother's voice. She pushed Billy forward. 'Ma, I'll see you at home.' Billy didn't move and his mother grabbed him and they went off. Julie waited for Brendan to come up to her. 'Hello,' she said. 'Were you at Mass?'

'I was. Can I accompany you?'

'If you want to.'

They walked in silence for a while.

'What do you want to talk about?' he said.

'I don't know.'

Brendan scrambled to come up with something. 'Have you got any girlfriends?'

'Of course. I'm not a tramp living under a tree.'

Brendan was startled. 'You don't have to be rude.'

She glanced at him. 'I'm sorry. Look, I get skittish with you. You pop up everywhere like a jack-in-the-box.'

'I did say I'd be at Mass.' But Brendan understood what she meant. 'Is that because I'm different?'

Julie broke off a twig that was hanging from a low branch. She didn't reply for a while. 'You're not like the other boys I know. They're simple, easy to read.'

'And how do you read me?'

'I don't know.'

'Is what you feel for me—?'

Her eyes flashed at him. 'I don't feel anything for you.'

Brendan was disappointed. 'But you don't hate me so much as to run away from me?'

As she looked at him, her eyes softened. 'No, I don't.'

'So maybe,' he said, 'if we got to know each other, things might change.'

'They might, but you might find we *don't* like each other.'

'We won't know till we try, will we? Can we go out?'

Julie stopped. 'I'm not a moll, Mr Leary, and that's what you want. A bit of fun.'

Brendan took hold of her hand. Her skin felt coarse. 'That's not what you are and it's not what I'm after.'

'They all say that.' She said this in a slightly challenging way but did not withdraw her hand.

'I like you.'

'They say that, too.'

'Who says that? Boys you've known?'

'All boys want one thing. You do too, otherwise you'd be a fancy one.'

He was lost for words. Only men talked like that about some men who didn't like women. A girl never talked about it.

'See,' Julie said and smiled. 'Got you there.'

He strode on with her, still holding her hand. 'I like girls, all right,' he said firmly.

Julie walked closer to him, her lemon scent attractive. 'I know. I can tell.'

'You can? How?'

'It's just something we women sense. But you don't know nothing about me, nothing.'

Here was a chance. 'Then let me get to know you. There's no harm in that.'

Julie stopped at the corner of Hunter Street and let go his hand. 'I don't see this going anywhere, and I do have men friends.'

Brendan was taken aback. But then, Julie was attractive and single. She would have many male admirers. 'I want to see you again, but if you're betrothed, then I won't.'

Julie looked at him. Those deep hazel eyes seemed to seek some sort of assurance. 'I'm not spoken for, but I've friends I want to see.'

'Fair enough,' Brendan said. 'Look, there's a dance at the Tivoli on Saturday, the sixth of June. Would you like to go? I'll come to your place at seven.'

Julie glanced down the street and turned to him. She paused and Brendan waited. 'All right,' she said. 'I'll go with you, but think about what I've said. I've warned you.' Julie walked off. 'See you then, Mr Leary.'

Brendan watched her go and turned around, happy. Saturday couldn't come soon enough.

Catherine sent Uncle Gerry and her daughter Mary home in the carriage. Then, having spoken to the priest about the date of a charity fundraising event, she and Agatha caught a cab. Agatha wanted to know the price of a new gown that was featured in David Jones shop front, so they headed down Macquarie Street on their way to Elizabeth Street. The cab stopped to let a tram pass and Catherine looked out. Brendan was not twenty feet away and was ... holding a girl's hand! Holding hands and talking to her.

'That's Brendan!' Agatha said. 'And with a girl.'

He was. But that wasn't what surprised Catherine the most. It was what the girl was wearing. Just a jacket and dress of simple weave and of the same colour—a girl from the lower classes. Brendan's look shocked her even more: smitten, that's what he was.

'Mother, what—?'

'Say nothing, dear, nothing.'

The cab moved off and Catherine sat back, trembling.

The gas fire warmed the Glebe bedroom but they'd made their own heat. Richard was to be married and there was no future with him, but that was for another day and Gillian revelled in his body beneath her. His hardness was intensifying, exciting her and she relished the pleasure she was giving him. She climaxed, inhaled his heightened scent, wanting him locked within her. Resting on his chest, her panting quietened and she slid to his side. It had been the second time in an hour that they'd made love.

She brushed her hair aside and looked up at him. 'Penny for them?'

'Nothing. Just work. Did you know that Morgan Stanley's a queer?'

'A fancy man you mean?' she said.

'I do.'

'No! The barrister who's always in the papers?'

Richard patted her rump. 'The same, married and a shareholder of the Imperial Hotel.'

Gillian got up and said, 'I'll be right back.' She closed the bathroom door, turned up the gaslight and ran the tap. Douching under the warm water, she concentrated. She had been careful before but she had lost count since her last monthly cycle. She shook her head. No, she'd be all right. Richard was dressing when she opened the door. 'So soon?' she said. 'You said you'd be here a while.'

He smiled. A grin that melted her. His eyes roved over her. 'Sorry, I have a game.'

She was surprised. 'On a Sunday?' Then she was annoyed. 'So that's what you prefer? Not my company! Richard, you gamble a lot, don't you?'

His smile went and what replaced it shocked her. It was as if he'd been told some terrible news. 'I enjoy it, Gillian, but it's just for fun, like you.'

'That's charming,' she said as she began putting on her undergarments, followed by a skirt and blouse. She then sat and watched as Richard completed dressing. She could watch him for hours; order and firmness, confidence and balance. Getting up, she did his tie for him and his hands touched her, sending pleasure pulses through her. Richard stared at her, his blue eyes unsettling her again.

'Gilly, this is the last time,' he said. The words didn't register at first. 'I'm sorry, but I'm soon to be hitched. It's too risky.' He pulled on his coat. 'I'll see you around, I'm sure.' He nodded to the tousled sheets. 'But this stops, now. Goodbye, Gilly.'

'Richard? No ... please.' He made for the door and Gillian grabbed his sleeve. 'Just like that? You don't love me any more?'

Richard shrugged his shoulders. 'I've never said that, have I?' he smiled. 'Come on, have I?'

No, he hadn't *said* it but she'd felt it. His closeness, his tenderness, all had made her certain. This was too soon. Not yet. 'We could still see each other ... after, you know.' Now *why* had she said that?

'Attractive,' Richard said. 'You would?' *Oh, blast him.* Richard kissed her then broke away. 'I might see you again, but that would be cruel.'

She didn't care. 'It wouldn't, really. I love you. I want to be with you.'

He kissed her forehead. 'Goodbye, Gilly. When I get back, you mustn't be here.'

She couldn't move. Her feet felt as if they'd been nailed to the floor, but the pain wasn't in her feet, it was everywhere. She couldn't speak. It was like a dream when you wanted to scream and nothing happened.

Richard stopped in the open doorway. 'I'm sorry, Gilly,' he said. 'I really am.'

Gillian looked at the door closing. She gripped the bedclothes to restrain herself from running after him and grabbing him. The front door banged and she collapsed and fell on the bed, drawing up her knees and biting her hand as the tears came.

The Imperial Hotel's project team came trooping into Richard's office, led by the one on whom much depended: John's general foreman, David Sullivan. Tom Prentice, the chief estimator, followed and was joined by John Gibson, Leary's chief buyer.

'It's crowded,' John said as they sat packed around the desk, 'but let's start. I want no interruptions for our first meeting. We'll bring in some food later. It's the first of June and Mr Turner, the architect, says the tenders will come out at the end of the month. Not long.' He tapped the plans in front of him and looked at Richard. 'These are good. How did you get them?'

'I worked on their draughtsman, David O'Mara. I reminded him we were on Turner's tender list. I told him we'd have the drawings soon anyway. Five pounds got me the tracings.'

'Christ, Richard, that's excellent.'

'And I got something else.'

'What's that?' Sullivan said.

'O'Mara told me who the other tenderers are: Bucknells, Branagan and Son, and Dennings.'

John smiled and said. 'Very good, but … it's too big for Dennings, they'll bid high.'

'That they will,' Prentice said.

'Bucknells, we guessed,' John said and paused. 'But Branagans … that's an odd call. Why them? No matter. Burgess told me nothing new. The Council have the plans but wouldn't show them to me. Burgess was waiting for clearance from Turner.' He waited till they all looked at him. He tapped the plans again. 'With these, we've got a start on our bid and we're going to keep it. This job is special and Sydney's seen nothing

130

like it. The contractor who wins the Imperial Hotel will have a huge advantage.'

He looked at each person and went on to explain. 'When we win this, suppliers who have quoted to the losing bidders will hammer down our doors, demanding, pleading for our order and—an order on our terms, our price. Our margin will be skinny, but we'll build up that profit by buying in bulk.' He looked at David Sullivan and prepared himself for an argument. 'Dave, you'll be job leader. I've picked you as you're the best and you need a challenge.' He smiled. 'You seem to have that wool store on a string.'

Sullivan spluttered. 'I wouldn't call that an easy job, Mr Leary.'

'Then,' John said, 'you need a monster job. To make you sweat at night and make the most of your talents.'

'Father?'

'David is our best, Richard.'

'But I can do the job,' Richard said. 'It's what I wanted.'

Silence filled the room and some heads were down. John had to cut this short. It wasn't the time for a family argument. 'I've made my choice. I'll discuss my reasons after this meeting.'

Richard threw a pencil on the desk, folded his arms and looked out the window.

Not a good start. John turned to Sullivan. 'Dave, you'll be responsible for winning this. This is a war and it'll be dirty. Find out who's supplying to the other tenderers. Get exclusive deals. Gibson here will help you, but do what you have to do.'

'Mr Leary,' Sullivan said as he rubbed his shoulder and glanced at Richard, 'if I'm to lead, I want a free hand.'

'You'll have it,' John said and stood up. 'You'll get coopera- tion from everyone here. If not, I'll want to know why. Dave's in charge.' John pulled out his watch. 'I have to see Mrs Mansfield for five minutes. Dave, this will be the first of many meetings. Get your planning started now. Richard's done some already. I'll want reports at every meeting till we bid.' John looked around the office. 'Next time we'll have more space to plan. The extended meeting room should be finished by then.' He left the room and Richard followed him.

'Father, why not me? I want an explanation.'

Mrs Mansfield waited outside John's office. 'I'll be with you in a moment,' he said to her. 'Come in, Richard.'

John closed the door as Richard sat down. 'You'd be like a fifth wheel during the tender with Sullivan there.' John said, 'But you're good at hunting. I want those investors found. I want to know where they buy, who they bed and if their bowels are healthy. When I put my bid in, those men will be in my palm.'

'I'm more experienced than Sullivan.'

John had to placate his son. 'On projects we've built, yes, but not on this monster. You accept that?'

Richard folded his arms. 'I don't. Sullivan has no more skill than I do.'

John sat down at his desk. 'We have ten other projects that need you more than this pub.'

Richard hesitated. 'I can do it alongside them.'

Now he was being naïve. 'No, Richard. You're needed elsewhere.'

'I don't like it.'

'Well, that's how it's going to be,' John said with finality. John knew he was right and that he wanted Richard for other tasks … but did he? Was he starting to doubt his son because of his gambling? Was he starting to lose confidence in Richard running a big job, especially with all that cash around, cash that could be stolen for … gambling? He wasn't sure. But for whatever reason, he knew he could trust Sullivan, and Richard would be free to keep the other projects in line, the new George Street bank project for one.

'Sullivan will fail,' Richard said. 'He won't win you the job.'

'The Leary team will win this tender, Richard. Now, are you going to be a part of that or not?' Richard did not answer. 'Richard?'

'I'll win the Imperial Hotel for you, Father, and when I have, we can talk about who's going to run it.'

John knew that would give him time. They had to win it first. 'I'm not going to argue with you. Will you help me get more information on these investors? Yes or no?' John waited and trusted his judgment.

'I've warned you, Father—'

'Richard, I want an answer.'

'All right. I'll find them and their dirty linen. I already know about one of them.'

'You do?'

'Mr Morgan Stanley.'

'The barrister? Good. I'll give you the others.'

John opened a file cabinet next to him and took out a slim folder. 'Here are the details. It's a beginning but there's more to add. This is the only copy. Keep it tight and get to work. I want a report in a week. Now leave me; I've got to see Mrs Mansfield.'

Richard remained seated. 'I've looked at the plans and I have an idea on how to save a fortune. Steel. We'll build in steel.'

John tapped his fingers on the desk. 'Go on,' he said, then paused and raised his voice, 'Mrs Mansfield!'

'Yes, Mr Leary?'

'Come in, please.' His secretary came in with notebook, a document and pencil and sat down. 'We won't be long,' John said to her.

'I've scanned the plans,' Richard said. 'There's masses of brickwork through the job, huge basement walls, some up to three feet thick in places to support the floors above, and between the lower-level hotel rooms, walls two feet thick. That many bricks spell trouble, big trouble.'

'A job like this has never been done in steel.'

'I know that, but millions of bricks mean massive handling, from drays to site and up to each floor, then onto the floor itself. All takes valuable time. And the mortar they'd need—a nightmare.' Richard's face was alive with excitement. 'If you can reduce the bricks, you save time, lower the risk and handling.

Steel is the answer—replace massive brick columns with slimmer steel ones.'

An idea, John thought, but then there was a hurdle. 'Yes, but bricks are fireproof and steel is not: it buckles and fails under fire.'

Richard sat back and pursed his lips. 'That's right, so we have to find a way to prevent steel from being affected by heat. We have to work out how to fireproof it.'

'Leave the design as it is. We'll just have to find a smarter way to win.'

'I'll still work on it,' Richard said.

'Just don't let it stop you finding out about those owners.'

John turned to his secretary. 'Now, Mrs Mansfield, that George Street contract, please. I'll sign it then take it with me to the bank.' John executed the deed and Richard witnessed it. 'Thank you, Mrs Mansfield. If you could put those in an envelope, I'll collect it on my way out.' As his secretary headed to the door, John turned to Richard, 'When I get back, we can continue our talk. In the meantime, study those owners in that file.'

Richard left John's office and entered his own, charged with excitement. It was like his time at the tables, but not as sweet. He closed his eyes to fight off the urge to think about another hand and another win. It was a drug to him and he loathed himself for it. *Come on, man!*

Steel. He wouldn't give up on either count: steel *was* the answer, he was sure, and he *had* to be boss on the Imperial. Richard had met representatives from Brunels, the English engineering experts. They'd excited him with their early work in steel design, combining the best of bricks and steel. That was the way to go on the Imperial Hotel. Restless, he thought about going back to the meeting. No, Sullivan, the golden-haired boy, would have it under control. He would go and see Brunels in Pitt Street. He was determined that those engineers would work for Leary's and no other tenderer. An advantage: he had to have an advantage.

John sat back as Delia served his evening meal. The feel of the knife beside his plate reminded him of the steel design Richard had mentioned that morning. Fantasy stuff. Bricks were predictable, plentiful and priced right. But Richard was thinking in the right direction: they had to find something that shortened their construction time. Steel? Maybe, but with dinner on the table he gazed around at his family. Mary was looking down in the mouth and she sat staring at her plate. 'What's wrong, Mary?' he said.

Mary looked up, startled, as if her father had jumped out of a cupboard in front of her. She glanced at her mother, sister and brother. 'Nothing,' she said. 'I'm tired that's all.'

'She's been working too hard,' Catherine said. 'She needs something different. Being an English tutor can be demanding.'

Mary was a problem, John thought. She didn't want to get married and no boys interested her. John had tried, pulled in favours from acquaintances with eligible sons. Mary had rejected them all. John sensed an ambush and put his cutlery down. 'You want to do something different, Mary?'

'Yes, Father, I want to do something that challenges me.'

'Challenge? I thought all young women wanted to get married and have children.'

'*I* do, and can't wait,' Agatha said, grinning. 'I'd love to get married.'

'You will, dear, you will,' her mother said. 'And to someone of substance.' She looked at Brendan and raised an eyebrow. 'It's only a matter of time. Mary would like to work at Leary's. Can you find her something, dear?'

'I just don't want to do *something*, Mother. I want responsibility.'

John said automatically, 'It's out of the question.'

'Why?' Mary asked.

He took a sip of wine. He had to admit, his first wife Clarissa had been employed in her father's business, and done it well.

Mary wasn't Clarissa's daughter but Catherine, too, had worked in business and been very competent at it. So why not her daughter? 'Are you sure that's what you want?'

Mary's face showed an eagerness John hadn't seen before. 'Yes, Father I do. I'd really like to work in the family company.'

He hadn't expected this. He was about to give a sharp negative when he saw Catherine's look. She was sympathetic to Mary. He said slowly, 'If I can find something ...'

'Oh, Father,' Mary said, getting up and giving him a hug.

'I said *if.* There'll be no going back if you can't face ink staining your hands or someone yelling at you.'

'I'll stay. I promise,' Mary said, sitting down with a big smile on her face.

John sighed. 'All right. This new project, if we win it, is going to need a lot of people. I'll see what I can do.'

'Father's right,' Brendan said completing his meal. 'There'll be plenty of jobs, and it's good to keep some of them in the family.'

'Why isn't my uncle here?' John said, desperate to escape the subject.

'He's taking dinner in his rooms,' Brendan replied, putting his glass down.

'And Christine?'

'Lying down,' Catherine said. 'She's unwell.' She looked at him. 'Just our merry team.'

'Quite.'

Brendan stood up. 'May I be excused?'

'In a moment,' Catherine said. 'Girls, you may go.'

'Is Brendan in trouble?' Mary asked.

'I think he is,' Agatha said, smirking, 'and I know why.'

'Please leave us,' Catherine said, 'and tell cook not to come in for five minutes.'

Catherine waited until the dining-room doors were closed and turned to Brendan. 'I saw you yesterday after Mass, fawning over a common girl in Macquarie Street.'

'Her name's Julie, Mother.'

'You're using her first name! You were holding hands, in public! Have you no sense, Brendan?'

'I do.'

'Not, it seems, when it comes to young women.' Catherine's face was flushed. 'A girl like that will take you for everything. She—'

'You don't know her. She's not like that. She's not.'

John had to help his son out. He was annoyed, though: chasing a bit of skirt was natural, but his son should keep it simple and out of sight. 'There was no harm done, I'm sure.'

'You're not to see that kind of girl again,' Catherine said. 'Is that clear? You should see Anne Connaire more often. She's just right for you.'

'I don't know what you mean by "that kind of girl", Mother, but it sounds like an insult. Julie had just been to Mass, and so had I.'

It wasn't often John saw Catherine so worked up. 'I forbid you to see her again!'

Brendan said, 'Julie is a modest and good girl.'

'I don't want to discuss her,' Catherine said. 'You know what you must do. Do it.'

Time to leave this alone, John thought. 'I want to see you tomorrow about your project,' he said to Brendan. *Now, how to say this without giving the boy a big head?* 'It's going well. Call in and make an appointment to see me.'

Brendan looked at his mother before replying. 'I will, thank you, Father.'

He got up smiling and left the room.

John waited till his son had gone. 'He's a young man, Catherine. All young men have to sow their oats.'

'That's as may be but Brendan should be paying court to Anne Bonnaire, not consorting with dollymops.' She stared ahead and John thought it best to keep silent.

Brendan got down from the cab in Princes Street. 'Wait here, please,' he said to the driver. He pulled his collar tighter against the cold air and walked the short distance to Julie's gate. By seeing her again he was rebelling against his mother and that didn't sit easily with him. Julie was not dear to him, yet, and she might never be. To what lengths would he go to win her over? And what if she turned out to be a gold-digger? His mother's words resounded.

Stamping his feet, as if to quieten his conscience and fears of rejection, he went and knocked on the door. A pause, scuffles, then the door thumped and it lunged open. Brendan smiled as a yelling Billy ran from the door, holding onto his ear. Julie's pinch would have made a torturer smile and Brendan wondered what Billy had done. Julie looked good in a fitted, deep blue dress, which showed off her trim figure, with a matching bonnet. The dress didn't seem to billow out like Agatha's, but Julie's eyes sparkled and her face was clear of powder.

'Come in, Mr Leary,' she said.

Brendan stepped into a tidy room with a warm fire. Julie's mother entered the room. 'Good evening, Mrs Carson,' he said.

Mrs Carson smiled and ran her hands down the front of her dress. 'Please sit down, Mr Leary.'

'Ma, we're off. I won't be late home.'

'Nice to meet you again, Mrs Carson.'

'Julie, take your coat,' her mother said.

Julie reddened. 'I won't need it.'

'It's cold outside. I'll go and get it.' Julie's mother turned and disappeared.

She returned with a dark-green coat, the same one Julie had worn in the gardens. It was clean but it didn't match her dress. Her mother put it on her. 'Better to be warm,' Mrs Carson said as Brendan opened the door. 'Have a good time.'

Julie's hand was damp as Brendan helped her up into the waiting cab. He got in and she pulled the coat around her. 'My other coat's being cleaned.'

He was sure Julie had only one coat but it was her he liked, not her clothes. The cab moved off and he said, 'There should be a big crowd because it's Saturday and there's a new orchestra.'

'That all sounds good to me.'

At the Tivoli, they alighted from the cab, left their coats in the cloakroom and walked into the hall. Smoke, heat and laughter greeted them. The place was packed, couples were on the floor, dancing to the music, flushed faces and smiles all around. 'A dance or a drink to start?' he asked.

'A dance, please.'

Brendan waited for the music to begin and took Julie's hand, which gripped his. Off they went, the beat pulsing through him. Her lips were drawn tight but as she moved to the rhythm, her grip and her face relaxed.

Brendan looked at her. 'It's nice to dance, isn't it?'

'You're good,' she said.

'You are too. See, there's something we have in common.'

She nodded and looked at him. 'There is.'

'I've met your mother a few times now, but not your dad. How is he?'

'Fair to middling, thank you. He's away at the moment. He works at a station in Coonamble as a muster boss.'

'What's his name?'

'Bert.'

They danced the next two songs and she dabbed her brow. 'I'd like a drink now, please. You go and I'll find a place over there for us.' She pointed to a corner.

Brendan went to the trestle table set up with refreshments. By the look of some flushed faces, there was plenty being drunk. There were one or two people he knew but the rest of the huge crowd were strangers.

Balancing the drinks, he squeezed his way through the throng to Julie, who was speaking to a solidly-built young man dressed in coarse but clean woollen trousers and a white shirt with no tie.

'I'd like to dance,' the man was saying to Julie.

'Julie?' Brendan said.

Julie looked at him, her eyes wide. She looked back at the man. 'Aiden,' she said, 'this is Brendan Leary.'

Aiden's handshake would have crushed walnuts. 'Are you a builder, Mr Leary?' he said. 'If you are, you have a site in Darling Harbour.'

'I am and we do.'

'I'd like to dance with Aiden,' Julie said. 'He's a friend. All right, Brendan?'

At least she had called him Brendan! He hesitated then nodded. 'Of course, but maybe have a sip of your drink first.'

Julie took one of the glasses from him, took a sip then handed it back to him before heading on to the dance floor with Aidan. Brendan swallowed half his drink before putting both glasses on a nearby ledge.

Leaning against the wall, he watched them dance. Julie laughed at something Aiden said, raising Brendan's pique. But it was understandable. She was attractive, and would know men; he had to accept that. Beside him three girls were seated; one was looking at him with a cheeky smile he had to return. She got up and sidled up to him. Her bodice was low, revealing her cleavage.

'Like to dance?' she said, smirking and looking him up and down.

'I'm taking a breather.'

'That's not an answer,' she said, her big eyes attractive.

He looked over her head and lost sight of Julie in the crowd.

'Your girl's busy. It's just a dance I'm asking.' She touched his arm and showed a slip of tongue. 'Nothin' else, handsome.'

'Some other time.'

The girl sniffed, smiled and moved away.

After Julie's third dance with Aiden, Brendan had had enough. He'd brought Julie here and he was going to take her home. Walking out onto the floor, he made his move and cut in. Aiden had the grace to smile and make way.

Brendan stepped off with Julie. 'He seems a nice bloke.'

'He is. He works near me.'

'So, you see him often?'

'I do.'

'Do you like him? The way you laughed with him, it seems you do.'

Julie patted her brow with her hanky. 'He's a nice boy and I'll see him again. Don't get jealous on me, Mr Leary. I'd like that drink now, please.'

'If it's still there.' They found two vacant chairs and their untouched drinks. They sat in silence for a while. 'Thank you for this,' Julie said and took a sip. 'Do you come to these dances often?'

'Not these but—'

'Balls, I bet.'

'Yes, but I like these dances.' He paused then plunged in. 'And I like you.'

Julie looked down. 'I know.'

Brendan felt a thrill. 'Feel like dancing some more?'

She put her empty glass under her chair. 'I do, but I promised Aiden another one.'

Brendan swallowed his pride. Julie was worth the effort to win her over. 'That's all right.'

Julie looked as though she hadn't expected that answer. 'Thank you ... Brendan.'

'When is Mr O'Connor coming to Enmore?' Rob Jenkins asked.

'Today,' Brendan said, 'and he's due soon, so let's make sure things are all right. But first, have a look at this.' Brendan handed a two-page document to his sub-foreman. 'It's our copy and it's all there. It's Mr Dawkins's end of May report and he can't praise us highly enough.'

Jenkins looked at it and grinned at his boss. 'Stan the plumber said he saw you last Saturday night at the Tivoli. You were dancing up a storm with a good looker.'

'Just read, Rob.' Brendan smiled. 'A boss has to have some distraction.'

Jenkins went on, 'Stan said she *was* some distraction.'

'Rob.'

'All right.' Jenkins started to scan the report. 'Above average ... best he's seen, none better. Is this right?'

'It is.'

Jenkins gave the report back to him and pulled out his notebook. 'Most times, a clerk of works has a cushy full-time job reporting to his client. The boys distrust them. They add nothing to building a job, just whinge to their client about our little mistakes.'

'Well, this bloke's different,' Brendan said. 'It's nearly knock-off. Let's look around before O'Connor gets here.' They left the site office and went up the completed stairs. Brendan entered the manager's residence and said, 'Is the plasterer right to start on the outside?'

'The scaffolding's ready for him.'

'Let me see,' Brendan said. He leaned out of a window and inspected the timber-framed falsework which covered the front of the two-storey building. 'More braces here. Tie this post back to the wall with an extra clip.'

'Right. Is it true that O'Connor's brother was killed on a site?'

'Sad but true, Rob. Rory O'Connor is an advocate, and a good one. I like his style. I met him at a Leary's site three years ago where its drunken foreman had sacked two carpenters. With some deft footwork Rory had the two workers back on the job and the foreman sent home. We've been friends ever since.'

Jenkins picked up two empty cement bags, folded them and stuck them under his arm. 'That's good.'

'Rory was in his final year as an articled clerk with a bright future. Then his younger brother died on a site in a bad accident. Rory got his ticket to practise and decided to do something to change the building industry, to make it safer. Come on, we've got more to check.'

There were always things to fix on a site, but Brendan knew he shouldn't be nit-picking about things. It was hard. An unfinished wall caught his eye and he made to say something and stopped. He forced his eyes away and kept walking. The wall would be finished tomorrow and, with Jenkins supervising, it would be right. Safety first, and he wanted fewer accidents. 'I told Father that we need a man just to check on safety and hazards around the sites.'

'What did he say?' Jenkins said.

'He'll think about it. Meantime he says let the leading hands do it and I suppose he's right.'

'I've got too many things on now,' Jenkins said.

Brendan slapped him on the shoulder. 'You're a sub-foreman now, Rob. Get Johnny your new leading hand to do it. I'll help you.'

'Good.'

'How are the furnishing orders?'

'Just about let,' Jenkins said.

'Look, are they let or not?'

'All but the window blinds. The supplier wants more money.'

'You want me to talk to them?'

'I'll have another go. If that doesn't work, I'll get you in.'

'Right,' Brendan said. 'When we get back to the office, I'll go over the accounts with you.' Jenkins rolled his eyes. 'Being a sub-foreman on site is essential but it's not everything. You have to understand the payments. You don't look convinced?'

'I am, but that's for the clerks.'

'No, you're responsible to help make a profit on this job. We're here to build safely and to quality but we're here to make a quid too, right?'

'I spoke with Mr Prentice the other day,' Jenkins said. 'I have a new iron girder supplier for him with a good price per ton.'

A voice came from below, 'Boss!'

Brendan looked down the stairwell. 'What's up, Johnny?'

'A man here to see you. Rory O'Connor.'

'We'll meet him in the site office in a few minutes, and tell him not to sample that bottle of whisky in the bottom drawer of my desk.' Laughter drifted up and Brendan smiled. The site was getting better. People had a spring in their step. Jenkins pitched his cement bags into a nearby rubbish bin.

A heavily-built man of about thirty with red hair and freckles looked at them as they walked into the site office. He smiled and said, 'You took your time.'

Jenkins looked puzzled but Brendan smiled and said, 'This is Rob Jenkins, my sub-foreman.'

The man stood up. 'Rory O'Connor, advocate and friend of the workers.'

'What's happening?' Brendan said.

'Not a lot, but then, maybe a lot.'

'Make sense, will you?' Brendan said.

'I will,' O'Connor said and smiled, 'if there's a drink to partner it.'

A drink? Brendan was curious. 'Don't you want to look around?'

'I did, first thing this morning, and your site passes.'

Brendan smiled. Rory was a smart one. An unscheduled site visit was likely to show up a few safety breaches. He turned to his sub-foreman. 'We'll talk accounts tomorrow, same time, Rob. Enough for the day.'

'See you tomorrow, boss ... Mr O' Connor.'

'Rory, please, good man. Nice to meet one of Brendan's team. Come Mr Leary, the beer beckons.'

As they walked to the pub on the corner, darkness settled on the streets. Brendan shivered in his jacket. 'Winter stinks,' he said. 'Summer's best for building.'

'It's the eighth of June. Winter's just a pup, my friend, and any time is best for the law, it makes no difference. Jenkins seems keen.'

'You only just met him,' Brendan said as they stopped to let a loaded dray pass them.

'I saw you two coming to the site office. He's as keen as a kid in a lolly shop with a pound to spend.'

Brendan nodded. 'And he'll get better.' He pushed on the hotel door and they stepped into warmth, a crowd and smoke. He spied a table. 'The usual, thanks Rory.'

Brendan settled back until his friend returned with the beers. 'So what's doing?' Brendan asked.

'The big pub's all the talk. Who'll get it and what it'll mean.'

Brendan sipped his beer and grimaced, his mood dampened. Richard was all over the Imperial Hotel bid like a tarpaulin on a wool wagon and Brendan knew little. 'What have you heard?'

'Groups I know see it as a *cause célèbre*.'

'Groups? Like the unions? The TLC?'

Rory leaned closer. 'Groups, my friend. Workers who meet and talk about their rights.'

'Tell me why we need a new Trades and Labour Council,' Brendan said.

'I'd be delighted to. The times need it,' Rory said, pulling his chair closer. 'The jobs are getting bigger, immigrants are pouring in and bosses are getting lazy.'

'Lazy?'

'Lazy, Brendan. The TLC stirred things up two years ago. It frightened the bejesus out of dodgy contractors—and no, Leary's isn't one of them. Some of the rest just didn't know what they were doing wrong. Can you believe that?'

Brendan could. 'No more slave-wage deals unearthed? No more death threats?'

'The odd one, but the contractors have settled down.'

'There are enough cranks out there spruiking the workers' paradise, Rory, and thank God you're not one of them. Set your builders onto them.'

O'Connor smiled. 'I'll try that.' He looked at his empty glass. 'Your shout.'

Brendan squeezed through the packed throng and thought about his friend. Rory wasn't popular with Leary's. He was seen as a nuisance. 'Two pints of Bass,' Brendan ordered. He grasped the drinks and headed back to their table. But Rory wasn't a zealot. That's why Brendan liked him. He could see both sides and used logic to solve problems. He put the beers down and picked up a copy of the latest *Bulletin* magazine lying on the table. 'Is this for me?'

'It is. There's a good article on wages pressure on page three. I commend it to you.'

'I'll read it. So, these workers who meet and talk about their rights. Pretty scattered are they?'

Rory put his drink down. 'They were—not now. They've got organisation and leadership within their unions.'

This was troubling. 'Who are they? The Society of Carpenters? The Bricklayers' Union?'

Rory smiled. 'They've taken me into their confidence, my friend.'

'I need to know who they are.'

Rory held his friend's stare. 'You do, do you?'

'I do. If Leary's is to be great, it needs to get its house in order.'

Rory paused then said. 'All right, I can tell you this. Whoever wins the Imperial Hotel had better watch out.'

'For what? A push for higher wages?'

'And other things. Do you think Leary's will win it?'

'Maybe, Rory. So, tell me more.'

Rory drank the last of his beer and wiped his mouth. 'You're persistent. I'll tell you what you'll find out anyway, eventually … but not some things.'

'Fair enough. What can you tell me?'

'Your shout.'

Brendan grinned. 'No, it's yours.'

Rory pulled himself up and advanced to the bar. Brendan's father loathed the unions and Brendan admitted that some were out for their own ends, but you could not just ignore them. They were a fact of life.

Rory sat back down with the beers. 'Improved ratios, that's what they want. At present, there's one apprentice for each three tradesmen, carpenter or bricklayer.' He paused. 'What they want is one apprentice for every two tradesmen.'

'That's madness.'

Rory shrugged. 'That's not all. A smoko of fifteen minutes in the morning and half an hour for a noon feed, but the big things are a guaranteed minimum wage and a pension.'

Brendan was amazed. 'A what?'

'For when they've retired—and they retire early because their limbs are buggered.'

Brendan thought of Alan Clancy, the foreman at the Bond Store warehouse job. He said, 'All very nice, but builders—general contractors especially—can't afford that.'

Rory sipped his beer and placed the glass down. 'I'm just telling you what's coming, that's all.'

'Wonderful. It's a rosy future we're going to have.'

They finished their beers in silence. Richard had called a meeting at Annandale for the following day to review the costs on the Enmore project. That would take five minutes, all was square there. What wasn't square was what Rory had just told him, and Richard had to be told.

Chapter Six

THE NEXT DAY, BRENDAN WALKED INTO RICHARD'S OFFICE AND SAT down opposite his half-brother. 'Morning,' he said, as he placed his report file on Richard's desk. 'It's all there, Richard: Enmore's costs, orders, commitments and profit.'

Richard looked up from the document he was working on and glanced at the folder. 'I'll look at that later. I have to see Father in ten minutes for an important meeting. He's with Prentice now.'

'On the Imperial Hotel?'

Richard grinned. 'It might be.'

'Good, then you've got nine minutes to hear me out.'

Richard put his pen down. 'What about?'

'I'm worried about it, Richard. It'll get us into trouble.'

Richard got up and sat on the corner of his desk. 'It certainly will, with Sullivan running it.'

'David Sullivan?'

'Father thinks he's the best, but I don't.'

Brendan had assumed Richard would be leader of the project. 'We have to win it yet. Is Sullivan leading the bid?'

'He is.'

'Well, that doesn't mean he'll get the gun job when we win it.'

Richard slapped Brendan on the shoulder. 'No, it doesn't! So, how's that job going to get us into strife?'

'The unions. I've got it on good authority that they'll go after us if we win it. They'll demand more apprentices, shorter hours—'

'Who's told you this?' Richard said.

'O'Connor. He's up to date with what—'

'He's a ratbag, Brendan. Ignore him and anyway, we have to win it first. That's the key.'

'We do, but as soon as we win it, the risk starts. Look,' Brendan said, pulling some papers from inside his jacket and opening them up, 'there are other things besides the unions: delays, materials . . .'

Richard glanced at Brendan's notes. 'You've been busy and that means your bank project's not getting attention.'

'I've got the bank under control.' Brendan touched his job file on the desk and said. 'It's all in there.'

'Confident little sod, aren't you?'

Brendan counted to five. His brother always got him going but he had to convince him. 'You're welcome to come to the site at any time and check it.'

'I don't need an invitation to do a site inspection on one of *my* sites.'

'It's my site, Richard.'

'I'm the Construction Manager, Brendan. You report to me. You ask *me* if you want to sack someone. I've seen Enmore. It's not bad. Pity you had to get rid of Dougherty. Good man, Dougherty.'

'He wasn't. He was disruptive.'

'But you should have told me before you sacked him.'

Richard was right again. 'All right, I should have told you.'

'You've still got a site to run, so let Father and me sort out the Imperial Hotel. We have the experience. Now, off you go and make sure that project of yours finishes on time and to budget.'

Brendan flicked the edge of his notes. 'These are important, Richard.'

'To you, brother, to you.' He looked at them again. 'Are these your thoughts?'

'Yes, though I think you should speak with Sean. He'd know a thing or two.'

Richard shook his head. 'Sean's old-fashioned. A job like the Imperial Hotel would be beyond him.'

'Maybe. But we're all new to big projects. Won't you at least look at these?'

'Nothing there about wet-nursing our men, I hope.'

'No,' Brendan said, irritated. 'But ways to reduce our costs and our risk. Richard, there are other things we could do. The Imperial Hotel won't be just a one-off. There'll be more like it and we have to plan. The colony will grow and we need to be prepared for that. We will have to adapt to new thinking and new ways.' Brendan leaned forward. 'Like when we had a recession, back in '78. I was at school then but I well remember Father worrying about the survival of the company. There was no work to bid on, and what little work Leary's did win had no profit. We need to make Leary's cash-wealthy, so that we can build our own buildings with tenants already signed up. Not be subject to the whims of the construction tender cycle by trying to win projects with low profits.' Brendan tapped his knee for emphasis. 'By getting a tenant to agree to pay rent in our own developed buildings, we could build and get good cash. After a year or two we wouldn't need to tender on jobs but would have our own projects.'

'I'll not stop being a builder.'

'We won't, Richard. We'll build our own buildings and enjoy doing so, but we'll control the architects because *we'll* be paying their fees.'

Richard seemed to be really listening to him. 'Architects should work for us, indeed. But what you're saying sounds as rosy as a nun's prayer group and I'll have none of your mad ideas about workers. The Imperial Hotel needs strong men, experienced men. You don't pass muster to comment.'

Brendan became angry. 'Why do you say that, Richard? I can see risk. I can see trouble. Don't you care about those?'

'Opinions and theory don't build you a landmark hotel, little brother,' Richard said, pointing at him. 'Guile, cunning and being tough get results. And that's plain to me.'

'I don't agree.'

Richard stood up. 'I don't care. You have no say. And I've got to see Father now.' He glanced at the notes. 'Oh, very well, leave them here. I'll look at them later.' Richard opened his office door.

Brendan paused at the doorway. 'That's not just opinion, Richard,' he said, pointing to his work, 'there's some good stuff in there.'

Richard folded his arms. 'Brendan ... I said I'd look at your notes. All right?'

'You don't believe in me, do you?'

'No,' Richard said, and moved closer to him. 'No, I don't. Keep your station, half-brother. Don't get beyond yourself. You might get hurt.'

'What's the matter Richard? Jealous?'

Richard gripped Brendan's forearm and forced it back. 'You need a lesson.'

Brendan grimaced but pulled Richard's hand off. 'Not from you. Never.' He pushed the door wider and left.

Richard was worried about him! That was good. It meant he was getting close to besting him. Brendan wanted his ideas heard. He'd have a chat with Sean.

Richard closed his office door. *Bloody hide of him. Give him one project and he's an expert. We'll fix that.*

He collected Brendan's notes, moved to put them in the waste-paper basket, then stopped. He tapped the papers on his hand, then folded them and stuffed them in his jacket before making his way to his father's office. He knocked on the door and entered.

John looked up. 'Ah, Richard, just the man. Come in, come in. Tom here has a question about one of the tenderers. What do you know of Branagans?'

Richard sat down and acknowledged Prentice. 'They're a medium-sized contractor with a few jobs around.'

'Right,' Tom said. 'Then why are they tendering on the Imperial Hotel?'

'They know someone,' John said. 'I'm certain.'

'They do,' Richard said. 'Mr Branagan is the cousin of Mr Cunningham, one of the Imperial's investors.'

'I knew it,' John said and slapped his hand on the desk.

'There are three investors in the Imperial Hotel, Father: Cunningham, a pastoralist, Morgan Stanley, and Grimshaws. Cunninghams have the majority investment.'

John looked at him. Richard had done his stuff in just seven days. 'Well, we know the link now, but Stanley with Cunninghams?'

'They don't like each other,' Richard said, 'but business is business. Cunninghams have a thirty-five per cent share of the St Peters Brick Company.'

'Really?' John said. 'That's interesting.'

'More than that,' Tom said. 'Branagans will get the bricks at cost price, a very big edge, because they're a shareholder relation.'

'And there's something else,' Richard said. 'The Bank of New South Wales is stumping up the funds for the project.'

John looked out the window. 'It all fits.'

'I've got something to show you both that might help us,' Richard said. 'I'll be back in a moment.'

He returned with a roll of plans and a folder of notes and placed them on the table in his father's office. Tom and his father stood each side of him. 'Brunels,' Richard said, 'have done a steel design for the structure—iron girders in the old language—which reduces the brickwork by forty per cent.'

Tom whistled. 'That'll help. Fewer bricks for us to buy and lay.'

John put on his glasses and scanned the plan that Richard had pulled out of the roll. He patted the notes. 'You've been busy.'

'Burning the midnight oil.'

'So, how much did Brunels charge you for this?'

'Nothing, Father.'

'It had to cost something,' Tom said.

'I convinced them,' Richard said, 'that if the steel design is used, they will get a lot of publicity and more work as a result.'

'Good work, son,' John said, 'but let's see.' He looked more closely at the plan. 'How do you fireproof the steel?'

'We encase the steel columns that support each floor with bricks.'

'Ah, so you still have bricks.'

'But not as many, Father. The steel will take the entire load.'

'Take Brunels' plan, Tom,' John said, 'and give it the once over. I don't trust fancy engineers. See if what they've designed can be built. Declan can help you.'

'It can, Father, believe me.'

'I have faith in my God, Richard. Everything else, I get the facts and ask a lot of questions.'

'You say I'm wasting my time?'

Tom rolled up the plans. 'I'll leave you two to talk.'

John leaned against his desk. 'It's too risky, Richard. Steel's not been done before and—'

'That doesn't mean it can't be done.'

'That's true, but at what cost? And there's the time it will take.'

'Steel will be quicker,' Richard said with confidence.

'It will ... after the third or fourth floor, when everyone's used to it. Let's talk again after Tom's measured the differences between your plans and our conforming bid.' John patted him on the shoulder, 'Don't get your hopes up.'

Brendan watched Sean Connaire enter Cochrane's Hotel and make his way towards him. Over the last six days, since he'd had the run-in with Richard, Brendan had worked out the way to plead his case to his father's former partner.

Sean sat down and smiled. 'You're looking tired. Hard work agrees with you, it does.'

'Thanks for the compliment.'

'You're welcome,' Sean said and looked at the bare table then at the bar. 'Dry argument?'

'I'll get us something,' Brendan said and headed to the bar for a lemonade for Sean and a beer for himself.

'This place is different,' Sean said, when Brendan returned. 'Your father and I spent some good times here in the original Cochrane's. It was our first job. From small pub to big pub in what ... thirty-five years, my goodness.'

'That's what I wanted to talk about,' Brendan said.

'What? This place?'

'No, the Imperial Hotel.'

Sean's broad shoulders sagged and he sat back in the chair. 'It's all I'm hearing. It's a monster, Dave says, and Declan agrees. He's working on it.'

Good, thought Brendan, Dave has been talking to Sean about it. 'How's he going?'

'Who? Declan?'

Brendan was more interested in Sullivan's opinion but remained polite. 'Yes.'

'My son's a devil with the costings, Brendan. Me, I was happy on the tools but not him, no. And he said the numbers are staggering, the sheer volume of all the stuff.'

'And Mr Sullivan?'

'He's got the big challenge. Where do you start? Materials, labour, handlin'? They're all there, in spades. I don't know. Why does your father want it? It could kill Leary's.'

Brendan looked at his untouched beer. 'I know. All our eggs in one basket. I told Richard of my doubts a week ago. Has he said anything to you?'

Sean shook his head. 'No, but this is your Da. He's had the banshees in his bollocks from a young age.'

'Hard to pin down was he?' Brendan said and smiled.

'Bagging a breeze would be easier. So, he's going for it; he's the boss.' Sean slapped his knee. 'We've got to help him.'

Brendan took a sip of his beer. 'The risks are huge.'

'Aye, they are, but what can we do?'

'You limit the risks or get others to pay for them.'

Sean scratched his balding head. 'What others? Leary's might be building the thing, Brendan. You're taking the risk. What are you on about?'

'It's not easy, I know. I did some planning over the weekend—'

'On the Imperial Hotel?'

'Rob Jenkins has a good hand on the bank job now. It's turning around.'

'I know,' Sean said. 'John and I have seen the effort you've made and Dave wants to see it, too.'

Brendan sat back. 'Really?' This was a turn up.

'Your Da was pleased. The job was too much for Dougherty. Anyhow, about the new pub?'

'I've been reading up on articles from the Builders and Contractors Association where they listed the things that could happen on a job this size.' Brendan counted them off on his fingers: 'Poor weather, suppliers running late or going broke, bad ground, accidents and unions.' Brendan reached into his jacket pocket. 'I've listed them here with a plan to tackle them.'

Sean put his hand up. 'No use showing them to me, boy. I know you like the details and such but I'm used to building things from the plans and fixing things when they need fixin'. Now, don't look so glum.' Sean rubbed his whiskered chin and he seemed deep in thought. 'Dave might have a use for them.'

'You think so?'

'I said might,' Sean said.

It was worth a try, Brendan thought.

'Right,' Sean said. 'Today's ... Tuesday ... yes the sixteenth of June. What ya doin' Saturday morning? Busy?'

Brendan thought quickly. He had a few things on, but nothing that Rob Jenkins couldn't handle. The Imperial Hotel was too important. Richard hadn't spoken to him about the notes he'd left him; they were probably in the rubbish now. Maybe he should wait and get Richard to speak to Sullivan. No, he would risk Richard's ire. 'Where?'

'I'll get Dave to come to your site. You can show him around, then talk to him.'

Sean had pull. He might be small, ageing and wiry, but as a former owner of Leary's and a highly experienced ex-foreman, he was respected by the workers. When he spoke, people listened—well, those who had brains did, and Dave Sullivan would. Brendan had made a second copy of his notes and now both Richard and Dave would know of his concerns. 'Good.'

Sean smiled. 'And I'll get Declan to have a chat with you too. Now, I know you're like your Da,' he said, 'like a bull at a gate, but hear me. Dave's a senior site man, sensitive like to criticism—'

'I'm not throwing rocks at him, Sean. Leary's depends on this.'

'Now, as I said, mete out those things you've got there in your jacket, a bit at a time. Dave will see, but you've got to land him like a trout, not club him like a salmon.'

'I just want to show him my thoughts.'

'And good ones they are, Brendan, I'll bet. But a word. You're a demon with detail—'

'Sean!'

'You are and you've got to learn to see things from above. Like the God we love. The art's in the convincing boy, not the facts as such. Now, how's that great-uncle of yours? Still causing mischief?'

'He is. But his health's not good. Coughing up a storm he is. He could do with another visit.'

'I'll see him,' Sean said, 'and I'll see your father, too. Try to talk him out of the tender.'

Brendan stood up. 'Good luck. He wants to win it and he hates losing.'

'Ohhh,' Sean said getting up, rubbing his knee. 'Glad I'm not going to be working on it if he does win. It's a young man's game it is.' He smiled. 'Or should I say a young person's game. Saw your sister Mary in the office t'other day. More bloody Learys! And Richard? He's stopped the gambling, I suppose?'

Why should Sean ask that? 'I don't know, Sean. Why? Have you heard something?'

'A few whispers. Ah well, it's not your problem.'

It wasn't, Brendan knew, but then if Richard was still gambling that was a problem for Leary's.

Sean sighed. 'I have to go. Look after yourself,' he grinned. 'You didn't hear this from me but Dave Sullivan's next meeting on the big pub is at the end of the month.' He gripped Brendan's hand and said, 'Get yourself an invite to it.'

Brendan watched as the ferry crewman cast off the line on the foredeck. He turned to Julie seated beside him. 'It'll be blowy out here but the sun's out.'

'I don't mind,' she said. 'I like the trip to Manly.'

As the boat made its way, the smoke from the funnel drifted away. Fort Macquarie stood clean and proud in the mid-June Sunday afternoon. 'We're preparing a bid for a big new hotel,' he said.

'Where?'

'In Clarence Street. It'll be sixteen storeys.'

Julie laughed. 'Sixteen? It'll fall over.'

'No. But it will be the biggest building in town. Dave Sullivan will be the trump on it. I saw him about it yesterday.' Julie pulled her collar up to her neck. 'You're not cold are you? We could go inside.'

Julie looked at him. 'You worry about me, don't you?'

Brendan more than worried about her! 'I do. You're special.'

'To you? Or just special?'

'Both.'

Julie smiled at him. 'How is your family? Your sisters are Mary and Agatha? Yes?'

'That's right. They're well, thank you. And your family's health?'

'The same, thank you,' she said. 'You know, you're nice to me, Brendan and I like it. I said that it wouldn't work out but ... so far it's been all right.'

'I always said it would.' An attractive, well-dressed lady inside the ferry came close to the window and looked out at the view. She then looked at them. Did he know her? The woman stayed for a moment then turned and walked back to her seat.

'Was that always a fort?' Julie said, pointing to Pinchgut.

'As far as I know,' Brendan said, reaching to hold Julie's hand. She didn't resist. Good, he thought. 'We are friends, Julie. I like to be with you and share things with you.'

'I do, too.'

'How's Aiden?'

She let go of his hand. 'We still see each other. He's a nice boy.'

Brendan forced himself to keep civil. 'That's nice.'

They kept quiet for a time, taking in the view and the freshening breeze. Julie was a big part of his life now and he liked that. A family near him was sharing a thermos of tea. He'd heard that there were people who could foretell your life from the pattern of the tea leaves: romance, health, career, all that. Agatha knew of a girl who wanted to know her future and she'd paid someone in a circus who had told her. He wouldn't waste his money on some charlatan to tell him his future with women.

Julie was the first girl he'd felt this way about, but was she the right one for him? Should he see other girls? No, romance wasn't as easy to solve as ordering bricks. He was an organiser and he took minimum risks. Yet here he was letting his heart lead him along a path he hadn't planned and to a destination of uncertainty. But he had to admit he was enjoying the trail with the girl sitting beside him.

'I have to go away,' she said.

'Oh? Where?' he said, surprised.

'Coonamble. My father says the station owner needs a seamstress for three weeks, starting in a couple of days. The wages are double what I get in the factory.'

Brendan forced a smile because he knew her family could do with the money. But three weeks without seeing her? 'Good on you,' he said and took hold of her hand again. 'I'll miss you. But how will you get time off from the factory?'

'I've told them that Dad's crook. I'll have time off with no pay.'

'Fair enough.'

'Will you write?'

'Of course,' Brendan said.

'Good. I'll be back by the twelfth of July.' Point Piper came into view. 'That's where you live?'

'It is.'

'Posh.'

'It's not. It's—'

Julie squeezed his hand harder. 'I'm joking,' she said. 'Now, what are you going to treat me to when we get to Manly?'

'Why Miss Carson, you are demanding.'

'Just want to see if you like ice cream. I do.'

'Then that's what we'll have.'

Sitting at the desk in his bedroom, Brendan sighed and put down the report on a new type of brick tie. It had been four days since the ferry trip and he missed Julie already. It was no use reading any further; all he could think about was her. There was a knock on the door. 'Come in.'

His mother entered and clasped her hands in front of her. 'I met Mrs Bucknell today. She said she saw you last Sunday with that girl again. I told you not to see her.'

Brendan tried to think who Mrs Bucknell might be, then he remembered: the lady near the ferry window. *So be it.* 'Yes, I was with Julie.'

'You disobeyed me, Brendan. That makes me sad and angry.'

'Sit down, Mother, please.'

She sat in a chair near his bed. 'Why do you do this to me? I'm trying to protect you.'

He appreciated it but he had to make a stand. 'I know and I love you for that.'

Tears filled her eyes. 'But you still do the wrong thing.'

'According to you,'

'Don't be impertinent,' she said. 'Stop seeing this girl or else.'

'Or else?'

'I mean it, Brendan. You are a kind, sensitive young man and a girl like that will break your heart. See her no more.'

'You're prejudiced, Mother. You don't know her.'

'And you do? Well?'

Brendan didn't answer.

'See?' his mother said. 'You don't.' She reached and took his hand. 'I've seen what these girls do. I've seen the way they trap young men like you.'

'Julie's not like that.'

'Are you sure?'

He wasn't about to argue over uncertainties. 'It's my life, Mother.'

Her eyes hardened. 'Oh dear me. Then be it on your head. But, I'm still convinced that girl's motives are not genuine.'

She stood up and left the bedroom.

Brendan was shocked. To hurt his mother was anathema to him and he would have to build a bridge back to her. But now, he had to get out of this room. He went downstairs to the kitchen where Mary sat drinking a mug of tea.

'What's wrong?' she said.

'Is it that obvious?'

She nodded. 'Want some tea?'

He poured one from the pot and sat down. 'I'm seeing a girl and mother disapproves.'

'I know. Agatha told me and it's all over the office. You were seen at the Tivoli.' Mary smiled. 'Is she nice?'

'She's more than that to me.'

'Stan the plumber said she was a looker. You like her, don't you?'

'I do.'

Mary pressed his hand. 'Does she work?'

'At McIntyre's in Newtown Road. She's a seamstress.'

Mary shook her head. 'Be careful, Brendan.'

'Don't you start.'

'All right. What's her name?'

'Julie Carson.'

'Julie Carson is a lucky girl.'

Brendan sipped his tea in silence. He was sad. His mother was angry at him and he could understand why, but he couldn't and wouldn't stop seeing Julie.

A warm mug eased the cold in Brendan's fingers as he sat in the empty room waiting for the meeting to start. Someone must have left food somewhere because the place reeked of cheese. He put the mug down to pull out his papers, notebook and pencil from his satchel and placed them on the table. He opened his notebook to a blank page and wrote at the top of the page: '29 June 1885, Annandale'. It was a quarter to seven.

'I knew you'd be early,' came a croaky voice as Richard sat down opposite Brendan. His eyes were bloodshot but he was grinning. 'Sullivan told me you tried to win him over with new ideas.'

'They're the same ones I gave you, Richard.'

'You had quite a chat together, didn't you? Christ, it's cold. Where's the damn heating? I'll see if the boiler's on.' He got up and left the room and Brendan thought about his notes. Yes, Dave had given him a good hearing but he hadn't sounded convinced ... yet. Today would be an opportunity to push home his ideas.

Richard breezed back into the room. 'Fixed that,' he said. 'Should be better soon. See how I look after you?' Richard drew up his chair. 'Sullivan's gullible. He's open to fancy ideas.'

Brendan moved his chair back. 'He's not a convert yet, Richard.'

'Nor am I.'

'But he said I could come today and have my say.'

'Brendan, it's a waste of time.'

Where were the others? Richard and he would be yelling at each other soon. 'There's always room to improve. No one has all the answers. Not even you.' Brendan sipped his tea.

Richard tapped Brendan's notes. 'I looked at these and they don't hold water.'

Dave Sullivan came in with files jammed under his arm, nodded to them and sat down. Brendan waited, worried now about whether anyone else was coming. Maybe they weren't interested in hearing what he had to say. His anxiety waned as Tom Prentice, the chief estimator; Mr Judd, the office manager and the stenographer, Miss Daley, all trooped in. Brendan was surprised to see his sister come in and close the door after her.

'What is she doing here?' Richard asked, pointing to Mary.

Dave motioned Mary to sit beside him. 'Miss Leary asked if she could sit in and see how a big tender's brought together.'

Richard rubbed his head and smirked.

'I approve,' Sullivan said. 'Any problems?'

Richard looked at the others. 'Doesn't worry me. She'll be bored in five minutes.'

Mary glared at her stepbrother. Brendan touched her sleeve. 'We promise not to swear too much.'

'It's smelly in here, isn't it?' she said.

'All right,' Dave said. 'We've got a full load. I've invited Brendan because he's got some contributions for our bid. Brendan, go ahead, but keep it tight.'

The door opened and his father came in. 'Good morning,' he said and sat on a spare chair near Brendan. 'Carry on.'

Brendan drew breath. His father would be tough on him but he'd have a go. Brendan looked from person to person, stopping at Richard. 'Thanks for the opportunity to present some of my ideas.' He glanced at his notes then at his colleagues. 'There are three items: insurances, advance payment and program. The first is insuring our cash flow against slow payments from our client. I've read that some London insurance companies will cover, for a small premium, the amount of the monies we are owed at any time if the client defaults or is slow in paying us on a month-by-month basis.'

Prentice wrote down some notes.

'The second thing,' Brendan continued, 'is we request a ten per cent advance payment from the client before we start work.' He waited as this idea settled on the group.

'Why?' Prentice said, then he smiled. 'Of course, to pay for our start-up costs.'

'Yes and no. When we start a job, we have to pay for all the start-up costs—set up, mobilisation, wages for a month, lease of equipment, Council charges ...'

'That's right,' Prentice said. 'We're out of pocket till we can claim and we then don't get paid for thirty days.'

'We could use some of the advance payment money for that,' Brendan said, 'but we could also place it in a contingency fund and let it earn interest. If we need it in an emergency, we still could use it.'

'Clients won't buy that,' Judd said shaking his head.

'They will,' Brendan said, 'if we give them a guarantee from our bank for the amount of the advance payment. It's a small fee we add on the tender. It'll cover the cost of the advance payment if we go broke.'

'Explain about the insurance again,' John said.

'It's straightforward,' Prentice said. 'You just pay a premium, yeah?'

'Sounds too easy,' John said. 'Has any other builder done it?'

Brendan paused. That was a good question and he should've done some checking. 'No, I don't think so.'

'Right,' John said. 'Untried and risky.'

Brendan wasn't to be put off. 'Nothing like the risk of not being paid.'

'I agree,' Dave said. 'I think we should do it. All agree?'

Nods all around, except Richard who looked out the window, and his father, who scribbled some figures down. Richard stood up and got himself a glass of water. Fighting an alcohol head, Brendan thought. Drink was a close partner of cards. Was his half-brother still gambling like Sean had said?

'These things added to our tender will make us uncompetitive,' John said. 'We need things that will reduce our bid price, Brendan, not increase it.'

'We can get our suppliers to heavily discount their rates,' Brendan said.

'We're already doing that,' John said.

Something Brendan didn't know. Richard sat back down and grinned at him.

'But if we can pass on part of our advance payment to the suppliers, by way of a deposit, especially for bricks,' Brendan said, 'they'll discount their prices further.'

Judd the office manager pursed his lips. 'They're always complaining about us paying them late. It's worth a try.'

Brendan had kept his best point till last. 'Now, about the program. To get the interest and attention of our clients, I suggest that we understate the program time to build the job but at the same time allow extra time in our costs for probable delays.'

'So,' Dave said, 'my estimate to build the pub is twenty-five months, give or take.'

'If we break ground this October,' John said, 'that means we won't be finished till November '87. That's too late. We have to be finished by end of July that year.'

'I'll still need to price in the costs for supervision and atten-dance costs for the full twenty-five months,' Dave said.

'Do that,' Brendan said. 'But we state twenty months in our bid, but allow ourselves the *cost* to build the job that would have taken twenty-five months.'

Richard slapped the table. 'This is madness. If we're late we'll be held to twenty months plus have to pay damages after that for not completing the project on time.'

'No,' John said. 'Brendan's tactic is a good one. Go on, son.'

Brendan was gaining confidence now. 'It's likely we'll be able to get extension of time approvals from the client. They'll give us the time extension for bad weather and such but are not likely to pay us for the delay in lost wages, so we'd best allow for those in our tender. We will have an additional advantage because our shorter time to build will be attractive to our client in our bid.'

Dave got up and stood beside the stenographer. 'Got all that, Miss Daley?'

'Yes, sir.'

'Good. Please write up the notes.' He turned to Mary. 'Did you learn anything?'

'I did. Because this is such a new project,' she looked at Brendan, 'any ideas should be looked at in detail.'

Dave smiled at her. 'Good. You may go now.'

'Yes, Mr Sullivan.' Mary winked at Brendan and, on the way out, clear of the others' eyesight, she put her thumb up. The door closed and Dave faced Brendan and said, 'Good contribution. Good ideas.'

'I don't think any of them are worth pursuing,' Richard said, looking at his half-brother.

'Dave,' John said, 'what do you want to do?'

The bid leader looked around the room. 'Let's talk about them.'

'Insurance and program stuff are good,' Prentice said. 'The advance payment is a sound idea but the clients won't give us that.'

'They will if we give them a guarantee,' Judd said. 'Any idea of its cost?'

Brendan looked at his notes. 'Point one per cent of the tender sum, if that.'

'Cheap. We could do that.'

'It's all too fancy,' Richard said. There was silence. Richard's grin was familiar. He was up to something and stood up. 'I've got to go, problems to sort. Let's leave things, Father. No need for these changes.'

'What do you men think?' Dave asked as he scanned the room. 'I'd like to go ahead.'

Brendan felt a glow of achievement. He'd got a tick from the leader.

'We should go ahead,' Prentice said.

'I agree,' Judd said.

Richard grabbed his files and made for the door. 'I don't. Father?'

Dave looked at Richard then John. 'Your father left the job to me,' he said. 'It's my call. That right, Mr Leary?'

'That's correct,' John said, looking at Richard. 'I'm all for taking these ideas to another level. Get more facts. It's the twenty-ninth of June and we submit in a week, but what I've heard so far is good.'

Richard turned and looked at his father. 'You're responsible,' he said and left the room.

'Thanks, Brendan,' Dave said. 'You can go. Enmore still needs you.'

'Glad to be of help,' Brendan stood up. He glanced at his father who also stood up, nodded to him and left.

'Brendan, you should've come to our last meeting,' Prentice said as he leafed through his diary. 'If that's a taste of your ideas, I'd like to hear more.'

'I agree,' Judd said, 'especially as we're putting in two bids.'

Brendan's brow creased in confusion.

'Yes, two bids,' the chief estimator said. 'One conforms to the architect's plans, and one, our own, is building with steel and fewer bricks.'

'The steel design was Richard's,' Dave said.

That's a smart move, Brendan thought. He tapped the desk. 'But has it been done before?' He paused. 'I don't think it has. A steel-framed building that tall? It will be a special.'

'I'll get Declan to send you a set of plans and Richard's notes,' Dave said. 'You can give me your comments. *Any* comments would be good. We have finished measuring the plans and are starting to price them. Now, off with you. We'll see you next week, same time.'

Brendan left the room and went down the hall, passing Richard's office. A hand came out and pulled him inside.

'What was that all about?' Richard said as he squeezed Brendan's arm, the pain burning him.

'What?'

'You were showing me up.'

'Dave asked me to the meeting, Richard. I said my bit. That's all; now let me go.'

Richard loosened his grip. 'And I suppose Father just happened to drop in?'

'I had no idea he'd be there.'

Richard's fist cracked into Brendan's jaw, the pain something fierce.

Brendan dropped his files and, grabbing Richard's hands, he pulled them down, hard. 'Don't *ever* do that again.'

Richard broke free but stayed close, glaring. 'It's to knock some of that cockiness from you. I'll clean you up in a stoush, never fear. Don't undermine me, Brendan.'

'I'm not.'

'Make no mistake, I run construction in this firm.'

Brendan managed to keep calm. 'Dave's the leader on that job.'

'Sod Dave. He'll come a cropper. And you're green. Don't be smart, you don't know how to be. Did Sullivan tell you about my steel design?'

Brendan stepped back and rubbed his sore jaw. 'It sounds like a good idea.'

'Don't patronise me. *Don't*. That steel's a good thing and it is *mine*. Now I'm off to St Peters to get a firm quotation on the bricks.' He pushed a finger into Brendan's chest. 'You never know, I might have a job for you on the Imperial Hotel—if you behave.'

Richard walked away and Brendan counted to ten as he picked up his files. He wouldn't be bullied by his brother and he wouldn't be bashed again. If it was a fight Richard wanted, then he'd give him one. He was glad his father had been at the meeting. Sound planning would win out and Brendan knew he had the right ideas.

✦

'Mr Richard,' Brian Murphy said and grinned, 'welcome to St Peters, once again. It's good to see you. Sit down. How's business?'

'Fair to middling but I hope it'll improve ... very soon.'

'Good, good. Now, what can St Peters do for you?' he said, sitting back in his chair.

God, that cologne again, like a cheap whore's perfume. 'We're nearly ready to bid,' Richard said.

'I know, face and commons,' Murphy said, rubbing his hands together. 'It'll be the biggest brick order we've ever had.'

Murphy didn't know that Leary's brick order would be a lot less than St Peters would expect because of the steel alternative. 'Leary's will win the Imperial Hotel. I have no doubt of that.'

The fat face kept grinning. The same grin he'd use for anyone sitting in Richard's place. 'Excellent.'

'And you'll make good money.'

'We hope so.'

'But you're not the only supplier,' Richard quipped.

The man blinked. That stopped him, Richard thought.

'It's too big for Classics,' Murphy said, 'and Vanguard isn't quoting. I know that.'

'They are. And their price is five shillings per thousand cheaper than you.'

Murphy leaned forward, his finger raised. 'That's impossible. Must be cheaper bricks in there somewhere.' Then he smiled again and said, 'You're pulling my leg, Mr Richard.'

Richard adjusted his cuff. 'There're no seconds. Vanguard's rate is for all first-quality facing bricks and their common bricks are four shillings cheaper than yours. We're considering them seriously, very seriously.'

Sweat filmed on the fat man's forehead and he tapped his fingers on the desktop. 'They won't be reliable. They'll drag out their deliveries. I know that from other contractors.'

'They're still cheaper, Mr Murphy. I have it in writing from their managing director.'

Murphy shook his head. 'That can't be. I'll need to check this. Their rate sounds ... they'd be mad to quote that. You have to give me time. We don't want to lose your order.'

Richard smiled. 'You do your checks, but in the meantime, I'm making you an offer.'

Brian Murphy patted his brow with a handkerchief. Richard sensed that he knew the scuttlebutt that Leary's could be the preferred tenderer; otherwise he wouldn't be bothered haggling.

'Offer?' Murphy said.

'If we win the tender, Leary's will buy bricks from you on three conditions. The first is, I want sixty days credit.'

Murphy grinned again. 'Forty is our best offer.'

'Sixty,' Richard said. 'Or I leave now.'

Murphy slapped the desk. 'You're a hard man, all right. The second?'

'That St Peters make a donation into something which I hold dear.'

'You and Leary's Contracting are one and the same.'

'Don't make assumptions about your buyer,' Richard admonished him.

Murphy appeared to understand. 'What's on your mind?'

Richard thought about this, needing to be discreet. He still gambled and he had broken his deal with his father. He'd lasted a week before he was into the cards again. He wasn't happy about that, not by a long shot. Yes, it was fine in the lead-up to the game and during it, but immediately after, there was a sense of hollowness and something different—fear. He suspected that his gambling now controlled him. And now he was resorting to extortion. Bloody hell. The brick maker would know of the side deal, a risk worth taking, especially with the money he'd earn as a commission. He said, 'We'll pay you the prices you want for your bricks and you'll put fifty per cent of the difference between your price and Vanguards into a trust, a charitable trust to which I subscribe. I have to do something for the downtrodden. It's the Imperial Beneficial Charitable Trust.'

Murphy paused, reached for a pencil and started scribbling. He looked up. 'A trust you said?'

'A trust.'

The man pursed his lips. 'A very worthwhile cause, I've no doubt,' Murphy said without blinking.

Richard had done it, but there was no pleasure in it.

'I'll check those brick prices,' Murphy said. 'If they are true, and it's a big *if*, I'll consider your offer. So, let's say our price to supply a rough split of commons and face is twenty shillings per thousand bricks and Vanguards is fifteen shillings?'

'Leary's would buy your bricks then at twenty shillings per thousand,' Richard said. 'You would pay into the Imperial Beneficial Charitable Trust two shillings and sixpence per thousand.'

'Half the difference between our price and Vanguards.'

'You've got it, sir,' Richard said. 'And the third condition is this. From now on you'll also donate into the same trust two shillings per thousand for all bricks that you supply Leary's for all its jobs. That's—'

'I can't agree to that.'

Richard paused, thinking he might have over-reached. 'Very well, after we win the Imperial Hotel, and for the next two years, Leary's will buy all its bricks only from St Peters.'

Murphy eyed him for a long time. 'Agreed.'

'Good. The Imperial Beneficial Charitable Trust is a confidential body and should not be discussed with anyone.'

Murphy kept his face impassive. 'I understand.'

'Its Trustees would be gravely embarrassed if it was made public and will resist any attempts at crude enquiries made into it.'

'I'm sure you'll provide all the details of the, er ... trust at the appropriate time.'

Richard stood up. 'I will, on Saturday morning when you're satisfied that what I've told you about your competitor is true.'

Bill Bucknell got down from a cab, crossed the footpath and climbed the stairs to his Redfern business. He paused on the landing to draw breath, tightness spreading across his chest. Wiping his brow, he walked inside, nodded to his secretary and entered his office where three men sat around a table near his desk—his chief estimator, Stan Jarvis, Jack O'Hearn, the construction manager, and Tom Burns, a clerk. Bucknell sat down at his desk. 'I got your note,' he said. 'It's bloody unbelievable!'

Stan Jarvis threw up his arms. 'Branagans might pull out.'

'Better for us,' O'Hearn said. 'Now, there are three tenderers left.'

Bucknell shook his head. 'Don't count on that. The architects might ask another contractor to quote if Branagans withdraw. It's only the third of July. I've contacted Dennings. They'll put a price in that's higher than ours. I'll tell them our price before we tender.'

'A cover price?' Jarvis said.

'What's that?' Tom asked. Bucknell and O'Hearn exchanged glances.

'Tom,' Bucknell said, 'go and help get more suppliers for the joinery tender. We're light on.' Bucknell waited till his clerk had left and he turned to O'Hearn and said, 'I don't want it to get out that we helped Dennings. They'll still have to bid. If they don't, then Turners will take them from their tender list and won't ask them to bid on any of their work again.'

The tea lady brought in a tray. 'The usual, Mr Bucknell?'

'Thanks, Lucy,' Bucknell said as she poured his tea. 'Family well?' he asked her.

'Yes, thank you, sir. Mother's better now. Say thanks to Mrs Bucknell for that remedy.'

Bill snorted. Some smelly Spanish brew Connie had knocked up. 'I'll tell her.'

The tea lady left and Bill looked at his men. 'The Imperial Hotel's too big for Dennings and their boss is worried. He told me he's still wounded from the Customs House job. William Turner's a friend of mine, but he won't stick his neck out that far and have only three tenderers.' Bucknell brought his tobacco pouch out. 'All right, get back to it,' he said. 'I want to review the final bid price on Wednesday. There's still Leary's to beat and maybe Branagans.'

Stan and Jack got up to go.

'Jack, wait up,' Bucknell said. 'I was at the club the other night and ran into Williams.'

'The steel merchant?'

'He told me about a possible order he'd heard about for a big job in town, nothing definite. He mentioned the tonnage and it's staggering. Heard anything?'

'Odd, that. I'd heard the same and did some quick checks. There's no job that size in Sydney.'

'Well it can't be the Imperial Hotel.'

Jack laughed. 'No. Anything else?'

'That's it. I'll try and get more details at the BCA dinner tonight.' Jack left and Bucknell sat back and filled his pipe. A big steel order? The Imperial Hotel was a big job and it was all bricks. Interesting, he thought. Bucknell sighed, put his pipe down and reached for a folder containing items for his review and authorisation. He opened the folder and sipped his tea. It contained a report on new steel products out from London. It had been published a month ago. Bucknell still found it amazing that it could get to Sydney this quickly. Given the talk about a big steel order, he read the report closely. Bucknells needed to keep up to date to keep their place as the top construction firm in Sydney.

Catherine Leary stood outside the tea room and smiled as Constance Bucknell approached. 'Good morning,' she said, and extended an arm towards the door. 'Shall we?'

'After you,' Constance said, who then followed Catherine inside where they stood near a table with a 'Reserved' sign on it. 'Is this where we sat before?' Constance asked.

'Yes. But it seems it's taken.'

The waiter appeared beside them and removed the sign. 'Welcome again ladies. Tea for two?'

'Thank you for remembering us,' Catherine said smiling. 'And reserving a table. Very thoughtful.'

'It's our pleasure, madam. We hope you will frequent us on a regular basis.'

'We might,' Catherine said, 'if those pastries in the window are as good as they look. Could we have a plate please?'

'Of course, madam.'

Constance sat down. 'A *whole* plate. I thought you wouldn't, but I'm game.'

'It's a treat,' Catherine said, sitting down opposite her friend. 'Just for us.'

'This time, after we leave here,' Constance said, 'I'm escorting you myself back to the cab stop.'

'I'll be all right, Constance, but thank you.'

'Please call me, Connie.'

Catherine seemed pleased at the gesture. 'Very well.'

Connie smiled. 'Your dress is stunning but you still look a little thin, I'm sorry to say.'

'No, don't apologise. I need to fill out some. That's why I ordered a tray of pastries.'

'Good,' Connie said and touched Catherine's sleeve. 'How is your memory? Last week, when I saw you at David Jones, you said there was still no ... oh, how to say it, recollection of what happened? Is that right?'

'You know, it's strange. No matter how hard I try, even after four months, I can't remember a thing. No, that's not right. I remember the dark alley and how I had difficulty seeing my way, but that's all.' Their teas and treats arrived and Catherine poured for the two of them. She said, 'Someone took my cash but left everything else.'

'The man who found you might have taken it.'

'He might have, Connie, but it could've been anyone. Anyway, enough about that.'

'I have to ask you,' Connie said. 'Did you talk with Brendan?'

'I did, but he's rebelling. He's still going to see that ... girl.'

'She didn't appear to be cheap.'

'Connie! You're defending her?'

'No, I'm not, but I think I know the scheming ones, and she didn't seem one of them.'

'I don't care,' Catherine said, 'it's a serious problem and I'm adamant Brendan must see sense.'

'I hope you're right. Brendan does seem a nice young man and then there are those two lovely daughters of yours. It must be quite lively at your place with all of them at home. Our home is a lot quieter than yours.' She sounded wistful.

Catherine glanced at her friend as she prepared to cut a pastry in two. 'Would you like children?' Catherine asked.

'I would, but I'm not getting any ... younger,' Connie pressed her lips together. 'It's just ... I can't have children.'

'I'm sorry to hear that.'

Connie blinked twice. 'It's all right. It's something I live with.'

'Do you think about it often?'

Connie paused. 'Yes ... no. But when I see a perambulator or a child holding his mother's hand, I get a tug at my heart.' She shook her head. 'It's as it is and God has chosen. My husband is a good man and right now he's a busy one.'

'John tells me little but I gather the bids are going in soon for the Imperial Hotel. John's going to the BCA dinner tomorrow night.'

'Bill as well. Yes, I know it must be close because Bill's temper is short.'

174

Catherine took a small bite from her sweet. 'John's getting impatient with me, too. Does Bill tell you what he does each day?'

'Are you trying to get hints on the bid?'

'No, of course not,' Catherine said. 'It's—'

'I'm only teasing,' Connie said and smiled. 'Bill sometimes tells me but it's—how you say—building and I don't understand a lot about it.'

'I'm the same. Still it's a thrill to know that the men we love are the fiercest rivals.'

'As long as we can still be friends,' Connie said.

Catherine tilted her head to one side. 'I think we can. Now, there's one sweet left. Please have it. Talking about my son just then has upset me.'

'I'm sorry.'

'It's not your fault. So tell me something interesting about Spain to distract me.'

From his table in the gallery in Sydney Town Hall, John had a good view of the attendees below on the ground floor. The Builders and Contractors' Association dinner had finished and cigars and spirits filled the hands of Sydney's master builders. As it was 4 July, there were a few red-white-and-blue neckties worn by Americans celebrating their Independence Day. Bill Bucknell and Jim Denning chatted away and when John shifted his gaze, he spotted Noel Branagan. Glancing around the Hall he remembered the work he'd done on the building. It seemed a lifetime ago.

Friday was bid day. He'd read over the tender and agreed with most of it. Steel was a winner, thirty thousand pounds cheaper than the conforming brick design. David Sullivan had done more homework since their last meeting—things that covered risk but didn't cost much. Sullivan was the right man, but then Brendan had provided most of the smart ideas. His uncle was right: Brendan was one for using his head.

'Mind if I join you?' Bill Bucknell said, smiling.

'Of course not. Are you enjoying the evening?'

'Usual faces, same food,' Bill said, unbuttoning his waistcoat. 'Ah, that's better. Big week this week.' He pursed his lips and caught John's eyes. 'Branagans are not bidding.'

John held his competitor's look. 'Really? Who told you?'

'Jim Denning,' Bill said and hailed a waiter. 'Whisky, John?'

'Yeah, why not.' The waiter refilled their glasses and left a jug of water. This was startling news, but maybe not. Was Bucknell throwing him a red herring? Any tactic was accepted in their stoush to win. He said, 'Dennings might be foxing. I wouldn't trust them.'

'You think so?'

A rowdy bunch of men passed their table and John raised his voice. 'I do.'

'Denning will struggle. I told him that if either of us wins it, we'd give him something.'

'What?' John asked.

'Part of the job. They're special at joinery. Maybe something like that.'

Not a bad idea, John thought. 'Maybe. How long do you reckon it'll take to build?'

'Hard to say. Thirty months, I think.'

Liar. 'Yeah, that's what we think.'

Bill slouched back and rubbed his forehead. 'There's talk around town about a bloody great steel order. You heard anything?'

John kept his face impassive. 'Steel? No. Not a new bridge, is it?'

Bucknell placed his glass down. 'Might be,' he said and grinned. 'Anyway, we're getting too old for this, should give it up. I've got a sharp construction manager who's keen to bust his balls.'

'Jack O'Hearn?'

'That's the man. Maybe flick him some shares. What about you? Richard's likely, I suppose?'

'Yeah, he's the one.'

'Thought so. What about your other one, Brendan?'

'He's having a go,' John said. 'I'll give him that.'

Bill pushed himself from the table. 'I'll leave you,' he said and held out his hand. 'Best of luck with the bid. In one respect, I don't want to win it.'

John, surprised, took the hand and held it. 'Come on, it's a trophy.'

'It is that,' Bucknell said in a soft voice, 'but it could kill us as well. Goodnight.'

John thought about Bucknell's comment as he finished his drink. The Imperial Hotel was the project to win and it would top out his career. It would make Leary's famous; big clients would come cap in hand to get Leary's to build for them. It would be John's last hurrah in the industry and what a triumph it would be. Also, the Imperial Hotel would be the job to test both his sons and how they would rise to its challenges, including controlling all costs. Costs reminded him of the price difference between brick and steel. It would be a massive advantage, but not a guaranteed advantage. They had four days left to get the best submission possible.

Making his way down the stairs, John felt a surge of excitement about the future and tapped the handrail. Richard would need to be groomed to take over. He had to be able to handle himself in boardrooms, yet still be able to deal with the workers. Richard had John's passion and he had ability.

Brendan was at the bottom of the stairs. 'I hoped I'd find you,' his son said. 'I thought we could go home together?'

'Good idea. We'll see Gibbs on the way out and tell him.'

'He's waiting for us.'

'Good,' John said.

They walked together towards the entrance. Richard would lead Leary's but it was interesting that Bucknell had asked about Brendan. John glanced at his son. Brendan was straight and true as a spirit level. He was putting the runs on the board and had come up with some smart things for their bid. John shook himself. *Maybe Richard has a competitor?* John smiled. Maybe.

Chapter Seven

John closed Dave Sullivan's file of notes, picked up the final draft of the tender letter from his desk and concentrated. Sullivan fidgeted in front of him but John ignored him. The sums tallied and the details on the conforming design were complete. His heart raced as he read the steel-design bid, offered as an alternative, the one he was sure would win over the Hotel's investors. Dave Sullivan and Tom Prentice had given the radical design the thumbs up for constructability and cost. In seven days John would have dinner with the Imperial's single largest investor: Miles Cunningham. The architects were a necessary hurdle but the investors, as owners, would make the decision on money.

'Looks good,' he said and reaching for his pen, signed the submission letter and two copies and dated it, Friday, 10 July 1885. 'Who's lodging the tender? It has to be you or someone you can trust.'

'Brendan's lodging it, Mr Leary.'

'Good,' John said and blotted the signatures.

'He's been a real help on the bid, Mr Leary. I'd like to keep him on the team.'

John rubbed his eyes. It was one-thirty and he'd been in the office since five that morning, checking all the details and reviewing the chief estimator's file and last-minute price quotations from suppliers. 'Brendan will be on the team, Dave, but right now he's got enough on his plate on the bank job.' John handed over the letter to his general foreman. 'Just get this in before three. This is your future you're holding—and Leary's.'

'That's what I wanted to ask you about. Can I be straight?'

John smiled. 'You can.'

'Richard hasn't been keen on me fronting this bid.'

John had heard the scuttlebutt and had seen Richard's attitude at first-hand. 'Let's win the job, Dave, then we can decide.'

'I can do it, you know I can build it.'

'I'm sure you could, but it's going to challenge all of us. Get going Dave.'

'I'm gone.'

Sullivan departed and John sat back. He would give himself an early afternoon. 'Mrs Mansfield, get Gibbs, please. I'm going home.'

Later, he was in his dressing room after a bath. He let his towel fall while he looked to see what he might wear.

'Coming down to dinner?' Catherine's voice drifted in from their adjoining bedroom.

'Of course,' John replied.

Catherine pushed open the dressing-room door, came in and stopped, her eyes taking him in. 'Oh,' she said, smiling. John smiled in return and pulled her close and kissed her. She returned his kiss then said, 'It's eight o'clock. Dinner is nearly ready. Get dressed.' He still held her and she moved against him. 'Later,' she whispered before breaking away with a laugh. 'Now, put something on.'

'Are you sure?' John said. Then he laughed too. 'Okay, later it is.' He quickly dressed, then, carrying his boots, he went into the bedroom and sat on the bed. 'I want to talk about Brendan and his future.'

'Now?' asked Catherine who was sitting at her dressing table, doing her hair.

'I just want to hear your thoughts on what I'm thinking.'

Catherine put her hairbrush down. 'All right, go on.'

'I've always believed that to be successful you have to be tough, even ruthless, so that no one could get the better of you. I've worked hard and I've made everyone who worked for me do the same. And it's paid off. Leary's is one of the top construction companies in Sydney. I haven't done what I've done to be popular and I'm aware that we have entrée to society because of my success, but I'm not sure that people like me—not that I care about such things at all. Now, Richard is like me. He's not too worried about what people think of him, despite his weaknesses, in fact because of them. Richard is ambitious and ruthless and doesn't let anybody stop him.'

'That's his hard side,' Catherine said.

'Yes, it's the part that drives him. He doesn't care if he gets people off side in his quest to replace me. But Brendan is different.' He paused.

'Go on,' Catherine said.

John exhaled and glanced out the window at the harbour. 'All right then. Brendan does consider people's feelings. He works with people to achieve what he wants. I'm starting to believe that Brendan is earning respect from others by doing things his way.'

'That's good.'

'Yes, but he's more successful in the way he achieves things than Richard and that's my dilemma. Who is going to succeed me? Brendan *worries* about things and people; emotions that sit better on the shoulders of women than men. But he's not soft. I used to think that he wasn't tough enough to make it in the construction business. But he epitomises the future and I've seen that. Look at the Enmore job where he's successfully managed a build, and that hasn't resulted from luck but hard grinding work, and perseverance at anything is admirable.' He brushed the front of his trousers. 'And on the Imperial Hotel, he's come up with ideas that will save money and people respect him. I can see now that Brendan has achieved things his way, and the result is that Leary's is better for it.'

Catherine smiled. 'I'm pleased to hear this, both for you and for Brendan.'

'My problem is this. Is there a risk in challenging Brendan further?'

'I guess you won't know unless you give him the chance to prove himself. I think Brendan is stronger than you give him credit for. If he fails, he will learn from that—but I don't think he will fail. Do you?'

John thought about that and realised that Brendan was ready for greater challenges. 'No.'

She stood up. 'Good. I only wish he'd get that girl out of his system. Until he does, he and I are somewhat estranged. I want to talk more about this, I do, but I've got to see to the soup. Cook's trying a new recipe.' She kissed him and left the room.

Brendan would see sense about that girl, John thought, it was a matter of time. He finished getting dressed, feeling much clearer about his thoughts in relation to his two sons, but perhaps less sure about which one should take over Leary's.

In the dining room, Brendan, Mary and Agatha were seated. John sat in his chair and began buttering a bread roll. 'Did you get the tender in?' John asked Brendan.

'We did,' Brendan said, 'with half an hour to spare.'

'Good. There were some smart things in our bid. That's great work, son.'

Brendan was pleasantly surprised, 'Thank you, Father. Richard didn't want us to put them in.'

'Well, it's one thing to present new ideas, it's another to back those same ideas with all you've got.'

'I'll do that.'

'You'd better,' John said, 'because, if we win the Imperial, you'll be working on it.'

Brendan put his bread roll down. 'Are you serious?'

Catherine walked in and stood by John's chair. 'What's that, dear?'

John looked at her. 'I'm going to put Brendan on the Imperial Hotel, if we get it. I've seen what my son's done on the bank job and it's … acceptable. More than acceptable.' He looked at Brendan. 'So, don't let me down.'

Brendan shot out his hand, his eyes glistening 'Thank you, Father. Thank you very much.'

'You'll be a success,' Agatha said. 'Good on you.'

'Well done,' Catherine said.

Mary patted him on his shoulder. 'You deserve it, Brendan.'

As she settled in her seat at the other end of the table, Catherine glanced at John and mouthed, *Thank you.*

'That's settled then,' John said releasing his son's firm grip. 'I'm hungry, let's eat.'

Delia served chicken soup, its steam wafting over them. Catherine picked up her spoon and looked at Mary. 'Tell me dear. How are you finding work? Not sick of it yet?'

Mary said. 'It's better than I thought but there are some things I'd change.'

John spluttered and wiped his chin. 'Are you now an expert in office administration?'

'No, I'm not,' Mary continued, 'but some things could change, little things. However, Mrs Mansfield won't hear of it. She's too old, too set in her ways. I'd—'

'When you've worked there a long time,' John said, 'which, because of your attitude, doesn't seem likely, you can contribute. Till then, you can learn.'

'I don't know how you do it,' Agatha said. 'It's so dirty, all that ink and dust … ugh.'

'Henri says all girls should work unless they're married,' Mary said. 'Even after that, they should work.'

'Who's Henri?' John asked.

Mary rolled her eyes. 'Henrietta Flemming, Father, I've told you before, my friend.'

'She'll never marry,' Agatha said. 'She scares the boys.'

Mary blushed and looked annoyed.

'Agatha,' Catherine said, 'have you chosen your dress pattern for the ball?'

Mary sighed and turned her attention to the roast dinner that Delia had just brought in.

'Mother, there's nothing around that's new,' Agatha said. 'And my dress is last season's. I'm panicking, just three weeks to go.'

'Well you'd better decide, because we're all going. We have to, it's at the Governor's invitation.'

'I'm going,' Brendan cut in. 'It's the first of the month, yes?'

'It is. And who are you bringing?' Catherine asked.

John hoped that this would not develop into a row.

'Since you don't like Julie, I—'

'Don't mention her name in my presence.'

Brendan looked at his mother. 'Very well, I'll go by myself. Can I be excused?'

'Of course,' Catherine nodded. 'But think—you might consider inviting Anne Connaire.'

'I'll see, Mother.'

Brendan had eased himself out of that one, John thought, as his son left the room.

'Dear,' John said, looking at Catherine, 'forbidding the lad to see a girl will only push him further from you and closer to her.'

Catherine looked at her daughters, who'd finished their meal and who seemed interested in Brendan's dilemma. 'You girls can be excused,' she said, and waited till they'd gone before replying. 'You consider this girl suitable?'.

'If, as you say, she's after him for his money, then I have to say no. But he's young and marriage is furthest from his mind.'

'Is it? Can you be so sure?'

No, he couldn't but Brendan wouldn't be that stupid, would he?

'There are ways that common girls trap sensitive boys like our son,' Catherine said.

John agreed. Brendan appeared to have little experience with females. For him as a young man, it had been the other way around: he had come from humble stock and he'd faced opposition from Clarissa's parents. To be fair, he didn't know Julie and perhaps his mind and Catherine's should be more open to the girl as well. 'I have a suggestion. Why don't we invite her here to Christine's seventy-fifth birthday party? When Julie is among us and our friends, she may behave in a way that could open our son's eyes.'

Catherine appeared to think on this. 'She might, or she just might see the trap and act the innocent. That would only make her more attractive to our son.'

'Perhaps. But it's hard to change a Rocks girl. I think she'll be true to form. That may well be her undoing. I think the Connaires are being invited as well, aren't they?'

'Including Anne,' Catherine said. She suddenly looked hopeful. 'Dear, it's a good plan. We're only trying to help our son not make a lifelong mistake.'

'We are. But be warned, dear, that if she is straight and her morals and values are high, which they very well could be, then she may be the girl Brendan ends up with.'

'She most certainly will not be that,' Catherine said.

'If we see this ... Julie ... at Mass,' John said. 'We can invite her then.'

'Good,' Catherine smiled. 'Don't work too long in the study.'

John leaned forward and kissed her. 'I'd be foolish to.'

Brendan was upstairs, his mind full of his parents' prejudice. He'd go to the ball by himself rather than invite Anne Connaire. Julie was the one he should invite but if they went together, all sorts of embarrassments might arise. Walking in the gardens, talking in the Rocks, a ferry ride and meeting at Mass were simple pastimes. Explaining Julie to his friends posed problems—not so much for him as for her. That type of society exposure might make her nervous and she could well find it humiliating, and blame him.

Entering his bedroom he looked again at the envelope on his desk. It bore the coat of arms of the Commercial Bank of Sydney. He knew what it contained. Donald Dawkins, the Bank's clerk of works, had told him two days ago: the Bank was offering him a job, and not just any job. During the interview, the bank had stressed that they wanted to reduce the time that their branches took to build new premises, and to build them smarter. Picking up the envelope, he opened it, took out the letter, read it and smiled. There it was: a contract for three years to be its Head of Construction, responsible for all the Bank's new branches, with a fat salary and all the perks. He would be twenty-three next month and it was a mighty compliment.

If his father wasn't convinced of his ability, he had the option to leave the company. Then, when he'd made his mark with the bank, he'd return to Leary's and demand his rightful place. Undressing for bed he smiled again. What he really wanted was a top position in Leary's—but it was always good to have a back-up plan, just in case.

John knocked on the door of a private room at the Australian Club and wished himself luck to win over Miles Cunningham. The door opened. A good-looking man in his late thirties held out his hand. 'You're punctual, Mr Leary. Right on six.'

'Thank you for meeting with me.'

'Come in,' Cunningham said. He closed the door after John and smiled. 'Would you care for something to eat?'

'Thank you.' John would have preferred to get the deal done first, and apprehension had replaced his appetite, but he didn't want to appear rude. He took a plate from a side table and selected a slice of baked chicken and one of ham. His host poured a claret and handed him a glass.

'Sit down and relax,' Cunningham said as he glanced around. 'I like it here. It's discreet. How's building?'

'I can't complain, but we'd like to build bigger projects, like the Imperial Hotel.'

'Let's just get one monster project done at a time,' Cunningham said. 'Our investments, as you know, are on the land and we can't complain either. Big is better and Father is currently negotiating to buy another 300,000 acres. Wool's good as gold and more stable than shares.' John did have an appetite after all and was hoeing in. His host gestured at the food and said, 'Take some more, that's what it's there for.'

John took a drumstick. 'Were there any surprises with the tenders?'

Cunningham's reaction was as if he'd been asked the time. 'No, but Dennings' was a very high bid. Turners said it looked like a ... cover price? You wouldn't know anything about that, would you?'

'No,' John replied innocently and took a sip of his wine. So, it seemed there had been some collusion. No matter. Leary's bid was a stand-alone and Branagans must have bid despite the rumours. 'What do the other investors think?'

Cunningham refilled their glasses. 'They'll follow my advice. The Imperial Hotel is our dream. Many of our clients are well-heeled country people. Like us, they want luxury accommodation when they get off the trains from Scone, Inverell and wherever, and we'll supply their needs.' He reached for a cigar and clipped it. 'Our accountants have done the numbers, and we could build another two of these massive pubs and still not meet the demand.'

'And we'd be up for that,' John said. The aroma of the tobacco was attractive. 'May I?'

Cunningham offered him the humidor. John said confidently, 'You have three good bids from reputable builders. The decision should be straightforward.'

Cunningham nodded. 'I can't say much, but the steel option you offered is very attractive. I think that alone could influence us.'

'That's what we intended.'

'Except for one thing,' Cunningham said. 'It affects our brick-works shareholders. They're disgruntled at the small number of bricks required.'

John coughed out smoke. 'I wouldn't call nearly two million bricks a small order!'

Cunningham spread his hands and said, 'Nevertheless, that's what we're up against.'

'I take it that the steel option is way below any other bid. That is, so far below that a counterbid is out of the question.'

'That's so,' his host replied.

And Dennings was out because their price was too high. Good, thought John. One down.

'Whisky?' Cunningham offered. John shook his head. 'The architects are pushing Bucknells.'

'Why?' John asked.

The Imperial's biggest investor looked surprised. 'They're architects, Mr Leary. Don't you see? You, a builder, have shown them up. They have to support the brick design because they didn't think of the steel one, or if they did, they didn't champion it.' Cunningham put his whisky glass down. 'How far can you move on your bid?'

Here it comes, thought John. 'You mean reduce our price?'

'Our brickworks shareholders estimate they'll lose two thousand pounds in sales due to the smaller brick order. We wouldn't want to lose that income from the companies we control.'

Within their tender, the Imperial Hotel's profit was twelve thousand pounds plus a five thousand pound contingency for unforeseen costs during the build. John knew that steel was risky but he backed himself. All problems could be solved and he had to win this job. He was so close but, as in hunting, he didn't want to spook his prey, even though he could just about taste the meat of the kill. 'One thousand pounds is as much as we could move.'

Miles held John's stare and he counted to five. 'That's unfortunate,' Cunningham said.

John's stomach tightened. 'We're in business to make a profit; we can't build at a loss.'

'We're not asking you to,' his host said and sipped his drink. 'But you are preferred.'

John tapped his cigar on the ashtray. There was still some room to move ... but not much. 'All right,' he said. 'We'll reduce our tender by two thousand pounds.'

His host examined his glass and John held the smoke in his mouth.

'That could make our decision easier,' Cunningham said.

John exhaled. 'Very good. Is there anything else?' Branagans and Jim Denning were out because their prices were too high. Bucknells had a conforming brick design, which was probably just below Leary's own brick-price bid. And now with Leary's lowering their own steel price, the brickworks owners wouldn't lose all their profits. John was sure he had his project.

Cunningham stood up. 'I think that's all we need. Now you must excuse me. I have another appointment ... with a young lady.' Miles put out his hand and winked. 'Good evening, Mr Leary, and good luck.'

John rode down in the now familiar lift in a daze. He'd done it. They had grabbed the prize, *the* prize and his blood pulsed. Tonight he'd won. He got into his carriage and on the way to Point Piper he thought about all the details he'd need to manage when they got the contract.

Delia, their maid, opened the door when he got home. As John gave her his hat and cane, Richard came out of the drawing room. 'Good evening, son,' he said.

'Father.'

John hesitated. No, he'd hold back on his news and see how the future unfolded. 'You're visiting us?'

'Grandmother sent a note for me to see her at eight. Could you excuse me?'

'Surely. I'll work in my study. Goodnight.'

Richard went down the hallway, through to his grandmother's newly constructed bedroom. What did she want to talk about? The room was clean and there was still a faint enamel paint smell. He knocked on the opened door.

His grandmother shuffled up behind him. 'Go in and put the gas on, for goodness sake,' she said. 'It's the seventeenth of July, in case you didn't know.' Richard grinned, went in and lit the gas heater. The room started to warm at once. 'Pull my chair up to it,' she said.

'Hang on, dear,' Richard said, and did the honours.

Christine put out her hands to the heat. 'That's better. Bring your chair and face me, I've got a crick in my neck.' Christine sighed as she watched his movements. 'You're gambling again, Richard.'

Richard was surprised, but kept his face impassive as his insides started to churn. If there was one person in the world he did not want to hurt, it was his grandmother. 'What have you heard?'

'Enough to worry me.'

He tried to keep the issue light but was struggling. 'I play for enjoyment, Grandmother. It's not a crime.'

Christine clucked. 'It's been corroborated by two people, Richard, so don't deny it. You're betting big sums, and often.'

'It's not a problem,' he said. 'I can stop any time.' Richard stared at the fire, not wanting to look at her.

'Ha! Your great-grandfather used to say that.'

He looked at her. 'My great-grandfather?'

'He was an inveterate gambler. Why do you think I married into money? It was to pay my father's debts. He was a gambler like you.' She tapped his leg with her cane. 'And he made us penniless. David McGuire, your grandfather, paid for my wedding dress— my wedding dress.'

'It's all in fun, Grandmother, really.'

'Well, laugh at this, then. John and I have withdrawn your nine per cent share in Leary's.'

Richard felt a coldness, despite the room's increasing warmth. It was as if he was hanging on a cliff edge and his grip was failing. 'What?'

'You heard me. It's gone into a trust until you can be trusted.'

Richard stared at her. This wasn't happening. His grandmother was just threatening. 'You can't do that!'

'We can and we did.'

Richard now felt hot. 'Why?'

She tapped him again with her cane. 'Why do you think? You'll get to a point where you need real money.' She coughed. 'The way you're going now, you'd sell your shares in a heartbeat.'

Richard sat back, shocked at her words. Yet she was right. The other night, he'd been losing and was seeking, no *begging* his playing companions for money. Hideous. 'You believe that? You, who hold your shares so close they've got mildew from your sweat?'

'Colourful but vulgar, Richard, and yes, I do,' she replied in a steely voice. Her anger waned and her voice became quieter. 'I have shares but I've got a plan to divest them. Also, I've agreed with your father that your salary will be controlled, and you will have to account for your money.'

Richard stood up. He needed space. He pressed his hands against the mantelpiece and leaned on it. This was bloody unbelievable. 'I'm not accepting this. I'm not. I'll get legal advice. I'll fight this!'

Christine's eyes narrowed. 'That's your prerogative but understand, it will be a temporary thing only. Prove to us that your gambling's under control and we'll reconsider.'

He turned towards her. 'That's great. Treated like a child.'

'That's what a gambler is, Richard. He doesn't have control. Now, look, dear, I've got people who can help you. They—'

Richard walked to the door. 'If I'm to be treated like an idiot, then I'll choose the company I keep.'

Christine pressed down on her cane. 'I'm not doing this to hurt you,' she said, reaching out for him. 'I love you. Please know that.'

He held the door open and looked at her. 'Of all people, I thought you were one who believed in me.'

She looked upset. 'Stop your gambling,' she pleaded. 'Stop, before you destroy yourself.'

He closed the door behind him, anger surging through him. His father, that's who was behind this. His bloody father and his precious Leary's! Well, the gloves were off. Thank God he'd seen Murphy and got that income sorted.

He stormed down the hallway. He should tackle his father but he knew that would be a waste of time. He looked at the clock in the foyer. It was just before nine. The players would just be warmed up. He had cash in his pocket and he was going to play. The adrenalin charge when he won was like sex ... but better. It would be his night tonight, he could tell. He grinned as he closed the front door after him. He'd work on his grandmother and father later. He was sure he could get them to give him his shares back.

His good mood lasted till he got to the gate. What was he doing? He knew he was using his anger at his father and grand-mother as an excuse to gamble, which really only confirmed what they thought about him. It seemed the only person he was fooling was himself. But he couldn't help himself; the pull of the cards was too strong.

Julie hesitated outside St Mary's. She was late and Brendan's family was inside, she was sure. What would they say if Brendan spoke to her and they saw her with their son? This was a big step for her; she knew she wouldn't be acceptable to them despite what Brendan might think. What to do? Go home where life was simple and where she felt safe with her people, or take the risk of encountering Brendan's family? Oh, she had missed him. Three weeks working in Coonamble had given her plenty of time to think and he'd occupied a lot of her thoughts. Taking a deep breath, she pushed open the church doors and went inside.

She scanned the congregation. Brendan was there, with his parents, she assumed, and two girls, who must be Agatha and Mary. The priest made the sign of the cross and Brendan bowed. She passed him in the aisle, genuflected and knelt four pews down from him. For the next fifty minutes she tried to concentrate on the service but couldn't.

The Mass ended and she stayed in her pew. Turning, she saw Brendan smile and she decided to walk straight up to him. This was the moment. Following the Learys outside, she would have to face them all and she'd rather have fronted a group of drunken leering men.

Brendan took her hand and greeted her but he didn't seem to know what to do next. He was half turned away from his family.

'Brendan,' a woman's voice sounded. 'Would you please introduce this young lady?'

Brendan looked surprised at his mother's question but he responded. 'May I introduce Miss Carson? Miss Carson, my mother and father, Mr and Mrs Leary, and my sisters Agatha and Mary.'

Julie felt the drabness of her woollen dress and bonnet compared with the silks and satins of the Leary women. However, Mary's dress was of a simpler design, like hers. Julie decided to behave with pride. 'Hello,' she said, 'pleased to meet you.'

Brendan's father touched his hat and both the Leary girls smiled. Julie was relieved. Those smiles seemed genuine and the daughters looked right at her and not at what she was wearing. She was feeling better still. 'I was late for Mass,' she said, trying to keep her voice steady. 'Mum was having some trouble with my brother, Billy, you see; he had lost his best shirt.' She was rambling on and conscious of it. Despite the chill, she was perspiring.

Brendan's mother was attractive and had a confident air about her. She looked Julie up and down. 'You've been seeing my son on a number of occasions, I'm told.'

Right to the point. 'I have, Mrs Leary.'

'And it seems that my son likes your company.'

Julie felt uncomfortable, especially since Brendan, too, looked taken aback. 'We see each other.'

'Then, please come to a family birthday celebration. It's on the fifth of September at our home in Point Piper.'

Brendan's eyes expanded and his mouth opened. 'Mother?' he finally said.

'Of course Miss Carson must come,' his mother said.

Julie was astounded. Invited, just like that, to a family gathering! It was too sudden. 'I don't think that would be right,' she said, 'to a private turn out. I'm just friends with Brendan.'

Brendan shot her a searching look.

Mrs Leary insisted. 'Do join our guests. It's a small gathering of forty or so.'

That was a mob in Julie's world. Both the Leary daughters smiled at her again but Julie couldn't make up her mind. She looked at Brendan for a clue but he didn't meet her gaze. Was he embarrassed? Maybe he didn't want her to come. He might want to protect her, shield her from making a goose of herself. But all at once he looked at her with affection and she knew what she must do. 'Thank you, Mrs Leary, I'll come.'

Just for a second, Catherine Leary lost her composure, but she quickly regained it. 'Excellent, we will see you then. Goodbye, Miss Carson.'

Brendan said, 'I'd like to walk Miss Carson home, if she'll join me. I'll see you back at Point Piper.'

Catherine hesitated, then nodded.

Brendan took Julie's hand and led her away. 'Well, there's a turn-up!' he said when they were out of earshot.

Julie's heart sank. 'What?'

'Mother inviting you to Grandmother's birthday. You see, we've talked about you and well ...'

'She doesn't like me, does she?'

Brendan shook his head. 'She doesn't approve of my seeing you. I had no idea she'd invite you like that.'

Julie understood. So, the mother was keen to expose her amongst a crowd of toffs. Cunning. 'I think she's hoping that I'll act common and embarrass you.'

'You couldn't do that.'

'No? You want me there at your grandmother's party, a working girl from the Rocks, who don't speak proper?'

Brendan took hold of her hand. 'I want you there because I like you.'

Her lips trembled. 'I might do something stupid. Make you ashamed of me. No, I won't go. Please tell your mother that.'

'No. You'll come. I want you to meet my friends and after that, if you feel uncomfortable you can leave at any time.'

Julie was wary. 'I'll think about it. I'm glad that I didn't keep rambling on just then. I sounded so stupid.'

'You're not, so there.'

She squeezed his hand and they headed across Macquarie Street. 'I can't believe it's the nineteenth of July; the year's going quick.'

Brendan stopped near the kerb and she stood in front of him. 'I missed you when you were away,' he said, his eyes on her lips. She felt an urge to kiss him, too, but later, somewhere private. She glanced down the street. 'I'll say goodbye now. Will you be at next Sunday's Mass?'

'I will and we can talk about the party and such.' Brendan took her hand, 'Just one thing.'

'And what's that?'

'Look after yourself.'

She smiled and touched his cheek and walked away.

The waltz ended in the crowded ballroom and Catherine sighed and dabbed her forehead. 'Oh, this is wonderful,' she said.

'Let's go and sit down,' John said.

'But it's just the fourth dance! I could go on for hours.'

John patted his stomach. 'I shouldn't have eaten so much.'

Catherine was disappointed. 'Oh, all right. I have some names on my card. Have your rest but I still want to do more dancing with you.'

John excused himself and went and sat down at their table. He pushed aside his half-filled wine glass and poured a whisky, drank that, then poured another. It would be the third of August on Monday and the bid for the Imperial Hotel had been in for over three weeks. John had heard nothing and wanted certainty.

'Mind if I join you, Mr Leary?' William Turner said. The architect didn't wait for a reply and sat beside him. 'These balls are damn fine. Governor Loftus knows how to do it—good food and good grog.'

'I'm glad you're enjoying yourself,' John said.

A waiter refilled Turner's wine glass. 'We make our choice on Monday.'

Turner's half-smile irritated John. 'I hope you make the right one.'

'I can't say much, but you're favoured.'

John feigned surprise, 'That's great news.'

'But you're not favoured if we choose brick,' Turner said and pursed his lips.

John placed his glass down. 'Steel is cheaper. It has to be the go.'

'It's never been done, so it's a risk for our clients.'

More like the architects protecting their own backsides, or the investors looking out for their business interests. John was not giving up. 'Money saved is money saved.'

'Maybe. But steel is new and it will come with problems. Have you solved them all in your planning?'

Turner had a point but now wasn't the time to admit they hadn't. John was sure that, with Brunels on side, problems would be sorted out. 'Most of them, yes.'

'So, hypothetically, if you were to win it, when could you start?'

'The site is cleared, Mr Turner. We could have men there in a week and start digging in a fortnight.'

'That soon?'

'We won't wait for the weeds to grow any taller,' John said. 'Time's money.'

'Who'd be the gun?'

John didn't hesitate. 'My best, David Sullivan.'

Turner stood up. 'Bill Bucknell's looking our way,' he said. 'I'd best go and say hello.' As he turned to leave, he whispered, 'Good luck, Leary.'

John pressed his hand around his glass as adrenalin flooded him. The Imperial Hotel was theirs! Cunningham must have talked Turner around.

Richard passed near his table with a full bottle of wine and two empty glasses. John knew his wanted to talk to him about his shares being withdrawn, but he wouldn't tackle him tonight. John caught Brendan's eye at the adjacent table, raised his glass and smiled.

Victoria Hughes, Richard's fiancée, was not particularly enjoying conversation with him tonight. He seemed distracted. She let him pour her a glass of wine, then said before he sat down, 'Would you excuse me? I want to speak to your stepmother.'

Richard grinned. 'Want to find out about what happens on the wedding night, eh?'

Victoria brought a hand to her face. 'Richard!' She got to her feet. 'I'll certainly excuse myself from remarks like that!'

Richard bowed and saluted her with an empty glass. 'Certainly, my love.'

Victoria walked through the ballroom until she found Catherine, who was talking to her dance partner. The orchestra started the next waltz. 'Excuse me, Mrs Leary,' Victoria said, 'but may we have a moment?'

Catherine smiled at her and turned to her partner. 'You don't mind?' she said.

'Not at all,' the man said. He nodded to Victoria, turned and walked away.

Catherine took hold of Victoria's forearm. 'I'm glad you rescued me,' she said. 'I've got bruises on my instep. That man must have been a drill sergeant at some time, the way he slammed down those shoes of his.'

Victoria gave a wan smile.

'What's wrong?' Catherine asked.

Victoria's lips trembled. She closed her eyes and shook her head.

'Come on,' Catherine said. 'Let's sit down. You're upset about something.' They walked to a quiet corner and sat on a couch. 'Now, tell me.'

'It's Richard.'

'What's the matter?'

Victoria placed her hand on Catherine's. 'I need your help.'

'What can I do?'

'Richard is behaving ...' She took a breath and started again. 'He's gambling ... a lot.'

Catherine said cautiously, 'All men like a flutter. It's part of their character.'

Victoria shook her head. 'He seems to be in very deep. Twice now, when we've been together, a man has come up and confronted Richard and demanded money. The first time it happened, Richard just fobbed him off. But the second time frightened me. Oh, Catherine, it was awful.'

'What exactly happened?' Catherine said.

'The second time, Richard looked angry and took the man away some distance from me. I could see them arguing. The man was angry and he prodded Richard's chest then he pointed to me. I was scared and Richard pulled the man's arm down. The man removed a piece of paper from his pocket. Richard read it, glanced at me then scribbled something on the paper and gave it back to him.'

Catherine said, 'The argument might have been about a debt. But it doesn't prove gambling.'

'When Richard came back to me, I asked him what was that all about. He said that the man was just a disgruntled supplier who hadn't been paid. Richard had authorised an invoice for him, that's all. That's all I'd seen, he said.'

Catherine smiled. 'Well, there you go.'

'No. The man found me … again.'

'What? The same man?'

'He confronted me, Catherine, and told me that Richard owed him £150 for—'

'That's a lot of money.'

'I know. It was for a gambling debt and he said if Richard didn't pay up, he would be … cut. The man said I was not to go to the police because Richard would be hurt. It was horrible. I told Richard that night, and he got angry. He said that it was all a misunderstanding and that he would pay the next morning. I wanted the truth and asked for details and Richard told me that it was all over a business deal.'

'But you didn't believe him?'

Victoria looked down. 'No. Amongst him and his friends I often overhear talk of bets and wagers, horses and odds, but when I enquire, the conversation is changed to something else. I'm so worried that gambling is a big part of his life but he won't admit it to me.'

Catherine glanced at the ballroom, where laughter and music filled the air. She looked lost for a moment. 'Leave it with me, dear, and my husband and I will see what we can do.'

Victoria reached out and squeezed her hand. 'Thank you.'

Catherine tried to enjoy the ball but her happy mood had gone. She did not see John until just before it came to a close, when he sat down beside her. 'Are you nearly ready to go?' Catherine asked him.

He leaned over and squeezed her waist. She eased herself away. 'What's wrong?' he said.

She could not contain herself. 'Victoria told me something disturbing.'

'About what?'

'She's convinced Richard is deep into debt for gambling. She says thugs are after him.'

John sat back and loosened his tie. He didn't speak for a while. 'If that's true, then we have a problem ... a big one.'

Agatha came towards them and Catherine rose abruptly. 'Come, let's go home and I'll tell you the details. You need to have a serious talk with your son.'

Chapter Eight

JOHN LEARY HELD UP A SHEET OF PAPER AS BRENDAN AND RICHARD walked into his office. 'It's the letter of acceptance. The architects wrote to me yesterday accepting our tender to build the Imperial Hotel.'

Brendan grinned and shook his father's hand. 'Congratulations, Father. Today, the seventh of August, is a great day for Leary's.'

'I'll tell Sullivan,' Richard said. He made a fist and punched his other hand. 'I'll get the team together this afternoon here at Annandale. What I want Sullivan to do is—'

'Can I see the architects' letter?' Brendan asked. 'I want to check if there are any special clauses.'

John handed it to him and said, 'David Sullivan will manage the project and he will report to me.'

'But—' Richard exclaimed.

'I'll talk to you about this later,' John said. 'And other things.'

Brendan put the letter down. He looked to his half-brother, then father. 'It looks all right to me. They've accepted the steel design.'

'Brendan, you can leave,' Richard said. 'Tom Prentice and I will get together and review costs for set-up and the steel order. There's a lot to do.'

'The acceptance letter,' Brendan said, 'talks about us providing details of the advance payment. I can stay and help with—'

'We can do that,' Richard said. 'Off you go.'

'No,' John said, looking at Richard. 'Brendan will do that and he will set up the contract administration on the project. That's his job, for now.' John said to Brendan, 'Can Rob Jenkins finish the bank job without you?'

'Yes, he can.' Brendan grinned.

'Good,' John said and smiled. 'Come on, I'll see you out.' He looked at Richard. 'Stay here. I won't be long.'

John and Brendan walked down the corridor together. John said, 'I'm looking to the future and want to talk to you. Come to my office after work. But now, get two kegs of beer and some food: pies and sandwiches. Get a note to the sites and invite everyone. We'll have a party here at Annandale tonight to celebrate. A Friday night to remember.'

'Great idea.'

'One thing more. Get Dave Sullivan to go to the City Council today. I want a copy of their consent approval for the Imperial Hotel.'

'I will, Father, and I'll see you at five.'

On his way back to his office, John snapped at his secretary, 'Mrs Mansfield, get me that wool-store cost report I asked for yesterday. And where's my tea? It's ten minutes late.'

His secretary scurried off, leaving John feeling guilty at his ill temper, but he had reason to be irritable. He closed the door to his office and sat down opposite Richard.

'Father, giving Brendan responsibility on the Imperial Hotel is not wise. I think—'

'It's done, Richard and I'm happy about it. Now, about you.' John paused to suppress his anger. 'It's clear you haven't stopped the cards and your stepmother and your fiancée are not only devastated, but involved in the consequences.'

'What do you mean?'

'You know exactly what I mean.'

'I don't have a gambling problem, Father. I don't know how to say that more simply.'

John closed his eyes and shook his head. 'Good God, son, a £150 debt and your own fiancée accosted in the street!'

Richard cleared his throat. John could see that his son was agitated. 'All Victoria saw was a disgruntled supplier. I fixed his late payment and that was all there was to it.'

'I don't believe you,' John said. 'You're gambling and you're in trouble.'

Richard sat stony-faced. 'Who says I am?'

John pointed to himself. 'I do.'

The door opened and Mrs Mansfield brought in the report and a cup of tea. 'Would you like a cup, Mr Richard?'

'No, thank you,' Richard replied, and waited till Mrs Mansfield had left before speaking again. 'You've taken my shares and you talk like I'm addled.'

'In one respect you are, son, and because of that Christine and I agreed to relieve you of your shares.'

'That was *your* idea.'

'No, it wasn't, actually. It was a joint decision. I trusted you to handle your habit and look what you've done—gone back on your word. Your nine per cent share of Leary's will be withheld until you've proved you can be trusted.'

Richard slammed his fist on the table. 'You can't take that from me!'

'Don't yell at me, Richard. I haven't started on you yet. We *can* take your shares under the rules of the company. Meanwhile Christine has with extraordinary generosity agreed to gift half her shareholding to you. Half of her fifty-one per cent will be held in trust in your name, and—'

'So in effect I don't have that either!' Richard stood up. 'I still do my job well, Father. You know that.'

John sighed. 'Yes, I do.'

'So let me keep my private life to myself. It's my business.'

'But when it affects your judgement Richard, it's *my* business,' he said angrily. He pointed a finger at his son and said, 'If I hear one more bad report, just one, I'm going to demote you.'

'It's a joke. I want more. I need—'

'No Richard, no. You'll still be Construction Manager, responsible for all our other jobs, but if you fail again you'll find yourself down on the tools again. You'll be a carpenter, swinging a hammer, hauling timber and busting your gut. Now, I ask you again. Do you have a problem with your gambling?'

Richard held his father's stare. 'No, I do not.'

John exhaled. 'Then, Richard, your future is in your hands. You hear me? I'm still in charge here.'

'But when you go, I'm the only one to replace you.'

'Until you've got your gambling beaten, you're a bloody liability to me,' John said, angrily.

Grim-faced, Richard walked over to the window.

John paused before speaking again in a calmer voice. 'Brendan is not being favoured over you in terms of company ownership. He has to prove himself too. The other equal half of your grandmother's shares will be held in trust in your brother's name, just as yours are. Neither of you will get your shares until such time as I step down from my position, which I must do, sooner or later.'

John waited for Richard to say something but he just stood there, staring out the window.

'Richard, your position is unchanged and rests entirely on your good behaviour. This is what's going to happen. You will continue as Construction Manager, get married and go on your honeymoon. After that, we'll talk again about your role.'

Richard shook his head in disgust and left the office.

John heard his staff going downstairs and preparing for their party. Popping sounds meant two kegs were being tapped and the beer would start flowing. It must be near five o'clock, and he thought about his run-in with Richard that morning.

Footsteps sounded in the hallway and John closed his folder. He looked up as Brendan stood in the doorway, a heavy satchel slung from his shoulder. 'Come in,' he said. Brendan sat down. How different his two sons were: one was a building specialist with a major flaw and the other enthusiastic and capable but still learning. 'Right,' John said, 'we need to plan the administration on the Imperial Hotel.'

Brendan patted his satchel and said, 'Dave Sullivan gave me the files. I'm taking them home to read over the weekend.'

'That's the way. Did he go to the Council?'

'I think so.'

'Right. We'll talk to him later. This job will be a massive challenge. We need to be on top of our payments to suppliers and get our cheques from our client in time. Cash will be king.'

'I know and thank you for your faith in me.'

John grunted. 'Don't let me down, Brendan, and I don't want to hear any of your talk about a workers' paradise. They'll build for me hard and they'll be well paid. You remember our talks? Right, so head down, get all the buying done and control our costs.'

'I've got something to say. What if I can get more out of our men without paying them extra money?'

'That's laudatory,' John said and smiled, 'but impossible.'

'No doubt. But I'm going to try. The Imperial Hotel will be a good project on which to run some of my ideas.' Brendan opened his satchel and rummaged around.

'Don't worry about them now!' John said. 'I've got something important to tell you. I'm giving you an incentive. If you achieve, and I think you will, you'll be rewarded.' Brendan looked up, interested. 'Your grandmother is going to gift her shares to you and Richard. Half of her fifty-one per cent share will be held in your name and the other equal half in your brother's, until I step down. Neither of you will get the shares until then.'

Brendan was silent for a moment. 'That's wonderful of her. But if we both get half of grandmother's shares, Richard will still be in front with his nine per cent.'

'Your grandmother and I have withdrawn your brother's nine per cent, for the time being.'

Brendan was shocked. 'Why?'

'That's not for you to know.'

'Can you do that?' Brendan asked.

'We certainly can.'

'What did Richard say about that?'

'Brendan, it's done and one day I'll tell you why. Anyway,' John continued, 'Richard's going to be married soon. It's not long till his wedding and honeymoon. He's still Construction Manager but while he's on leave, you'll be my second-in-charge. Our clients want me day-to-day and I need time to concentrate on the future of the business. So, Brendan, you'll have to be my full-time proxy at these client meetings, about a day a week. Are you up to it?'

Brendan stood and slung his satchel back on his shoulder. 'I am, Father.' He patted his bag. 'I've a lot of reading to do, but that's for later. Let's get into the party. From the noise downstairs, it's already started.'

Dave Sullivan met them as they got to the bottom of the stairs. 'Not good news, Mr Leary,' he said. 'The Council still need to give their consent to our steel design. They've only approved the brick one. I've got a meeting scheduled with them and us first thing Monday morning.'

John's good mood faded, but he was surrounded by employees—some ruddy-faced already—patting him on the back. Soon he was swamped by well-wishers. He smiled at them. Now wasn't the time to tell them bad news. Now was the time to party. He'd stay long enough to see they were enjoying themselves, then leave them to it.

'Let's talk later, Dave,' John said. 'We'll solve this.'

Richard finished his fifth beer, placed some loose change as a tip on the bar top and left the Annandale Hotel, pulling his jacket together to ward off the cold. It was seven o'clock. The party would be well under way and he had to sort things out. Brendan had outdone him for the last time and he needed attending to. It was always the same with his half-brother. Even as young-sters, they'd fought. Brendan the thinker, the idealist and now Brendan on the path to the top. He wouldn't have his half-brother best him.

Walking back to Leary's, Richard festered: the damned cheek and damned hide of Brendan, sucking up to their father, showing off with his facts and figures. Well, it was time to act and he'd enjoy doing it. He entered the noisy downstairs area at Leary's where desks and chairs had been stacked to one side. In the open space, over thirty men were sharing yarns and laughing in a fug of smoke and hops: a bit like the pub he'd just left.

By now some of the workers would know that he hadn't got the top post on the Imperial Hotel job. And he felt, as he moved around, that every eye was on him, every person sensing his loss of face and power. By tomorrow all would know, and that he couldn't take. His father wasn't there and that was something. His half-brother was deep in conversation with Tom Prentice. Even with everybody laughing and drinking around him, Brendan as usual was talking about *work*. Pitiful. It was time.

Richard smiled at the chief estimator and said, 'You can spare Brendan for five minutes, Tom, I think. Congratulations, by the way, on the win.' Richard took a grip on Brendan's arm. 'Come with me.'

Brendan shrugged off the grip and followed him.

Richard stepped into the chill of the rear yard and walked onto a gravelled patch surrounded by empty drums, rolls of rope and stacks of timber. 'You need a lesson, Brendan,' he said. 'A lesson in knowing your place.' Taking off his jacket and necktie he placed them on a drum and rolled up his sleeves. 'I'm not talking books and blackboards. They won't teach you what you need to know.' He brought up his fists, the skin taut on his face. 'These are my teachers.'

'You don't need to teach me anything,' Brendan said, and went to go back inside.

Richard threw a straight left that landed on Brendan's chin. Taken off guard, his half-brother lost balance and fell down. 'That's lesson number one. I'm your boss. That's how it is and always will be.'

Brendan stood up, feeling his jaw. He stripped off his jacket and raised his fists. 'If that's all you know how to do, Richard, then let's do it. Come on.'

'Good,' Richard said with an ugly grin on his face and anger coursing through him. He feinted with his right and used his left again. Brendan blocked it and jabbed his fist into Richard's eye. Richard staggered back and doubled over.

'Finished?' Brendan said.

Richard charged him, butting his head against his Brendan's stomach, catching him by surprise. 'This is for being a brown nose to Father.' Raising his head he bashed his forehead against Brendan's nose, hearing the sound of broken cartilage. Brendan raised his hands to staunch the flow and Richard gave him two short jabs in the stomach. 'Do what I say, just do what I say!' Richard said. Brendan fell to the ground and Richard pulled his boot back for a kick.

'That's enough, Richard,' Sullivan said.

Richard turned to the general foreman. 'Sod off, Sullivan. This is between us.'

'Then no kicking.'

A small crowd had joined Sullivan, with Mike Finnegan and Brendan's favourite, Rob Jenkins, among them.

'Watch yourself, Brendan,' Jenkins said.

Brendan staggered up and wiped his face. He raised his fists again. Richard came in swinging and Brendan blocked the blows with his forearms held upright and together, protecting his face. Jumping nimbly sideways, he landed a straight left at Richard's temple and a right to the throat. Richard stood there for a second, his eyes wide in amazement and fell forward, gasping, his breath misting in the cold air.

'That's it,' Sullivan said. 'Go on, all back to the party.' Most didn't move. 'I said, let's go! And not a word to the boss—those two need to sort it out alone.' Slowly the onlookers started to peel away back inside.

Brendan picked up his jacket and using his handkerchief, wiped the blood from his nose with care. Richard's back rose and fell. He'd survive. Bringing a hose from the shed, Brendan turned it on and washed his own face, the cold-water pressure adding more pain.

'Can you see?' Sullivan said to him.

'I'll live,' Brendan said and turned the hose onto his half-brother.

The water roused Richard and he sat up, peering through his matted hair and shivering. He grabbed a handful of gravel and threw it at Brendan 'You'll keep, brother. You'll keep.'

Brendan ignored the scattered stones, turned the water off and flung the hose aside. 'I'll be here, Richard, any time there's another lesson to be taught. Come on, Dave,' he said to Sullivan, 'there must be whisky somewhere in my father's office.'

On the Monday morning after the party, John, accompanied by Dave Sullivan, stepped out of Leary's George Street offices. They had a problem, a bloody big one. Why in hell had Turner awarded them the project when the City Council had not approved the steel design?

'Mr Burgess was blunt on Friday, Mr Leary,' Sullivan said. 'They only have the brick design approved.'

'You've told me that already. What else did he say?'

'Not much. I told them I wanted Mr Burgess to meet you first thing, when they open for business. I thought you might have some ideas.'

Not likely, but at least John could front the council in person. Perhaps all they needed to do was to submit an amended application for approval, one in steel. They weren't changing the outside look of the building or its height, just the structural skeleton, so it should be an easy matter. Pausing on the corner of King and George Streets, he glanced at a banner of a morning newspaper: 'Broken Hill Propriety Company floated.' An interesting move by the miner. Worth keeping an eye on them, John thought. For now, though, he had more pressing concerns. He stepped off the kerb and they continued along George Street.

'After the Council,' Sullivan said, 'I went to the architects. Turners don't want to talk to the Council. When I asked their rep, he said that since the steel design was ours, *we* had to get approval of it.'

'Did you see Mr William Turner? Talk to him?'

'No, Mr Leary, he was busy.'

'William Turner's playing a dangerous game, I suspect,' John said. 'There was no mention in their acceptance letter that the City Council had to approve our design. It's a ploy. They want us to kneel and worship their brick design. Well, they can wait. I'll get this through.'

Crossing Market Street, John picked up his stride. They had to be punctual for their nine o'clock meeting. Turner's brick design was at least £30,000 more expensive and it would take longer to build. Could Leary's build it? Of course, but it would mean a tight job. The Imperial Hotel had to be finished by the end of July 1887—not a day later. What if there was not enough time to get the steel design approved and still meet that completion date?

Doing up his jacket he mounted the Town Hall steps. 'Beard the lion, Dave,' he said, 'we'll get the upper hand.' Accompanying his general foreman into the City Council offices, John wished he felt as confident as he was pretending.

When they were admitted to Burgess's office, Burgess asked them to sit down.

John sat with his general foreman on one side of a desk that was broad, high and perhaps fifty years old, much like Mr Burgess himself. The Council officer sat down and dragged a heavy file in front of him. The noise from the Druitt Street traffic seeped through the top of the open windows, into the sixteen-foot high room. Burgess placed his hand on the file and said, 'The Imperial Hotel approval, gentlemen. I have the stamped blueprints downstairs.'

John had no strategy, but he had to get Council on side. 'We need our Imperial Hotel design approved, Mr Burgess: the steel one.'

Burgess stroked his moustache. 'I haven't seen your design in detail but Mr Turner explained it to me. By all means it can be submitted for review and we will comment, but that does not mean approval. Steel is new, Mr Leary. If we and the Fire Brigade approve the general principles, you'll have to build an actual steel-framed hotel room and test that under real fire conditions. If all that passes, then the Fire Brigade will have to agree with the final details. Their approval is mandatory.' Burgess steepled his fingers and said, 'That's the run of it, but'—he tapped his thick file—'you already have an approved design that's all brick. Build that.'

Yes, John thought, he could but he wouldn't, not yet, and not until he had proven these people wrong. 'We would submit an amended application for approval. That should be easy for you.'

'The steel design is too radical a change to accept as an amendment,' Burgess said. 'I'm sorry.'

'But all that testing and stuff,' Sullivan said, 'that'll take months, even a year. We haven't got that long.'

Burgess opened his hands to them. 'That's not my issue.'

John had to think. There had to be a way. 'The brick design is sixteen floors, with enclosed fire stairwells from top to bottom.'

'That's right. The whole structure is an interlocking grid of brick. It can withstand a huge fire and still stand, unlike your steel one. A bit like ... yes, the chimney of a bush hut ... it'd still be intact long after the fire had destroyed the rest of the house.'

'But our steel columns are encased with bricks, so they're just as fireproof!' Dave said.

'And the floor beams?' Burgess said.

'No, they're not.'

'Then, gentlemen, you have an issue.'

'Dave,' John said, 'take some notes. He waited till his offsider was ready. 'So Mr Burgess, what are the things that Council will accept to approve the steel design?'

'You have to know that a sixteen-storey building is a first for this city. That's two hundred feet high. The Australia Hotel is ten floors and that *just* got our approval, despite fierce opposition. The Imperial Hotel had a hell of a fight in Council. There are powerful lobbyists who would relish opening up the approval process again. Please understand this.'

God, John thought, even if they got their steel design approved by the authorities, they would be in for a fight with the politicians. John's breathing quickened. *Keep calm. That's for another day— technicalities first.* 'But,' he said, 'the building will look identical to any other from the street. The internal structure will be invisible.'

'The structure will still come into question. Then there's the fact that the fire brigade's ladders only extend to a height of eighty feet from the footpath.'

'Yes,' John said as Dave scribbled away, 'that's their height limit to rescue people.'

'Well, any storeys above that height are at risk,' said Burgess. 'That's why we have brick-enclosed stairways above that ladder height so all the people can get down from the upper floors, then out onto the ladders, or continue down the stairs to the ground floor. And that's just the start. Your steel floor beams are a problem; steel buckles and fails under fire. The brick design has hardwood bearers and joists of ironbark. The bearers are virtually fireproof: with that kind of timber, it's generally just the outside surface that burns.'

'And the floor structure stays sound,' Dave said.

'Yes, but scorched,' Burgess said. 'Your design has steel floor beams instead of timber bearers, naked and unprotected.' Burgess paused. 'Solve that and we might—I say might—be interested. You'll need insurance cover and an engineer's report that will say the steel building will not collapse under a fire.' He sat back. 'A big task and as I said, is all that worthwhile when you already have an approved design?'

John stood up and ran a hand through his hair. 'Thank you, Mr Burgess. We know where we stand. We'll come back with some answers.'

The council man shook both their hands. 'See Captain Martin of the city brigade in Castlereagh Street. He'll be tougher than me. Convince him of your steel protection and you'll get me interested.'

Ten minutes later, John stepped onto the footpath. 'Let's get back to George Street. I want Tom Prentice in on this and Brendan. We have to meet Martin too, as soon as possible. Getting costs for all these things will add to the job.' They crossed Druitt Street. 'Steel might be the go but it's got to be able to accommodate these extras Burgess wants.'

John rubbed his whiskered jaw and reached for the teapot. Brendan's nose was taped and John mused again how he might have copped it. His son said he'd had a fall but John had a suspicion there had been a scrap after he'd left the site party on Friday. Richard's face sported a black, half-closed left eye and a bruised neck. A coincidence? No. But he didn't feel like broaching it with them— there were more important things to discuss.

He refilled Brendan's mug from the pot. 'Another half an hour and we'll call a stop.' He sat down and rubbed his eyes. Twelve hours was enough for today. 'Let's see what we've got.'

Brendan looked at his notes. 'I'll start with the cost we have to beat. The brick design is £30,000 more expensive than the steel. So any cost we have to add to our steel design has to be less than this.'

'Agreed,' Tom Prentice said. 'Maybe £25,000, which will allow a £5,000 buffer for unknown costs.'

'Absolutely,' Brendan said. 'Otherwise we build in brick.'

'Which,' John said, 'we don't want to do. And there's another thing; I don't trust Turner. If we cave in and agree to build in brick he may want to have a new tender and that we can't have. I *won't* have.'

The room was silent as Tom sorted through his notes. 'Encasing the steel floor beams with concrete is the killer. It's only been done twice in the town and on small jobs. It'll set us back—'

'Wait,' John said. 'The brick design has hardwood joists which sit on ironbark bearers.'

'Which are toothed into the brick walls at each end,' Brendan said. 'In normal buildings, these ironbark bearers just get burnt on their outsides. Their insides remain intact. In the steel design we still have hardwood joists but they are fixed on top of steel beams that are not fireproofed. That's our Achilles heel.'

'So,' Tom said, 'we haven't got hardwood bearers because we have steel beams instead and our steel beams are connected to the steel columns. We have no choice, we have to enclose the steel beams to fireproof them.'

John drank the rest of his tea. 'So, we're in a pickle. Tom, what's the damage if we fireproof the steel floor with concrete?'

'I'm guessing. I've added some buffer but you won't get those beams protected with concrete for under £50,000.'

Brendan sat back and exhaled. 'Then we build in brick.'

John slammed his open hand on the table. 'We bloody won't!'

'But Father—'

'No, Brendan. There has to be a way. Steel will be easier after the first floors and it will save us time. Tom, are you sure of your costs?'

'I've been at it since midday and no ... not absolutely sure, but we can't fool ourselves. It's expensive.'

'Well, that's that,' John said disappointed. 'Let's call it a night, but be here, all of you by seven tomorrow.'

They stood up. Brendan stretched. 'Let's go home.'

✦

In his study that night, John's eyes were tired but he continued to scribble.

A hand squeezed his shoulder and the scent of talcum made him close his eyes. 'Come to bed, dearest,' Catherine said. 'It's after one. The problems will be there in the morning. You'll solve them.'

John covered her hand with his own and nodded. 'I promise. Five minutes.'

'No longer,' she said.

After she'd left, he shook his head and examined his notes. It was all about wrapping, he thought, about protecting the beams by encasing them with fireproofing materials, probably concrete. All to be built using overhead work, temporary supports: all tiring, dirty, risky, time-consuming and costly. What if they did nothing? Then the beams would be exposed to fire. *That's that.*

He glanced at his half-finished model ship, the three masts now standing with their yards crossed. How good it would be to spend some hours on that? But not now. He turned down his study gaslight. As the light went out, he stopped. A germ of an idea started. What if he could extinguish any fire on site *before* it attacked his exposed steel floor beams? He walked up the stairs and turned off the lamp on the landing. He could have hose reels and hydrants on each floor—but that would only serve to fight a fire after it had started. How to *prevent* a fire? John went into his dressing room, got changed then went into the dark bedroom, felt for the bed and got in. Catherine's breathing was even—she was asleep. His eyes closed as his head sank onto the pillow. Firefighting ... Martin. Fire Brigade.

✦

John munched on a crumpet that a staff member had prepared for him in the George Street kitchen, the butter and honey making it very tasty. He drank his tea and its heat soothed him.

'Tom's not with us,' Brendan said. 'He's getting his costs checked at Annandale.'

'Like any good estimator,' John said. 'Well, Declan, you're here in his stead. Any ideas that could help?'

Sean Connaire's son was tall and big like his mother and had her broad features. 'I've been racking my brains for some ideas, Mr Leary, but I've got nothing to add, I'm afraid.'

'We'll get there, Declan,' John said. He sat quietly thinking for a little while, then said, 'We have to be smarter, gentlemen. We're missing something here.' Maybe Richard should be here, more heads were better, maybe more ideas.

Brendan was tapping on the desk and John looked across at him. There was no tape across his son's nose but it was still bruised. Brendan's eyes were as alert as ever. He said, 'The Fire Brigade has good pumps on its wagons.'

'They do. But their pressure only gets water to a certain height. Maybe on the Imperial Hotel we could have stronger, permanent pumps in the basement. Then we could push water to hose reels and fire hydrants on every floor, right up to the sixteenth.' John finished his crumpet and sat back. 'Perhaps that's the way to protect the steel.' The GPO clock struck the hour. 'It's eight, we have to meet Martin at eight-thirty. Let's get going.'

'I'll do a bit more reading up,' Declan said. 'There might be something that's been done overseas that we haven't tried here yet.'

'Good one,' John said. 'Come on, son.'

Captain Martin shook John's hand with a firm grip. With his build, it looked as if he could carry two people at one time out of a burning building. Martin's brass buttons glinted as he sat down, his jaw jutting forward. 'Mr Leary,' he said, 'all you businessmen want is to build bigger and taller and we don't like it.'

Right to the point. 'We are builders only, Captain,' John said.

'And you'd be building a death trap, had I not demanded essential fire-extinguishing inclusions. Mr Leary, I protect people. They are my only responsibility.'

John wanted answers, not an argument. 'We want to build safely in steel. We have the columns encased.'

'In brick, solid, fully sealed?' the fire captain asked.

'Exactly,' Brendan said, bringing out a pad and pencil.

Martin turned to him. 'What about your floors?'

'That's where we need your help,' John said.

'Fireproof those. You can get halfway with having concrete floors.'

'We have looked at encasing the beams in concrete,' Brendan said. 'But it's far too costly.'

'No. Not the beams,' Martin said, 'just the floor. The practice is new and not used much, but it works. Here, let me show you.' He sketched in a firm and confident hand and handed back his work.

'You should be a draughtsman,' John said as he studied the sketch with Brendan. 'Corrugated iron sheets?'

'Placed over and fixed to the top of the timber joists,' Martin said. 'Then two inches of concrete laid over the iron, like a topping.'

'All from above,' Brendan said. 'Then you add the floorboards on top of that screed. It's possible, father.'

John looked at Martin. 'But we have to do more than this, right?'

'You do,' Martin said. 'You have to protect your steel floor beams from *below*. The plaster ceiling there isn't enough.'

'So, what do we do?' Brendan asked.

Martin hesitated and then stood up. 'I'm no engineer, gentlemen. I can't help you any more.'

John looked at the man. The fire captain had hesitated just then and seemed a little too keen to end the conversation. John wasn't being told the facts. 'Are you saying there are no other ways to protect structures from fire than fully enclosing them with concrete?'

Martin sat down and looked straight at him. 'No.' He kept up his stare. 'Nowhere here on this continent of ours.'

John saw the hint and welcomed it. 'But overseas?'

'Mr Leary,' Martin said, 'if what I tell you gets out, I'll deny this conversation ever happened.' He stood up and withdrew a file from his cabinet. 'In Philadelphia in the United States, a water sprinkler system has been used to protect a building. The system consists of a network of water-charged pipes fixed under the roof that connect to sprinklers set out on a grid pattern. Each sprinkler has a plug of material called a head that melts under heat and releases the water in a spray. It's been tested and approved ... for warehouses.' He took his pen and wrote something on a plain piece of paper and closed the file. 'Not on office buildings or hotels. But I see a time when this will be needed everywhere.' He handed John the paper and said, 'Here are the telegraphic details of the supplier. It's a start. If you can prove to me that you can get sprinklers to work in a tall building, I want to listen.' He sat back. 'But you have a major problem: at present I don't believe our city water supply could provide you the continuous water quantity you'd need to feed thousands of sprinkler heads during a fire.'

Hiding his excitement, John handed the paper to Brendan. He got to his feet. 'Before we leave, may I use your lavatory?'

'At the end of the corridor.'

John relieved himself, then before leaving the lavatory he looked with new eyes at the water system that served it. Above him on the wall was a cistern full of water. When he pulled the chain, water flowed down a connecting pipe to flood the bowl below. The cistern then refilled itself via a valve. Simple and effective.

John washed his hands and returned to the office. 'Thank you, Captain,' he said. 'We have work to do. Come, Brendan.'

Their carriage was waiting for them outside. 'Annandale, Gibbs,' John said. He sat back and brought out Martin's sheet of paper, put on his glasses and said to Brendan, 'Right, telegraph these people and get the facts, I want specifications of pipes, heads, pumps, the

217

lot. I'll even pay to get people out here. Within a month we should be able to do a detailed design. Get in Anthony Simpkins, our plumber foreman, and Tom or Declan. They can estimate a rough price of the pipework needed. We'll work through our tucker.'

Brendan paused in his note taking. 'It may all be too expensive, Father.'

'I know that, but we have to pull out all stops. We have to.' John thought about the time needed. Martin sounded genuine and wanted a job like the Imperial Hotel to prove new fire engineering. 'And Tom has to price the concrete topping and the corrugated iron.'

'I've got that already.'

'The water supply. That's the worry. Even if we get the sprinkler system designed, get it tested and passed, we still might not have the water.' He racked his brains all the way to the office. John had no ideas yet, but something kept niggling at him.

Brendan came into the meeting room, sat down and helped himself to a sandwich. 'I've sent off the telegrams. We should have something in a day or two.'

'Right,' John said. 'Tom's working on the other stuff.'

'If the cost of the sprinklers and the concrete floorboard topping come in under £30,000 with a buffer,' Brendan said, 'we may have a case. But we still need the water supply.'

John breathed out. That was the crux. Solve that and they had a chance. The town water supply came from the pipes in the street. Those street pipes were fed from reservoirs from Busby's Bore. Reservoirs ... cisterns. *That's it.* 'Tanks,' he blurted out.

Brendan looked at his father. 'Tanks?'

'Brendan, what if ... what if we built a tank in the roof of the hotel and put in pipes connected to the floor sprinklers? Like a WC. The water would flow down by force of gravity. If the tank was constantly topped up from the water supply and held enough water to fight any fire—'

'There'd need to be enough to extinguish it completely—'

'Then we have an answer,' John said, excited now. 'Get Simpkins back in. I want that tank sized, and get Brunels to design beams to support it. And we'd have to fireproof those beams. We are back in business, son. Get everyone back and we'll work all afternoon, we—'

'Mr Leary,' Mrs Mansfield said from the doorway, 'I've postponed your meetings for today but I'm running out of excuses. You have a lot to catch up on.'

John looked at her. Until he got the details from America he couldn't go much further with the new sprinkler-system idea. 'Right, I've got the next two days available. Get my meetings scheduled for that time.'

Mrs Mansfield smiled. 'Very good.'

'Go, Brendan, let's solve this. Get Prentice, Simpkins and Brunels onto those estimations. I want answers in two days.'

Forty-eight hours later, John entered the Annandale meeting room and closed the door behind him. Brendan, Simpkins and Prentice sat in front of him. John held up a paper in his hand. 'It's a letter from William Turner,' he said. 'He's asking us when we'll start the Imperial Hotel. He's putting the pressure on. It's the fourteenth of August now and we have to sort this out—quickly. Tell me some good news.'

'You tell him, Tom,' Brendan said.

Tom's face was earnest. 'Mr Leary, I think we can get all we want for just under £20,000.'

'And the tank?' John said.

'Including that. That's the costly bit. We can build it in sections on the floor and put it together up in the roof. But there will be extra time needed with the concrete topping on each floor and installing the sprinklers.'

'So for £20,000,' John said, 'we can build in steel with some fireproofing and sprinklers?'

Brendan smiled. 'We can,' he said, opening his folder. 'Here are the telegrams. On your instructions, Father, I've paid passage for their engineers to come out and help us.'

A hugely relieved John sat down. 'Good, very good.' They had a plan.

'We still have to convince the Fire Brigade,' Brendan said.

'We will! Then we'll have to preempt the politicians, in case they try to white-ant this. Get to work, men, get everything double-checked. You've got some "fat" in that cost of yours, Tom?'

'About as much as two beef steaks, Mr Leary, that's all.'

'That'll do. Now I've got to get to Cunningham and his cohorts. Brendan, set up meetings with Burgess and Martin. Martin first. I want our design approved ... in principle at least.' John leaned over and put out his hand. 'And happy birthday.'

Brendan smiled. 'Thank you, Father. We have something to celebrate.'

'It's encouraging so far,' John said, and left them to their work.

The Imperial Hotel's biggest investor opened the door of the now familiar private room at the Australian Club.

'Mr Cunningham,' John said. 'It's good to see you again.'

John's client shook his hand then closed the door after him, cutting off the noise and smoke of the Club's lounge area. Cunningham gestured to a vacant chair. Already seated were Morgan Stanley and a stranger.

John put his hand out. 'Evening, Mr Stanley.'

The big barrister stood and shook hands. 'Mr Leary,' he said.

'Mr Leary,' Cunningham said, 'this is Mr Alan Harris, chief accountant for Grimshaw's, the third investor of the Imperial.' John shook the small man's hand, who nodded at him and sat back down. 'Please sit down,' Cunningham said. 'We need to understand what's happened. We were expecting Leary's to get on with the project. It's the end of August, three weeks since we gave you the job. Mr Turner said you haven't started.'

'Why is that, Leary?' Stanley asked.

John looked at all three men. The architect could be playing him, expecting him to fold and build the brick design. But he wouldn't. He thanked the Lord that Cunningham had been hard to meet; he'd needed the last two weeks to get the fire brigade on his side. 'All's well gentlemen,' he said. 'We're ready to start, but it's going to cost you more.'

'More?' Stanley said. 'What do you mean, more? We have a contract with you, Leary, at a fixed price.'

'No, what I have is a letter from the architects agreeing for Leary's to enter into a contract with you.'

Harris waved his hand in dismissal. 'It's much the same.'

'No,' John said again. 'The contract to build the Imperial Hotel is between you as the investors/owners/clients, and us as the builder. The architects administer the contract only.'

'I know that,' Cunningham said with irritation. 'What's this extra cost?'

John noted the rudeness but wouldn't react. They were the owners, after all. 'We want to build in steel. It's simpler, it's cleaner but it needs to be fire rated.'

'I don't understand ... fire rated?' Harris said.

'Fireproofed, then,' John said. 'I've given my report to Mr Turner, which includes a sign-off from our engineers, Brunels, and has approvals from the Fire Brigade and Sydney City Council. The cost of fire rating, gentlemen, is £20,000 and that's all I'm asking for. Fireproofing the Imperial Hotel with a sprinkler system added is cheaper than encasing the steel with concrete.'

'We should stick with brickwork,' Harris said. 'The architect says that it's more proven.'

'But using bricks alone is more expensive,' John replied. 'Our figures show that. Unless you've had cheaper estimates from someone else?'

None of them responded. John felt certain that Bucknells' bid on the brick design had been more expensive than what John was now recommending.

'And the time?' Cunningham said.

'It will take an extra two months to build.'

Cunningham sat back and sipped his drink. John hadn't been offered one and these investors had been very matter-of-fact with him. This meeting had a single agenda and John was glad that all the owners were present. Their joint approval was needed.

'You expect us to take the risk on this ... fire rating,' Cunningham said, 'when it hasn't been done before?'

Fair comment. 'AMP Insurance has backed us,' John said. 'I can give you their letter.'

Cunningham raised his eyebrows. 'Send it to me. But this extra time you need, Mr Leary, that's not acceptable. We may pay your extra cost, as long as every pound is scrutinised by our own quantity surveyor. Please submit your costs to the architect. But the extra time—that's not negotiable.'

John knew he was on thin ground here. To meet the end of July '87 deadline and with all the fire-rating and sprinkler work to do, he'd have to accelerate the works, put more men on and work more shifts, all costing money. Tom Prentice's cost for this was £2,000. Well, he'd have to cop it. Leary's would have to make savings elsewhere. 'Very good. To show good faith, I agree to meet your deadline.'

Cunningham glanced at the other two owners. 'Are there any further questions, gentlemen?'

'I'm not happy, Leary,' Morgan Stanley said. 'This is not a good start.'

John looked at Harris, who looked at the carpet.

Cunningham stood up. 'We need to check your costs, Mr Leary and seek our own advice on your scheme.'

John stood also. 'Then there are the politicians to consider.'

'If we approve your scheme, and it's a *big* if,' Cunningham said, 'we will get the aldermen on side.'

'Good,' John said and reached for the door. 'I'll get the contract over to you to sign.'

'When we have approved the extra,' Cunningham replied. 'Not before.'

'Good evening, gentlemen.'

As John went down in the elevator, it stopped between floors. Not an omen for his future, he hoped! He rattled the doors for a time but nothing happened. Suddenly the car continued its descent. In his carriage on the way home, John thought he'd done as well as he could at the meeting, but he had no sense of the likely outcome.

Chapter Nine

William Turner refilled his glass from a decanter on the table. The Lord Mayor and two aldermen from the Sydney City Council sat opposite him in the Council's drawing room. Turner drank the water and put the glass down. 'It has to be brick gentlemen,' he said. 'It has to be.'

The Lord Mayor tapped the papers in front of him. 'But you approved the steel design, Mr Turner.'

'With respect, I did not recommend its acceptance. The investors made that decision, based on their return on capital, together with support from Brunels and the AMP.'

'Then surely that's sufficient,' one alderman said.

Cunningham and his ilk had got to the Lord Mayor. Three nights previously, a friend of Bill Bucknell had seen Leary leave a private room at the Australian Club, followed a little while later by the Imperial Hotel's three investors, and Cunningham was a big supporter of the Lord Mayor. 'And you'd risk a sixteen-storey monster in steel?' Turner said. 'If it collapsed, you could sue the engineers and the insurance company, but think about the catastrophe. You'd be voted out before they even started cleaning up the bodies and the debris.' The other two aldermen glanced at each other, one easing the tension of his necktie.

'Clearly,' the Lord Mayor said, 'we want the safest structure for the Imperial Hotel.'

'And that's brick, gentlemen,' Turner said with emphasis. 'We've spent the best part of an hour discussing it.'

'The fire brigade has passed the steel design,' the alderman with the itchy neck said.

Turner knew that this man held a big swathe of stock in Sydney Steel and he would benefit from a steel structure. He would be the hardest to convince. 'It hasn't been done before on this scale,' Turner said. 'You cannot risk it, gentlemen; you cannot.'

'Thank you for your valued opinion,' the Lord Mayor said. 'Our meeting is tonight and we will vote on it.'

Turner stood up. 'I'll be there. I hope you make the right decision.'

Christine McGuire sat in her chair in the drawing room at Point Piper, with family and friends gathered around her. Outside, a southerly blasted the grey water on Blackburn Cove and a few raindrops spattered the windows. 'The fifth of September, 1810,' Christine said, 'the day I came into the world. My, my. It seems an eternity ago.' She smiled and nodded to all of them. 'Thank you for coming and celebrating this day with me. Now, for the cake. Son-in-law, will you do the honours?'

John took the knife and bisected the numbers seven and five through the icing. A round of applause sounded around the room. 'Many more years to come, mother-in-law.'

He stepped back to let Delia cut the cake into portions and distribute them to the forty or so guests. Glancing at the group in the corner with Brendan, he smiled. Julie Carson looked about as comfortable as a Baptist holding a beer. She must be over-whelmed by the surroundings and anxious about what she might or mightn't say that would embarrass her. He had had similar feelings when he'd first gone to the McGuire house during his courtship of Clarissa.

Meanwhile Agatha was asking Julie, 'And you sew? You made your own dress?'

'It's not silk,' Julie said.

'But it's so fashionable!'

'I work in a factory,' Julie said, and looked at Agatha for any reaction but there was none, just curiosity. 'That's what I do.'

'I wish I could use my hands,' Mary said. 'My job at Leary's isn't much. I'd like to do more.'

'Come, Mary,' Agatha said, 'I want to show you some daguerreotypes. They're of Greece and I know you're interested in that country. Excuse us, Miss Carson.'

They went off and Delia offered Julie a piece of birthday cake. She tried to juggle her crystal glass with the cake on its fine china and the plate fell, hitting the hardwood floor with a bang. This raised giggles from a nearby group of girls.

'Let me help,' Brendan said.

She looked at him with thanks, her face red with embarrassment. 'Could we sit for a bit? These new shoes are hurting me. That's what made me wobble.' Brendan smiled, helped Delia clean up the mess and joined her on a couch.

'Brendan? You haven't introduced me to your friend.'

Anne Connaire looked at Julie as Brendan stood up, noting the contrast between the two young women. Anne was petite with solid hips, black curly hair, and a sweet smile. Julie was a true beauty, statuesque, with ravishing lips.

'Miss Carson,' Brendan said. 'This is Miss Connaire, the daughter of Mr Connaire, father's former partner.'

'How do you do, Miss Connaire,' Julie said.

'How do you do,' Anne replied. 'Where did you meet our Brendan?'

Right to the point, Julie thought and she thinks he belongs to her already. Well, let's see how far this will go. 'Oh, Mr Leary met me at home, if you must know.'

'Really?' Anne said, trying to hide her surprise.

'Yes, he came to my house, in the Rocks.'

Anne forced a smile. 'That must have been cosy.'

Julie wanted this girl to know that she wasn't easy. 'My Mum was with us all the time.'

'Of course she was.'

'The Rocks is a safe place, Miss Connaire,' Julie said with confidence. 'You won't get hurt there.'

'So you do like living there?'

Julie was getting impatient with this banter but noted Brendan seemed interested in the exchange. 'I do and I'm proud of it.'

'Charming. I hope to see you again, Miss Carson,' Anne said and reached and squeezed Brendan's hand. 'See me soon, please. It's been too long.' She walked off.

'Well, that ain't half plain,' Julie said watching her go. 'She likes you, a lot.'

'Anne's a friend,' Brendan said.

'She thinks she's more than that to you.'

'I don't want to talk about her.'

Julie didn't either. She glanced at the guests and the hosts. 'Right, so are your parents ... close? They look it.'

'Yes. And I think mother's accident has brought them closer. It's nice to see.'

Brendan stood up as Agatha joined them again. She sat down and linked her arm with Julie's. 'You should go outside and show Miss Carson around, Brendan. The weather's cleared.'

'Good idea,' he said.

Agatha squeezed Julie's arm. 'Are you having a good time?'

Julie smiled. 'I am. There are so many beautiful dresses, and the food.'

'You're the one being looked at. Better watch her, Brendan, the word's out. Sydney's bachelors are lining up.' Julie looked down and coloured. 'See,' Agatha said, 'even when she's shy, she's beautiful.'

'She is,' a young man said sidling up to them.

'James Johnson,' Agatha said. 'Where did you come from? Sneaking up like that.'

Johnson bowed to Julie. 'May I have the honour of escorting Miss Carson outside? The rain has cleared, the sun is out and I'm sure she would like to see the harbour.'

Julie looked at Brendan, who smiled at her. She took James's arm.

'Be careful of him, Miss Carson,' Agatha said as he led her away. 'He's a smooth one.' She turned to her brother. 'Sit with me Brendan. Let's talk.'

Agatha settled her dress and said, 'She's sweet, Brendan, she is. Drops her "aitches" a few times but that's endearing. She said little at first, shy she was. Maybe she thought we're rich and snooty. But she relaxed when I told her a few things.'

'What things?'

'Just about us. How we're a simple family. How Mother was a milliner. She told me about her family. Her mother's a tireless worker, and she's close to her.'

'It wasn't easy getting her to come today,' he said.

'There is an issue, though, and don't get upset when I tell you.'

Brendan took a guess. 'She doesn't know what I see in her?'

'Something like that. I put her straight and said that you weren't playing games and that you were serious about her. That's right, isn't it?'

'It is,' Brendan said, and stopped a waiter and got himself a beer. 'Do you want anything?'

'A glass of water, please.'

The waiter poured a glass from a jug.

'What do you think I should do?' he said.

'Go easy,' Agatha said. 'Don't crowd her. She likes you, Brendan.'

'She does?'

'She told me something when you were out of earshot.'

'What did she say?'

'I said I wouldn't tell, and I won't. But be easy with her. She does have another admirer.'

'Aiden. I know.'

'He's a boilermaker. No reason why she shouldn't have friends like that. Father is a carpenter, after all. I told Julie that and she felt better.'

'I'm glad.' And Brendan was, very glad.

On the veranda and out of sight of other guests, James Johnson stood beside Julie. She was self-conscious with him and on her guard. She sensed his type but would not be rattled.

'It's a beautiful vista,' he said. 'Don't you agree?'

'It's pretty,' she replied.

'So, Miss Carson, where do you come from?'

'The Rocks.'

'The where? Did you say ... the *Rocks*?'

Julie blushed; her temper was being tested. 'Yes.'

Johnson grinned. 'Oh, now I understand.'

'And what's wrong with where I live?'

He kept up his smirk. 'But you look so grand and ... where did you get the dress?'

'I made it.'

He laughed. 'Really.' He pressed against her and she moved away, trying not to get angry. He moved closer again. 'Until you spoke,' he said, 'I thought you were one of us, but then you opened your mouth. It shows.'

Julie went red and tried to keep control. 'I speak like I speak. You talk like a toff. I'm not.'

'That's more than obvious,' Johnson said. 'Come on, a girl from the Rocks knows how to have a good time.'

'I do, but not the sort of time you have in mind.'

He smiled and stroked her arm. Julie shivered. 'You're teasing me now,' he said.

'I'm jolly well not.'

He put his lips close to Julie's ear. 'We can go to a quiet place and —'

Julie stood back and slapped him. People nearby stopped talking and some came to look.

'I think you should go,' Julie said trying to contain her anger.

'Go?' he said. 'I'm not going anywhere. You're the one who should leave. You don't belong here.'

Julie was about to reply when Brendan appeared. 'What's wrong, Julie?'

'I shouldn't have come here,' she said.

'Johnson?' Brendan said. 'What happened?'

'It's of no consequence, Leary,' he said and smiled. 'I was just talking with your little *Rocks* girl, here.'

There were a few gasps and Brendan looked at Julie, who went to move away. 'Stay, please,' Brendan said.

'He might be dressed proper,' she said, 'but he ain't a gentleman. He wanted to feel me up.'

'Oh dear,' one woman said.

'Let's go inside,' Brendan said.

'I think you'd better take Miss Carson home,' his mother said, a look of triumph on her face.

'Mother, I want to find out what happened. It's—'

Julie turned on him. 'Don't you believe me?'

'I do,' Brendan said and turned to Johnson. 'You owe Miss Carson an apology.'

'Come on, Leary, it was all in fun.'

'Brendan,' his mother said, 'take Miss Carson home.'

Julie turned on her, 'You don't believe me, either.'

'A young lady doesn't ever get herself into this position. You may have perhaps invited the attention.'

'Invited? Well, that's lovely. Brendan? Please take me home. I'm not staying here if no one believes me.' She turned to Johnson. 'Don't come down Princes Street any time soon and try that, mate, or you'll get stitched up.'

There were more gasps and Brendan took her hand. 'Come on.'

Julie kept quiet on the way through the house and out the front door, a look of defiance on her face. 'You didn't say anything!' she said, once they were outside. 'You just stood there! Why didn't you get into him?'

Brendan had asked himself the same thing. Did he believe her? Yes he did and he should have done something more. 'I'll attend to Johnson later, don't worry.'

They were walking down Wolseley Road and Julie stopped. 'Leave me here, Brendan. I'll get a cab home. I have money.' Just then it started to rain again.

'I'll come with you.'

Julie hitched up her dress and set off. 'Go back to your people. Goodbye, Brendan.'

Victoria loved all this pomp and ceremony and Richard was excited for her. They were in St Mary's Cathedral and on his right were his three groomsmen, trying to suppress smiles, and on Victoria's left were her bridesmaids.

'Keep still, Richard!' Victoria whispered. 'Just a minute more.' She looked either side of her and said, 'All right everyone, pay attention. These are the places you'll have next Saturday the nineteenth. Remember them. They are between the windows and the statues. Thank you.'

'Miss Victoria,' the priest said. 'May I see you for one minute?'

'Of course, Father. Wait for me near the carriage, Richard. I won't be long.'

Outside, Richard leaned against the warm sandstone of the church wall. More by need than inclination, he'd found a few card games the night before. Just to be at a game seemed to satisfy him and yet he knew he had become an addict to it and hated the pull that the cards had on him. He'd won some ready cash, enough to square his debts.

The seven projects he was responsible for were all going well, including the new bank in George Street. But he needed more and wanted the Imperial Hotel. After his honeymoon he would aim to get it back and tip out Dave Sullivan.

And he had something to use against the general foreman. His investigations had found that Sullivan had been the foreman at a Surry Hills site where a man had been pushed under a steam shovel during a fight and been killed. Richard could bring that to light again. Then there was the missing money. Rumour had it that a payroll had been stolen and Sullivan had blamed it on thieves. It was strange that, just before the robbery, Sullivan's wife had had a stroke and was comatose in hospital, requiring expensive care. Raising a murky past seemed just the thing to ease Sullivan out of his job, even if the facts weren't established. It would be a mean thing to do and Richard was amazed at his conscience niggling him about it. It never had in the past.

Victoria came up to him. Her coachman was leaning against a tree in the early September sunshine, having a smoke, and she got his attention. 'We need a few minutes,' she said to him. 'We'll call you when we're ready to go.'

The coachman acknowledged her and Richard helped Victoria into the carriage. Once inside he opened the roof hatch to get some air.

Victoria turned to him. 'Now, the itinerary …' Richard kissed her, cutting off her words. Victoria responded, her hands cradling his face, her mouth open, then she broke away and looked at his eye.

'It's healing nicely,' she said. 'You want to be more careful on sites next time. It could have been a worse accident.' She smiled. 'Let's try to talk about the honeymoon. Please.'

He'd forgotten about the fight, but not about Brendan. 'All right, my dear, but you know that I love you.'

Victoria's shoulders sagged and her eyes filled. 'You do? You're not just saying that to … you know.'

Richard took her hands. Yes, he wanted that. 'No,' he said, 'it's you … all of you.'

'Thank you, Richard.' Victoria kissed him, and for the next five minutes they talked about their plans. Richard then waved for the coachman to come and as he did, Richard saw someone familiar walking towards the church. He focussed. It was Gillian Thompson, her face pale and drawn. She looked at him, turned away and went inside the church. It was Saturday afternoon, three o'clock—too early for Mass or confession. *I wonder what she's doing?* She was a Catholic; she had told him that the first time they'd met.

The carriage jolted to a start and Victoria chatted on but Richard only half listened. Gillian looked like she'd seen a ghost.

Inside the cathedral, Gillian blessed herself and sat in the back pew. The crucifix above the altar seemed to loom over her, getting bigger and bigger—crushing her. Forcing her eyes shut to cut off its power, she knelt and tried to say The Lord's Prayer, but an image of a baby flashed in front of her. She pushed it aside, finished the prayer and sat up.

Footsteps came towards her: a priest with head bowed. The closer he came, the faster her heart beat. She lost control, lowered her head and sobbed.

'Are you all right, my child?' He genuflected and sat down beside her. 'Whatever troubles you, you're in the right place. God won't fail you.'

Seeing Richard in that carriage had been a sign, a sign to say that the time was right to tell. There had been a girl in the carriage with him, his fiancée no doubt. 'Oh Father,' she said, 'God can't forgive me.'

The priest smiled. 'God forgives anything, as long as the penitent wants forgiveness.'

'Oh I do, Father. I do.'

'Tell me what troubles you.'

Gillian took a deep breath. She dabbed her face and looked at the pew. She turned to the priest. 'Father I'm going to have a baby and I'm ... not married.'

The priest closed his eyes for an instant, then took her hand. 'All life is sweet to Jesus, child, whether it's in marriage or otherwise. Does the father know?'

Gillian shook her head.

'Well, you'll need to tell him.'

Gillian sniffled. 'He's getting married soon. It wouldn't be right.'

'Have you anyone to help you? Your family?'

'No.'

The priest looked at her for some time. 'I'll get Sister Benita to speak with you. She knows about these things and can advise you on ... what to do.'

'Adoption?' Gillian said and shivered. She withdrew her hand. 'I ... can't think about that now.'

The priest took her hand again. 'I understand. You've got time to consider it but would you like me to hear your confession?'

Gillian forced her mind to clear and to concentrate. *Richard must never know he's the father.*

'Bless me father for I have sinned ...'

In the early morning sunshine, Brendan alighted from a tram in George Street, near Margaret Street. It was six-thirty and he prepared himself for meeting Julie. It was twelve days since his grandmother's birthday and since then he had been desperate to see her and to find out whether she was prepared to see him again. He'd forced James Johnson into admitting that he might have taken liberties with Julie, and Brendan had left the man shaking and in fear of him. But that wouldn't win Julie back. He'd written two letters to her, one the day after the party and another a week after that. He'd only got her reply yesterday and she'd said she would meet him here this morning.

He was anxious because she mightn't even turn up. Entering the tea shop, he saw her and relaxed a little. She was looking down at her hands, and her face was pale. She looked up as he approached.

'I can't stay long,' she said. 'My tram is due in ten minutes.'

'Would you like a cup of tea?'

'No thanks. Brendan, I have to tell you something.' He sat down. 'What happened at Point Piper could've happened anywhere. I face men like that all the time. But that wasn't what upset me. We can't keep meeting. We are different and I told you that from the start.'

Brendan had feared she would say this. He had to make her see his point of view. 'Julie, do you like me?'

She hesitated. 'Yes. But I like many people.'

'Aiden?'

She looked down. 'Yes,' she said and looked up at him. 'He's ... simple, not stupid, mind, but I'm easy when I'm with him. There's no pressure.'

'Pressure?'

'When I'm with you, I have to try hard. I have to always think of what I have to do, what I have to say. With Aiden, I'm just me.'

Brendan was uneasy. 'You've not been tense with me when we've been together.' She had been, but he wouldn't admit to that.

'I've dealt with Johnson. He behaved like a bastard and he knows it. You didn't deserve to be treated that way.'

She shook her head and looked at him sorrowfully. 'I can't see you no more.'

'But you said you liked me!'

'I do, Brendan. A lot. But it can't work.'

Brendan felt himself slipping away.

Julie stood up. She had tears in her eyes. 'It's the only way. Please don't try to see me again, please. Goodbye, Brendan.'

He sat there and didn't turn around, didn't hear the tea shop door open and close. He just felt his heart breaking and nothing else.

On the third Saturday in September, some two hundred people were celebrating Richard's wedding on the lawns of the Hughes's Darling Point harbour-front property including Stella Fawcett,

Richard's former nanny and close family friend. She was seated at John's table, enjoying herself. Victoria glowed like the new bride she was. Richard had certainly married well and there would be many sons—John was counting on it.

John sipped his champagne. It tasted sweeter as he thought about the future and the new hotel. Cunningham's approval of the extra cost had meant work could commence and he was glad he'd backed himself and had started on the site before he'd got his client's approval. All power to Sydney City Council too; to his amazement, they'd come good in the end.

Catherine, sitting beside Brendan, caught his eye, smiled and raised her glass to him.

Joseph Hughes came up beside him. 'Enjoying yourself, John?' he said.

'Excellent, Joseph, thank you,' he said and gestured to the newly-weds. 'A great day; the youngsters did us proud.'

Richard waved his glass, spilling the contents, and Victoria shrieked as Richard's other hand touched her somewhere under the table. She scolded him but he just kept grinning.

'Excuse my son, Joseph. He's as passionate about his bride as he is about his work.' John hoped that Richard would turn some of that passion into fixing his gambling. 'That was a handsome wedding gift you gave them, a house in Glebe.'

Hughes said, 'It's a good start for them. Say, I passed your hotel site the other day and things are happening already.'

'Time is money,' John said. 'We'll have that site humming before you know it.'

Hughes chuckled. 'I'm sure you will. Richard says he's going to run it.'

Richard's got a big mouth. 'He's certainly capable.'

'But?' Hughes said.

John allowed a waiter to refill their glasses. 'He's got our other projects to run. When he's back from his honeymoon we'll give him something more to do.

We have new sites to manage and we're blessed with a glut of talent.'

'That bank building in George Street,' Hughes said. 'It's coming on.'

'It is.'

Hughes paused. 'Richard will run Leary's one day, surely?'

John sensed Joseph wanted some surety of Richard's future to support Victoria. He hoped Richard's new bride would be able to persuade his son to do something about his gambling, get him back on track. Richard was his clear successor but he had to reform. 'Yes, he could run it,' John responded honestly.

'Good. Everyone needs a succession plan. You and I are not getting any younger. I'm going to throw it in myself soon. Excuse me, John, I've got to see to my guests.' John raised his glass to his new in-law and his thoughts returned to the Imperial Hotel. David Sullivan had set a gruelling program on site for the next four weeks. Time had to be made up. October couldn't come soon enough.

John stopped under the street awning adjacent to the Imperial Hotel site. In the mid-October sun he had a clear view to count the men. There should be close to three hundred if Sullivan was right. John clicked his fingers. He didn't need to count them. There were more.

Far below the Clarence Street footpath, workers were pushing barrows, swinging picks and pouring concrete, their combined noise sounding like an open-pit mine, and that's what it was like—digging and shifting, sweating and swearing. In the dust-misted hole, the scream of steel wire running through blocks was drowning out the orders yelled by the overseers.

David Sullivan stood next to him. 'We're getting there.'

'You are.'

The blackened funnels of the steam shovels belched smoke as they strained to dig out the sides of the excavation, the sandstone, some smooth, some scarred for the first time in millennia. The bucket teeth of one machine had caught in the rock, its rear end lifting, but the rock gave up the fight, sheared and yielded up its fragments. An ox, tethered to five others, dropped a fresh pat as the shovel dumped its spoil in the tray. Another team strained under the whip to drag its load up the man-made ramp.

'We needed three shovels,' Sullivan said. 'It doubles the rate of excavation. They are costly but save time.'

John agreed. Wet weather might delay them, flooding the massive hole. John pointed to a dray-sized temporary drainage pit in one corner of the site, which was connected to a steam pump. 'That's good. Come on, let's get on site.'

They walked along Clarence Street. Dug into the sandstone at the base of the site were neat, square footing pits, laid out like a platoon on parade. Some had freshly set concrete in them and two had thick base plates for the steel columns which would rise to an amazing sixteen-plus floors into the sky.

'It's a fair start,' John admitted, more to himself than his companion. The site was orderly, no unnecessary clutter, with the materials placed at strategic points. John looked up and grinned. 'Couldn't you get a bigger sign?'

Sullivan stopped at the site fence and looked up. 'The letters are as big as me,' he said. They were brash and blatant: LEARY'S CONTRACTING, with the architects' names underneath. 'And, Mr Leary, you said you wanted it up before we broke ground.'

Sullivan opened the gate and John followed him into the site sheds where half a dozen men were busy; the air a mixture of sweat, smoke and fine dust. 'Come into my office,' Sullivan said.

John went in and sat down. 'Problems?'

'Nothing that won't be solved today.'

The right answer. Sullivan was king of his site and had to rule and solve a myriad of issues, as well as manage hundreds of workers. Sullivan could have dumped problems on John but hadn't—so far so good. But there must be a weakness somewhere. Perfection wasn't possible, even at this early stage.

'How is the steel?' John asked.

Sullivan stepped over to the plans laid out on a table and John joined him. 'There's an issue,' Sullivan said and cleared his throat. 'See these columns supporting the façade? They're sixteen inches thick and they're spaced at every twenty-five feet. We can't get them made in Sydney, they have to be imported. But we can get eighteen-inch-thick ones from Sydney Steel. They're more expensive columns but,' Sullivan smiled, 'we only need two thirds of the original number because they are stronger and we'll use fewer footings to support them.'

John put his glasses on and took a closer look. 'What do the architects say?'

'It's our call.'

This might be a problem, John sensed. Turners were not readily approving anything to do with the steel. 'What do Brunels think?'

'They're all right with it.'

John wanted more assurance. 'That extra insurance that Turners wanted for the steel design, have you paid it?'

'I have and our budget will be bruised. That's Turners for you. They don't trust the engineers and they don't trust steel.'

'I'll back Brunels,' John said. 'Go ahead. Just make sure the new column positions don't interfere with the window openings.'

Dave looked at his drawings. 'I don't think they do. But I'll check again.'

They went back to Sullivan's desk, where John resumed his seat. 'How's your team?'

'We're still below ground and we've got the lift pits to do. I can handle the in-ground services, drainage, water and gas for the time being, but this steel's got me up at nights.'

John understood but wanted the reasons. 'Why?'

'Mr Leary, we've got a rigging foreman and a rivet foremen. Both gun tradesmen who'll drive the teams well. But I need a steel-work overseer.'

John had heard of these men on bridges and gas works but not on building sites, although he understood Sullivan's need. 'Anyone in mind?'

'I do, but hear me out.'

John smiled. Sullivan would make a good advocate. 'Go on.'

'You'd know both foremen. They respect the company. But they're proud … need nursing,' Dave said and smiled. 'Not bandages and shit but they have to be moulded to a team. They're both critical to stringing the whole web together. There's someone I think can lead them. Brendan.'

John was surprised. 'Brendan? No, he's not for that. Let him do the contracts, just the contracts, for now.'

'Look … I know he's green on steel. We all are, but —'

'It's too risky, Dave.'

'Both foremen want him, Mr Leary. They've worked with him, know his experience, know he's good at details and can gee up a team. Do you want me to get him? He'll tell you what he's been doing.'

John hesitated but Sullivan had left the office. Brendan on the steel? That was a big call. John stepped to the window and opened it, letting in the site's roar. He had to think. Sullivan had this place running well. His judgement on Brendan would be sound and both foremen couldn't be wrong.

'Hello, Father,' Brendan said as he came in with Sullivan. He sat down on a chair next to him, his hand gripping a cardboard file.

'How are the contracts?' John said. 'Tell me.'

'Here—better, I'll show you,' Brendan said and tabled a thick sheaf of paper. 'All the main trades are accounted for, including the elevators, which we saved money on. The steel order can be placed today. That will result in a ten per cent reduction on the budget in our tender.'

That was about a five thousand pounds saving, a profit straight to Leary's bottom line. 'Well done son, well done. But you'd better speak to Dave. There's been a variation to the—'

'Façade columns?' Brendan said.

His son was all over it. 'Yes.'

'I'll make the change,' Brendan said, 'and it's all good to go.'

'Some of that saving will pay for the insurance.' John said.

'The saving could have been fifteen per cent, Father, but the steel price increased two days ago.'

'And the rest of the supply contracts?' John asked.

'All let and all orders issued.'

John sat back and was impressed. 'You *have* been working.'

'After hours, too,' Sullivan said. 'I want him for the steel erection.'

'These foremen,' John said looking at Dave. 'They really want my son?'

'I'll get them if you like. They'll tell you.'

John looked from his general foreman to Brendan. Things were moving too quickly and when that happened, mistakes would be made, but time was money. 'Brendan,' he said, 'make sure ... by God make sure all the contract administration is done. If I find one invoice is not paid, I'll yank you off the steel. Understand?'

Brendan looked at him and then at Sullivan. 'I think I can do it.'

'All right, Dave,' John said. 'You can have Brendan for three months if—'

'That's not long enough, Mr Leary.'

Sullivan's reply took John by surprise but he would compromise. 'We'll review it after Christmas. If Brendan's coping, which we're all hoping he will, we'll make it permanent. Brendan, you've got three months to show what you've got.'

As soon as Richard opened the door of their London hotel room a flushed Victoria grabbed him and pulled him inside.

'Look what I've bought,' she said. Richard stepped around a pile of opened boxes, tissue paper and ribbons, all adding the smell of new fabrics to the coal-heated room. 'Don't mind the mess,' she said. 'Just look at these.' She giggled. 'I didn't know London's prices would be so expensive, and for dresses already made. I hope you don't mind?'

Richard grinned and grabbed hold of his wife but she wriggled free, pushing his hands from her. 'Wait, wait,' she said and picked up a lemon silk dress, held it against her and walked to the full-length mirror. 'What do you think?'

Richard sat on a chair. 'It's lovely,' he said. 'Goes with your hair.'

'I think it does. And this?' She put down the silk and held another gown against her.

'Just as good.'

Victoria pouted. 'You're just saying that to get your way.'

Richard spread his hands and said, 'No, they're nice, all of them. Come here.'

She sat on his lap. 'I love you, Richard Leary,' she said, her eyes glistening. 'I want you to tell me again that you'll stop your gambling.'

Richard's smile faded. This was the second time they'd talked about it. 'I will.' He said that easily, too easily.

'Are you sure? I need the truth, Richard. I'll not stay married to a man who gambles. I'll even face the scandal of a separation. Do you hear me?'

Richard smiled at her but it was forced, and he remembered an incident the previous day that had shocked him. While Victoria had been shopping, he'd strolled to the Marlborough Club and was tempted to enter and play. But he'd hesitated and he was glad he'd done so. Near him, a young gentleman with an anguished face was wandering around outside the club. He suddenly jumped into a hansom cab and after it pulled away, Richard heard a loud shot. The cab stopped, people ran up, and someone called out that the man had shot himself. In *The Times* this morning he had read that the young man was a peer of the realm, and the reason for his suicide was thought to be his gambling debts.

'I mean it, Richard,' Victoria said. 'I do. Even though it would hurt me terribly, I'd leave you.'

Her face was unmoving. *She means it. This is a turn-up.* Well, he had a real job now—to keep his wife—and that was a job worth taking on. He wasn't going to kill himself and leave Victoria a widow. No way. And it was going to be hard, bloody hard but he was going to try. 'Dear,' he said. 'I'm going to make sure I stay married to you and that means giving up gambling.'

Victoria closed her eyes for a moment then opened them. 'Thank you. Because I don't want that horrid man coming near me again, like he did in Sydney.'

Anger filled him as he pictured Victoria being confronted by that thug. Something started a spark in him, something strange and different. She was his wife, and he needed to protect her. And when they had children, he would have to protect them, too. In the past he'd never questioned his gambling, as the consequences of his actions had only affected him. But now Victoria was his responsibility as well. It was a mighty load. Could he carry it?

'You look serious,' she said stroking his chin. 'Are you thinking how hard it's going to be?'

She was good, he admitted. 'I was, actually.'

'I want you to tell me the truth, Richard, whatever it is. I'm a big part of your life now and everything you do affects me. So if you have worries, share them with me, please.'

This was new, too, a mate to share his thoughts and his troubles. He could talk to her. 'I will,' he said.

She kissed him and happiness filled him. But here it was easy to make promises, snug and warm with her in the joy of their honeymoon. Back in Sydney, back in the smoke and the lure of the bright numbered cards, that would be the test. But he'd try. September was the last time he'd played—two months—and it had been hard on him.

Victoria broke away. 'Are you hungry?' she said.

'I am. Something to eat, something to celebrate.'

'Celebrate what?' she said holding onto his hand.

'Why, these.' He waved his arm at the dresses.

Victoria nuzzled his ear. 'The dining room's just opened. It'll be crowded.' She glanced at the bedside clock and fingered the button on her blouse. 'We've got half an hour yet. Have you got any ideas to pass the time?'

Richard looked around and picked up a daring silk nightdress, which he held up to the light. 'Pretty,' he said. 'Try it on.'

Victoria looked at him. 'It's the middle of November; I'll freeze.'

'I'll warm you up,' he said as he started undressing her.

She took his face in her hands and kissed him hard. 'Hurry, darling ...'

Brendan knew he had achieved a lot in a short time. The fourth floor of the Imperial Hotel, on which he stood, had been completed a week ahead of schedule and his foremen Jackson and Smith were on the money. Now to check for himself. He counted the covered stacks of timber floorboards. These were to be laid over the concrete fire-rated topping when the floor was ready and not rain-affected. Good, all accounted for. It was the busy period before year's end. This reminded him that Richard would be home from his honeymoon on Christmas Eve, in fifteen days' time.

The steel columns for the fifth floor shimmered in the heat and sweat dripped from workers' chins and foreheads. Brendan spotted his rigging foreman and raised his voice, 'Stephen, early meal today.'

A nuggetty rigger grinned at Brendan, his teeth shining in his tanned face, his shirt pungent from the grease of his tools. 'Good one boss,' he said. 'The boys'll kiss ya for that.'

'I'd prefer a pretty girl. Get some water into you.' Brendan said, raising his voice. 'All of you.'

The workers downed tools and slaked their thirst. Stephen Smith came up to him and said, 'Good idea. Some men are dropping, they are.'

'Can't have that,' Brendan said.

'Other bosses wouldn't have bothered. Now ... this new transfer beam design.'

'Let's get some shade,' Brendan said, and they headed into a lean-to built within the steel framework, which would be a future bathroom. He offered the hessian bag to his rigging foreman who grabbed it and drank. Brendan followed suit. The water had a metallic taste but was satisfying. He put the bag down and smoothed out the plans.

Smith placed a gnarled finger on the drawing, smudging the ink. 'Transfer beam over the fourth-floor reception room. It's the second big bastard after the ground-floor ballroom one. Trouble is, we've just got new plans and the two columns that support it are already erected. Their gusset plates are too small. We'll have to get them remade to suit the new beam.'

It was best practice to take the loads of a building on each column, one above the other, all the way from the roof to the ground. But on the Imperial Hotel, where the upper columns came closer to the lower floors they encountered ballrooms and other large spaces that needed to be 'column-free', so transfer beams had to be built over these large spanned spaces to take the loads of the columns above.

Brendan ducked out into the heat and looked at the rogue columns. He came back inside. 'Leave the columns there. Connect up what you can with the existing gussets. Then bolt bracing at forty-five degrees from below the column gussets back to the transfer beam.' Brendan looked at the plan. 'There are nib walls that encase those two columns. They'll cover the bracing.'

Smith closed one eye and paused. 'That'll work.'

'I'll sketch it and the engineers can check it.'

'Good.'

'Are we right for tomorrow morning's staff meeting?' Brendan asked.

'Yeah. Them meetings are good. Jackson likes them too. All the boys know what they've got to do for the next day's work. I'll grab a bite. You eatin'?'

'I'll have something later,' Brendan said. 'Off you go.'

'I ran into Rob Jenkins the other day. He finished that Enmore job in October, two weeks early.'

Brendan grinned. 'He had a good foreman, Stephen.'

'Don't know him,' Smith said, grinning back at him, then he went off while Brendan took another drink. His eyes felt as if they were rimmed with sand. Not enough sleep—but working long hours had paid off. He was thankful for being on the steelwork and he was keeping up with the contracts each day after knock-off.

Paul Jackson, the rivet foreman, came under the lean-to. 'Got time, boss?' he said.

'What's up?'

'Rivet stocks are down. There's a strike at Mackay's. In about a week we'll be stopped on the fifth floor if we don't get some.'

Brendan had heard the rumours. Without rivets on a steel job, it would stop. He looked at the foreman and waited. He'd been encouraging his team to solve problems. Jackson dropped his gaze. 'What are you going to do about it, Paul?'

The foreman shrugged his shoulders. 'What can I do?'

'You know how important rivets are?'

'Bloody oath, boss.'

'Can you get another supplier?'

'Maybe.'

The air was getting hotter. 'Yes or no?'

Jackson took off his hat and scratched his bald head.

'Try McPhersons,' Brendan said. 'Find out if they have any, and order enough rivets to cover for the next month. We'll have to have the strike solved by then.'

Jackson went off and Brendan pulled out his list. The day was half over and he'd still a day's work to do. He thought of Julie. It'd been nearly three months since their break-up and he hadn't seen her, but he wanted to, he did.

Sullivan stuck his head into the lean-to. 'Got a moment?'

No rest. 'Yes.'

'After Christmas I want you here full-time. You want that?'

'I'll say!' Brendan said without hesitating.

'Good. I'll need to clear it with your father.' Sullivan looked at him. 'You'll be right, don't worry.'

'Thanks.'

'Let's hold fast for the present,' Sullivan said. 'Now, show me what you've got planned for the next week and tell me how you're going to get us more rivets.'

Bringing up his list, Brendan sighed—no chance to eat again. 'Right,' he said. 'This is what's on ...'

Bill Bucknell leaned back in his chair in his office and smiled. He placed the *Sydney Morning Herald* on top of his Christmas-present list. He had fourteen days to buy the presents and he'd best get cracking. 'Leary's have a problem with their steel,' he said. 'Good. The bastards deserve it for the way they got that job.'

William Turner glanced at the open door of Bucknell's office. 'Are you sure we're alone?'

Bucknell grinned again. 'We are, don't worry. It's after knock-off.'

'I didn't agree with the investors' initial decision.'

'I know.'

'Steel is too risky, Bill, and was not approved by the Council at first.'

'We know that, too.'

'I'm sorry, Bill, but I still can't get used to what happened. I had to recommend Leary's but I knew he wouldn't get his steel approved. The idea was then to get *you* in the door.'

'But he bloody did get Council approval.'

'Because he fought and won over the fire brigade.'

Bucknell grunted. 'He's still got to build it with its fancy fire rating and sprinklers. What rot. They won't work. How come the Council caved in? You told me you had aldermen on side to cancel the steel plan.'

Turner sighed. 'They tried. But the Mayor changed his mind and wouldn't listen to them. He wants a good story for the city, and the Imperial Hotel is it. He says he doesn't care if the whole thing's made out of cardboard as long as it stands up.'

'Well, we'll get Leary's another way. Mackay's are on strike, and the only other rivet mob is about to join them.' Bucknell patted his newspaper. 'It's in here. The socialists are into the factories and are stirring shit.'

'Bill, language please.'

'Leary's can't get rivets. No rivets means no steel, and no steel means the job stops.' Bucknell brought his tobacco pouch close and filled his pipe. 'Stupid wombats, to pick a steel design.'

Turner stood up. 'Leary's might get through this, and if they do?'

'If they do,' Bucknell said, 'there's still the fire rating, that'll nail 'em. And then, you're going to need help,' he smiled. 'We'll be here. We can always make sure that *this* time, *I'll* be building it.'

'Make sure? How?'

'Things always happen on building sites, nasty accidents, scaffolding failures.'

William Turner swallowed. 'Bill?'

'Just like I said, accidents happen on sites. I'm seeing an expert on safety in one hour. I'll be very interested in what he has to say.'

Turner nodded and said, 'I'll leave you to it then. Goodbye.'

An hour later, Rory O'Connor, the advocate, sat opposite Bill Bucknell in the builder's office. O'Connor considered Bucknell to be an honest contractor with a fair record. 'Yes, Mr Bucknell, steel's new to tall buildings, but that doesn't make it unsafe.'

'It's new, it's untested and anything that's not familiar to workers causes problems.'

'A fair point.'

'And by problems, Mr O' Connor, I mean accidents. You want to get accidents down, not up. Yeah?'

'I do.'

'So why can't you get Leary's to use brick, force them? Call on the workers you represent to boycott steel as unsafe?'

'You have an axe to grind, Mr Bucknell. Leary is your competitor.'

'The industry wants better safety, not worse. Can you guarantee that steel will have fewer accidents than building in brick?'

'You know I can't,' O'Connor said.

'Then, what are you going to do about it?'

'What I'm not going to do about it, Mr Bucknell, is close my eyes to a potential real hazard.'

Bucknell seemed encouraged. 'You stick to that, Mr O'Connor. You stick to it.'

In his father's office, Brendan stood his ground. 'All right, so there's a strike on at Mackay's. I'll solve this, Father, by seeing them face to face.'

'It's bloody serious, son. It's ten days to Christmas. If we run out of rivets, we stop work and lose money, a lot of it.' It was crucial that he escape the consequences of this strike. He shook his head. 'No, I'm going with you.'

'There are ways Leary's can be protected under the contract because of this strike.'

'I know that. But those are a matter for debate, Brendan, and I want to keep it simple, not get smothered in legal bulldust.'

'We've been over this for half an hour, Father. If you front Mackay's and this isn't resolved, where are we? If I go and have trouble convincing them, I can always come back to you for the final say, then we can have another go.'

'But you don't know how to—'

'What? You think I'll capitulate? Father, really, give me some credit. I've taken on architects and their products, sorted Enmore, got the Imperial Hotel's steel under budget—'

'All right, all right.'

Brendan continued. 'These are rivets, Father, the steel's life-blood.' Brendan glanced at the wall clock. 'It's seven-thirty. I'm due at Mackay's at eight. I have to go.' Brendan put his hat on. 'I won't let you down.'

'You won't, because I'm coming with you. This is my project, son, and we'll hunt in a pack. Come on.'

At five minutes to eight, they mounted the steps of Mackay's, the biggest rivet supplier in Sydney, and John opened the front door. The reception foyer was vacant and they sat down and waited. The wall clock struck the hour. A door opened and a tall man in his thirties emerged and came up to them. 'Good morning, gentlemen. I'm Andrew Mackay.'

'John Leary, Mr Mackay, and this is my son Brendan.'

'Pleased to meet you. Come with me and I'll show you around. Have you been to Marrickville before?'

'No,' John said.

They followed Mackay into the factory, its noise deafening. In fifty thousand square feet, scores of men hovered over machines that punched out hundreds of rivets at a time, the sound ear-splitting. Other workers were pushing sheets of steel around on trolleys. Showers of sparks engulfed some groups as ferrous-filled smoke shrouded men who were concentrating on their work. Overhead, travelling cranes rumbled with loads of steel plates. Along two one-hundred-and-fifty-foot aisles stood wire cages filled with steel coil and bars.

'We're not at full production,' Mackay said with his voice raised, 'and we should be at this time of the year, just before Christmas. This lot's for the military, a government contract.' Mackay opened an office door in the corner of the factory and Brendan followed him inside where a nuggetty, middle-aged man sat reading the newspaper. 'This is Mr Kent,' Mackay said, 'the owner of Mackay's. Mr Kent, this is John Leary and his son Brendan.'

The suited Kent stood up, a tad shorter than Brendan, and shook hands with both men. Kent's hand delivered a tradesman's grip.

'Please sit down, gentlemen,' Mackay said. 'Some tea, Mr Kent?'

Kent resumed his seat. 'No, thank you. I'm due in town at nine to talk to my bank, so let's make this quick.'

'I don't understand,' John said. 'You are the owner of Mackay's?'

'Mr Kent is the major shareholder,' Mackay said, 'with my father holding the smaller share.'

John came straight to the point. 'Your strike is going to hold up the Imperial Hotel and time is money.'

'Your problem is the industry's problem,' Kent said. 'Mackay's workers—'

'I'm not interested in your workers,' John said. 'I want rivets like we ordered.'

Kent eyeballed him. 'I know what you want, Mr Leary.'

'Right. So what are you doing about it?'

'Perhaps,' Mackay said, 'hear what Mr Kent has to say?'

John exhaled. Workers were making rivets fifty feet from where he stood. Why couldn't he get his?

'My workers want more money,' Kent said. 'They want to do that by joining the iron-founders union. Damned cheek and we're not going to pay them more. Bastards are on strike.' He pointed out the glass-front window. 'What you see out there aren't our workers, but contractors employed for just one job. Their wages are paid by the military—higher wages, mark you, than what they'd earn normally.'

'Good,' John said. 'When they've finished, hire them for longer, to make our rivets.'

Kent glanced at Mackay. 'That's what Andrew here says.' John went to speak, but Kent raised his hand. 'But that'll just inflame the mob.' He pointed into the factory. 'Two presses were wrecked before these boys took over.'

'And those workers in there,' Mackay said, 'are producing more rivets in a given time than ours do.'

John was not surprised. 'Who's got your own men organised?'

Kent slapped his thigh. 'Organised, now there's a good word. Yes, they talk as a group and a cove called O'Connor has them beating their chests.'

'I know him,' Brendan said.

'If you do,' John said looking at his son, 'then get hold of him and knock some sense into him.'

Kent slapped his thigh again. 'Good idea.'

'Before the strike,' Brendan asked, 'did Mackay's pay bonuses?'

Mackay looked at Kent. 'No.'

'The workers don't deserve them! They're lucky to have a job.'

'How long can you last without capitulating and bringing them back on higher pay?' Brendan asked.

'Wait up, Brendan,' John said. 'This is Mackay's problem.' He looked at both managers. 'And your solution to *our* problem? When do you start making the rivet's you're contracted for?'

Kent stood up and buttoned his jacket. 'I don't know, Mr Leary. I just don't.'

John stood as well, towering over him. 'That's not an answer. I have a contract with you. You break that and I won't stand for it. I won't lose money because of your incompetence.'

'I'll never give in to the bastards, Leary. Paying them more would just be the beginning. They'd never stop with their demands after that.'

'And your competitors?' Brendan asked.

'The smaller ones are watching what we do,' Mackay said. 'McPherson's are sitting on the fence but their men are grumbling, too.'

'Then I have no option,' John said. 'I'll get McPherson's geed up to give us what we want.' He poked his finger onto Kent's chest. 'Any costs for that, you'll pay for.'

'Don't threaten me, Mr Leary.'

A man tapped at the office window. Mackay looked up, acknowledged the man and left the office, closing the door behind him.

'So, Mr Leary,' Kent said, smiling, 'You want to step into the yard and settle this?'

John was surprised and admired the man's pluck. In a scrap, he'd get a few cuts. John grunted. 'We'd both ruin our suits.'

Mackay came back in. 'O'Connor wants to come in and see us now.'

'Damned cheek of the man,' Kent said.

'Have you met him?' Brendan said. Kent shook his head. 'I think it would be a good idea.'

Kent stood up. 'I'll not see him. I'm liable to hit him. You two meet him with Andrew. I'll see you tomorrow. If we don't solve this wages thing, we'll have to start closing down next week when the military contract's over.' He turned to John and stuck his hand out. 'My fight's not with you, Leary.'

John held onto the firm hand. This man was straight. 'I'll see you later,' John said.

Kent opened the door and left, ignoring the waiting O'Connor's nod to him.

Mackay went out and brought O'Connor into the office. 'Rory O'Connor, meet John Leary. You know Brendan, I believe.'

O'Connor smiled at Brendan. 'Good morning.' He put his hand out to John, who ignored it.

'Right,' Mackay said. 'We have to solve this. Do you have a way?'

'I do,' O'Connor said, 'if you get rid of your scabs.'

John had heard the word before.

'Scabs?' Mackay asked.

O'Connor pointed out the window to the workers. 'Them. They're taking over other men's jobs.'

'I've got no say on that,' Mackay said. 'They're the military's responsibility. You want to take *them* on?'

'Listen, Mr O'Connor,' John said. 'I need rivets and my job's stopped.'

'McPherson's are still supplying,' O'Connor replied.

'At fifty per cent over Mackay's prices,' Brendan said, 'and they'll be on strike soon, too, because of your stirring. Meanwhile we've got a pub to build.'

'My concern,' O'Connor said, 'is with the men who used to work here, not Leary's profit.' He paused. 'What's more, you're building in steel, and that's untested and unsafe.'

John stepped up to the advocate, who stood his ground. 'Don't dish up your socialist garbage to me, mate. Just get those men back here to work.'

'They'll come back,' O'Connor said, 'when they get the pay they deserve.'

John laughed. 'So now you're the judge of a man's worth are you? God spare us.' He turned away and shook his head.

'If we close our site, Rory,' Brendan said, 'all the men will be laid off. You hear me, all of them. Three hundred and fifty.'

'You wouldn't do that, Brendan! You'd be broke.'

John looked at his son, hoping he'd play hard. In a real pinch, they could close the site and claim costs from their insurer.

'If we had to close,' Brendan said, 'our costs would be covered but the men's wages would not. You want them without money ... ten days before Christmas?'

O'Connor put his hands on his hips. 'Not you! I can't believe that.'

'My son's right,' John said. 'It's your call.' John had the stirrings of an idea. It had to do with the workers outside the office and he concentrated as he thought it through.

'Those men on your site will get work somewhere,' O'Connor said. 'It's booming out there.'

A fair point, John thought. O'Connor was right about that for most trades, but not all. There was only one card to play: to call the bluff and then he could get down to a solution. 'You leave me no choice,' he said. 'I'm closing the site. Good day.'

John walked to the office door and opened it. Brendan followed him. This was dangerous but calculated ground.

'Wait,' O'Connor said. They stopped, and turned around. 'I don't want all the men to get hit,' the advocate said. 'We should talk.'

'Very good,' John said and glanced at Mackay. He should speak with him alone first, but he wanted to get this solved quickly. He came back into the office with his son and O'Connor. 'If I could get Mackay's men more money—'

'Mr Leary, I told you we won't pay them more,' Andrew Mackay said. He folded his arms. 'But have your say if you must.'

'Right. If we compensate you for the extra wages, in return Mackay's men would have to produce more rivets for us.'

O'Connor's eyes narrowed. 'How many more, Mr Leary?'

John glanced at Mackay, who sat stony-faced. He said, 'Give us twenty minutes alone *Mr* O'Connor. We might then have something to talk about. Brendan, you seem to know this man. Talk to him.'

O'Connor stood up. 'We'll see you then in twenty minutes. Come on, Brendan.'

Mackay closed the office door and looked at the retreating pair. 'I won't pay more money, Mr Leary, and neither will Mr Kent. You're wasting your time.'

'Mr Mackay, let's talk. There may be a way where you can gain and so will your men.'

'How?'

John grabbed a blank pad on Mackay's desk and brought out a pencil and his glasses from his jacket. 'What if we can get a method of paying your men for as many rivets as they can make? If they make more rivets, they get more money.'

'How much more?'

'I can answer that if I know how much it costs you to make an average rivet.'

Mackay paused, his look suspicious. 'Why would you need that?'

'To work out your unit cost,' John said. 'Then I'd see how that cost would come down if more rivets were made in the same time.'

'That information is confidential.'

John sighed. This was proving difficult, but he had an answer. 'Look, I'm not going to go into the rivet business and I'll sign a confidentially paper if you want. Do you have any other way?'

Mackay glanced out the window then back to John. 'You tell anyone about my costs,' he said, 'especially McPhersons, and we'll blacklist Leary's for ten years.' He grabbed the pad from John. 'All right then, the first cost we've got is ...'

Chapter Ten

RICHARD PAUSED NEAR THE OPEN DOORWAY OF HIS GRANDMOTHER'S bedroom. It was five days before Christmas and he wanted to make peace with her. He went inside, where she sat staring into space. Since October she'd aged at a pace. Her back was bent and her shoulders stooped. She pointed to a pitcher next to her bed and Richard poured her a glass.

She drank and placed the glass down. 'My throat's dry these days,' she said. Her eyes twinkled at him. 'Welcome home. So, you decided to see your elders? I thought you didn't want to see me any more. What's the reason? Money?'

Richard shook his head. Money was the last thing he needed. It was all too easy to give in to his addiction when he had some. 'I want to find out why you don't trust me.'

She looked at him for some time. 'Richard, when it comes to gambling, there is no trust.'

'That's not an answer.'

She squeezed his hand and drew breath. 'It is, boy. When you face the problem, when you realise that you have something you can't solve by ... yourself, then you'll be on the road to recovery.'

He tried to make sense of what she had said. A glimmer of understanding blossomed into full acknowledgement. He was addicted, no ifs or buts. And he had other responsibilities, great and glorious ones. Protecting Victoria and having her trust. 'I promise I'll stay away from the haunts.'

His grandmother looked at him for a long time. 'You mean that?'

'Yes. I've already made that promise to my wife.'

Christine patted his hand again. 'As a start, that's as good a reason as any. You're beginning to recover already, that's good.'

'Who knows, Grandmother? Life goes on, doesn't it? We'll see.'

'It does, my boy, and only you can make the call. Now, be off with you and go to your pretty wife. I want my last Christmas to be peaceful.'

Richard kissed her cheek. 'There'll be many more, dear.'

She said nothing and he left her. On his way home to Glebe, he considered the money accruing and earning interest in the Imperial Beneficial Charitable Trust. That money would stay in its account and earn interest. It was a temptation to dip into it, he knew. If he faltered he could get money to gamble, so he should terminate the trust now, inform St Peters Brick Company and sever all ties. But another way, a way that would strengthen his resolve, would be to let the money continue to build and at the right time he would have great delight in donating the proceeds to an orphanage.

Victoria liked Glebe and its genteel neighbourhood but she missed her harbour view. She was thankful, though, for the jacaranda that shaded their rear garden from the February sun. 'That will be all, thank you, Jane. Go and enjoy your afternoon off.'

Victoria waited till the maid went indoors. 'I have to say, dear, that since September you have been a changed man.'

Richard smiled. 'It's just five months of marriage, Victoria. It's not ten years.'

'But to me, Richard, you are different.'

'How so?'

She took a bite of her second macaroon. 'You are more patient. You speak with civility to the servants and are considerate to others.'

'Really?'

She smiled. 'You know you are.'

'It doesn't seem like I've changed, but maybe I have. I'm still bored with what I do at work, though.'

He was and that's what worried her. Richard was a driven, ambitious man and wanted the top job at Leary's. If he had too much idle time, the cards would claim him back. 'You know you're the best man in construction.'

He placed his teacup down. 'Thank you, but others don't share that sentiment.'

'It's not so much *others*, dear. It's your father. But give him time.'

'I've got to win him over.'

'How?'

'I want him to have the belief in me that you do, dear. He's got to believe that I've given up gambling. Meanwhile I'm doing things to win back his respect.'

She was curious now. 'Like what?'

'I'm making a real effort to be decent to people I work with. Especially Brendan.'

'Good. That's an excellent start. Tell me, how is he doing romantically?'

'Struggling, I think.'

Victoria remembered the Point Piper birthday party. 'Your grandmother's birthday—that was an awful afternoon. And yet Miss Carson seemed a nice girl. She must have felt mortified. I suppose it's over between her and Brendan?'

'I think so. But he'll find another, maybe another as good as you.'

'You're a dear,' she said and touched his hand.

'Gambling is still my challenge.'

'You mean the urge is still strong?'

'It's always with me, like an ache, something I have to live with.'

'Am I helping?' she said.

'You are. You are indeed.'

'I'm glad.' She smiled. 'Tell me, this new Richard who's the collaborator rather than the conqueror: is he getting results?'

He said wryly, 'Not long ago I would've bitten your head off if you'd said that to me.'

'Not now?'

'It's odd. I hate to grovel, so I don't. I just try to take a softer approach, and it's getting surprising results. People at work listen to me. My old aggression frightened them, I think.'

'A strong approach is good, though,' she leaned closer and squeezed his hand again, 'in the right place at the right time. Jane has the afternoon off. We are quite alone and I would welcome a little of the old Richard, if you know what I mean.'

Richard finished his tea. 'I don't know if I can be my old self,' he grinned, 'but I'll try.'

'Good,' she said, then stood up, took his hand and led him inside and upstairs to their bedroom.

Brendan was at the ten o'clock service at St Patrick's, Church Hill. He wanted to find Julie. He scanned the congregation but couldn't see her. Waiting outside after Mass, he had clear view of both exits, but still no sign of her.

It was 7 March 1886, a year since he'd first met her. Not seeing her today had him worried. She might have moved, got married or maybe something dreadful had happened to her. He had set himself six months to either get Julie back or get over her. He had two weeks left of the allotted time. He knew what he *ought* to do: be sensible and stop thinking of her. He had a job to do, a big one, on the Imperial. By concentrating on that and that alone, he would get by.

Terence Slattery placed his half-filled beer down on the bar in the crowded Ship Inn Hotel. 'It'll come in handy, it will, Mr Bucknell,' he said.

Bill Bucknell wasn't worried about treating Slattery. A little extra money given each week to a working man was a good gesture and he could get something in return.

'I'm sure,' Bucknell said. 'You know Terry, you slewed a good load on my last job. There's not a better crane driver in Sydney.'

'You're laying on the blarney, Mr Bucknell.'

'It's true. Now, you must have told me ten times that you'd never work for John Leary again after what he did to you. So how come you are on the Imperial Hotel?'

Slattery's lips firmed. 'Work's work, and the pay's good.'

'But you still don't like John Leary?'

'No! Back then, he sacked me for being drunk on the job.'

Leary probably did the right thing, Bucknell thought— a drunken crane driver could cause accidents. 'A miscarriage of justice, you reckon?'

'Aye.'

'So, if you still hate Leary, you're happy to do what I ask?'

Slattery emptied his glass and wiped his mouth with his sleeve. 'Just a little mischief, that's what you're asking for? Nothing too big that'll make a stink?'

'No. Just slow the bastard down. Any way you can.'

Richard tied up his gig to the Clarence Street kerb post. The cacophony blaring from the site was spooking his horse and he patted its flank. 'Let's see what my half-brother's been up to.' Shielding his face from the sun, he checked the structure of the Imperial Hotel. It was the middle of March, so by now the seventh-floor framing should be up. Sure enough, the steel web of columns and beams now rose above the seventh floor.

So, despite the rivet strike and a few steel problems, the site 'gun', David Sullivan, deserved huge credit for keeping the building on schedule. Since January the progress had been impressive. It all made Richard feel even more restless. He might be Construction Manager, but all he was doing was supervising efficient foremen, and checking orders and planning. The predictable routine was grating on him. He needed a real job!

Walking towards the site sheds, noises swamped him. Hammers clanged on steel, leading hands were yelling orders and gasping steam machines spewed smoke as the workers laboured at mixing concrete, riveting, moving bricks and sawing timber. He felt jealous of Sullivan and wanted his job but these days he wasn't prepared to go about that the wrong way. He had enough dirt on Sullivan to get him sacked from the site with the suspicion of the missing Surry Hills payroll, but he wasn't going to use it. He smiled ironically. It still surprised him, his changed attitude. Would it last?

On the first floor, he opened the door of the site shed and stepped into Sullivan's office. The general foreman wasn't there. 'Where's the boss?' Richard said.

A sweaty Mike Finnegan looked up and said, 'On site, Mr Richard.' The foreman turned to a labourer rummaging in a corner toolbox. 'Ronan, get the boss, will ya?'

'I'll find him,' Richard said to the labourer. 'Keep at it.'

'If he's anywhere,' Finnegan said, 'it'll be the elevator framing on level six.'

Outside, the reflection from the concrete floor dazzled Richard. He squinted, and his nose tweaked at the smell of ironbark, as giant saws ripped rough wooden slabs into finished timbers for the floor joists. A stiff breeze scattered the dust from the saws, and he coughed. It was messy cutting timber on site but there was no other choice. All of Sydney's sawmills were flat out and couldn't supply timber to the Hotel's tight deadlines. So on site it was. He stepped into the steam driven hoist.

'Mr Richard,' the hoist driver said. 'Up to the top?'

'Yes, Sam. A bit different to Moncur Street terraces, yeah?'

'That it is. The height takes some getting used to.'

'Better than labouring?' Richard said, smiling.

'Yes, sir,' the rangy driver replied as the hoist trundled up.

On this site Richard had no say and could only advise—if asked—and that wasn't likely. It was time to see his father, get back his role and make the Imperial Hotel and the other projects even better than they were now.

'I'm thankful to you for the promotion,' Sam said as the hoist stopped. 'Here you are sir: hardware, men's work clothes, nuts, bolts, pipes and sundries.'

Richard grinned. 'Thank you. You could get a job at Farmer's store any time, Sam!' Stepping out, he looked around. It was so hot, his back was wet with perspiration. In the corner of the evolving eighth-floor structure, Brendan was standing on a beam suspended sixteen feet above the seventh floor, balancing with the skill of a twenty-year veteran rigger and with nothing between him and death but eight inches of steel flange. Brendan's face was sunburned and his upper body had bulked up.

Richard spotted Sullivan squatting with another man near the elevator shafts. He cleared his throat and said, 'Got some time?'

'What's up?' Sullivan said, getting up and coming over to him.

'We need to talk,' Richard said. 'Over here ... please.' A section of the floor was completed and they sheltered under its connecting staircase. Richard wiped his face and glanced at the plumbers installing a section of the four-inch cast-iron main that would supply water to the future sprinkler tank on the roof.

Sullivan folded his arms. 'Warm, isn't it?'

'For March, it is. How's it going?'

'Good. It can always turn to shit, though. Just need two days of solid rain to slow us.'

Richard agreed. 'At least you're out of the ground. You're doing a great job.'

'Your father thinks so.'

'He does,' he said and clapped Sullivan on the shoulder, surprising him. 'Now for the winning straight, when progress can be gained and measured. You'll see the massive results from the street and so will our future clients. And father's seen what you've done with Brendan. Father was sceptical at first, but not now.'

'Brendan's got the touch,' Sullivan said with pride.

Richard stepped back to allow a labourer with a filled barrow to pass them. 'Father's got my half-brother as his assistant and—'

'And what's your job going to be, Richard?'

Richard tensed. 'Don't you worry about that.'

'I do. I know you. Now we've got this far, you won't be wanting to sit under a tree and watch us. You want to get back into the action. Yeah?'

Richard feigned indifference. 'Oh, I've got plenty on.'

The general foreman eyeballed him. Richard could tell he didn't believe him. It made him angry. 'Don't worry about my role, Dave. Just make sure you do your job well here.'

Sullivan's eyes narrowed. 'You think you have the stripes to order me around?'

A rigger near them swung a lump hammer, easing a bolt fixed in the slab to align it with its column plate.

Richard changed tack. 'Dave, Father put you in charge because you're the best. I didn't agree with him, but that's that. You've done well and you've picked and trained a winning team. That shows skill.'

Sullivan unfolded his arms and was quiet for a time. 'Coming from you,' he said, 'that's a compliment.'

'I mean it.'

'Good,' Sullivan said. 'I can rest easy, then.'

'How are Jackson and Smith going on the steel?'

Sullivan reached for a water bag. 'Want some?' Richard shook his head and waited till the man had slaked his thirst. 'They're getting better, and using their heads more.' Sullivan pointed the water bag to the steelwork. 'And Brendan's been a power of help. There's plenty for him to do here, till this lot's done.'

'Yeah, and of course I'd prefer to keep him here full-time: he'd learn a lot more. But he can't do that—he has to spend at least one day a week with our father. In the meantime you must get those foremen better trained at their jobs.'

'Thanks, Richard ... I'll think about it.'

Richard was about to chip him and stopped himself. Sullivan was right: Richard had no authority and could not order anyone on this site to do his bidding. Frustration built in him and he changed tack. 'Dave, just get Brendan up to par so Father can really use him. Fair enough?'

'He's coming right behind you. You can advise him yourself. I've got to get back to the elevators.'

Richard turned. 'Good day,' He said to Brendan. 'How's it going? Looks like you're in front.'

'I'm trying to be, but there are always challenges.' Brendan suddenly looked up. 'Here, step back.'

Richard hesitated and Brendan gripped him hard and moved him aside as a load of steel beams descended onto the floor nearby. A dogman unscrewed the shackles, freed the slings and blasted his whistle twice. The crane rope danced free of its load and soared into the sunshine.

Richard looked up, his hand shading his eyes. 'That's not a Bolton crane,' he said.

'No, but the Dunstans are just as good, and they're cheaper.'

'Brendan, nothing's as good as a Bolton crane: their joints are galvanised, the sheaves are high tensile steel, they have—'

'Just like the Dunstans, Richard.'

Richard wanted to argue and stopped—Brendan would have done his homework. And Richard had no say here. It was frustrating, like dealing with Sullivan. 'All right. This is your watch, after all.'

'Well, Dave's and mine.'

'Good. Now, you're busy, so I won't keep you from your work.'

Brendan gave him a puzzled look. 'I've got some time. It's smoko soon.'

It was early days in Richard's attempt to be amicable to his half-brother, and the right words still eluded him. But for a second he recalled Victoria and his promise to be amenable. His tongue loosened. 'How's it really going? Are you finding it a bit tough?'

'What?' Brendan waved to the frenetic activity around them. 'This? The steel?'

'This thing's new to all of us, Brendan. It's big and it's brutal.'

'It is, but in the end it boils down to materials and men. It's a matter of organisation, structure and direction. Look, the steelwork gets easier after the complications of the ground floor with its ball-rooms, shops and coffee rooms. Once we managed the first-floor steelwork we knew exactly what to do for the rest of the tower.'

'I understand.'

'It's become easier with each floor. We found and solved all the problems early on, especially the fire rating. We've done well with the brickwork enclosing the steel columns, and easier construction means faster time.'

Looking around, Richard could see that Brendan was right. There was nothing out of place and Sullivan had succeeded, with Brendan's help. It seemed Brendan had the talent to take on a big challenge like this and make it his own. Richard was impressed. 'Nonetheless, I'm thinking how all this must affect you. Don't you find yourself worrying about it?'

Brendan frowned at him. 'That's a strangely considerate question, coming from you!'

'I'm not getting soft, brother. I'm just interested.'

'What, in me?'

Richard gave up. 'Look, if you don't want to talk, that's all right. I'll go.' He made to leave.

'No,' Brendan said. 'Stay, it's just … I didn't expect you to … be like this. Nothing happened in London to addle your brain, did it?'

Richard smiled despite himself. 'No.' No need to tell Brendan about that horrible suicide he'd witnessed and how that incident had galvanised his commitment to Victoria and their relationship, a bond that was getting better each day. 'Do you need help here? Is Sullivan looking after you?'

'I can always use help. Are you offering?'

'I am.'

Brendan's eyes narrowed. 'Why, Richard? The only help you offered over this hotel was to bash me.'

His half-brother was right again. Brendan was suspicious, and gaining his confidence was going to take some time. Richard didn't blame him for that—he respected him. Brendan was growing up. 'I'd like to help. I know that's hard to swallow, but I would. Look after yourself. I'm going down to have a look at these fancy sprinklers.' He paused. 'Victoria and I look forward to spending Easter with you. The Connaires are coming.'

'Oh.'

'Come on, Brendan, Anne likes you and she's not going to drag you off to the altar on sight!'

'I'll be there,' Brendan said.

'Good.' Richard walked away and across the floor slab. As he descended the stairs he glanced back. Brendan was still looking at him. He walked on, feeling lighter. It was a pleasant feeling, something new and he didn't know why, but he gave in to it. Next stop, Annandale and his father, to test out the old man's attitude.

Richard poked his head into his father's office. 'Have you got some time?'

John looked at his wall clock and waved him in. 'Yes ... some.'

Richard sat down opposite him. 'I've just seen the Imperial. It's racing ahead. Sullivan has it humming and Brendan is pulling his weight.'

'Indeed. It's early days, but encouraging,' John said. He removed his glasses and rubbed the bridge of his nose. 'I hear you're doing audits on all our sites?'

'Yes. They have to be done, along with my work on the George Street job. I could be doing a lot more with my time. Now that I'm back, the more I have on my plate the better.'

'You mean you're not satisfied with what you're doing at the moment?'

'No, Father.'

John leaned forward. He wanted his son to feel the heat. 'Well, you know why I haven't given you any more responsibility lately.'

'I do and I've been thinking about your reasons, while I was on my honeymoon and since I've got back.'

John remained silent. He was a stickler for straight talking. He wanted Richard to name the big reason.

'I've been thinking about my gambling.'

'Go on.'

'I've decided Victoria is too precious to hurt.'

John said, 'Let's keep the women out of this. This is about you.'

Richard said firmly, 'It is, to be sure, but Victoria's a part of me now, Father. What I do affects her.'

John thought of Catherine and how he'd nearly lost her. Yes, the women were important. 'So, you're saying you now value another person over yourself?'

'Victoria is worth two of me. We will have children and my responsibility extends to them.'

John almost smiled; Richard seemed genuine. 'Go on.'

Richard exhaled. 'Everyone seems to think I have a problem with cards.'

'But you don't?'

Richard looked down at his hands. John sensed that Richard still wasn't acknowledging his addiction. However, it seemed that his son was prepared to fight it for his wife's sake. Richard looked at him across the desk. 'I'm trying Father. I am.'

John was pensive. 'So, you don't recognise your problem but you say you're making an effort to avoid your gaming. Why, when I've heard it all before, should I believe you now?'

Richard spread his hands. 'I wasn't married before. I didn't feel this way before. I've got a reason to try to give it up.'

Was his son being straight? Richard was a good manipulator. Was he doing that now?

Richard stood up. 'All I can say is that I'll try, and I think I can be more useful with a more challenging job. I'm asking for that chance.'

John shook his head. 'I don't know. I have to start again to trust you. I don't know if I can.'

Richard paused, then put on his hat. 'I'm just asking you to keep an open mind. Good day.'

On Easter Sunday, John Leary had chosen that the family should come to Mass at St Patrick's, Church Hill, rather than their familiar St Mary's. Brendan always found Easter Sunday's a moving service—majestic, mysterious and enduring.

Since achieving solid progress on the Imperial Hotel, he had been thinking about his future. He could be the leader of Leary's, the person who would direct all Leary's business for as long as he was able. That sounded straightforward enough and Brendan knew he could do it. His stint at Enmore and managing the steel on the Imperial Hotel fuelled that confidence. But there was still Richard to contend with. Richard expected to be the next head of the company, despite his setbacks. And then there was the Commercial Bank, which was waiting on Brendan's answer. They had agreed to keep the job offer open for him for twelve months, but that would expire this July.

Looking along the pew, he could see Richard smiling at Victoria, a smile of real warmth. His half-brother had changed for the better since his marriage, and Brendan hoped it would be for good. Richard was expert in his job and tough in business, traits Brendan admired. But Richard was still not in the fold and Brendan wondered how he was coping. Five weeks ago, on site,

Richard had seemed intent on offering his help for no reward. That was a dramatic change from the man who'd fought him, and he sensed Richard was trying to be closer to him. Brendan hoped this was true. He'd talk to him further.

Of the two of them, Richard was ideal to run construction and was well suited to his role. Brendan admitted to himself that it would be a few years before he could master the building skills his half-brother had acquired. Meanwhile, Brendan could perhaps concentrate on the business of winning new work. But in the end he wanted the top job—and Richard did, too. It was a race between the two of them. Brendan smiled. He told himself that if Richard won, that was all right. He could work with him and make Leary's great.

The priest's voice brought his attention back to the present. The family had been invited to Richard and Victoria's place in Glebe for an Easter Sunday lunch. Anne Connaire would be there in the afternoon and he would be polite with her and try to deepen the friendship. His self-imposed six-month period without seeing Julie had expired and it was time to try and move on. But it wasn't easy; Julie was still in his thoughts.

He stood up for the communion, the incense still pervading, when he saw Julie. She was walking down the aisle, with her back to him. All thoughts of Anne, Richard and Leary's evaporated as she made her way towards the altar in a fetching royal-blue bonnet and matching dress.

After the priest completed the final blessing, Brendan went out first. He slipped around the corner of the church and waited for Julie to come out. She would pass him here, he hoped. Richard and his father followed and stood in the sunshine while Victoria, his mother and sisters made their way to the carriage.

Julie was now near to him. 'Hello,' he said.

She was surprised. 'Hello ... Brendan.'

She continued on her way and he followed her. 'Please, I want to talk to you. It's been a long time.'

'I told you not to see me.'

He was at her side and kept up with her brisk pace. 'I didn't seek you out. I'm at Mass, for goodness sake!' She said nothing. 'I tried to stay away from you and it was hell. Seven months. That's how long it's been and I've missed you.'

'Brendan, please, leave me be.'

They were in Princes Street and Julie stopped. She glanced ahead and waved. Brendan looked and he saw a solidly-built man about his own age waiting outside Julie's front gate. It was Aiden.

She turned to him. 'Don't come any further, please. That's Aiden and I'm seeing more of him.' She paused. 'We have an understanding.'

Brendan felt a hollowness. 'Are you going to marry him? Are you engaged?'

She forced a smile. 'He's asked me.'

'And?' Brendan noticed Aiden walking towards them.

'Goodbye, Brendan,' she said and walked towards the boiler-maker. Brendan stood watching her go. He had never felt so bereft.

Meanwhile, outside the Church, John was talking to Richard. 'I've told the women to go ahead without us. We'll go to George Street and get a cab to Glebe.' They walked down Charlotte Place and skirted a broken bit of pavement filled with water from an early-morning shower. 'You'll be an old man before they finish the macadam on these city roads!'

'I will. And the timber paving blocks they've used as a base course are starting to fail as well. It's disgusting in summer and the dust is unbearable.'

'Writing to the Council does no good either. I'm sick of complaining about it. That and the sewage stink.' *Enough small talk.* 'I've been thinking about what you said.'

'And?'

'This isn't easy for me, Richard. I've changed my mind a half dozen times these past weeks.' He paused. 'But the company needs you. The Imperial Hotel's getting complicated now and the sprinkler work has its challenges. We can use every pair of hands.'

John stopped and gripped Richard's elbow. 'That's why I need you there—for your expertise. And don't get me wrong: if we didn't have this big pub, you'd still be on the outer.' John released his grip and started walking again.

'So where does that leave me?!'

'I want your knowledge and experience on that job. Sullivan will still be in charge and you'll report to him.'

Richard shook his head. 'I'll have no say about anything, then.'

They arrived at George Street and walked to the cab stop. 'You *will* have a say,' John said. 'I'm giving you a chance, just one more. Let me down again ... and you'll pay. Clear?'

'So I'm to work for Sullivan and impart my knowledge, without any authority. And how long will that last?'

John put his boot onto the step of the front cab and looked at him. 'It will last as long as I want it to. Now, do you want the job or not? The Imperial Hotel needs you, but if your self-love is bruised because you're not in charge, you can work in the plant yard for all I bloody care.' He got on and sat down looking ahead. 'Your answer?'

Richard got in and sat beside his father. 'I'll do it.'

'St John's Road, Glebe, driver. Now,' John said, 'our next project meeting's on the tenth of May. On the way, tell me what you would do on site to make it better.'

John stepped from the goods and passenger hoist onto the Imperial Hotel's seventh floor. The site meeting would start in ten minutes and he had some time to look around. The view astounded him, a full perimeter vista from Surry Hills to Annandale through to Cockle Bay, Dawes Point and the Domain. It was a perfect May day, crisp and clean, and he imagined how much more he'd eventually be able to see from nine floors higher.

He looked around. All the trades were here and space was scarce. It was only seven-thirty but activity filled the floor, with bricklayers and labourers laying and mixing, riggers awaiting their steel loads and carpenters fitting door and window frames. Bricks were stacked in neat piles. He thought about the notes in his pocket. They were Richard's recommendations and they were sound: better planning schedules and tighter inventory controls were the ones that stood out.

The steel frame was definitely the go. But, even with the steel, the brick quantities were significant.

Mounted on temporary platforms, one floor higher than the floor being worked on, stood two stiff-legged derrick cranes, on opposite corners of the floor. Each crane comprised a round base made up of linked beams, in the centre of which was a tower, held rigid by guy ropes and struts to the linked-beam base. The tower supported a jib that could turn and be raised or lowered. A driver in a cabin adjacent to the tower controlled the hoist wire ropes that threaded from an engine up through the tower and, along the jib, then through pulleys at the jib's point. At the end of the wire ropes there was a hook. The sling, attached to the hook, lowered the load to the crew waiting to fix it. As each floor was completed, one crane would be disassembled and its parts moved to a higher point by the other crane, to build the next level. That crane would then be reassembled and then it would lift the parts of the second disassembled crane to the new level and so the process would continue.

A shadow swept over John's feet as one of the two cranes slewed a load of timber and corrugated iron to John's side, its sling taut to bursting under the weight. The second crane slung the last of the steel beams the riggers would connect to the columns to complete the eighth-floor framework. Gas fitters were laying the vertical mains for the room heating alongside the electrical wiring for the new-fangled lights—a first for the city. John admired the work.

A sub-foreman came up to him. 'Mr Leary, the meeting's about to start. Mr Richard told me to get you.'

John wished he could have stayed longer to watch the lights being installed. 'I'm coming.'

The sub-foreman and John walked to the hoist and waited. The cage rumbled up, the gate opened and Sam the hoist driver touched his hat to John as the two men got in. As the cage descended, John saw that men were fixing the external stone flutes onto the brick walls. On the inside, bricklayers were building up the internal walls, the smell of drying mortar lingering in the hoist. Plumbers competed with plasterers and carpenters in the tight space to build their parts of the massive job. Men worked on these levels like bears in caves, labouring in semi-darkness.

The hoist stopped and John made his way to the second-floor meeting rooms. Richard would be there: he was on the Imperial Hotel as an observer, with some design coordination duties. John wondered how successful his son had been in coaxing the others to get them to agree with the recommendations John carried in his pocket.

A hum greeted him as he opened the door and heads looked up. Dave Sullivan glanced at him, Richard was talking to the steelwork foremen, and Brendan was writing notes.

'Right,' Sullivan said. 'Let's start. Jones will take notes.'

John sat in the corner of the room. He wouldn't interfere. If he needed to, he'd talk to Sullivan separately, outside of the meeting.

The steelwork foremen, Smith and Jackson, were sitting side by side and next to them were Simpkins, the plumber foreman, Barry Carrick, the electrical foreman, and Stevens, the maintenance fitter.

'I've been around the site this morning with Mr Richard,' Sullivan said, 'and we've seen a few things.' Sullivan smiled. 'Some good, like the carpentry for the floors, and some not so good. We'll talk about them now. Steelwork.'

Brendan cleared his throat. 'On program.'

'Whose program, yours or mine?' Sullivan said.

John looked to see Brendan's reaction. The room was silent.

'Both,' Brendan said, and John smiled. A few laughed.

'So,' Sullivan said, 'you'll have level-nine steel up by the end of May, in three weeks' time?'

'If the crane's serviced on Sunday,' Smith said.

Sullivan looked at the maintenance fitter and said, 'Stevens?'

'Yes, Mr Sullivan,' Stevens said. 'Both will need attention.'

'Right,' Sullivan said. 'I want more work out of the cranes. The drivers have to shake a leg and I want more steel up and braced. The brickies and carpenters are waiting for the riggers to finish and that's slowing us down. I want the steel two floors ahead. Clear?'

'The crane drivers,' Brendan said, 'are working double shifts. Any more hours and they'll foul up.'

'Get more out of them in the time they work,' Sullivan said. 'That's your job.'

Brendan said, 'O'Gara, the workers' rep, will stop the cranes if they work more. The drivers have bitched already. Slattery mainly.'

'Is O'Gara one of Rory O'Connor's mad apostles?' Richard asked.

Brendan nodded. 'He is.'

'But he's good at his job,' Smith added.

'If he weren't a good rigger,' Sullivan said, 'I'd sack him. You're sweet with him, Brendan. Keep him busy on other things.'

This O'Gara was a nuisance, John thought. Dave should piss him off. Workers' rep. What a load of rot!

Brendan shook his head. 'If the crane drivers work more, they'll lose concentration, and I won't be responsible if something happens.'

'*I'm* responsible for the Imperial Hotel, Brendan,' Sullivan said. 'Get the cranes working like they should.'

'They should have been Bolton's cranes,' Richard said.

John knew this was a sore point. Brendan had saved money with a different manufacturer by getting Dunstan's cranes and Dave Sullivan had supported him.

'They're just as good,' Sullivan said.

'We'll see, won't we?' Richard replied.

Sullivan checked his notes. 'Brick work is behind. We've talked about that. Services?'

'They're all on schedule,' Simpkins the plumber foreman answered, 'except the sprinkler pipe work.'

'Those Yankee engineers any good?' John asked.

'Not bad,' Simpkins said. 'But the work is taking us longer than we planned. I'll need more plumbers.'

Sullivan said, 'You'll get your plumbers, Anthony. We can't lose time. Brendan, get the costs of those taken care of. Gas?'

'Gas is ahead.'

'What about the lights?'

'Mr Sullivan,' Barry Carrick said, 'we're slow on them. It's all still new to the boys but we'll make up ground.'

'Be sure that you do,' Sullivan said. 'Now, what about design? Have we got detailed joinery drawings from the architect?'

'They're due this afternoon,' Richard said. 'I've got to—'

'They were due two days ago,' Sullivan said. 'What's the hold-up?'

'Turners need to cross check them with the plumbing drawings. They need—'

'Make sure you get them today,' Sullivan said. 'They're late and we've lost a day. You need to kick some heads to get what you want, Richard.'

It was a warranted criticism, John thought. But Richard would not be used to being corrected in front of others, and he was still the Construction Manager for Leary's. However, Richard said, 'Right. I'm onto it.'

'Thank you, Richard,' Sullivan said and his son nodded in reply. John was pleased by how both men had handled that, Sullivan showing his respect and Richard not showing anger. It would increase the team's esteem for both men. John got up and left the room. Things were under control here but he had to know that the fire rating would not lag behind. He'd be at the next meeting to make sure of that. Now, he wanted to get back on top to see the new lights being installed.

'So, Mr Leary, keeping an eye on things?' William Turner

stopped near him, accompanied by a younger man who was juggling rolls of plans.

'It's looking good,' John said.

'So far it is. Your son's a bright one.'

'Brendan? Yes, he is.'

Turner turned to his offsider. 'Go on to our site office. I'll join you shortly.'

Turner waited until his colleague was out of earshot. 'Mr Sullivan's got the job running well, Mr Leary. But Brendan—he's got the ideas.'

'Is that so?' John smiled.

'Absolutely. Keep him close, which I'm sure you are. If he leaves you ...'

John wiped a fly away from his face. 'Why would he do that? He loves the company.'

'I've heard a rumour that a bank is after him to work for them.'

John was surprised. 'A bank?'

'It seems. They want an expert on building.'

John kept his face expressionless but inside he was gobsmacked. 'Not Brendan. He's bolted onto Leary's.'

'And that's how it should be,' Turner said. 'But there can only be one boss. And Richard will be that one day, won't he?'

'Could be, but I've got a good role for Brendan as my second-in-charge.'

'Right,' Turner said, and started walking towards his site office. Then he stopped and turned to face John. 'I can't see Brendan working for Richard or as your second-in-charge. He's too smart. He's shared some ideas with me about building. Some are impractical, like us working for the builder, God forbid, but others are revolutionary. There, I've said it,' Turner said and smiled. 'And about a builder, no less.'

John shrugged as the architect disappeared behind the site hoarding. Brendan working for a bank? No, that was daft. Turner was confusing his son with someone else. The hoist doors jangled open.

'Mr Leary?'

John turned around to face Rory O'Connor. 'Ah.'

The big man stuck his hand out. 'How are you?'

John shook the proffered hand. 'I'm well, Mr O'Connor.' John entered the hoist and turned to the driver. 'Level seven, Sam.'

The hoist gate was about to close when O'Connor jumped in and joined him. John opened his mouth to speak but O'Connor interrupted. 'You're going to have problems with your cranes.'

John didn't respond. He waited for the hoist to reach its destination and hoped his silence would be a hint that he didn't want to talk to the man. Moments ticked by.

'Brendan's clued up,' O'Connor said. 'O'Gara convinced him—'

'O'Gara?'

'A first-class rigger, Mr Leary, but Sullivan isn't listening to either of them.' The hoist stopped and John stepped out. 'And it looks like you won't either.' O'Connor got out of the hoist and stood beside him.

'Look, O'Connor, I don't like your type,' John said, then started walking to where the lights were being fitted.

'My type?' O'Connor said, catching up with him. 'You don't even know me.'

'I've seen what you're doing in the factories and that's enough for me. You're unwanted and a pest.'

'But a necessary one.'

'What do you mean?' John said.

'Wait, Mr Leary, please, just a moment of your time.'

John glanced at the electrical fitters. 'You've got two minutes.'

'Leary's is better than most construction companies,' O'Connor said. 'It recognises the value of the labour put into a job. You pay the men well and Brendan has started a safety course.'

John was aware of that. 'Go on.'

'But the rest of the industry isn't coming up to par and that's why I need your help. I want to use Leary's as a guide on how to improve things across the building trade.'

278

This sounded sensible but John was still guarded. The man had a political motive and Leary's would not be the beneficiary of his actions, he was certain. 'If it doesn't cost me money and time, then I'll consider what you have to say.'

'While work on this site continues, Mr Leary, I beg you to consider that all life isn't measured in money. In practice, people's well-being is more important.'

'Is that all?'

O'Connor held out his hand. 'I can be a help to Leary's as well as a pest.'

John admired the man's demeanour and felt his own hand gripped with strength. 'Just keep out of my hair, Mr O'Connor, and keep your workers on this project moving. Understand?'

'I understand, and you'll be the first to know if there's going to be trouble. And watch those crane drivers, they're overworked.'

Richard wasn't concentrating when out of habit he took his old route home on horseback from the George Street office. During the last eight months, on purpose, he'd given the gambling dens a wide berth and he was starting to live with being able to avoid cards. The first month had been the worst, but then it had got a little easier. However, now, in the middle of May, he found himself outside an old haunt in Day Street. Damn, the urge was still there, as strong as ever. The dark entranceway seemed to expand, approach and absorb him. Richard closed his eyes and clenched the reins in his hand, the leather edges biting into him. *No.* His boots jabbed and his horse cantered on, taking a detour down Clarence Street and away from the need to play.

His breathing returned to normal and he kicked the horse harder and made for home.

Chapter Eleven

BRENDAN KNOCKED ON THE FRONT DOOR OF THE CONNAIRES' HOUSE and waited. It opened and Sean greeted him. 'Come in, Brendan, and out of this July wind. Anne is nearly ready.' They went into the parlour and sat down. 'You're off to see a play, Anne tells me. *Sleeping Beauty* is it? At the theatre?'

'That's right,' Brendan said.

'It's courting you are, lad?'

Brendan was surprised. This was just the third time since Easter that he'd seen Anne. 'We're good friends, Sean.'

'Would you like it to be more?'

Sean's wife, Vonnie, entered the room. 'Hush, Sean. That's a leading question to ask the man.' She smiled at Brendan. 'How are you?'

'Very well, thank you, Mrs Connaire.'

'Anne won't be long.'

Anne entered. 'Here I am. Hello, Brendan.' She glanced at the clock. 'We must go. We don't want to be late.'

'Goodbye, Mrs Connaire, Sean,' Brendan said.

Outside, Anne pulled her bonnet straps tight as they walked up Forbes Street. 'It's extra chilly tonight.'

'It is.'

'How's work?'

'Busy, Anne, but I like it.' Work reminded him of the letter he'd received the previous day. The bank had told him that their offer of a job had now closed but they would be interested in talking to him in the future if he wanted to work for them. It was flattering to know he still had an option, if Richard got the top job any time soon.

'Is working for Mr Sullivan easier than working for Richard?' she asked.

They stopped at William Street and Brendan hailed a cab. 'Hard to compare. I report to Sullivan, but I don't report to Richard. He's on site to give advice.'

The cab stopped and they got on. 'Theatre Royal, thanks, driver,' Brendan said.

'I'm looking forward to the play,' Anne said. 'I can't wait for Her Majesty's Theatre to open next year. They say it will be grand.'

'Aye,' Brendan said, looking out into William Street as their cab went up the hill to College Street. In the streets there were couples, families, people just like himself and Anne, going somewhere on a Saturday night. 'I enjoy your company, Anne.'

'And I enjoy yours,' she said and smiled.

He did like being with her. They both liked theatre and books and even had similar tastes in authors. Their first outing had been to the art gallery and they had enjoyed that. Yes, he did like her. He looked at her and smiled. Could he kiss her? Did he want to? Yes, he could, but didn't have an urge to do so. Maybe that was how love developed, from friendship.

The cab continued down Park Street, crossed Elizabeth and turned right into Castlereagh Street.

'I have a twenty-first birthday party to go to next month,' Anne said. 'Would you like to go with me?'

Why not? 'Yes, I would. Thank you.'

'Good.'

They passed by a seamstress's shop, where there was a sale on. The shop reminded him of Julie and he felt sad again. She was still on his mind. He didn't have to think about whether he felt like kissing Julie! But that was a fantasy.

'Here we are,' Anne said as the cab stopped at the theatre.

Brendan helped her down and she took his arm. Yes, Anne might not be Julie but she was intelligent, warm and affectionate. He still didn't have an urge to kiss her, though.

The Imperial Hotel's site meeting room was tightly packed.

John noticed that Dave Sullivan seemed worried—he was rubbing his shoulder, something he did when he was anxious. Brendan might be in for it, John thought. His son's section was next.

On cue, Dave Sullivan looked at Brendan. 'The steelwork's behind. It's the ninth of August, Brendan, and we should have the twelfth floor up and starting the thirteenth. We're only on eleven.'

'It's the cranes,' Brendan said.

'That I know.'

'I've slowed their output.'

Sullivan looked at him. 'Why?'

'If we keep the drivers at the pace we had them at before, they'll start making mistakes.'

'Well,' Sullivan said. 'Get some of the dogmen trained up to relieve them.'

'Dogmen,' Richard said, 'even well trained, couldn't work with this steel. Brendan's right.'

Sullivan slapped the table. 'Then hire more drivers, Brendan, and spread their hours with the others.'

'I'll try,' Brendan said.

'Do more than that! Make it happen. For two months now those cranes have dawdled. You've serviced them?'

'I have,' replied Stevens, the maintenance fitter.

Sullivan eyeballed him. 'And they're all right? Still going strong?'

'Aye, but they'll seize up again soon.' Feet shuffled and Stevens cleared his throat. 'They need a full check.'

'Not until you're ahead on program,' Sullivan said. '*Then* you can get the cranes fully overhauled.'

'But that means we have to accelerate our work,' Brendan said. 'Putting the cranes under more pressure.'

'I don't care how you do it,' Sullivan said, pointing at him. 'Just get back the lost time. The steel has to move faster. And don't argue with me: I know more about cranes than anyone on this site.'

'Except me,' Richard said with emphasis. 'I trust Stevens's opinion.'

'So,' Sullivan said, 'you're saying the cranes will break down?'

'Not for certain,' Richard replied, 'but the likelihood's there.'

'Will they have enough in them to get to thirteen?'

Brendan glanced at his half-brother.

Richard knew his cranes, John thought. This would be interesting.

'If they were Bolton's, Mr Sullivan,' Richard said, 'they would. But these ones, I'm not sure.'

'The cranes we've got are equal to Bolton's,' Sullivan said. 'Brendan's done the homework.'

'I'd like to check Brendan's paperwork,' Richard said. 'If that's all right?'

A conciliatory gesture, John thought. *This must be hard for Richard. He's used to getting what he wants.*

'I'll back Brendan,' Sullivan said. 'No need for further checking.'

Richard spread his arms in a gesture of capitulation and looked at his half-brother. 'I've tried.'

Sullivan paused, tapping his hand on the table. 'All right, then. When we're ahead of program and up to level thirteen, we'll get those cranes looked at.'

'You're the boss,' Stevens said.

'Simpkins,' Sullivan asked. 'What's the program on the basement?'

'The walls are nearly completed and the equipment's on site.'

'Good. Sprinklers?'

'Just one floor behind, Mr Sullivan, and I'm counting on Brendan getting the steel pushed harder. Got a team of plumbers itching to get stuck in.'

'There, Brendan,' Sullivan said. 'We all need that steel ahead. Anything else?' No one answered. 'Right then, back to it.'

John waited for everyone to go except his sons. Richard stood up to leave.

'Richard,' Brendan said. 'I've got the files on the cranes. You can look at them if you want.'

'Exactly what I wanted to do, too,' John said.

'Tell me,' Richard asked, 'in summary, what do they say?'

'Loads of both crane types are the same, with similar safety margins,' Brendan said. 'The jibs are made of identical steel and the test reports are validated.'

'That sounds encouraging,' John said. 'So there's nothing different that leaps out at you?'

'On balance ... no.'

Richard tapped his half-brother's shoulder. 'Good, then let's see if we can pinch some relief drivers. I know there's a gasometer just being finished in Canterbury and things are quiet in the industry. Maybe there're some experienced drivers coming free.'

'We have to get them, Richard,' John said. 'We have to. Come on, there's work to do.'

'We'll get the drivers,' Richard said. 'Are you still coming to dinner this Saturday night? Victoria's looking forward to it.'

'Can I bring Anne?' Brendan said.

Richard grinned and clasped his shoulder. 'She's expected.'

'Excellent.'

His sons left the office. This was better, John thought. They were getting on. Life was good.

Mary Leary completed the last sentence of her plan, an outline of a lesson, and reviewed it. Just right. She looked at the rows in front of her in the Campbell Street College classroom, an annexe of the Blackfriars School in Broadway. Thank goodness the space was no larger. Their little group would have frozen on this cold August night. Their teacher had given them twenty minutes to finish their work and that time must be about up.

The fifteen students were all women, aged from sixteen to Mary's twenty-two, and they were halfway through their year-long teacher-training course, Mary loved it, glad that she had taken the plunge. While waiting for the others to finish, Mary was sucking a lolly to placate her appetite.

The pencil she held reminded her of work: it was Mr Simpkins's, and she'd borrowed it for tonight. The Imperial Hotel had been busy since May and Brendan and Richard were working well together. The job benefited from that, Mr Simpkins said. It was good that Brendan and Richard were getting on. Maybe they had to, to make things work. Mary thought about Brendan and Anne. Although he'd seen Anne Connaire a few times, Mary knew his heart wasn't in it. And Mary knew what it felt like when you fell for someone that others found totally unsuitable. For Brendan's sake, Mary had had the idea of seeking out that young woman, Julie, whom Mary had liked. McIntyre's, that's where she worked. She would find out for herself what Julie's feelings were for Brendan.

The girl beside Mary put down her pencil and sighed. 'Glad that's over.'

Mary smiled at her. She had only joined their class in the past fortnight and she was attractive, with clear skin, bright eyes and a full figure. Mary had glanced at her a few times; she was sure that she'd met her before. Then it came to her: she was the girl Mary had seen that first night in February, when Henri had taken her to see the Darlinghurst refuge. Mary still felt the shock of visiting a place that looked after women who were destitute, or disowned by their families, unmarried and pregnant. Henri spent her mornings there helping out, and was paid a stipend from the refuge's charitable donations.

Mary closed her eyes. Henri, my Henri, my lover. There— she had said it, if only to herself. At Mass each Sunday her guilt weighed on her. From all her teachings, love between a man and a woman was the only acceptable love. All else was an abomination. And yet, Henri loved her too, cared for her and would do anything for her. Was that so wrong?

'Time's up, ladies,' the teacher said. 'Pass down your papers and I'll mark them.' He stood up. 'I'll see you on Thursday.'

Mary packed up and stood aside to let out the others in her row.

'Excuse me,' the girl next to her said, 'have I seen you before?' She leaned close and whispered, 'At the refuge?'

'I think so. I'm Mary Leary.' The other girl's face froze as if Mary had insulted her. 'Are you all right?' Mary asked.

'I am, thank you. I think I ... need to eat something.'

'Well, there's a place around the corner,' Mary said. 'Have you got time for a cup of tea? Sorry, I don't know your name.'

'It's Gillian Thompson. Yes, there is a place. No, I have to ...' She hesitated. 'All right.'

'Good,' Mary said and smiled. 'Let's go.'

Putting on her coat, Mary opened the door and exclaimed. 'Oh, it's freezing. I can't wait for summer.' They walked quickly and Mary ushered Miss Thompson into a teahouse in Elizabeth Street. They went to a table, where Miss Thompson sat down.

Mary stood near her. 'What'll you have? This place has a range of teas.'

'Just black tea, thanks.'

'Nothing to eat?'

Miss Thompson glanced at the counter where a rock cake stood alone on a plate. 'Looks like all they've got. I'll have that.'

Mary ordered and returned to the table with the teapot and some sugar. The tea was a dark Ceylon, its aroma pleasant. While she waited for her tea to draw she asked Miss Thomson, 'So, how do you like the course? I think it's grand.'

'I like it, too. I worry, though, whether I'm going to be any good. I've really just started and I had to convince the teacher to take me on. I'll finish the course after you, about July next year.'

'You'll be all right,' Mary said and had an idea. 'I'll help you.'

'That's very kind of you, Miss Leary, thank you! The course gives me something to look forward to.'

The waitress brought over the teacups and the rock cake. Miss Thompson said to Mary, 'Would you like to have half?'

'I would, I'm starving,' Mary said. As she watched Miss Thompson cut the rock cake, she leaned forward and said in a quiet voice, 'I hope you don't mind me mentioning this, but did you have a baby at the refuge? Was it a good place? It seemed clean enough to me when I visited.'

'Yes. In February. And yes, the ladies at the refuge were wonderful.'

'Are you recovered? How do you feel?'

Miss Thompson stared at the pieces of rock cake. 'Terrible right after and even now it's hard, as if I've been robbed.'

Mary poured the tea for them both. 'I can't imagine how awful that must be. You had help, am I right? There was another girl there with you.'

'Lucy.'

'That's right. Was she caring?'

Miss Thompson smiled and covered her mouth. 'A marvel, really. We still see each other. She had her child before mine. She knows what it's like.' She drank her tea, her eyes fixed on Mary. She put down her cup. 'I recognise your surname.'

'My father has a building company. It's—'

'Leary's Contracting. I've seen the signs on that big site in Kent Street.'

'Clarence Street,' Mary said. 'I work there now.'

Miss Thompson's eyes expanded. 'What? On site?'

Mary sipped her tea, delicious. 'No, in the office, just a couple of days a week. I'm doing the course on other days.'

Miss Thompson stared at her.

'What's wrong?' Mary said.

'Nothing, it's just a surprise that you're working in a building company. That's very unusual.'

'It's not easy. I tell you, I've learned a few words I've never heard before, and a few about building.'

They both grinned.

'I've met your brother,' Miss Thompson said.

'Brendan or Richard?'

'Richard. We saw each other a few times before he ... he was engaged.' She glanced out through the window.

That's a coincidence, Mary thought. 'He's married now.'

'Any children?'

'No, but I know his wife would like a child.'

Miss Thompson's eyes flashed back at her. 'A baby she could keep?'

Mary could hear bitterness in her voice. 'Yes,' she said gently.

Miss Thompson looked down at her plate again, her eyes glistening. Mary reached out and covered her hand with hers. 'I'm sorry.'

'It's all right. I have to get used to talking about children ... babies. That's part of life. You know, my baby boy went to a good family—country and wealthy at that. That's all I was told. He'd be six months old now.' She finished her cake and opened her purse. Her hand was shaking.

'I'll pay for this,' Mary said. 'You can pay next time.'

Her companion sat silent for a moment. 'Thank you.' She stood up and put out her hand. Mary took it and for some reason, she felt that Miss Thompson wanted to talk some more.

'I'll see you on Thursday, Miss Leary.'

Mary moved aside to let her new friend pass.

There's a small world; fancy Miss Thompson knowing Richard. Mary wondered whether to mention the young woman to Richard.

Then she had a thought. *Goodness, Richard might be the father*. He had had quite a reputation before he was married.

Her companion hadn't mentioned the father of her child, and Mary hadn't expected her to. Maybe she would talk more on Thursday. Tonight she'd sensed the girl's distress about losing her baby. She'd keep an eye out for Miss Thompson; maybe she could help her and put some sunshine into her life.

On the twelfth floor deck of the Imperial Hotel site, Richard knew the man needed a serve. 'Come on Slattery,' he said. 'Stop playing with your gearbox and get cracking.' A few men near Richard laughed.

Terrence Slattery scowled and stuffed a rag into the pocket of his overalls. 'It's the twentieth of September, Mr Richard, and this crane needs servicing. So does the other one.'

'It's eight-thirty,' Dave Sullivan said. 'Just get in your cabin and get that crane working again.'

Slattery did just that and Richard eyed the two beams that were ready for lifting.

'Right,' Sullivan said. 'Let's strike a blow.'

At the same time down on the second floor, John pushed his chair back from the table and warmed himself in the morning sunlight streaming through one of the Imperial's suites. He gathered his scattered meeting papers and looked at the group in front of him. 'We'll take a breather for five minutes.'

Ronan O'Gara, the site workers' representative, stood up. 'Will do, sir.' He and Rory O'Connor left the suite and Brendan got up, stretched himself and stood by the window.

'O'Connor seems straight,' John said. 'I mistrusted the man when I first met him but he's got my attention today.'

'He had you going on the unions, Father.'

'Bloody unions! They'll never take root. They're just a place for bludgers and layabouts.'

'Probably,' Brendan said, 'but like O'Connor said, he has to protect the weak and exploited.'

'Bulldust, Brendan. Have you ever seen a sixteen-stone weak and exploited bricklayer? They don't need a union to be intimidating. But I did agree, you noticed, that there are unscrupulous builders who are taking advantage of some workers. Best ways to handle that is men like O'Connor and the Association working together and weeding out the bastards.'

Brendan resumed his seat. 'We shouldn't be much longer. We just need to conclude the agreement.'

'Load of rot, if you ask me. It's a try-on by O'Connor to get more money from me.'

Brendan glanced at the open doorway and said, 'It might be rot to you, but it costs us little and we agreed to sign it by the twentieth and that's today.'

His son was right. At the last Builders and Contractors Association's meeting, concern had been raised that the organised tactics of the workers were starting to bite. John looked at Brendan. 'Is Richard still up top?'

'Yes, on twelve with Dave.'

'Is he earning his keep?'

'He is. He's different, Father.'

'So I've noticed.'

'I don't know what's behind the way he works now,' Brendan said, 'but he's mellowed.'

'Mellowed?' John smiled. 'Richard's not my age yet! That's when you mellow.'

Brendan smiled with him. 'Maybe, but he's ... working *with* us here, not dictating.'

O'Connor came back in with O'Gara and they sat down. O'Connor began, 'Right. The last thing we have to agree on is the apprentices. At present there's one to every two tradesmen and their mates. We want to make sure enough are employed to keep that rate up.'

'Mr Sullivan is against that,' Brendan said. 'Adds to costs.'

O'Connor tapped the table. 'This is about jobs, not money.'

'Without investment in hotels like this,' Brendan said. 'There'd be few jobs.'

Good point, John thought.

'I agree,' O'Connor said. 'But that doesn't mean you have to—'

John grabbed the table as a shudder vibrated through the suite.

Brendan turned to O'Gara. 'Ronan. Find out what that was.'

John glanced at his son as the rigger left the suite. Brendan met his father's stare. 'That sounded bad, like a collapse,' John said. He looked at Brendan with a concerned look on his face. Like sailors and miners, builders were instinctive and superstitious. Only one thing was certain about that shudder: it wasn't good.

'Right,' Brendan said, 'until O'Gara comes back, what about the apprentices?'

John forced himself to think about the issue. 'What's Dave's complaint on the costs?'

O'Connor's eyes locked onto John's. 'Every two apprentices add a hundred pounds a year to a project cost.'

John did some calculations on a medium-type job, urging himself to concentrate and avoid thinking what was happening above them. 'That doesn't sound like a lot.'

'It isn't,' O'Connor said. 'Nothing compared to the training and job opportunities and the extra hand.'

'I agree,' John said.

'Then it's settled?' Brendan said.

'I'll get Dave Sullivan to sign it off,' John said. 'It'll take some time to—'

O'Gara ran into the room and stopped. His flushed face was perspiring. He stared at Brendan and said in a strangled voice, 'I grabbed a man on level five who's just come down from the top. It's the cranes. One's toppled and has trapped two men. The other's on fire.'

Brendan blinked and paused, just for a second. 'Let's go.' O'Connor pushed past him and he said to John, 'I'll go and check, Father, you stay here.'

'Not bloody likely,' John said. 'I'm coming.'

John merged with the pack of men in the stairway already congested with workers coming up to look at the damage up top. He slowed on the next floor and the mob pushed past him, oblivious to who he was, and he stepped inside and onto the fourth floor. Entering an unfinished room, he got his breath and went to the window, where he leaned on its sill. His heart punched his chest as though it wanted to burst from his rib cage and he struggled to control his breathing.

Muffled shouts penetrated the stairwell and he tried to think. Big accidents on building sites weren't new but *here* it would be a disaster. He opened his eyes and concentrated on the Town Hall extension under construction and the Sydney Central railway station. For some reason he couldn't move from this spot or breathe properly, so he focused on their features: facades, flutes, domes and columns. He tried to replace his shock with logical thoughts. Cranes didn't collapse like that. They'd been overworked. Brendan had been right. It had been Sullivan's decision to push on regardless, and it had been the wrong decision. The Imperial Hotel, the trophy job in town, was blighted.

Dave Sullivan coughed from the smoke. Through the mangled jib and flames of one crane he could see three men. The first, the driver, was lying pale and lifeless. A carpenter near the driver, bare-chested and kneeling in blood, was pressing his own bunched shirt against another man's leg. The man was a rigger, whose artery was pumping like a fountain.

Close to them Richard, stripped to his singlet, was using his shirt to beat out the flames that threatened to engulf the trio. In the opposite corner of the floor, the second crane stood like a beacon, its cabin on fire, flaming oil dripping onto the deck below. A safe distance from that crane, its driver Slattery was sitting and rubbing his head as workers applied a splint to his leg.

Another rigger was running around, his wild eyes focused on nothing. 'Ambulance,' he yelled. 'Where's the bloody ambulance?' He ran into Dave Sullivan and stared at him as if he was a stranger. 'Is there nothing for their pain?'

Sullivan grabbed him and shook him. 'Bring up the first-aid box. Go.' He turned to another group as the rigger raced away. The hose reels. Thank God, they had them charged with water. He pointed to a leading hand and said, 'Get below to level-eleven hose reel. Start the pump, then get up here with a hose and soak everything that's not on fire. The rest of you rig up a bucket brigade to the crane.'

'Look!' Stephen Smith yelled. Burning oil was lapping at the first crane's diesel tank.

'Richard!' Dave yelled. 'Get down!' Richard looked at the burning oil and dived onto the floor slab. The tank exploded and a loud whoosh rushed over his back, its heat searing him. Richard stayed down and grimaced in pain. In the fireball of the crane, the rigger and carpenter were screaming and alight.

Sullivan raced over to Richard, lifted him up and carried him clear. A stockpile of timber stored next to the tank began to crackle and burn.

Brendan and O'Connor arrived on the floor. Brendan ran towards the two screaming men who were trapped, with the dead driver, in the first crane's wreckage. But he had to stop, pushed back by the heat.

A worker threw a bucket of water onto the fire, which did nothing but spread the flame. The cries of the trapped workers ceased. There was just the roar of the fire engulfing the space.

'To the other crane, come on!' O'Connor yelled. He headed a group of workers, sprinting across the twenty-yard space. They upended a bin full of sand just as the flaming diesel was about to engulf the second crane's fuel tank.

Richard yelled over the din, 'We haven't got enough water pressure to put out the fire. But we can use it to isolate what's still burning.'

'We have to do more than that,' Sullivan said. 'We have to.' But he knew it was hopeless. The men carrying the hose from the floor below had arrived and were soaking everything but the flames. The wind changed and the smell of roasting flesh overcame him. Sullivan gagged. Three dead, at least, and all Sydney would know that the Imperial Hotel was on fire. He stood transfixed at the destruction around him.

Brendan shook him. 'Dave? Come on man, help me get Richard away.'

Sullivan helped Brendan pull Richard to the stairway. Brendan stood aside as the firemen arrived with the ambulance crews. Workers jammed into the stairway, O'Gara in front.

'I need five of you to help the brigade,' Sullivan said to him. 'Rig up some scaffolding so we can get up that crane. The rest of you, get more sand from the floor below.'

O'Gara led the first group and started work. Within five minutes, they'd erected a lattice of timbers on the windward side of the first crane, where some steel still burned. While three men braced the framework, fireman clambered up and the rest of the crew set up a sand-bucket brigade.

When that looked to be working, O'Gara herded another group and a scaffold took shape adjacent to the second crane.

From both scaffolds, the firemen hurled bucketfuls of sand and were winning the battle; soon everyone was pitching in and the flames were ebbing.

O'Gara came over to Sullivan and said, 'We'll hold a meeting this afternoon. This'll knock the lads, it will.'

'Have your meeting O'Gara ... but make it short. Get news to the families of those injured.'

O'Gara paused. 'I'll do a roll call. What about the dead?'

'I'll attend to those,' Sullivan said.

Brendan pulled Sullivan out of earshot as O'Gara left. 'If you don't close the site today, you'll have a big problem.'

Nearby, an ambulance man was applying balm to Richard's back.

Richard grimaced but joined the argument. 'Brendan's right, the site closes.'

Sullivan stared at him. 'You don't run this job, Richard.'

Brendan gripped Sullivan's shoulder. 'The site closes, Dave.'

Dave Sullivan took stock. Both cranes were useless. Timber, scaffolding, pipework and bags of cement were either scorched, water damaged or destroyed and he had to concede that no work could be done that day. 'All right. Do it. But it's back to work first thing tomorrow.'

Some wreckage of the first crane still burned and one ambulance man, shielded by a fireman, was peering at the three smouldering, blackened human remains. After a moment, he shook his head, turned and walked away.

The fire captain came over to where they stood. 'Who's in charge here?'

Sullivan tore his eyes away from the three bodies. 'I am.'

The captain took off his brass helmet and wiped his face, smearing further grime and sweat over his eyes. 'We'll be here till all the fire is out. Get that second diesel tank drained just in case. I've got men below making sure there are no embers threatening your neighbours.'

'Brendan,' Sullivan said, 'do what the captain says.' Sullivan pointed to the charred bodies. 'Who were they?'

Brendan said, 'The crane driver, a ... carpenter and a rigger.'

'Names, Brendan! I want their names, for Christ sake.' He shook him by the shoulders. 'They're bloody dead. You hear me! They're dead and we've ... killed them.' Dave Sullivan released Brendan and beat his hand against a steel column, once, twice, then again. He heaved and panted and hung his head.

At last John Leary came onto the twelfth-level deck, sucking deep breaths. He looked at the devastation and faltered. He couldn't believe how long it had taken to drag himself to this level. The fire was still smouldering, its smoke pungent. The ambulance crews were covering the bodies on stretchers. He leaned against the stairwell.

'It's grim, Father,' Brendan said coming up alongside him. 'We've lost three men.'

Three ... John shuddered. *Dear Lord.* 'What happened?'

'Richard's going to be all right.'

'Richard! Is he hurt?'

'Just his back. Some burns and he's on his way to hospital. He'll survive. It's contained, Father.' Brendan called out to Sullivan and he joined them.

John said, 'You saw everything? How did this happen?'

'It was the cranes,' Sullivan said, his voice strained. 'Both were lifting a beam, like we've done plenty of times. The first jib sheared. Then the second crane's jib failed, because it couldn't take the whole load. Sparks, then the fire.'

John moved closer to what was left of the first crane, its heat still strong. 'How come they couldn't lift the beam? Did you overload them?'

Sullivan scratched his head. 'No. There was plenty of margin.'

'One jib failed,' John said, 'then the next?' He was silent for a moment. 'So how? How?'

His son and general foreman just stared at him.

John sat with his sons as their carriage made its way to Randwick. The previous forty-eight hours had passed in a blur. Uniforms, paperwork, interviews and questions, all mixed in a process that seemed endless. 'Have you sent money to the bereaved?'

'One hundred pounds,' Brendan said, 'to each family.'

'It's the least we can do,' John replied. Richard winced as their carriage hit a pot hole. 'Your back, Richard?' John said.

'On the mend, Father, thank you.' He slapped his thigh. 'I'm damned if I know what happened on that deck. But I'm getting some clues.'

'Well, you'd better crack the whip. The Coronial Inquest could be just weeks away.' An inquest … that was the worst. He had fronted Turner and O'Connor, both of whom warned of further and worsening actions, but talking about the death of his men in front of strangers and the law made the incident seem unreal and nightmarish.

'Father, it was my fault,' Brendan said, his chin thrust forward, his lips firm. 'I selected the cranes. I did the checking and yet they failed.'

John forgot his worry and admired his son's forthrightness.

'Brendan,' Richard said. 'This is Leary's problem, a damned big one, but we'll beat this … together.'

John agreed. They all shared this, himself the most. 'Get the facts, Richard. I want those Dunstan's, or what's left of them, examined over every square inch. What are Dunstan's doing about the failure of their cranes?'

'They say we overloaded them,' Richard said.

'That's bulldust, Dave reckons,' Brendan said.

'I know that,' Richard said. 'And we have to prove it and I'm onto it. I need to find the real cause.'

'And Sullivan?' John asked.

'I've got him busy on site. He's cleaned up most of the mess.'

'We're here,' John said looking out.

Their carriage stopped at the entrance to the Sacred Heart Church. The three hearses and their loads were a reminder of the disaster; a reminder as well of the deaths, in the same month and nearly to the day, thirty-one years ago, of another three men on one of his sites. Sean had been that site's general foreman then.

You never get used to it. John flexed his arms and forced the sadness away, to give him strength to endure the service for the next hour or so.

He and his sons walked up to the Connaire family. John's former partner looked like death itself and Anne had a firm hold of his forearm.

'Good morning, Mr Leary,' Anne said. She nodded to Richard and Brendan.

'I wish it were, Anne,' John replied. 'Come, let's make our respects to the widows.'

'We already have,' Sean said. He looked at John. 'They don't want your sympathy. They don't want to talk to you.'

John stiffened. That hurt.

'They only spoke to me,' Sean said, 'because they think I'm not really a boss at heart.' He glanced at the hearses. 'I didn't think I'd ever see more deaths on a Leary's site and yet here we have it.' He looked at John in desperation. 'You'll have to find out the cause this time, my friend. I don't think I'm up for it.'

'I wouldn't ask you to, Sean,' John said. 'Besides Richard's already on to it.'

Brendan scanned the crowd outside the church and saw Julie, who was consoling a middle-aged woman. 'Excuse me, Father,' he said. 'There's someone I have to see.'

'Of course,' John replied.

Brendan went over to the two women.

Julie looked at him. 'Mr Leary, this is Mrs Thackery. She lives near us. Her nephew, Harry Somerfield, was one of those killed.'

Brendan touched his hat before addressing the woman. 'I'm very sorry, Mrs Thackery.'

'Oh,' the woman moaned.

'Come,' Julie said to her. 'Let us go to the others. I know they'd want you with them.'

'Thank you, Julie,' Mrs Thackery said.

Brendan followed at a distance as Julie escorted the grieving woman towards the three widows. The four women, handkerchiefs grasped and heads bent, waited for the coffins to pass them by, then they followed their departed loved ones into the church. Julie waited till Brendan came up to her.

'I knew Harry,' he said. 'He was a good man.'

'He was,' she said and brought a handkerchief to her face.

Just to be beside her again seemed to give Brendan a sense of belonging, of being a whole person, even on this wretched day. It was as if, over this last year, he'd lost a part of himself and had almost grown used to not being complete. Now he'd found that part again.

'I'm sorry for you, too, Mr Leary,' Julie said. 'I know how much you love your job and Leary's. It must be hurting you.' She reached out and touched him. He looked at her left hand. There was no ring on her finger.

'Thank you,' he said. 'Shall we go inside?'

'Yes.' Julie took his proffered arm as if she'd been doing it all year. Brendan's guilt over the deaths was eased a little and he knew the reason. He would not see Anne Connaire again. Julie was the woman he loved and he was going to get her back.

Bill Bucknell glanced around the bar in the Ship Inn Hotel. It was nearly closing time. There were only three other drinkers there. 'You're a damned idiot, Terry.'

'Keep your voice down, Mr Bucknell,' Slattery replied.

'What were you thinking, man?'

'It wasn't me, Mr Bucknell. It wasn't.'

'It had to be!'

'I didn't get the chance. Every time I thought of doing some damage round the site, young Leary would come by and I couldn't do anything without him seeing.'

Bill Bucknell stared at the crane driver. 'Are you sure? Someone else caused the accident and the fire?'

'As I am about the plaster on my leg.'

'How is it?' Bill looked down at it.

'It'll heal.'

'Then, if it wasn't you,' Bucknell said, 'who did the damage? How did it happen?'

Slattery scratched his head. 'That's what's got me foxed. I'll get the blame, but.'

'Why?'

'I'm the driver, well the senior one, any road. I was on the crane that failed first. Tim Stevens, the fitter, won't cop it. No, it'll be me.'

'What will you do?'

'I'll lie. I'll say Richard Leary overloaded the cranes.'

'Did he?'

Slattery gripped Bucknell's wrist, pressing hard. 'He did. I'm sure of that. That's what I'm going to say in court and that's what I said to the police after the funeral yesterday.'

Mary Leary got off the tram at Broadway and walked up Newtown Road, glad that she'd been able to leave the office early. It was just before four. She had checked the newspaper advertisement for McIntyre's again in her bag. Yes, they closed at four and she stopped and waited outside their factory.

Julie Carson came out. She was as good looking in her simple work clothes as she had been dressed for Mary's grandmother's birthday party.

Julie stopped in front of her with a questioning look in her eye. 'Miss Leary. Mary Leary?'

'Good afternoon, Miss Carson.'

'What brings you out here?'

Mary decided to be up front. 'I came to see you.'

'Oh. Did Brendan ask you to come?'

'No.'

'I'm on my way home.'

'I'll come with you,' Mary said.

'Then let's go.'

Agatha had told Mary that Julie was linked with another man. She needed to find this out first, because if she was, Brendan would be heartbroken. 'Brendan told me he saw you at the funeral.'

'It was a terrible day, Miss Leary. It was just a week ago and I still feel low about it.'

'I know. Brendan's taking it hard. He's sensitive to our workers and their plight.'

They stopped at the corner and crossed Parramatta Road.

'What did you want to see me about?' Julie asked.

'I'd like us to be friends.'

'Just like that?' Julie said. 'I'm a working girl, Miss Leary.'

'Please call me, Mary. So am I.'

'But your family is wealthy.'

'We are,' Mary conceded, 'but we come from humble stock.' She paused. 'I know Brendan likes you—no, more than that—and I want to get to know you.'

Their tram arrived and they got on board and found a vacant double seat.

'Miss Leary ... Mary, your brother's a good man and—'

'Do you love him?'

Julie's eyes expanded. 'You're very forward, aren't you?'

Mary persisted. 'Do you?' she said.

'Mary, like I said to Brendan, we're different, too different to have a life together.'

'Would you try?'

'Try?' Julie said with a puzzled look on her face.

'Yes,' Mary said. 'If you love him and he loves you, would you try to make things work?'

Julie said nothing for a while. 'Aiden has asked me to marry him. I may not marry him but I will marry a man like him.'

'But you love Brendan?'

'I didn't say that,' Julie said with force.

'I think you do and he loves you.'

'He said that?' Julie's voice was soft.

'Julie, I know my brother. He's gone.'

Julie's eyes started to glisten and she looked away. 'The foolish boy.'

'He really loves you.'

Julie looked back at her. 'I didn't ask for this, Mary. I didn't! I didn't trap him. We ain't even kissed yet. I don't—'

'It's all right. It's all right. I know you're not conniving ... Brendan said you broke up with him. You could have been devious and snared him but you didn't. I respect that and that's why I want to get to know you, to be your friend. If you'll have me.'

Julie kept quiet till Central Station. 'All right,' she said. 'I'd like that, but Brendan mustn't know. If he wants to be with me, to try and make this work, he's got to make the move.'

Mary smiled. 'I think you're right. But you might have to help him a little. Men are such simple souls.'

'Men like Brendan are,' Julie said, smiling 'Well then, before you get off, tell me about your work. I want to know.'

'We have to beat this, Richard,' John said. 'If we don't, we'll go bankrupt.' He looked at his two sons and Dave Sullivan sitting in front of him in his Annandale office. 'It's the fourth of October and we've been closed down for two weeks and stuck on the twelfth floor. If you get this report finished, with the results you're expecting, back to the Coroner next week, he should let us open for business. How certain are you about those results?'

'Not certain, Father, but pretty convinced.'

'The Coroner will want to know why the cranes broke down,' John said. 'Have you found out anything?'

'Tell me, Richard,' Sullivan said. He had lost weight, his face was gaunt. 'Please, if you know something, anything.'

Guilt must be killing the man, John thought.

'Dave,' Richard replied, 'like I told you three days ago, I've got an independent report that either the jib steel or the sheave blocks *may* have been faulty, but I don't know for sure. Don't worry, I'll tell you when it's definite.'

Dave rubbed his shoulder. 'You think the cranes could be faulty? *Both* of them?'

The man had a point, John thought. It was odd that both cranes had failed.

'I'm still waiting on the findings,' Richard said. 'And forget about Dunstan's. I wouldn't wrap garbage in their preliminary report. Their conclusion was that we overloaded their cranes. What rot.'

'We'll sue them,' John said.

'We will, but that'll take months. No, we have to nail them with facts.'

'I should never have used them,' Sullivan said.

The office was silent for a time. 'The inquest's just the first hurdle,' John said. 'We've got the architects threatening to cancel our contract'—he tapped a letter on his desk—'and we've got insurers who are walking away, saying we've been negligent.'

'I know, I know, Father,' Richard said.

'Here's their letter,' Brendan said pulling it out from a folder on his lap. 'The insurance company isn't interested in settling the fire-claim damage, as we neglected to service our cranes properly. I'm looking into that.'

'Don't just look into it,' John pointed a finger at Brendan. 'Solve it.'

'I will, Father. We'll get out of this.'

John wasn't so sure. A coronial inquest was serious. They had to have every risk and outcome quarantined. He looked at Sullivan and said, 'What's the report on the structure?'

Dave jerked as if awoken from a dream. The man was still skittish and who could blame him. 'Below the level-twelve deck, the building is sound. Brunels have given it the all clear.'

'That's something,' Brendan said. 'The architects will want a copy of that report. Send it to me and I'll get it to them.'

Richard stood up. 'We will make up the time lost.'

John pursed his lips. 'And the cost?'

'We'll make that up too, Father.'

John picked up a letter on his desk. 'This is a notice from Turners to show cause. Reply to it, Richard, under the contract—'

'I can do that, Father,' Brendan said.

'I want you concentrating on the job, Brendan,' John said. 'I want your program back to me this afternoon on how we are going to make up time. We still have four floors to build. Off you go.'

Brendan stood up. 'I'll do everything I can to repair this mess.'

Richard smiled encouragingly. 'Go on. Get busy and start thinking about smart ways to get us out of this. You're good at that.'

For the first time since the accident, Brendan smiled, just a little. 'I'm off.'

'Get back to town, Dave,' Richard said. 'And don't dwell on this. Just keep active.'

Dave stood up. 'I'll try.'

'Good advice, Richard,' John said after Sullivan had exited the room. 'And with his wife ill ... is she still the same?'

'No change in her condition, Father. Still comatose.'

'Poor bastard. Now, why are you so convinced about the cranes?' John looked out the window. 'This is Sullivan's fault. It was his insistence that those cranes work beyond their service recommendation.'

'It was, but the evidence wasn't obvious.'

John looked back at him. 'So what does your gut tell you about the cranes?'

'I wanted to act right after the fire but the cranes were still too hot. Dunstan's were happy about that—no evidence. So I got onto Bolton's.'

'Why?' John said.

'They've kept in contact with me. They were keen to get the

Imperial's crane contract. But I didn't get the Imperial Hotel, Sullivan did.' John shrugged his shoulders. Now wasn't the time to do a witch-hunt on that. 'And Sullivan used Dunstan's for the stiff-leg derricks on the tower.'

'On Brendan's advice,' John said.

Richard winced. 'Which I checked. All cranes have a safety factor built in to them. Ropes, pulleys and frames are all tested beyond their specifications.'

'I guess they have to be.'

'They do, Father. Bolton's agreed to strip down all the parts and test them for us.'

'Did any survive the fire? They must have been damaged, surely?'

'That's what I thought, too. But Bolton's tell me that cranes are resilient. I'm confident that those two cranes could have handled the duty we expected of them, despite the whingeing of the site crew, Brendan included. Therefore only two things could have caused that fire—shoddy fittings or sabotage.'

'Sabotage?' John was surprised. 'Is that likely?'

'Remember Bucknells' angst when we won?'

John's eyes narrowed. 'Go on.'

'Bucknells or Branagans might have arranged to fiddle with the cranes during their assembly—after all the Imperial Hotel was *the* project in town—but I don't think so. I'd put money on the problem being shoddy fittings: the sheave blocks and jib sections. According to Bolton's, those are the parts where Dunstan's might have chosen to cut corners in their manufacture, to save money.'

'Find out, and quickly.' John paused and looked at his son. 'This is our future, Richard!' he said and pounded his fist on the desk. 'I'll fight right to the end.' Richard looked calm but John could tell it wasn't because of indifference to the accident or arrogance. Brendan had said that Richard had changed ... maybe he had. The instances John had seen pointed to that. But he wanted to probe. 'On another matter, how's the tug of the gaming table?'

John expected a curt reply or more of the usual blarney, but Richard said, 'When I'm near a game, I have an overpowering urge to go in and play.' John was about to speak, then stopped. 'The need has no timetable,' Richard went on. 'When I wake in the night I might get it but not all the time. When I'm not active, it's worse.'

John opened his mouth to say something, but Richard raised his hand. 'Father, don't say anything, please. All I can tell you is that I haven't played at cards for nearly a year.'

John sensed an honesty in his son that he'd not shown before. 'It's a start. A bloody good one.' He pulled his watch out and looked at it. 'I'm seeing O'Connor now. On your way out, get Brendan will you? I want him here with me.'

'Keep the line, Father. I'm sure the facts will come out on this mess. O'Connor will sniff any opportunity to get what he wants.'

'Noted,' John said.

Bill Bucknell looked up from his office desk and stood up. He extended his hand. 'William, welcome,' he said. 'Take a seat.'

William Turner sat down and mopped his brow, his face paler than usual. 'Thank you.'

'This is a pleasure. We were going to see each other next week at the school meeting.'

'This can't wait,' Turner said, looking around Bucknell's office. 'You've had this painted. Nice choice.'

'It needed it.' Bucknell knew Turner hated small talk and it wouldn't be long before he'd come to his point.

'Now,' Turner said. 'A messy business, the Imperial Hotel.'

'A tragedy. Three souls lost and a project half-built. Cigar?' Bucknell offered his humidor.

'Thank you.' Turner took one and lit it while Bucknell filled his pipe. 'When you and I last talked, Bill, you said you might have ways to influence the schedule on that job.'

'You mean slow it down?'

Turner eyeballed him. 'Did you do something?'

Bucknell smiled. 'I tried to get something done. On a small scale.'

Turner looked shocked. 'You caused those deaths?'

'No!'

'But—'

'I asked Slattery, the crane driver, to slow the job, slow the pace.'

'My God ... but deaths.'

'I didn't cause those.'

'I asked you to be cautious, Bill, to be prudent.'

'William, I believe Slattery when he says he had nothing to do with it,' Bucknell said. 'He's not a killer. Sure he's simple but he's cunning, in small ways. What happened on that deck wasn't Slattery's fault.'

'And you believe him?'

'I do.'

'But the inquest, Bill. He'll talk, he'll implicate you and then I'll—'

'Steady my friend, steady. We don't want to lose our heads. Our tack is to nail Leary. Slattery is certain the cranes were overloaded and that's what he'll say at the inquest. Leary will be implicated and you'll need a new builder to finish that job.' He smiled.

Turner sat back and drew on his cigar. 'I don't know, Bill.'

'You believe me, don't you? Slattery didn't cause those men's deaths.'

'So you say. It looks like Leary will go down for negligence, and if that's the case I have an obligation to my clients to complete the Imperial Hotel ... if the current contractor cannot.'

Bucknell held his unlit pipe. 'Bucknells is ready to be of service, at your clients' pleasure.'

'It's the thirteenth of October,' Turner said. 'The coroner has announced that the inquest will begin on the twentieth, so Leary's got a week to complete his preparation. I don't think that will be long enough and he won't convince the Coroner. He looks set to lose the Imperial Hotel. Let me be frank, Bill—that building is all steel. Could you finish the project in steel?'

Bill lit his pipe and puffed away. There was a way to make a quid here but he had to go carefully. 'We both know bricks are the best way,' Turner waved his hand in agreement. 'It's going to be hard in steel, bloody hard. You see what's happened to Leary's. They, like all of us, are new to steel. There'll be more site foremen needed, more inspections, putting in those bloody sprinklers, more—'

'Yes, yes I know, there'll be more cost.'

Turner knows it. Good, that's good. 'But we could have a crack at it ... on a cost plus profit basis.'

The architect coughed out smoke. 'I don't think we could go that far. Open-ended financial arrangements aren't favoured by my clients.'

Bill pursed his lips. 'How about this, then? We'll check everything that's been built and what needs to be done to make up the damage and we'll give you a price to complete. Fair enough?'

'You'll get a quantity surveyor to verify your costings?'

'Yes, a partnership we will nominate.' Bill knew he could get the right QS to agree that his price was fair and reasonable. But Turner might want his own man to ensure that costs were above board, and that might test Bucknells' price. He held his breath.

'You can name the firm,' Turner said.

Bill sat back and smiled and Turner did, too. 'Are you going to talk to others about the Imperial?' Bucknell said. 'Branagans and Dennings, for instance?'

'No, we won't go to tender,' the architect said and smiled again. 'As long as the quotes you give us are reasonable.'

'That's my middle name. You can cancel Leary's contract if the inquest brings a finding against them?'

'Yes,' Turner said.

Bill Bucknell stood up and proffered his hand. 'Then I'm sure we can do business.'

Bolton's technical manager put on his gloves and picked up a sheave, the size of a large dinner plate. 'We steam-cleaned it to remove the fire residue but you can see the crack.' Richard leaned forward and so did John. There it was, the thickness of a human hair, running across the face of the metal.

'Mr Dawson—'

'Call me Harry, Mr Leary. All the men here at Lidcombe call me Harry.'

'Very well, Harry,' John said. 'Could the fire have caused that crack?'

'No. That's a stress failure in an inferior grade of steel and that's what caused the crane to jam.' He crossed to another workbench and picked up a similar sheave. 'This is the sheave of the second crane. It did not appear to have a crack when we cleaned it up, but we put it through continuous testing and after thirty hours it also failed, resulting in a similar crack.'

Richard took the sheave, looked at it and glanced to his father. 'So that's what caused the accident?'

John was pleased and relief spread through him.

'No,' Harry said.

John's pleasure turned to surprise. 'No? But ...'

Harry took off his spectacles and placed them in his dustcoat pocket. 'The sheave jammed, Mr Leary. But that didn't cause the jib to fail. Here, I'll show you. Follow me.'

Harry led them out of the testing laboratory and into the Bolton rear yard, where crane components of all sizes were stored, ready to be assembled. They walked for some time and John pondered the future. It wasn't sounding good. Leary's had nothing to fight with. Richard glanced at him and John forced himself to smile. Harry stopped and John recognised the remains of the Imperial's two cranes, tagged number one and number two, their jibs side by side, their main charred sections held together with a lattice of bracing.

'Number one crane jib failed,' Harry said, 'but we still don't know why. We've put the main framing under tensile stress and it passed. The second jib also failed, as you know. Here you can see the top member bent because it couldn't take the combined load.' John could see the fold.

Richard put his hat on; the October sun had a bite in it. 'But something made that jib fail!'

'Sure,' Harry said. 'That is, if it wasn't overloaded.'

'Harry, it wasn't,' Richard said. 'I was there.'

Up to now John had believed him, but maybe Richard wasn't telling the truth? Maybe he and Sullivan *had* overloaded the jibs. The program had been behind and they'd had to make it up somehow.

'The fractured sheave would have jammed the ropes,' Harry said. 'And the resultant friction may well have caused sparks to ignite the grease and surface oil that always coats hot crane parts ... but that would be open to challenge in any court. And, if the load was within limits—'

'It was!' Richard said. 'I'm telling you Harry, it was.'

'Then the jibs would have just remained stationary, both of them. No, my opinion is that the jib failed for reasons not associated with the materials of the crane.'

Richard squatted down next to the framework of the jib. John remembered the funeral and thought about the three dead men who had once visited him in a dream, their bodies faceless.

'The bracing,' Richard said, pointing. 'Did you test the jib bracing?'

'No need,' Harry said. 'It doesn't take the load ... well not all of it.'

'Test it, Harry,' Richard said. 'Test it today.'

'I can't today, Mr Richard. I'm due at—'

Richard clamped his hand on Harry's shoulder. 'I'll pay what it takes. Do it.'

John surfaced from his depression. 'Bracing? That won't prove anything. The load is mostly taken on the jib framing. Even I know that.'

'It does,' Harry said, 'but it's worth a try, I suppose. I'll use random sections of bracing from the number one jib.'

Richard turned to John, his face alight. 'We've still got a chance, Father.'

John glanced at Harry but the Bolton man looked down. Harry Dawson knew that it was a long shot. John forced his hand out. 'Thanks for your efforts, Harry. Come on Richard, let's get back to town. There's plenty to do.'

He walked with his son to their carriage. Perhaps all this was a sign. He'd battled to get the biggest pub in Sydney and he'd done so ... but at what price? John closed his eyes ... three deaths, that was the price.

Chapter Twelve

On 20 October, John, Richard and Brendan mounted the George Street steps of the Coroner's Court. John knew he must steel himself for a possible recommendation of criminal prosecution, and a resultant trial that could only have one outcome— guilty. So be it. The guilt that seeped through him from the deaths would be somewhat assuaged by a time spent at the governor's pleasure. That would bring equilibrium back to his life. There was no one to blame but himself. If Richard had overloaded the cranes, if Sullivan was irresponsible, it made no difference.

John ushered his sons into a quiet corner of the vestibule. 'Listen, both of you. I'm responsible for my employees and I will take the consequences of any findings. I make that absolutely clear. Now, let's go inside.' Catherine and he had talked late into the night and his eyes were red-rimmed from lack of sleep. Like a pub brawl, you got knocked up but then you lived for another day. That's what would happen. It wasn't giving up— it was accepting the reality. There had been no further word from Bolton's and he hadn't expected any.

They walked in and sat in the front row. In front of them were two tables: at one sat the Counsel Assisting, Lawrence Barker, who, on behalf of the Coroner, would be presenting evidence and questioning witnesses, and at the other table sat Leary's lawyer, Conrad Harrison QC, a full-barrelled man with impeccable tailoring and a moustache of rainforest proportions. In front of them was the Coroner's bench.

Sitting in the row behind John and his sons were three ladies in black—the widows. One held rosary beads. John felt their misery and sensed their anger at him like a pressing force.

There was no blame attached to his sons. The Imperial Hotel had been his dream and now it had become his nightmare.

The Coroner appeared and they all rose. There was the usual preamble but John wasn't listening. Chairs moved while people sat down. Catherine's face appeared in his mind, drawn and lined. This had all been hard on her. Footsteps sounded nearby.

Richard leaned towards him. 'There's someone in the ante-chamber who needs to see me.'

'Now?' John said.

'Yes.'

Richard left. John only half listened to the proceedings, which listed the history of the event. Who wanted to see Richard? At this time? John tried to concentrate on what was being said.

'... that said cranes caught alight causing the deaths of three workers ...'

Richard sat back down beside him and placed a thin, bound copy of a report in front of him, Bolton's logo the single item on the front page. 'It's the bracing Father, it—'

Conrad Harrison, hearing them talking, turned around.

'Mr Harrison,' the Coroner said, 'is there some problem?'

The QC turned to the Coroner. 'May I ask the court's indulgence to enquire?'

'Proceed.'

Harrison approached the Leary table and pointed to the folder. 'Is this pertinent?'

'Yes,' Richard replied.

Harrison lifted it, opened it at the first page and read it.

'Mr Harrison?' the judge said.

The QC turned again. 'Your Honour, I have here, just delivered, a report which the Crown should consider.'

'A report? Does it have a bearing on this inquest?'

'I believe it does, your Honour, from my initial perusal. May I tender it to the court?'

'Bring it here, please.' The Queen's Counsel walked the short distance to the bench and handed the report to the Coroner, who put on his spectacles and began to read. After five minutes he put it down and announced, 'We will recess for fifteen minutes. Mr Harrison and Counsel Assisting, please come to my chambers.'

A murmur sounded in the seats around them.

'What was in that report?' John said.

'Come outside,' Richard said. 'I've got an extra copy.'

John, Richard and Brendan filed outside and stood on the footpath in the warm sunshine.

Richard opened a loose-leaf, bound document. 'It's all here. The jib bracing steel was of the same quality as the sheaves—inferior. The bracing failed in all four tests that Bolton's used, and Bolton's are certain that all the jib framing was made from the same quality steel. Father, the cranes are at fault ... nothing else. The jib on the first crane failed because all its *bracing* failed.'

John took hold of the report. 'But the bracing doesn't take the entire load.'

'It doesn't, but the right bracing steel stops the jib from twisting. The jib's torsion failed because of the poor bracing steel. The resultant collapse added the necessary friction to start the fire at the jammed jib sheave.'

'Let me read it, Richard.' John concentrated on the summary, then breathed out and stood upright.

Leary's were not at fault. They were not to blame. John felt numbness only. Three men had died tragically but it wasn't Leary's fault. He said, 'But will the Coroner accept this? It's just Bolton's opinion.'

'Dunstan's supplied us with faulty cranes,' Brendan said, closing the report. 'There's no question about that.'

'We'll be right,' Richard said.

John wasn't so sure.

'Mr Leary,' Conrad Harrison hailed them from the Court's entrance. 'The inquest's recommencing.'

They trooped up the steps into the darkened space.

'All rise,' the sheriff called out.

John stood with the rest of the courtroom. The Coroner's face was expressionless. Surely, Leary's would be exonerated? John's stomach rumbled. Surely.

'I have reviewed the document submitted to the court,' the Coroner said, 'and prima facie it has merit. However, it needs to be scrutinised and verified by a court-appointed expert. Additionally, the manufacturers of the cranes, Dunstan's, will also need to be called and asked to explain their interpretation of the report and if necessary provide their own. On that basis, three things will ensue. First, a full safety report on the Imperial Hotel site is to be undertaken and if the site is found to be safe, then, secondly, Leary's Contracting will be permitted to continue with the Imperial Hotel project until this inquest resumes. Thirdly, this court will reconvene in twenty-one days.'

'All rise,' the sheriff intoned.

John remained sitting. Around him chairs moved and people made their exit.

Conrad Harrison came up to him and said, 'You have some more time, Mr Leary. The Coroner told me to tell you that the report seemed professionally prepared and comprehensive, but he did not commit himself to an opinion either way, nor would I expect him to.' The QC tapped the report and said, 'If Dunstan's cannot contradict the report, the inquest may well have grounds for recommending criminal proceedings against them.'

'That's good news, Father,' Brendan said.

Yes, John thought, it was encouraging, but he wanted to be sure and he had a few more rounds to fight. A tingling ran down his left arm and he shook it. 'I want to meet with Bolton's and get the top and tail of their report. Thank you, Mr Harrison, for your attention on this.' John stood up and motioned to his sons. 'Come, we have a business to run.'

Harry Dawson looked out over the Bolton yard and tapped his fingers on his desk. He looked back at John. 'It's all there, Mr Leary. Over this last week I've had another opinion, which agrees with our first findings. Additionally, I've tested seventy per cent of the jib bracing. Every piece failed.'

John wanted certainty. Since the inquest had gone into recession, he'd grown more sceptical about their chances but he couldn't put that down to anything concrete, just a feeling. 'Will Dunstan's have any grounds to challenge it?'

'They may link the supposed overloading to the jib sections failing, but that's all. You know, there's one thing I don't understand in all this.'

'What's that?' John said.

'Neville Waters. He was a lead foreman here at Bolton's for six years, knew cranes inside and out. Now he's with Dunstan's. An honest man and one for absolute integrity in all things he did. There's no way he'd use second-rate steel in his cranes, never.'

'He may not have known about it,' John said.

'Maybe.'

'And people can change, Harry,' John said. 'Why did he leave here?'

'More money and a promotion. Is that all you need, Mr Leary?'

John stood up. 'Thanks, Harry. We now wait.' John walked out to his carriage. The site had passed muster for safety and work had started two days previously. He would have to wait two weeks till the inquest reconvened and those two weeks would feel like two years if he kept inactive.

Gibbs looked at him as he approached. 'Any luck, sir?' he said.

John shook his head. 'George Street, please.' John sat back as the carriage took off. Luck, that's what they needed now, barrow-loads of it.

John shook his head. 'George Street, please.' John sat back as the carriage took off. Luck, that's what they needed now, barrow-loads of it.

'Call Mr Richard Leary,' the court attendant said.

This would clinch it, John thought. Richard would be under oath and had to tell the truth one way or another. Dunstan's had documents in their defence, which Counsel Assisting had given them access to. John was glad that they had had the last two weeks to examine them in detail. Some of the affidavits were laughable but one of them could blur the facts.

Richard took the oath and sat down.

Lawrence Barker, Counsel Assisting, approached Richard. 'Now, Mr Leary, you have read the affidavit from Mr Terrence Slattery, crane driver, of 10 Castle Street, Redfern?'

'I have.'

'Mr Slattery was the driver of number two crane on the day of the incident.' He leaned towards Richard and said, 'Do you agree with the content of his sworn statement?'

John turned to see the crane driver, his leg still in a minor splint, his eyes directed towards the floor. Bloody man.

'No,' Richard said. 'The cranes were not overloaded.'

'Mr Leary, Mr Slattery clearly remembers you ordered him, and the other crane driver, to ignore the load-scale tables affixed in their crane cabins and instead lift the beam in question.'

John waited for his son's response. He hoped it was the right one.

'I did not so instruct him,' Richard said.

'And that beam,' continued Lawrence Barker, 'was in excess of the loads the cranes were designed to lift and it caused the cranes to collapse.'

'That's not correct.'

'That is all, Mr Leary, you're excused. I'd like to call two other witnesses, Your Honour.'

John knew that Slattery was on thin ground, as there were no other witnesses to corroborate his story. John felt a tap on his shoulder and turned around. It was Rory O'Connor.

'Mr Leary,' he said, 'could I see you, please?' John hesitated. 'Please?'

John got up and followed O'Connor into the antechamber, where the advocate ushered him to a corner.

'Terry Slattery's a liar, Mr Leary, but I can't prove it. But what I can say is that he's been seen with Bill Bucknell.'

Bucknell? Richard had mentioned possible sabotage.

'I know what you're thinking and I'm guessing the same,' O'Connor said. 'If Bucknell had anything to do with these deaths, all bets are off. But I'm a lawyer first. I need proof. That'll take time.'

'Which we haven't got.'

'No. But I can get Slattery to withdraw his version of events.'

'How?' John said.

'Leave that to me. Just be assured that I won't have to break his leg again to do it.'

John went on alert. 'Why would you help us, O'Connor? We're the ones you want to ringbark, not one of your workers.'

O'Connor exhaled. 'I don't like lies and will not tolerate injustice, whoever causes it, labour or capital.'

John looked at the advocate, whose face seemed sincere. 'Do what you have to, then and … thank you,' John said, pulling his watch from his waistcoat. 'I have to go to the office now, but I'll be back this afternoon.'

The vestibule clock struck two as John sat back down in the courtroom. The three widows were still there, as silent and unmoving as their sandstone sisters in the Blue Mountains.

Harrison came up to him. 'It's all over, Mr Leary. The Coroner is deliberating in his chambers. Slattery had a change of heart after

I grilled him. He seemed to forget about a few things and I went for his jugular. That was good for you, Mr Leary.'

John turned and found Rory O'Connor, who winked at him. How had he done it? It didn't matter, he supposed. A man he now owed a favour to, but that was all right. A tingle ran through John's left arm. He rubbed it.

'All rise,' the attendant said.

The Coroner came in and sat down. John felt his spirits lift: he'd leave the court this afternoon and his life would restart.

'I have made a finding on this inquest,' the Coroner said. 'There is evidence that a failure of equipment caused the accidents at the Imperial Hotel site.' Good, John thought. 'Equally, however' the Coroner continued, 'there is no clear, unchallenged evidence that poor materials caused the resultant fire and tragic loss of three lives. Therefore, today the tenth of November 1886, I am bringing a finding that the deaths of Harry Somerfield, Ian Muncaster and Francis Delaney were caused by negligence. I recommend that a criminal prosecution for manslaughter be brought against Leary's Contracting.'

The tingle turned to a sharp pain and John felt as if his chest was strapped tight, the pressure increasing.

'Murderer!' screamed one of the widows behind him.

'No, no!' This was a shout from another voice, male and deeper. John blacked out.

John's mouth was dry and he squinted at the sunlight coming through his open bedroom window.

Catherine was there, smiling at him. 'Just rest, dear. The doctor has given you a sedative.'

'Water, please,' he asked. Catherine helped him drink and he lay back. 'What day is it?'

'It's just after ten on Thursday, the day after the inquest.' John closed his eyes. He would have been better off dead. But that seemed petulant and Catherine's smile was comforting. Criminal proceedings and a possible prison term? Well, he'd have to cop it. 'You have to take a complete rest for ten days.'

'With what I've got to face, I'll need it.'

She touched his cheek and caressed it. 'The doctor's diagnosis says that it was most likely your heart, my love, but it was just a turn. All is well.'

'My heart! But what about the business? What's happening?'

'Richard will tell you, though I wanted him to wait till you're better.'

John raised himself up. 'Catherine, will they prosecute us?'

She pressed him back down onto the bed and held his hand. 'No, they won't.'

John forced his eyes shut.

'Are you up to seeing Richard?' she said.

He nodded and Catherine left the room. No prosecution? How? He felt the wool of his blanket, pinched his wrist and inhaled the hint of salt on the breeze from the harbour. He wasn't dreaming.

Richard entered and sat down. 'How are you, Father?'

'Not bad. So, tell me.'

'Can you believe it? A Dunstan's employee made a full confession just after you ... blacked out. Brendan took you to hospital and I stayed in court.'

John's tiredness lessened a little. 'Was he the man that Harry mentioned to us?'

'Yes: Neville Waters, the foreman. He said that he'd used inferior steel under instructions from the business owners to save on costs. After the accident, when the inquest came up, he hoped that the Coroner would find Leary's not liable. That didn't happen and he reckoned we were poorly served. More importantly, he couldn't live with three deaths on his conscience and he wanted to tell all. When Waters waived his rights, the Coroner set up the appropriate papers and made an amended finding. It's *Dunstan's* that are to be prosecuted for manslaughter. Father, it's all over.'

John grasped his son's hand. It was hard to believe. 'Excellent ... excellent.'

Richard released the grip. 'Rest now, please.'

John sank back, exhausted but relieved.

❖

It had started in Norway, or somewhere up in that region, and immigrants had brought the custom to Sydney. When the structure of a tall building was erected, a tree, usually a fir, was fixed to its highest point. A nice touch, John thought. Hung from a crane, the big tree hovered over the top of the Imperial Hotel's uppermost tip, with the sprinkler tank behind it.

The tree showed Sydney that the core of the building was completed, even though on the floors below hundreds of workers toiled at the external walls, finishes and fitments. Standing before the tree, John blinked as the morning sun broke through its branches. The men who'd built the structure—the lean and wiry riggers and their foremen, the labourers, carpenters and bricklayers—crowded around him and stared at the fir being lowered to the roof. They stood sixteen floors above Clarence Street, higher than any other building. A December haze had settled on the harbour but the view was breathtaking. It was a bit like being on the top of a mountain.

'A great day, Father,' Richard said, standing next to him.

'Indeed. The fire slowed us down but we got here.'

'We did.'

Following the Coroner's final finding, the insurance company had had no option but to pay Leary's claim for fire damage. He was glad the AMP had then pursued Dunstan's, who were now the ones facing manslaughter charges. John shook his head. 'But the deaths are still a tragedy.'

'They are,' Richard said.

They both looked up as the tree was lowered. 'Bolton's came up trumps,' Richard said.

'We should have used them in the beginning and from now on we will, on all our jobs.'

'Agreed,' Richard said.

Ronan O'Gara walked up to them. 'Move back, please, gentlemen,' he said, 'just to be sure.' The tree was above them and John and Richard stepped back. Conversation died away as the rigging crew secured the tree and removed its slings from the crane. Applause erupted and John looked over at Brendan, who was standing with the rigging crew. Were his eyes glistening?

Richard shook hands all round but Brendan stood looking at the tree and smiled. The job had months to run but the fir marked a milestone. Brendan caught John's eye. A lump formed in his throat and he continued clapping.

John blinked as a photographer's flash erupted near him. Someone pumped his hand, another hand patted his shoulder.

'Well, we got there,' Brendan said coming to stand next to him.

'We did. The steelwork was done well, son, especially the last four floors.'

Brendan grinned at his father, basking in the compliment.

'I mean it,' John said. 'That steel's coated with Leary sweat, your sweat.'

Brendan's smile faded. 'Thank you, father. But it cost us three of our workers.'

'God rest their souls.' The deaths reminded him of the funeral and how that Rocks girl had accompanied his son into the church. Anne Connaire had seen them, and from her look, she hadn't been happy. Brendan's love affairs were his own business but what Mary had told him the previous night had piqued his curiosity. Mary. Always forthright, she'd come into his study and had told him that Brendan still carried a torch for Miss Carson. John wanted the facts before he'd tell Catherine.

'And you?' he asked Brendan. 'Are you seeing a girl?'

'The one I want, Father, isn't acceptable to you and Mother. You remember Julie Carson? The girl at Grandmother's party?'

'Yes, and at the funeral.'

'After Grandmother's party, Miss Carson ended our close friendship.'

'Friendship?' John said, surprised. 'I thought it was more than that.'

Richard joined them.

'I have to get back to work, Father,' Brendan said, looking at his half-brother. 'There's much to do.'

There always was, but John wanted to know about this girl. Brendan was still keen and that was a worry.

'Stay for a bit,' John said. 'Richard, I need a few moments to talk to Brendan.'

'What's he done now?'

'Nothing,' John said and waited for Richard's customary anger.

'Certainly, Father, but I've got news, too.' He smiled and left them.

'He is different,' John said, watching Richard go. 'He would have wanted to know what we were going to talk about. He used to be suspicious, but not now. Well, Brendan, about this girl.'

'She broke it off because she couldn't fit in with us.'

'Did you think she ever would? Really, you were asking a lot of her.'

'But we're not like that, Father. You started in the colony as a chippy's mate before you got your carpenter's job. And Mother was a milliner. We aren't pure bloods.'

John admitted to the point. 'But we've risen, son, with grind and making our own luck. That's brought us wealth and that changes people. Changes us.'

'For the better?'

'We're still moral, or try to be,' John said. 'Miss Carson couldn't be accepted and should never be.'

'I don't agree. She has no mercenary intentions.'

'How can you be sure?' John replied. But then, the rest of what Mary had told him now made sense. Mary had said she had a woman's intuition about gold-diggers and she was sure Julie Carson wasn't one.

Brendan spread his hands. 'I love her and I'm going to try my hardest to get her back.'

'Look, son ...'

Richard came back up to them. 'Sorry to interrupt, but what I've got to say can't wait.' Brendan and John looked at each other.

'It sounds serious,' John said.

'It's joyful, Father. Around May next year, you'll have your first grandchild. And Brendan, you'll be an uncle.'

John smiled and slapped Richard's shoulder. 'That's great news, son! Wonderful news. When we get downstairs we'll knock the top off a bottle of champagne.'

'Good on you, Richard,' Brendan said. 'I'll join you both soon.' Brendan turned and left.

Richard watched his half-brother as he walked down the stairs. 'He's still a serious soul, isn't he?'

Serious and in love. 'He is that, but I admire his diligence. Come on I'll walk downstairs with you.'

'All the way down? What about the doctor's advice?'

John looked around the top floor. The crowd had thinned as bricklayers resumed their work.

'He said some movement is beneficial. Anyway, Catherine's keeping me on the rails. Just the two floors below,' he said, grinning. 'I want to see for myself what you and Sullivan have been hiding from me.' John strode off and Richard followed him down the stairs.

On the floor below, Richard stood aside as two men pushed a trolley full of plaster mix in their direction. John stopped at three different places on the floor and took in all the progress. The brick-work encasing the steel columns was being laid hard up against the floor above and John was satisfied. He took the next stairway down. 'Sullivan's got his confidence back.'

'It took a while,' Richard said and looked up. 'Speak of the devil.'

'There you are,' Sullivan said. 'They need you two down on the footpath for a group photograph.'

John put his arm on Sullivan's shoulder and smiled at the man's surprise at the gesture. Sullivan then smiled too. 'Let's go,' John said and turned to Richard. 'Come on. We've got a bottle to drink.' He smiled. 'Well, a glass at least.'

Their carriage was making its way past Woolloomooloo in the morning humidity. It was quiet for the festive season.

'It feels like Easter was yesterday,' Catherine said, 'now here it is, Christmas Day, 1886. I have to say, dear, that I'm happier because ... well because you're more content.'

John smiled. 'I'd like to think it's acceptance, more than contentment.'

'Yes, you're right.'

'Our industry is a dangerous one, Catherine, and serious accidents happen. Even though we weren't at fault, it doesn't diminish the deaths of those men.' He kept silent for a minute. 'But I'm better now, and worrying less about it.' He shook his head. 'We have a grandchild on the way and that's one reason to keep my health under control.' John looked out of the carriage into the December heat.

'Indeed,' she said. 'Now I have something to tell you. I've been keeping something a secret and it's time you knew.'

'What?'

'Connie Bucknell and I are good friends and we see each other often.'

'That's grand!'

She clasped his hand. 'Thank you. I thought you might be angry?'

'Of course not.' He smiled. 'Could be useful. If she talks about work and, well—'

Catherine dropped his hand. 'If you think I'd spy!' Then she saw his eyes twinkle. 'Oh you ...' She smiled with him. 'Now, about today, I thought we'd do something different.'

Always thinking about the family, that's what made her special. 'I've got something to tell you in return,' he said. 'Brendan still wants Julie Carson.'

'*What?* I beg your pardon, dear. Our son with that girl—again?'

'I'm afraid so.'

Catherine looked harassed. 'How do you know?'

'He told me two weeks ago. They met again at the funeral. He wants to get her back.'

'But he can't, John!'

'Catherine, he can do what he pleases.'

Her head jerked. 'Do you condone this, dear? Surely not!'

He paused. 'We should keep an open mind about her, don't you think?' Before Catherine could reply, he said, 'We don't know anything bad about her except her upbringing. And after all, you and I are both from trade backgrounds.'

Catherine sat back and looked thoughtful. 'Maybe you're right ... I said, maybe. But she could still be a little hussy. She's scheming. She's manipulating Brendan. He's blind to it.'

'I don't think so.'

'You men! You're all the same. You see an attractive face and ... all the other ... and you can't think straight.'

'That's as maybe, but Mary thinks differently.'

'Mary? Our Mary?'

'The same,' John said.

'What has she got to do with this? What has she said?'

'She's met Miss Carson a few times now since Christine's party. They are friends.'

Catherine said more quietly, 'I see. I'll talk to Mary myself. I need some time to think about all of this.' The carriage stopped outside St Mary's, its bells pealing, and they joined the rest of the family in church.

John was annoyed at himself for telling Catherine today but she had to know. And Catherine was smart: he hoped that in time she might soften her views about Julie Carson.

Today was all about family: Catherine had been adamant that the whole family be together and in the public eye. As their carriage pulled up, he could see Victoria, who was smiling at something Brendan had said, her teeth flashing white and her skin glowing.

After Mass, the family gathered outside. There was Brendan standing alone. Richard, Victoria, Agatha and Mary were chatting in the shade of a tree. John looked from one son to the other; this time next year one of them would lead Leary's. Which one? Just then, there was a gust of wind and John smiled. A sign that, yes, a new broom was needed?

At home, Catherine helped prepare the Christmas feast, glad that all the fuss had stopped her thinking about Julie Carson. But when they were seated, her thoughts of the girl returned. Could Mary be right about her? Was Julie genuine in her affection for Brendan? She caught Brendan looking at her. 'Merry Christmas!'

'And to you, Mother.'

She should feel happy, but her equanimity vanished. Pent-up frustration made her want to scream at her son, to force Julie Carson from his mind. She glanced at Mary, who was focused on eating, which was not unusual: Mary had a healthy appetite.

'We might have to leave early,' Richard said. 'Victoria needs to lie down and rest.'

'Of course.'

John was looking at her. Was he right about Brendan? Was she wrong? Distressed, she looked around at her family. There was conversation happening and one or two laughs, but she was disappointed in Brendan. When was he going to tell her about his real feelings for Julie Carson? Maybe never? What if he decided to elope with her? *God forbid.* Christmas Day, 1886—not one of their best Christmases.

Brendan walked along Princes Street. It was five o'clock and there'd been little movement in the town on his way here; most people were relaxing indoors or full of cheer after their Christmas Day meal. For him, there'd been better Leary Christmas dinners. He suspected his mother knew about Julie, which would explain why she'd looked at him at the dinner table as if he'd insulted her. His father must have told her. It couldn't be helped. He loved his mother but Julie had his heart.

The air was thick with moisture and a slight breeze wafted the dust around as he closed Julie's front gate behind him. He knocked on the door.

When it opened, he took off his hat and said, 'Happy Christmas, Mrs Carson.'

'It's been a long time, young man,' Mrs Carson said and smiled at him.

'And your health?'

'I can't complain.'

Julie came to the door. 'We'll walk off our meal, Ma. I need to and I'm sure Brendan does, too.'

'Goodbye, Mrs Carson. I hope to see you soon. If not, have a Happy New Year.'

'Thank you, Mr Leary, same to you and your family.'

They headed off down Princes Street to Millers Point. 'I've seen your sister Mary a few times,' Julie said. 'She's nice.'

'She is. We are close.'

'That's what she said and that's why she wanted to see me in the first place.'

'So, what are your thoughts?'

'About?'

'About us.'

'What do you want me to say?'

He stopped and turned to her, taking her hand. 'Julie, I've made up my mind. I want you in my life and my family can go to the devil for all I care.'

'You don't mean that!' She was shocked. 'You love your family.'

'If they don't accept you, I'll leave Leary's and go my own way. I think the bank might still take me on. If not, I can look after myself.'

'But I could never come between you and your family. You'd be angry with me for it, afterwards.'

'Julie, I want us to be close.'

'So do I, but we have to work this out.'

'Tell me you like me, then.'

'All right,' she said. 'I like you a lot.'

'Enough to be my girlfriend?'

She pulled him along. 'Come on. There's a band playing in the pavilion. We can get a cool drink there.'

'Julie?'

She came close to him and she kissed him on the lips. 'There,' she said. 'Now, come on.'

It was the third Saturday night in February, and Sydney society was on show. The Governor, the Most Honourable Marquis of Lincolnshire, was hosting his first ball of 1887.

John drank his whisky then stood up and said to Catherine, 'I have to meet some people, and I mightn't see you again before the ball ends. I'll get a cab back to the house. Gibbs will take you and the girls home whenever you like.'

Catherine smiled. 'All right, dear. Just go easy with the drink.'

'Will do,' he said and made his way through the throng, the air a mix of perspiration and the alcohol that was settling in abandoned glasses. He saw some familiar faces, smiled at some and acknowledged others.

At the same function, Brendan was making his way back to his table when he ran into Richard, who was holding a bottle of champagne and two glasses.

'Come on brother,' Richard said, 'let's talk.' He pointed to an empty table in the corner of the ballroom and Brendan followed him.

Richard placed the glasses down and filled them. 'Victoria's having a rough time,' he said, as he gave Brendan his glass. 'She was too unwell to come tonight, but she encouraged me to, against my will. She's wonderful. I'm going to leave early and see how she is.'

This new side to Richard was still surprising Brendan. And it seemed Richard's concern for Victoria was genuine.

'Here's to the little fella,' Richard said.

They clinked glasses, then Brendan, said, smiling, 'You're certain it's a boy?'

'As certain as the bubbles in your glass,' Richard said, slapping his brother on the shoulder. 'You should get hitched, Brendan. It would do wonders for you. Miss Carson has the goods, a fine girl.'

'What makes you think I'm seeing her?'

'Mary told me. Work on your mother, Brendan. She'll come around. Now, about the boy. I think you'd be a good godfather.' He took a long gulp of the bubbly, wiped his chin, then grinned. 'Yes, you would be.'

'Thank you, Richard. I'd be proud to be his godfather.'

Richard's brow wrinkled. 'You'll not be too strict? I don't want the little tyke brought up a priest.'

Brendan was about to make a sharp reply when he saw the gleam in Richard's eye. 'It could be a girl, Richard.'

'It could and if it is, I'll still love her.'

This might be a time to raise a touchy subject. 'You're in a good mood and I want to offer my ear if you need it.'

'Your ear? Why?' Richard grinned again. 'Do you want to part with one?'

'No ... but if you ever want to talk about your gambling, I'll listen ... just listen.'

Richard filled his glass, spilling some on the tablecloth. 'I live with it,' he said, and stared at his half-brother. 'But don't get righteous on me.'

'I'm not,' Brendan said. 'I'm here if you want to talk about it.'

'Honourable in all things. That's my brother.' He picked up the bottle and stood up, his face now serious 'Thank you for accepting to be godfather, Brendan. The offer of your ear,' he winked, 'is also appreciated. See you around. I have more drinking to do and people to see before I leave.' He walked away.

Agatha settled back in the carriage as it departed from the ball. Mary was beside her and their mother sat opposite. 'That Mr Davidson is a cad,' she said.

Catherine flinched. 'Agatha!'

'Well, he is. Colleen Davies is in love with him and he didn't talk to her all night. She's broken-hearted.'

Running footsteps sounded beside their carriage and Mary sat up. 'What's that?'

Catherine looked out. 'Oh, no! It's larrikins,' she said. A flush of fear surged through her. The carriage leaned to one side, there was a yell, then someone was on the roof. Catherine felt her heart racing, and said, 'Quick, shut the windows.'

Sounds of thuds filled the carriage as the women slammed the windows closed. There was a grunt, then the carriage lurched as one attacker seemed to fall off.

'Gibbs!' Catherine shouted in panic.

The carriage's overhead hatch opened. 'Sorry 'bout that, ladies,' Gibbs called down. 'I had to hit the mongrel with my club. It was the same cove who attacked us before. I got him a good one, right across his hooked nose.' Gibbs closed the hatch.

Catherine's heart was pounding and a face flashed in her mind. 'My God!' she said.

Agatha took her mother's hand, her face anxious. 'It's all right, Mother, there's no threat.'

'No, no … the larrikin. The King, or whatever he's called. The man who threatened us before. He hit me. That man hit me.'

'Mother?' Agatha squeezed harder. 'What do you mean?'

Catherine looked at her daughters. It was now clear as new glass. She opened the roof hatch. 'Gibbs, are you sure it was the same man?'

'Sure enough, Madam.'

'Thank you, Gibbs,' she said and closed the hatch. She looked at her daughters' worried faces and smiled despite her shock. 'It's quite clear in my memory, all of a sudden. The man who held up our carriage two years ago on the way to a ball was the same man who attacked me at the markets. He caught me in that dark lane and attacked me.'

'Oh, Mother!' Agatha said.

Catherine smiled. 'No, actually, I'm glad to know exactly what happened. Wait till I tell your father.' She paused. 'It's getting close in here. Open the windows, girls.'

John followed Richard into a fourteenth-floor Imperial Hotel room and pointed. 'Look at this,' he said, 'bedhead, dressing table, cabinets, the lot, unfinished and costing us plenty.' It was the same on the two floors below him. 'Three weeks before Easter and a stoppage—a critical one.'

'Indeed,' Richard said. 'If this lot's not done, we can't hand over the rooms.'

'Any news of the meeting?' John said.

Richard shook his head, pulled out his fob watch and glanced at it. 'My spy said they'd be finished by now. I wonder what's taking them so long.'

'They shouldn't have had the meeting!' John said. 'They've got no right to stop work.'

'I know.' Richard leaned against a windowsill, hands in his pockets. 'Bucknells might have joiners, or Dennings. We should have given them the job.'

'It's too late to get Dennings in now, but Bucknells?'

'We could pinch some of their joiners,' Richard said as he bent down, closed one eye and looked along the edge of a bedhead. 'Offer them a contract.' Richard stood up. 'Speaking of our competitor, I had dinner with Miles Cunningham last week. He let it slip that Mr Turner offered Bucknell this job if we failed at the inquest.'

'Bloody hell. But then, they know each other, Richard. The school reunion, remember?'

'Yeah. Cunningham said he wouldn't have told me if he'd found that we had caused the accident. But back to our joiners. They still get paid well for what they do. I'm paying our joiners more than Bucknell did for his little fart hotel.'

'But you've cut their pay,' John said.

'I had to, Father, just till this job's finished. There's not much work out there for them and I needed to make up for the loss caused by the fire. The insurance didn't cover everything.'

'And have you?'

Richard spread his hands. 'I had, up till last week. Now the wheels have fallen off.'

'They certainly have, brother,' Brendan said walking into the room. Rory O'Connor followed him.

'They're out,' O'Connor said. 'Indefinite.'

'What do you mean?' John said.

'It means, Mr Leary, that the joiners have agreed to leave the site and not return until their old wages are paid ... with back pay.'

Richard stood up. 'They've gone?'

'Yes,' O'Connor said.

'But they can't,' Richard said, and swung towards his brother. 'You're in charge of finishes now. You should have stopped them meeting. Made them go back to work.'

'There're fifty of them, Richard,' Brendan said. 'I can't force them all.'

'You should have tried. This is blackmail.'

'Well, Brendan?' John asked.

'The lad's right,' O'Connor said. 'Fair made up their minds, they have.'

John had had enough. 'With your help.'

'You may not know this Mr Leary, but it's *you* I'm here to help. You see—'

'No. You're part of them, always will be.'

'If it wasn't for Mr O'Connor,' Brendan said, 'we'd be in a lot deeper. He stopped the joiners from getting the whole site closed down.'

John looked at the big advocate. He owed O'Connor a favour because he'd provided them with a vital witness at the inquest, but that just made him angrier.

'No need to defend me, Brendan,' O'Connor said, and glanced from Richard to John. 'This industry has to change. It's 1887 and there are still too many slaves and scabs.'

'Change for the workers, yeah?' John said. 'Not the bloody builders.'

'For both,' O'Connor said as he sat on a window board.

'You really believe that, don't you?' Richard said.

O'Connor paused. 'I do. You're both needed, labour and capital.'

John leaned on one of the unfinished cabinets. All right, he'd find out what made this man tick. 'We're not capital.'

'You want to make a profit on the job?'

'Of course.'

'Then, you're capital, Mr Leary, and that's all right. I'm not against making money. I just want equity.'

Again O'Connor had restated his Coroner's Court sentiment. The man was consistent, but to force workers to strike wasn't on. No one said anything for a while. The cabinet work was critical to completion. John made a fist, punched his other hand with it and said, 'All our joiners are well paid but there's a downturn now and joiners are plentiful. Now, let's see. We can hang in there. They haven't got us over a barrel yet—we've been fortunate on the structure. Good weather, sound planning and double shifts have made up our lost time, with no foul-ups.'

Richard pursed his lips. 'I agree. The joiners will fold. They'll be back to work in two days.'

'They won't be,' Brendan said.

Richard turned on him. 'They will,' he said, 'and you know why, because this is new to them Brendan, new. It's the first time they've taken on Leary's and they feel the power. I feel for them because once they're alone, facing the people who depend on them, they'll change their minds and come back.'

'Richard's right,' John said. 'Let them get a bellyful in the pub tonight. Tomorrow they'll feel different.'

O'Connor stood up. 'That's your final word?'

'Yes,' Richard said. 'And I don't want this talk to get back to them, either. You understand, Mr O'Connor?'

O'Connor shook his head. 'They won't be back until you pay them.'

Richard smiled. 'Wait till Easter. Then they'll be back.'

'I don't think so,' O'Connor said and left the room.

John said. 'The man did us a favour at the inquest and he's straight, even if we disagree. And he's confident. That's not a bluff.'

'It is, Father,' Richard said. 'You wait. They'll scream to be back by Good Friday.'

'And the alternative?' Brendan said.

Richard turned to him. 'That's the difference between you and me, brother. I stand up to them. They know who I am and they'll fold.'

Brendan glanced at his father. 'I hope you're right, but I've got a better idea.'

'Go on,' John said.

'Negotiate,' Brendan said.

John thought about that and a doubt crept in. Brendan was embedded in the Imperial Hotel, had picked up years of experience in a short time but there was still a weakness here, just a little one, but an important one. 'No. I won't.'

'Father's correct,' Richard said. He paused and looked around. 'Get as much finished as you can here. We normally wait for the joinery to be done before painting but now we have no choice.'

Brendan nodded. 'Good idea.'

'You give in too easy, Brendan,' John said. 'You have to be assertive. They'll be back to work soon and this will all be over.'

Brendan looked from his father to Richard. 'I hope you're right.'

'Don't get too close to O'Connor,' John said. 'Keep your own counsel. He's got his own plans—political—anybody can see that. But he's fair.'

'He is,' Brendan agreed. 'A lot of things are being made in factories now. Just look around you. Plaster cornices, metal fittings, hardware. It's a big change and the men doing that work are being paid more. Workers understand that their labour is valuable. It's just the joiners at the moment who are plentiful. Leary's is well placed—better than others. I can work with O'Connor.'

'Work with him, son,' John said. 'But not for him.'

Dave Sullivan walked into the room and looked at John. 'What's the decision? I've got people wanting to know.'

'Brendan will tell you,' Richard said.

'Good,' Sullivan said.

The priest closed Christine McGuire's bedroom door. He came into the Point Piper foyer where John and the doctor were talking together.

'How is she, Father?' John asked.

'Her body? Failing, but that's best left to the doctor's opinion here.'

'I've told Mr Leary,' the doctor said, 'that she's very ill and I don't think she's got long.'

John studied the doctor's face. 'She's been close before.'

'Not like this,' he replied putting on his coat. 'Send a message to me. Till then.'

'Thank you,' John said. He closed the door after him and faced the priest.

'If you want to see her, John, now's the time,' the priest said. 'She's lucid and she's made her confession.'

His mother-in-law was at heaven's gate. John walked down the hall and opened her bedroom door. She lay on her back, her arms by her side, her eyes closed. Candle smoke hovered near her bed and the smell of beeswax was strong. A floorboard squeaked under him.

'Don't tip-toe,' she said, 'I can still hear.' John sat on a chair beside her bed. Christine's eyelids opened as she turned to him, just enough to see. She gave a wry smile. 'Well, son-in-law, have you come to watch me go? At least I made it to Easter.'

The gold cross on the bedside table reflected the flame of the flickering candle.

'Are you in pain?' he asked.

'Not much. That's at least a blessing.'

'Richard will miss you.'

Christine forced her eyes shut and a tear slipped down her cheek. She felt for the boy, always had. 'I know.' She coughed. 'But few others.'

'Catherine.'

'Yes, she will. A good woman, John.' She paused to get breath. 'I'm glad she remembered who had assaulted her. Who'd have thought it? And I'm proud of her going to the police about it.' Christine winced. 'And you son-in-law, will you miss me?'

Would he? Really? Yes, he had to be honest. 'Yes, I will. We've had our moments, and you were always a match.'

'A drink, John, please?' He filled a glass from a pitcher and supported her while she drank. She settled back. 'That's better. Richard will be all right?'

John looked down, then back at her. 'I won't lie to you, especially now. He still is a risk to himself, but he says he hasn't gambled for over a year.'

'And you believe him?'

There had been no reports, no rumours and Richard seemed content with Victoria. 'Yes ... I do.'

'I've never asked you for anything, but for Clarissa's sake I ask you this: protect him from himself.'

Hearing Clarissa's name at this time brought back sad memories for him. 'I will. I don't know how, but I'll try.' She concentrated on him for a long time. 'I will try. He's my son.'

'I know you will.' Christine squeezed his hand. 'In the bureau ... over there ... two envelopes. Bring them here, please.'

John got up, opened the bureau and brought the documents to her. He put on his spectacles. The first envelope held her will. The second was addressed to him. He was about to open it.

'No, not now,' she said. 'When I'm gone. It's an authority from my lawyer ... that you're the only one to read my will and carry out the wishes it sets down.' This sentence had tired her and she panted and closed her eyes. 'You look after yourself, John. You are a good man and a good father.'

Despite himself, he was moved. They were words he never expected to hear from her. This frail, dying woman was no threat and though he hadn't felt any great affection towards her, he would miss their relationship.

'I want the baptism to happen,' she said. 'Don't delay it. I'll tell Richard the same. Let me see him now.'

He stood up. 'I'll get your grandson.' He pressed her hand and felt his pressed in return.

John opened the bedroom door and a red-eyed Richard went past him and into the bedroom. John closed the door behind him and went back down the hall, placing the envelopes in his pocket. Catherine came up to him with Brendan and the girls. She took his hand.

'John,' she said. 'You're pale.'

He was sad and that sadness was real. 'I'm all right.'

'And Christine?'

'Fading. Richard's with her. The doctor is on standby.'

'Let's go into the drawing room,' she said.

He squeezed her hand. 'Yes.'

The May sunlight spread over the assembled throng gathered in St Mary's Cathedral following the eleven o'clock Mass. John and Catherine stood in the front pew and nearby the godparents and proud parents clustered around the baptismal font with the priest. The baby gurgled and Brendan grinned as he held the lace-wrapped bundle closer to him. A stranger would have thought it was Brendan's baby and not Richard's.

'Don't crush him, brother,' Richard said.

'No. He's precious, our little Mark.'

Victoria smiled at Richard and he returned the gesture as the priest held out his arms to take the baby. Mark cried, and John smiled. Mark, his first grandson, a 'Cornstalk', a native-born New South Welshman, like Richard.

The priest recited the Latin blessings and Victoria's eyes glistened with happiness. And Brendan was the baby's godfather; a Leary was godfather to a Leary. Seeing the joyful face looking at his little nephew, it was clear that Brendan would stand by the lad in all weathers.

Mark Joseph they christened him and then Brendan and Mark's godmother, Victoria's bridesmaid Felicity Turner, made their commitments to their godson as the smoke of the incense settled over them in a mist.

In the vestibule, after the baptism, John took Richard's elbow. 'Blessed day, Richard.'

'It is, Father. Indeed it is.' He forced a smile. 'It's a pity Grandmother just missed it.'

'She's here, don't worry. Another Leary is born and has received the Holy Ghost, and for that we thank God. Let's enjoy this day and what your son might bring to all of us.'

'Richard,' Victoria said, holding out her son. 'Here, hold him.'

Richard took his son. Mark's eyes twinkled and his mouth opened in what looked like a little smile. That smile increased John's contentment. Leary's could go away for a day. What he had now seemed more valuable to him than anything.

Chapter Thirteen

Brendan pressed close to Julie as the cab clipped along down George Street on a cool June Sunday afternoon. Life was good. They'd just had a meal with his sisters at Point Piper. His parents had been absent, as they were spending the weekend in the Blue Mountains.

Julie patted her stomach. 'That food! My goodness, it could've fed an army. And that Mary, she puts it away.'

'She does,' Brendan said, grinning. Their cab passed Margaret Street with the massive hotel up on the hill. He had a good position on the Imperial Hotel now, supervising all the internal finishes, joinery and painting. The joiners had folded like Richard had said they would, and had returned to work after Easter. They'd had no choice really. Once the word was out that Leary's might need joiners, the company had been overwhelmed by out-of-work tradesmen who wanted the labour. It was a better outcome that Leary's had the original workers back at their jobs.

'That was nice of Agatha to say that she could have me for a sister any day,' Julie said. 'Dumbstruck I was to see how they took to me. Makes me locked in with you lot.'

'Do you want to be locked in? It sounds like a prison.'

She smiled. 'No, not like that.'

Brendan loved her, had for months; well, from the very beginning really, and Agatha and Mary had welcomed her, too. He was sure of his feelings for her and he hoped she felt the same way.

'Your sisters are grand,' she said. 'Each time I'm with them I'm more easy with them.'

The cab went up Grosvenor Street towards Julie's house. Brendan said, 'Father, I think, might accept you, but Mother we'll have to work on.'

'But what if we can't? What if she never likes me?'

'If that's the case, then I'll choose you above them.'

'I hope that never happens, Brendan. Mary said to me that her and Agatha don't like going behind their mother's back by seeing me. I don't either.'

'We'll have to find a way to get you to meet my parents again, without fuss.'

Julie looked excited. 'You know you told me how your mother remembered her attacker after the ball in February?'

'Yes.'

'You also told me what he looked like.' Brendan nodded. 'Now, I ran into Aiden the other day and we chatted.'

Brendan was irritated by this news but tried not to let it show.

'We talked about larrikins,' Julie said, 'and I told Aiden how angry I was that another woman, and your mother, especially, had been attacked. I talked about the King and what he looked like.' She squeezed his hand. 'Brendan, Aiden says that he knows him. His name's Jimmy McNab and he was an apprentice along with Aiden before he went off the rails. Aiden is going to keep an ear to the ground. Maybe he can find out where the King is living. I didn't want to say anything in front of your sisters today.'

'That'd be wonderful,' Brendan said pleased. 'I'll tell Mother and the police.'

'Not the coppers, Brendan. They do nothing to larrikins. You should have seen Aiden's face when I told him about your mum. It was like it was me who'd been belted. If I know him, he'll stitch up Jimmy.'

Brendan was not keen that Aiden was back in Julie's life and he didn't like owing the boilermaker a debt. 'Just get Aiden to find out where McNab lives. My mother will confront him with the police and see him go to jail. She's not scared of him.'

She nodded. 'All right, I will.'

The cab stopped and Julie pressed his hand. Brendan alighted and helped her down. She took off her bonnet and walked up to her front door. 'Would you like a hot drink?'

'I would.'

He followed her inside, his eyes adjusting to the darkness. A hint of lavender settled on him. The room was cold. It was winter after all.

'Sit down,' she said. 'I won't be long.'

Brendan collapsed on the lounge. 'Where's your mother and Billy?'

Julie raised her voice over the noise of the sink pump. 'Gone to be with Dad at Coonamble.' She came in a minute later with two cups and some fruit.

'I couldn't eat anything,' Brendan said.

Julie sat beside him. 'Can you take time off from your work?'

'Like a holiday?'

'Yes.'

'Not until the Imperial's finished.'

The kettle whistled. 'I'll be right back,' she said.

Brendan thought about his future. The job offer with the bank had lapsed and he understood that. God, they couldn't wait for ever but they knew he could build their branches. His experience was evident to them. He'd have to start small, but his great-uncle was on side to back him, although Gerry still wanted him to have the top job at Leary's.

Julie came in with the teapot and placed it down. She sat beside him. 'I need to let it draw. Now, what could we do in the meantime?'

She moved closer, her eyes on his lips. 'I've had a lovely day,' she said as she stroked his cheek.

He shivered. 'I've had wonderful days with you.'

She moved closer. 'Each time we've been together it seems right.' Brendan agreed. She took his hand. 'I've got feelings for you, Brendan, deep feelings.'

Her face was earnest and Brendan didn't hesitate. 'I have feelings for you too.'

'Kiss me,' she said.

He closed the distance, her mouth cushioning his lips, her hands holding his head. Brendan ended the kiss and hugged her. 'Julie, I love you.'

She laid her head on his chest. 'Do you?'

'I do. I always have.'

She raised her head and he kissed her again. His hand slipped to her breast and he pressed it. She moaned and broke away, took his hand and kissed it. 'I love you, too, and I want you, Brendan … but if we do what we want, then what happens?'

Her eyes were intense, her face was flushed and he sensed that her need was as strong as his own. He wanted her, all of her, to love, here and now. She held his gaze and she seemed to ask a question of him. He loved her, wanted no other man to have her, and the position was simple. 'Will you marry me?' he said. Julie looked away. Brendan turned her face to him. 'I want you, Julie. I want us to be together. Well?'

'But your mother?'

'We talked about that. Will you marry me?'

'Yes, oh yes. When?'

Brendan grinned. 'Well, I'll have to ask your Dad formally. Will he be in Sydney soon?'

'I'll make him come, don't worry. Then you can ask him.'

'Grand. We'll have to have a decent engagement period. What about spring?'

'And I'll get a ring?'

'The best I can buy.'

'Don't be silly,' she said, and bit her lip. Her eyes became moist. 'I'm not like that. You know that.' She turned away and started crying.

'What's wrong?'

Julie turned and smiled. 'Nothing. I'm just lucky, that's all.' She wiped her face.

'No ... *I'm* the one who's lucky,' Brendan stood up. 'Now, I best go before I do something we might both regret.'

'What about your tea?'

Brendan grinned. 'I'm so excited. I couldn't drink it.'

She stood and took his hands in hers. 'I love you and want to show you how much I love you.' She stroked his cheek. 'And you want me, I can tell. When it happens it will—'

'I know. Now let me go ... please.'

She walked him to the door. 'Sunday?'

'I'll pick you up and we'll go sailing.'

'Grand,' she said. 'Till then, goodbye ... my love.'

Brendan skipped up Princes Street. On the way home he thought about his future, how great it looked. There was one dark spot—his mother. He had to convince her.

Richard walked with purpose along Pitt Street to the bank. He smiled as he thought what his father's face would look like when he saw the money. It was true that Richard had acquired that same money underhandedly, and the brickworks could still unmask him, but he wouldn't spend a penny of it himself. And he was proud that he hadn't touched it after all these months. Now, the money would go to a proper charity, an orphanage ideally. Here it was, July, and he had not gambled for twenty-two long months. Once he placed the money on his father's desk, he would prove he had beaten the cards—for good! Then he could get his authority back and continue to be vigilant with his addiction. Reaching the bank in Martin Place, he sprinted up the steps and made his withdrawal.

'That's £300, Mr Leary,' the bank teller said, handing over the crisp notes. 'Please let us convert it to a draft for you. With larrikins afoot, it's too dangerous to carry around all that cash.'

Richard smiled at the anxious man. 'It'll be right, thank you.'

'Very well. The Imperial Beneficial Charitable Trust account is now closed. Would you like an envelope for the notes?'

'Yes, thank you,' Richard said, and took the money. He went to sign the receipt and paused.

'It's the twenty-fifth of July, Mr Leary,' the teller said.

'Thank you.' Richard signed and placed the money into his jacket pocket.

'Good afternoon, sir.' The teller said and glanced at the clock. 'You're our last customer.'

Striding from the bank, eager to see his father, Richard headed into George Street and spotted Simon Spencer, one of his cardplaying friends, walking out of an office. The man, nattily dressed in a new suit and hat, was coming towards him. Richard didn't want to meet him and slipped into a men's clothing store.

'Yes, sir,' the salesman greeted him, 'what can I do for you today?'

Richard scanned the selection of suits on display, all cheap and of poor weave and cut. 'I'll just look myself, if that's all right.'

'Look around my friend, look around our wonderful selection of fine cloth.'

Richard ducked behind a rack of suits, which shielded him from the street. He felt one garment and left a damp imprint. He was perspiring and hiding in the musty fabrics, certain that if Simon saw him he'd convince him to join him in playing. This was silly, wilting like a girl, afraid to face up to him, but he couldn't move. He forced his eyes shut and a tremor passed through him.

Twenty-two months he'd lasted and he'd been good: he'd built his armour against the pull, and he needed that protection now.

Simon must have passed by now and Richard could cover the short distance to Leary's city office with the money that weighed like a brick in his pocket. He ventured a look around the rack. The shop door opened and Simon stepped in.

'Richard,' Simon said, spotting him. 'Nice to see you.'

The shop assistant came up to them. 'Mr Spencer, welcome.'

'Afternoon, Jack. Have you got that scarf I ordered?' Simon turned to Richard, his cologne strong. 'I won't be long.'

'Come to the counter, please Mr Spencer,' the assistant said. 'I've kept it for you.'

Richard could leave. He could go without saying goodbye. That would be bad manners but he'd keep his money and his determination. That's what he should do, but his feet would not move. Perspiration trickled down his back. It was the worst he'd felt for a long time. *Keep the line and keep Victoria.*

Simon came up to him, carrying his parcel. 'It's been a while, Richard. It's after four. Are you free?'

Richard felt the urge returning, just a spark but it was there and he hated himself for it. He pushed against it. 'I have to see Father, Simon, I'm sorry.'

'Pity, because I've got time and there's a game on in Sussex Street. You must still be playing all these months, surely? Not with me, it seems, but others?'

'With others ... yes.' Richard blurted out the lie. He didn't want Spencer to know he hadn't played for a long time. But why couldn't he tell him that he'd stopped? *Be assertive, man!*

Simon smiled. 'Just the four of us; that sound all right?'

Just say no, turn and walk away. Do it. Leave. But he couldn't.

Richard felt hot because he was losing—badly. The Imperial Beneficial Charitable Trust money was gone and, worse, an IOU he'd pledged—all lost during the last two hours. The remnants of his weekly wages stared up at him from the table. He held three jacks—a fair hand, and at least he might be able to keep what was in front of him. Sweat filmed on his forehead and he wiped it away. Nearly two years he'd lasted, a lifetime between games. Well, he'd been kidding himself! The first hour had been brilliant, the excitement had built and peaked, and the other two players had left, but now he was here with Simon, at the bottom of the pit once again.

Simon eyeballed him. 'What have you got?'

Richard exposed his hand and waited. He couldn't look at the cards Simon displayed but heard them brush the green felting of the table top.

'Three kings. That's it, my friend.'

Richard exhaled, his mouth dry. He owed five hundred pounds. His eyes filmed over—five hundred pounds, a fortune! 'That's me for tonight,' he said in a quiet voice.

Simon coughed. 'I'd think so. Five hundred.'

Richard pushed himself up. 'I'll have to give you a note.'

'Leary, you're good for it, but it's a big sum. How about in ten days? That's ... the fifth of August?'

Richard was hoping for a month, his usual time in the past, but he had no choice. 'I'll give you a bank draft, Simon.'

Simon grinned. 'Good man. You'll win it back. See you next time.' He nodded to Richard and left.

Richard concentrated on moving. He had to think about motion and balance. Reaching like a blind man for the door, he left the club by the staircase to the rear lane. He mounted up. The wind pierced through him and he shivered, just as his horse did. Riding home to Glebe he thought about what he had to do. *Five hundred pounds*. It was still not sinking in. After such a long period of effort, he'd given in so easily.

He formed a fist and pounded his thigh in anger, the pain coursing through his leg, then he pounded it again and again until his tears blinded him. There was no other way. He'd have to borrow from the loan sharks, and pay their 30 per cent obscene interest. On the way, visions of Victoria and Mark appeared and he pushed them from his mind. They were too good for him: a man who was weak and helpless, and too soft to say no. Too rotten to fight back and ignore his need.

His house came into view. He pulled himself together to give a semblance of normalcy. He got down from his horse, stabled it and walked into the parlour.

'Hello, dear,' Victoria said, looking up from her seat by the fire. 'You're very pale. Are you ill?'

'No, I'm all right.'

'The site work is tiring you too much. You should speak to your father about getting some assistants.'

Richard bent down and kissed her, his hand lingering on her cheek. 'Yes, I might. But now I just want to sleep.'

Victoria didn't answer but her worried look remained. Richard turned and walked up to his bedroom, each footstep heavy with guilt and something worse, a chill of fear.

Richard climbed the staircase of the Paddington Hotel, disturbing the smoke rising from the lower bar area, the smell of hops redolent in his nostrils. Reaching the top landing, he scanned the crowd and spotted his man, who was in conversation with a companion sitting opposite him. Richard approached the table, bile rising from his stomach at the thought of what he had to do.

The suited man looked up and smiled. 'Mr Leary. Now, there's a face I haven't seen for a long while.'

'Mr Clark,' Richard said.

The man held out his hand. 'Jordan, please, Richard. We're old friends, surely. Come, sit down.' Clark eyeballed his partner, who stood up and left. Richard sat down. 'A drink?' Clark asked.

'No, thank you.'

'Ah, then it's business.'

'I need a loan,' Richard said.

Clark sat back and remained silent for a moment. 'Of course, our usual rates will apply.'

'Five hundred pounds.'

Clark whistled. 'My, Richard you have been naughty. Not like last time. A sum that big, well ...'

'I'll pay your thirty per cent.'

Clark smiled. 'You will indeed and you'll have it all back to me in twenty days.'

Richard's eyes expanded. 'No, it's forty,' he said.

The loan shark opened his hands in a pleading gesture. 'Times have changed. Last time we had to remind you and we had to speak to your pretty wife. How is she? I see from the papers you've had a son. Congratulations.' He leaned towards Richard. 'But if you think you can do better than me, there are always others you can go to.'

Richard shook his head.

'Very well,' Clark said and brought a notebook and pencil from his jacket. He wrote something in it and smiled back at Richard. 'It's the twenty-eighth of July today and the seventeenth of August is my reckoning. We'll meet again and you'll give me £650.'

Richard's anger rose. He pondered the alternatives. Jordan Clark was a bandit and a thug, his dapper clothes, gold cufflinks and handmade shoes notwithstanding. It was a pity Victoria had seen them together the last time. Her suspicions had been right. But he had no choice. Better the devil you know, and it had taken him two days to get to see Clark. 'You'll get your money back,' he said.

Clark slapped him on the shoulder. 'Good man.'

'But keep away from my family.'

Clark had a hurt look on his face. 'I'm a businessman, Richard. Just keep your side of the contract and all will be well.' He looked up and signalled to a man in the corner who had a bent nose, forearms like skittles and shoulders wide as a barrow. He came over to them, carrying a leather bag. 'Gus,' Clark said, 'go down below with this ... gentleman, find a quiet corner and give him five hundred pounds.'

Gus looked at Richard and started for the stairs. Richard stood up and followed. He felt his coat sleeve pulled.

'Remember, Mr Leary—twenty days.'

John placed his napkin down beside his plate and smiled at his family seated around him. 'The first of August, horses' birthday,' he said. 'That reminds me to place a bet at Randwick this Saturday. Imperial is favourite in the fourth and I'll have a flutter.'

It had been another tense dinner at home and Brendan wanted to clear the air. It was necessary, one way or the other. 'Mother, could I talk with you?'

'If it's about that young lady,' Catherine replied, 'both your father and I want to be present.'

'It is.'

'Mother,' Mary said, 'if you want my opinion, Miss Carson's a nice girl and just right for Brendan.'

'I think so, too,' Agatha added.

Brendan was chuffed that his sisters had spoken up.

'Thank you, both,' their mother replied, straight-faced, 'but this needs to be settled between the three of us. Come, Brendan, into the drawing room.'

Brendan sat opposite his parents with his back to the fire. He could've done without the extra heat. 'I'm going to get married,' he declared. 'I've asked Julie and she's accepted.'

His parents just looked at him, shocked. His father recovered first. 'So, you've declared yourself.'

'Yes.'

'Brendan, you're a fool,' Catherine said. 'This girl—'

'Her name is Julie, Mother. Please call her that—if not, Miss Carson.'

'She will ruin you,' she said.

'I don't think so.'

'You wouldn't know. She's blinded you. You can't think straight.'

'When is the wedding?' John asked.

'Wait, wait,' Catherine said, looking at his father. 'No one said anything about our approval.'

Brendan had to make this clear. 'I don't need it, Mother.'

Catherine sat back. Her lower lip trembled and Brendan felt sad for her. 'You would do this?' she said. 'Inflict such pain on us. Rebel against sound advice?'

Brendan sighed. 'I'd like your blessing, but if not that, then at least your acknowledgement.'

'I don't understand you,' she said. 'All these years you've acted in a mature way, then as soon as one dollymop turns your head, you become a blithering idiot.'

'Catherine, it's done,' his father said. 'The boy has decided.'

'Against all good sense.'

'I understand how you feel, Mother. I do. But believe me, Julie has been the hardest to convince. You don't know her. You've never spent time with her. You are prejudiced.'

'You are impertinent!'

'But honest.'

Catherine stood up. 'I'll not accept your manner. I will not accept your decision to marry and I will not accept that woman into this house.'

She was beyond trying to reason with, and Brendan had no option. 'If that's the case, I'll move out. I should have done so by now, anyway. The wedding is in November at St Patrick's, Church Hill. You are both welcome.'

'Oh, Brendan,' Catherine said, and brought out a handkerchief and dabbed her eyes. 'How could you do this to me?' She got control and stood erect. 'If that's how you feel, then there's no more to say. Goodnight.' She turned and left the room.

His father watched her go and went to the drinks trolley. 'Would you like one?'

'I think I'd better,' Brendan said and sighed.

Brendan took the whisky. 'I can't convince her, can I?'

'It's been a shock, son.'

'But she's fighting me on it.'

'She is. I'm not happy either, but it's your life and you have to make your own choices.' John sat down.

'Julie isn't a mistake, Father.'

'Your mother thinks she is, all right. But, I think Julie's made of the right stuff, even though I don't know the girl.'

Brendan was pleased. 'Thank you, Father.'

'Your mother might come around. Not fully, mind, but we have—what—three months to get resolution?'

'End of November's the date.'

'Right,' John said and refilled Brendan's glass.

'Thank you, Father,' Brendan said. 'And while we're talking about my future—I want the top job in the company.'

John sat back and smiled. 'You do, do you?'

'I think ... no, I know ... I can make Leary's great. But if you can't agree, then I have no option but to leave the company.'

'This is sudden!' his father said.

'I've been thinking about it for months.'

'You can't leave, Brendan! You're part of the place, part of the fabric.'

He'd never seen his father so shocked and Brendan worried that he might have another heart attack. 'Maybe, but if I can't have the top job, then I'll go out on my own. Gerry will back me.'

'My uncle?'

'Yes, Father.'

His father said nothing for some time. 'Brendan, think. I have to hand over soon and you've got the goods.'

'So, have I got the job then?' Brendan said and his father paused. 'I see, I haven't. It's Richard and that's that.'

'I don't like being pushed.'

Brendan felt confident and strong and had no qualms facing his father. Quite a change from over two years ago. 'I know. That's why I have to go. You've made up your mind.' Brendan finished his drink and stood up. 'I'll work till the end of the year at Leary's, then I'll be gone. Now, if you'll excuse me I've got to grab the *Herald* and find some digs.'

'Got it all worked out, yeah?'

'No, Father. It's going to be tough, but that's how I've been brought up. It'll be more of the same. Goodnight.'

Mary Leary was tidying up her marked papers in the empty classroom on the first floor of the Elizabeth Street State School. It was only two years old and was near to Market Street, surrounded by a high wall. She searched for her diary and flicked the marker to today, 2 August. There were two students who had arrived late for class that day and she wrote down their names. Henrietta was due any moment and Mary was excited. Footsteps echoed in the hall outside. This must be her and Mary scribbled the final name, turned down the gaslight, exited the room and smiled at her friend. 'Hello,' she said. 'How was your day?'

'The boys were lazy again with their fractions, but we'll get there.'

Three days a week after school, Henrietta was tutoring two brothers from a wealthy barrister's family. The wages supplemented her meagre income from the charitable donations given to the Darlinghurst refuge.

Henri smiled. 'Finishing up?' She grasped Mary's hand, thrilling her. 'I've missed you.'

'Hush.'

'Is there anyone here?' Henri said and Mary shook her head. 'Then we're all alone. Quick, in here.' Henri pulled her friend into the darkened classroom. 'Oh God, you look good.'

Mary giggled. 'I look a fright and it's only been two days.'

Henri kissed her on the lips. Mary responded and her lover pressed her against a desk and started to caress her. Mary broke away, her face flushed. 'No, not here—at your place.'

'Right then, let's go,' Henri said. Outside, she linked her arm with Mary's as the night winds hit them. 'So, did you get it?'

'I did, but it took some convincing.'

Henri squeezed her elbow. 'I knew you'd succeed.'

'Father was dubious,' Mary said. 'He's generous, but to charities he thinks are straightforward. Your refuge is on the fringe, a little controversial, and he baulked. I said that downtrodden women needed all the help they could get. I mentioned his grandson and how would he cope without a family and he wavered, but your idea convinced him to part with his money.'

'Has he agreed to the presentation?' Henri said.

'Yes. Half of his donation would go to the Campbell Street College and the rest to your refuge. I suggested that his donation to the college could be called the Leary Prize and would be given to the best graduating student. When I told Father he could give the prize at the graduation ceremony he accepted. Both Brendan and Richard will be there too.'

They stopped at the tram shelter. 'Good,' Henri said, 'then let's get the cash.'

'I'll raise an invoice with Leary's tomorrow. We'll have the money at the end of the week. Here's our tram.'

Henri huddled closer as they boarded. 'Good girl.'

They found a double seat at the back.

'How's Gillian going?' Henri said.

Mary sniffed. 'It's smelly back here, isn't it? She's all right now she's graduated.'

'No sad regrets about the baby?'

'Sometimes, but she will be a good teacher. She's a natural.'

'Give her the job of organising the presentation,' Henri said.

'I was thinking the same thing.'

They sat in silence for a while then Henri prodded her. 'This is our stop. I can't wait for some tea and toast.' Henri looked around to see that no one was watching them, and then she brushed Mary's mouth with her finger. 'And other goodies.'

Brendan smiled at Julie, who cuddled closer to him in the cab. 'It was a good night,' he said. In the cold August wind, her body was warm against his. It had been three days since his announcement to his parents, and it was becoming impossible to live at Point Piper. His sisters had tried to speak with their mother, but she had resisted them. 'I have to look at digs this Saturday afternoon. Will you come with me?'

Julie became quiet. Her excitement following the dance seemed to have ebbed. 'This is getting bad. You having to leave home.'

'It's my choice Julie, and it's for us.'

'I know, but I feel sorry for your mum.'

'So do I.'

'All right,' she said, 'I'll come with you. Whereabouts?'

'Glebe. Richard said there's a room coming free not far from him. He said he'd put me up at his place but Mark's a handful and not sleeping well. They're up at all hours with the boy.'

The cab stopped and Brendan helped her down. 'Is your mother home?'

She looked down and shook her head. Brendan took her hand and led her towards her front door. Julie stopped. 'Please, don't come in,' she said.

'What's wrong?'

She kissed his lips lightly. 'I worry that we'll do ... things.'

'But I love you.'

'And I you, but I don't trust us.'

Brendan held her hands. 'Just for a little while? I promise I'll be a gentleman.'

Julie smiled. 'That's sweet, but you see, if we go inside ... I may not act like a lady.'

He pecked her nose. 'You are the wise one, my darling. I'll see you soon.'

Julie smiled. 'Thank you.' She hugged him and he kissed her again. She disengaged herself.

Brendan smiled. 'Saturday? About three?'

'Julie,' a voice near them said.

They both turned and Aiden stood there. He took off his cap and nodded to Brendan. 'Mr Leary, I hoped I'd find you here. I was coming to talk to Julie, anyway.'

'What do you want to tell me, Aiden?' she said.

'I know where Jimmy McNab lives.'

Brendan became excited. 'Let's go!'

Aiden hesitated. 'We could, but better if you tell your parents and they can bring the cops.' He smiled. 'He's not going anywhere. He broke his leg when he jumped off a roof getting away from a robbery. His gang took him to his place. He always was a bit stupid.'

Brendan was so relieved. 'Thank you, Aiden,' he said, extending his hand. 'We'll take it from here.'

Aiden took it and squeezed. He was looking at Julie now. 'No problem; here's the address.' He handed Brendan a piece of paper.

Julie pressed Aiden's forearm. 'Thank you.'

Aiden nodded to them both. 'Goodnight.'

Brendan watched him go. 'He's a good man.'

'He is. Now, my love, straight to your mum and tell her.'

'I will.'

Brendan turned and walked away. He felt good. He was in love, he'd found his mother's attacker and the big pub was to be opened in four days.

Outside the Campbell Street College hall, it was freezing, but in here the gas wall heaters were disgorging their breath like brick kilns and John could've stripped to his shorts. Sitting in the front row, he smiled to himself: that would surprise the ten rows of proud parents and friends of the graduating class of teachers seated behind him! The speeches had droned on and now shuffling feet, moving chairs and muffled conversation were signs of impatience. This was the last speaker and then the graduation prize-giving would start.

It had been a busy day. That morning he'd gone with Catherine and the police to capture the King in Harrington Street. It was pitiful really. The larrikin was incapacitated and quiet, with nothing like the arrogance he'd shown in the past. The police had arrested him and charged him with assault.

On Monday next, the Imperial Hotel would be officially opened, on time. There had been no trouble from the unions during the completion of the hotel; they were in disarray. A few key sites had jacked up against them and the big builders were back in control. Most of the afternoon he'd spent with Richard, Brendan and Sullivan doing the rounds and checking that all would be well. Cleaning crews would work all weekend, then they would be ready to unveil the great hotel to Sydney. That was the good news. On the home front, he had three months to get Catherine and Brendan reconciled and four months to keep Brendan in the company.

The applause died away and people started talking.

'Better get ready,' Richard said beside him, mopping his brow. 'Here's the presentation.'

The principal made a signal to John, who mounted the stage. The audience came into focus and the background noise died down.

'Madam Principal, distinguished guests,' John said, 'it is my pleasure tonight, Friday the fifth of August, 1887, to present the Leary's Award for achievement to the best graduating student ...'

As his father spoke, Richard battled with an urge to leave the hall. He had to find a game and to win with a new strategy. Forget about the carefree techniques he'd used in the past, no, now he had to play with logic, memory and reason. There was no thrill needed or sought now. He needed a win so that he could repay his debt. After that—finished, and he meant it; he'd never been as confident about anything in his life. It would be a campaign with an end objective. He smiled as he remembered Spencer's gratitude yesterday when his money had been repaid. Then he stopped smiling.

He had less than two weeks to pay back Jordan Clark. Would he find a game? And worse, could he play like an artist and not an addict? That was the challenge.

The room was full of women. Teachers, women teachers— a dull bunch, he thought, and not a sweet scent among them. The applause started for the recipient. An attractive woman approached the lectern and Richard looked at her. It was Gillian, his Gillian! She hadn't seen him yet; her eyes were downcast, then fixed on the silver trophy his father handed to her.

'Congratulations, Miss Thompson,' his father said to her, then he stood aside as she approached the lectern. The clapping died down and she caught Richard's stare. She blinked, then looked over him to the audience behind.

'Thank you to the College,' she said, 'and Leary's Contracting for this prize.' She raised it above her head. 'It proves that hard work can win out and ... women can do the work of men!'

Most women stood up and applauded, some stamping their feet. His father's mouth fell open at the sight and Richard looked around. The noise subsided as Gillian left the stage. He waited till the remaining winners had received their prizes and the ceremony ended. Richard scanned the room and saw Gillian leaving. He went to go after her, but a hand on his arm stopped him.

'Be on site tomorrow ... early,' his father said, 'for a final inspection. You have the nightwatchmen organised?'

'For the next three nights. Sam Shepherd, the hoist driver, and his mate.'

'Good,' his father said, moving off.

Richard ran out of the front door, the cold hitting him like one of the Imperial's fancy new freezers. Gillian was just turning into Elizabeth Street. She still looked good, nice figure under that coat. Memories of their lovemaking came to him. 'Gillian, wait up,' he said.

She stopped and turned as Richard pulled his coat closer around him. 'Richard. How are you?'

'I'm good.' He pointed to the trophy in her bag. 'Congratulations, it's quite an honour.' She looked at him, saying nothing. 'Would you like a cup of tea? Anything to get out of this cold.'

She looked past him, and he turned but there was no one there. 'Just for a little while. There's a place close by.' He took her arm and she didn't resist.

Ever since she'd met Mary Leary, Gillian had known that she might run into Richard at some time. Inside the tea shop she removed her hat and her hair fell free. Richard ordered their tea. He smiled at the waitress and Gillian felt a flutter at that smile and chastised herself. This man had dumped her and she was going to make him pay for the hurt he'd given her.

He returned to the table and sat opposite her. 'So, what have you been doing?'

'Swotting most of the time.'

'Why?' he asked surprised.

'Why?' she said.

'Yes.'

Still the same arrogance, she thought. 'I want to improve myself. Since … us, I've changed. I want to do things.'

'I thought all women wanted was to get married and have children.'

That jolted her and she looked down and pressed her lips together. Looking back at him, she composed herself. Now was the time. She felt confident that she could tell him and still not break apart. 'I did have a child. Your child.'

Richard looked shocked. 'You had a baby?'

'I had your baby, Richard. A boy.'

Richard's head jerked. 'But … how do you know it was—?'

'It was yours, Richard, yours.' Gillian leaned forward and noticed a drop of perspiration on Richard's cheek. Good, let him sweat. 'I'm not a trollop. You were not my first, but it's yours.' Their tea arrived and she poured them each a cup. 'My son,' she said, 'was adopted by a wealthy country family. That's all the refuge would tell me.' She took a sip of her tea.

Richard stared at her. He looked stunned and a part of her felt good about that. 'Refuge? Dear God, Gillian! Why didn't you tell me?' He placed his hand on hers but she slipped it away. 'I could have helped you.'

Her resolve weakened and she held her breath. No. She would be strong. She exhaled and said, 'Would you? You left me. Why would I think you would help me?'

'But I had to leave you. I was engaged.' Richard looked at his untouched teacup. 'A son,' he said quietly and looked at her. 'Victoria and I have a son, you know.'

'Yes, I read it in the newspaper,' Gillian said and sipped her tea. Her resolve ebbed from her but she would not show any sadness. Not to him. She put her cup down and stood up. 'I have to get home, Richard. Goodbye.'

Richard stood. 'But you can't leave like this!'

'And why not?' The tea shop had few patrons and she felt strong. 'I have a life, starting now. A profession that will give me a reason to wake each morning. That calling makes me forget, just for a little while, that I have a son out there whom I'll never see.' Gillian held her breath, stemming the emotion that threatened to break her. She regained her self-control. 'I'll live with that pain for the rest of my life.' Her eyes were moist now. 'But you have a son whom you'll see every day. Goodnight, Richard.' She turned to go and he sat down.

Gillian closed the tea room door behind her and walked past the glazed shop front. She glanced inside. Richard sat staring at his cup of tea, still untouched. Gillian wrapped her scarf tighter around her neck. *Good, I'm glad he's shocked, he damn well deserves it, and more!*

Chapter Fourteen

Just as the clock on the General Post Office chimed two, Sam Shepherd arrived at the Imperial Hotel. Rubbing his gloved hands to warm them in the morning chill, he felt important. Richard Leary was a champion of a man and Sam felt proud that he had been chosen to be on watch, to guard the colossus and protect it until its unwrapping in just over eight hours.

The Imperial Hotel was to him a magic thing, a giant sculpture, the biggest building in town. Leary's had done it and he, Sam Shepherd, was part of that team. From labourer to hoist driver to protector—not bad, he thought, and grinned. And as hoist driver he'd got to meet everybody, including the bosses.

The southerly whipping along Clarence Street felt as though it carried ice from the Antarctic. I'll have stalactites on my nose he thought, if I don't move. *I'd kill for a mug of tea.* But he knew as he set off down Margaret Street that he'd have to do without. He hoped Herb would turn up, but Herb had a habit of being late.

A stench as though from the open sewer hit his nose. He remembered Mr Simpkins showing him how the Imperial's drains were connected to the main sewer, all very modern, but not so the streets, which discharged their waste God knew where. The sound of a bottle smashing made him turn. Just across the lane, a drunk swore and vomited into the broken gutter.

A pity the Council couldn't fix their streets and their sewage. Leary's had had to build new kerbs along the boundaries of its site. It made no sense, the new meeting the very old and busted.

The street lights lit the hotel's nooks and shop entrances where tramps might be sleeping. All quiet. In any case, tramps were not a problem, because at six-foot-three-inches tall, Sam scared most of them away, even if he was as thin as a reed. No, it was the mess they left behind that he had a problem with. Turning around, he headed back to the corner and looked up, his neck stretching to take in the height of the grand building. The polished stone and brass façade reflected the street lights and the steel-framed windows glinted in their new sheen. The hotel was a colossal new piece of Sydney—beautiful.

A big man stood on the corner wearing an overcoat and a hat, which touched his ears. Herb, Sam grunted, about time.

'Morning, Tub,' Herb said as Sam approached him.

Sam liked the nickname, because he was more likely to slip through the deck boards of a jetty.

'Freeze the balls off, Herb.'

'Yeah. Anything happening?'

'Quiet.'

A laugh made them both look. A couple opposite were walking along the street and the man's arm was around the woman, his hand clasping her breast.

'Lucky bugger,' Herb said. The woman saw them and pushed her lover's hand away. The man muttered something.

'Come on Herb,' Sam said. 'Let's check the doors. I don't want no problems and it's too bloody cold just standing still. Are our boys coming?'

'At four-thirty. Mr Leary said he wanted men here just to help out if things went wrong.'

'Fair enough.'

Sam saw the wagon first and said, 'Here are the bench seats for the ceremony! Herb, come on!'

The wagon stopped outside the Imperial Hotel and the driver jumped down and started pulling benches from the back with Herb's help. But something was wrong. Sam looked for the legs to go with the benches but they weren't there. 'It's half past five, mate,' Sam said to the driver. 'Where have ya been? And where're the bloody legs?'

'What legs? No one told me about no legs.'

Great, Sam thought. Last-minute problems like this had been going on for two days. They'd had to ward off two separate attacks from larrikins who'd tried to break into the new pub. Then there'd been a rush to fix half a dozen doors that had come loose. Now this. 'There's got to be legs to fit the benches! Else how are they going to stand up?'

'Not my problem, mate.'

'Herb, grab Thommo from our team. He's a carpenter. He's got to fit legs to all the seats so the big nobs have something to sit on. Get some tools from the basement store and get the lads cracking.'

'I'm onto it.'

'What the bloody hell is that?' Sam said.

A tall man in a well-cut suit and overcoat stood on the footpath in front of the hotel. Leaning against his legs were two equal-sized pieces of timber as big as washboards, joined together with leather straps. The man stood the two pieces upright, lifted them above him and eased his head between the straps. The front piece read 'BABEL TOWER WILL FALL—UNSAFE'. Just as Sam went over to him, the man turned around and he saw that the other board read 'REPENT NOW'.

'Sweet Mother of God,' Sam said. 'Hey, you!'

The man faced him. 'Yes?'

'What are you doing?' Sam said.

'I'm here to protest, young sir,' he said and glanced down. 'I am on the public footpath ... or what exists of it. I am not trespassing. I will not cause you any mischief.'

Sam scratched his head, sighed and turned away. He'd deal with him later. 'Just steer clear of our boundary and out of my hair,' he said.

A rumble came from the pub opposite. A muscled brewery worker unwound a rope and harnessed another keg to drop into the pub's basement. What he would do for a pint now, Sam thought. An hour till light, thank goodness.

Sam drank his coffee—a luxury—gripping the cup with both hands in an attempt to warm them up. A council worker extinguished the last of the street lamps as daylight seeped across the still chilly forecourt. This Monday would be fine and sunny. Sam knew it must be around six and he could eat a horse.

'These are the last free cups of coffee we'll get from this place,' Herb said near him. 'From now on, only toffs will grace our Imperial Hotel's coffee lounge. I'll go and see if the area is clear for the barricades.' He sipped some more, then spotted men approaching and said, 'The Learys are here. Right on time.'

Sam looked up and was glad. All this responsibility had been hard and as Richard walked towards him, he saw his boss in a different light. Day after day, Richard Leary copped a load that he guessed at ten times what he had just put up with. He was worth the big wages.

'Morning, Mr Richard.'

'Hello, Sam. How's it been?'

Sam was all prepared to dump his problems, then changed his mind. No, he had learned a lot and maybe that was good for his future. 'Herb and me got it all under control. Here's the police.'

Richard turned around. 'Good, give them a hand with the street barricades, will you? Then you can go.'

Brendan came up to them. 'The cleaners are here, Richard. Will I get them started on hosing down the forecourt?'

'That first, yes,' Richard said.

Sam nodded to Brendan, who returned the greeting before heading off.

'What the hell?' Richard pointed to the well-dressed protester. 'Who's that?'

'Mr Leary,' Sam said, 'he's some ratbag, but a classy one. You could talk to him and I'll come with you. Mr Richard, I don't want to leave yet. After I get the barricades sorted, I'd like the job of taking the guests in the elevator to the top after the opening.'

Richard looked him up and down. 'Sam, that job's yours, but you'd better grab a shave and wash up. Help yourself to a feed in the kitchen, too. Tell them I sent you. But before that, let's see what your friend with the sign is going to do.'

John was proud to bursting that the opening of his biggest project was finally here. He had reached the zenith of his career and his goal was achieved. Now, he could plan with certainty the handover of his company, and Richard was the likely man. The signs were good that Richard had tamed his demon. Brendan was a close second and would be fine, too, provided Brendan stayed in the fold. But that looked far from certain.

At the junction of the two city streets, a big crowd had gathered, sprinkled with school children playing truant, one of them pulling the sleeve of the bedecked silent protestor. John smiled at the man with the boards, a harmless soul with something to say.

The official invitation to the opening was dated 8 August 1887 and, despite the challenges of steel, fire protection, strikes and the crane inferno, the pub had been finished on time at the end of July. John swelled with satisfaction. The footnote on the invitation honouring the three deceased workers pricked at his happiness. They wouldn't be a footnote to him. Should he tell Catherine about the trust funds he'd set up for the survivors of the dead men? No, and he hoped Miles Cunningham, the other benefactor, would also remain anonymous.

The flash from cameras caught his attention. Sydney's Lord Mayor, Joseph Riley, dressed in his mayoral robes, was standing before the seated guests in the forecourt, praising the wonders of the project. As Riley unveiled the plaque, the noise of the applause deafened John and his hand ached from the handshakes from well-wishers. Leary's employees escorted the guests of honour, including the Premier, Henry Parkes, the owners and invited dignitaries, to the elevators to take them to the top floor of the building. It was the start of a grand tour of the completed landmark.

John shook hands with the owners and architects. He held onto William Turner's hand a little longer. 'We did it, Mr Turner.'

The architect held John's look. 'William, today, please, John—if I may. Yes, we did.'

John saw Brendan coming towards him. He glanced at the architect and said, 'I'd like to join you in a drink shortly, but for now, please excuse me.'

'I'll hold you to that,' Turner said, before he himself was joined by other well-wishers.

'Just about done, father?' Brendan said coming up to him.

'Yes. Where's your brother?'

Brendan pointed to the lobby. 'He's talking up Leary's to a new client. Do you want me to get him?'

'No, I'll find him. Tell me, are you still keen to move on?'

'I am—that is, if you haven't changed your mind.'

'No, I haven't,' John said.

'Then I'm away.'

John was disappointed. 'It doesn't seem right.'

'You went out on your own, Father. Rupert Jenkins told me. I had a beer with him and Gerry two nights ago. Mr Jenkins said you left his employ to start your own business.'

Guilty as charged. 'I did.'

'So you can understand why I'm doing it.'

They said nothing more and watched as the crowd celebrated and marvelled at the magnificent building they'd built.

Brendan smiled and turned to John. 'But I'm not turning my back on Leary's. This company is my life, Father, and my family will fit within it. I want to run the company one day and I believe I can do it. If it's not for the foreseeable future, then that's all right.'

John smiled. 'That so?'

'Yes.'

John said, 'Look, go mingle and get us more orders. You're still here till Christmas.'

Brendan walked away and John looked for Richard in the crowd in the lobby. He spotted him talking to a well-dressed business-man. As John walked towards the pair, the man prodded Richard in the chest three times, turned and left. Richard dropped his head. When John came up to him, Richard turned, his face pale and perspiring. 'What's wrong?' John asked. 'Who was that?'

Richard grinned. 'That? Oh, just a disgruntled architect. Said he could build sixteen floors in brick in a shorter time. I begged to differ.' Richard wiped the perspiration from his face. 'It's hot, isn't it?'

Not in this weather, John thought. Whoever that man was had frightened his son, and that wasn't an easy thing to do—but Richard would deal with it. 'Tomorrow,' John said, 'I want you to make sure any defective work here is planned out to be completed.'

'I'm onto it already. Brendan and I will divvy it up. Sullivan has the list from Turners. We'll have any defects rectified.'

'Excellent. Now, let's celebrate.'

'I've just got a few things to do,' Richard said, 'then I'll join you.'

'All right,' John said, 'but don't be long. We're all due a celebration.'

Out of his father's sight, Richard loosened his tie and made his way to an office off the Imperial's lobby. Using a master key he stepped inside and stripped off his jacket. He had to be alone for a minute.

He was still rattled by his altercation a little earlier. The man had been no unhappy architect, it had been Jordan Clark. *Damn that mongrel!* Threatening him like that in broad daylight and in front of dignitaries. Richard still had time to pay and had told Clark that, but the loan shark had made it clear. 'Pay your debt on time Mr Leary,' he'd prodded. 'Pay your debt and life will be sweet.' Another prod. 'Don't pay your debt and life will be over for you.' A final prod and he'd left.

Richard had to get the money, but from where? If he couldn't win it back on cards, what could he do? If only he had his shares back, he could use those somehow. His stomach heaved. He could even sell them if need be. Rushing from the office, he vomited in the nearby toilet. Washing his face, he cleaned himself up and made his way back to the celebration. It was 8 August, so he had nine days to pay back a loan or if not … It didn't bear thinking about. He had to find a way to get that money.

Gerry Gleeson put the newspaper down on the drawing-room side table and watched his nephew fill their glasses. The *Sydney Morning Herald*'s article the previous day had been effusive in its plaudits for the majestic hotel and its opening. He took off his spectacles and looked out onto Blackburn Cove. 'So,' he said, 'the Imperial's made good money for you. Now, what's your next challenge?'

John sat down with his drink and looked at the flames in the fireplace. 'My next challenge, Uncle, is to stand down.'

Gerry was surprised at the suddenness of this, but then, why not? John was in his late fifties and probably that blacking out in court had been a sign, yet he wasn't the sort of man to give up such power easily.

John looked straight at him. 'I'm still hungry for it, the building side, and I'll still be a part of it, as a director. But, this business with the deaths and … other things has sharpened my decision.'

'When would you do it?'

'By Christmas,' John said.

Gerry smiled. 'You can't go on for ever.'

'Clearly.'

'So, who's it to be?'

John swirled the drink in his glass. 'I haven't decided. Richard is preferred but Brendan's an alternative, a real one.'

Gerry studied his nephew. John's eyes met his. 'Brendan's leaving though,' Gerry said.

'With you helping him.'

'Enough to help him survive, nephew, and no more.'

'I thought you'd be pleased that he was being considered.'

'What I want is not important,' Gerry said. He paused before he spoke again. 'Brendan's good, but you're not considering him because of that—you have lingering doubts about Richard. Am I right?'

John sipped his drink. 'I don't like to doubt Richard. He's fighting his demons, and I think he's winning. But I've had to do a mean thing. There're a few scouts I've paid to see if my son is keeping to his resolve. Either Richard is stealthy about where he plays or he's not playing at all. And he seems settled into being married. Victoria, I think, is a blessing for him.'

Gerry agreed. He held out his glass for John to refill. 'The christening was grand indeed. I've seldom seen happier parents.'

John nodded and stared into the fire. 'I can only hope Richard has given up his gambling. Then I may give him his shares back. There was a separate instruction for that, accompanying Christine's will.'

'You never talked about it.'

'No, she asked me to keep it confidential.'

'But you're telling me now?'

'Christine left it up to me,' John said, 'which is a compliment and a curse. If I feel Richard's in control, I'll give him his nine per cent shares back—with no conditions.'

'And I assume that now, with Richard's good behaviour, you're inclined to do just that?' Gerry pushed himself up and stood still while he got his balance. 'The only way you can control a gambler, John, is to watch him and pray. Richard will always have the weakness. If he's definitely not playing *and* getting help from the people we recommended, then there's hope. I'm going to bed.' He trudged across towards the doors and spoke without turning around. 'At least you're thinking seriously about Brendan and, for me, that's good. Richard will fight back, though. Goodnight, nephew.'

John finished his drink and walked up the stairs to his bedroom. He changed and got in beside Catherine.

She put down the book she'd been reading and placed her spectacles on the side table. 'We need to talk.'

Thank goodness. Catherine had been tight-lipped for a week. 'Brendan?' he asked.

'The marriage is one thing. My son leaving the company is another.'

'I don't think they're related.'

'Of course they are, dear. Brendan's angry with me for not accepting Miss Carson. I don't want this marriage, but I'm prepared to accept it, if Brendan stays at Leary's.'

'And if he doesn't want to stay?'

Catherine turned down the gaslight. 'He'll stay. He'll be so excited I've accepted his fiancée. No, he'll stay. I'll talk to him in the morning.'

'He won't be here. He's starting on the Imperial Hotel at five. He's helping Richard with the defect rectification. It's part of the completion process.'

'Then I'll see him now.' She got out of bed and donned her robe.

John settled under the covers. He wasn't so sure there'd be a rapprochement tonight but it was a start. A good one.

Brendan was placing a pair of old trousers into a cloth bag when the knock came at his bedroom door.

'May I come in?' his mother said.

'Of course.'

She sat on his bed and looked at the bag. 'What are you doing?'

'I can't take everything to Glebe, so I'm packing some clothes for the poor.'

'It's final then?'

'Don't be upset, Mother. You'll still see me around.'

'I don't want you to leave the company.'

He looked at her. 'I don't either. But it's Richard that Father's chosen. That's it.'

'What if I said that I'd condone your marriage? Would you stay?'

Brendan was overcome. 'You would accept Julie?'

'I don't know her,' she said and paused. Her eyes glistened and she touched his hand. 'But yes. Your happiness is paramount to me. You're right. I should get to know her.' He bent down and hugged her and her resolve broke, her tears wetting his cheek. 'I don't want to lose your love, my darling.'

'That you'll always have.'

She pulled away from him but held his hands. 'So you'll stay?'

'At Point Piper or Leary's?'

'I'd like both.'

Her face was pleading. He knew that the triple hit of an unwanted fiancée, and him leaving home and Leary's, had knocked her. He couldn't keep hurting her. His future might have to wait a while. He said. 'I can't stay for ever if Richard's the boss. You know that.'

'I know, I know, but just for a bit longer. Time for me to get to know this girl who's taken your heart.'

She had given ground, and that would've been hard. He would too. 'All right.'

John's carriage pulled up outside the Imperial Hotel. His beloved project was just two days old, guests were booking in and the hotel was a going concern. He brought out his watch—four o'clock.

Richard should be here soon and John had decided on his son's future. On cue, Richard walked out the front door of the hotel in the company of a Turner associate. The architect peeled away and Richard started walking down Margaret Street.

'Richard,' John called out. His son turned and approached the carriage. John opened the door and said, 'Get in. I'll give you a lift home, part of the way anyway.'

Richard hesitated. 'I have to go to a … meeting,' he said.

'Now?' John said. 'It's after four. You're very pale. Are you ill?'

Richard gave a faint smile. 'I think I'm coming down with something.'

His son was normally the epitome of health at all times and John was concerned. 'Well, you certainly don't look like you can work. Is it important? This other thing?'

'It is.'

'What is it?' John asked. Richard hesitated again and John became impatient. 'Well, at least get into the carriage and out of this chill. Come on.'

Richard got in and sat back. 'It's not important, Father, really. What do you want to talk about?'

'Right. How's the defect rectification coming along?'

'As usual. All minor, and done unobtrusively. We've only been on them two days. But we could have them knocked over in six weeks.'

That was encouraging. 'Good. Well before time.'

'It's just rectifying defects, Father. Nothing fancy.'

'But it's an essential job.' And now came the clincher, what he had to do next. 'I suppose I'll have to get you something to do after that.'

'I need to be useful, Father. But I'd like to ask something first.'

'Go on.'

'It's about my performance and my Leary's shares.'

John smiled despite himself. 'Well, let me tell you, son, since your wedding you're a different man, for the better.' Richard looked out the window. John continued, 'Your grandmother said that it was up to me when I could review your position.'

Richard looked back at him. 'What does that mean?'

'It means that if I felt you were in control of your problem, I would give you back your shares.' Richard closed his eyes and brought a hand to his face. 'You're clearly unwell, son.'

Richard shook his head. 'I'm all right,' he said and folded his arms. 'And what is your decision?'

Now, he couldn't turn back. Richard's face was pale but innocent and John had the feeling that his son would have expected to wait longer for his shares to be returned. He made up his mind. 'On account of your good behaviour and your encouraging sense of maturity, I'm giving you back your nine per cent.' Richard shook his head and held it with both hands. 'What's wrong? I thought you'd be pleased!'

'It's just a headache,' Richard said and looked at him. 'I am pleased, Father. I am. I'm just shocked.'

'Well don't be, because I mean it. I'm proud of you and the way you've struggled against your gambling. Are you seeing someone to ... help you?'

'I have a person.'

'Excellent. You can have your shares. There are no conditions. There, that's a demonstration of my faith—'

'When?' Richard. 'When can I get them?'

John hesitated. Richard *was* keen. 'As soon as I can sign the papers, a couple of days at the most.'

Richard closed his eyes and a rivulet of sweat ran down his cheek. He opened his eyes and gave a wan smile. 'I'm sorry, Father, I don't want to appear greedy.'

'Well, you'd best get home and get some attention. Now, when you get back on deck, I've got something for you to do.'

'What?'

John thought carefully. Committing himself to the share return was one thing; what he'd planned next was another. It was a risk, but a manageable one. 'I need a senior man to run another project for Mr Cunningham. Nothing's signed yet. Cunningham's wants another Imperial Hotel, in Melbourne.'

Richard's eyes expanded. 'Melbourne? We've done nothing down there.'

'I know. Turners have done the early plans,' John reached for his briefcase, and extracted a folded set of drawings. 'Miles Cunningham has allowed us to see these. I want you and Brendan to check them out, and plan the job from start to finish.' He handed them over. 'I want a report in a week. Mr Cunningham wants our building knowledge, especially fire protection, to be able to improve the design.'

Richard nodded. 'Are we preferred?'

'We are, but they still want to put it out to tender.'

'So that means Bucknells will have a crack.'

'They're on the tender list, yes.'

Richard slid the plans into his bag. 'Thanks, Father,' he said and patted his satchel. 'I'll get this back to you as soon as I can.'

'Get well first and none of your shenanigans. Don't act smart. Don't make decisions. I'll do that. Clear?'

Richard looked at him. John had seen the look before and knew an argument was near. 'I'll toe the line,' Richard said.

'Good. I'll drop you off here, if you don't mind. It's just a short walk home. Can you make it?' Richard glanced out and nodded. He opened the door as the carriage stopped. John placed a hand on his sleeve. 'You're back in the fold, son.'

'I know, Father, and thank you very much.'

'You've got a challenge to lead this company. Now, you've told me everything? There's no hidden secrets?'

Richard opened his mouth then closed it. 'No.'

John released his hand. 'On your way, then.'

Richard stepped down and John sat back. Richard had hesitated just then. Why? He hoped it wasn't anything about his gambling problem. Not now, after all this time, surely. Maybe it was just his illness.

Bill Bucknell examined the plans on his office desk. It was the end of September and they had four weeks to lodge a preliminary bid. 'What do you think, Jack?'

Jack O'Hearn, the construction manager, tapped the plans. 'It's steel again, not brickwork.'

'I can bloody see that. So, how are we going to win it?'

'Fred here,' Jack said, indicating the man next to him, 'knows Melbourne.'

'Born and raised there,' Fred said.

'So, Fred,' Bucknell asked, 'do you know the site?'

'I do.'

'Good, because you'll be the gun and you'll have to tell us how we are going to beat Leary's. Jack, get Fred here a desk and get him set up. Turners told me Leary's are favourites because of the Imperial. But we've got to get an advantage.' He glanced at the wall clock. 'It's nearly knock-off. Take Fred for a beer but be in here tomorrow at sparrow fart and get into it.' He stood up and went to a cabinet and withdrew a thick file. 'Here's all the stuff on the fire rating. Study it, and don't ask me where I got it.' Bucknell grinned at the men and waved them off.

The two men trooped out of his office and Bucknell sat back. Leary's had won the Sydney hotel with steel, luck and cheek. Well, he could price steel and sprinklers too, now, even if it was Melbourne. Bucknell grabbed his jacket and headed home.

Brendan and Richard were poring over their notes in John's Annandale office and John reached for another chocolate biscuit. No, the rich treat would have to wait, doctor's orders. Sighing, he glanced at his desk calendar, near the tempting snacks, 21 October. 'We've got nine days left to submit a tender for the Victoria Hotel,' he said. 'What did Captain Martin's final report say? They've tested the Imperial's sprinklers?'

'Yes,' Richard said, 'and certified them, including pressure testing on random sprinkler heads. All passed. We've been lucky we've had the last two months to get it in writing. The buggers have been slow.'

'But it was worth it,' Brendan said. 'The Melbourne Fire Brigade was none too keen until we showed them Martin's report. They're more open to the sprinklers now.'

'And the plumbing unions?' John said. 'Will they install them?'

Richard took a biscuit, much to John's envy. 'Simpkins came down with us. He convinced them.'

'But it's the other unions who are kicking their heels up,' Brendan said. 'They've got structure and money, according to O'Connor.'

'That's what we'll be up against,' Richard said. 'Here I'll show you.' He pulled up his briefcase, removed a wad of notes and placed it on John's desk. 'This is a list of contractors and suppliers in Melbourne, and their connection to their Associations or otherwise, plus their latest prices and labour rates.'

John felt reassured. Richard was taking on the responsibility and this was good, very good; a great harbinger for his future role, which wasn't far off.

There was a knock on the door and Mrs Mansfield entered. 'Mr Leary, it's your eleven o'clock appointment, Mr Johnson. I've placed the gentleman next door in the vacant office. The meeting room is booked.'

John had forgotten his meeting with Johnson in his excitement at this new project, and the way his team was working. 'Thank you,' he said.

Mrs Mansfield turned and left.

'I won't be long,' John said to Richard and Brendan. 'Keep working.'

John stepped into the adjoining office. A man with a drawn face and sallow complexion sat beside the table. He was not Johnson, but a stranger, and yet he looked familiar. John closed the door behind him.

'Mr Leary,' he said. 'Johnson couldn't come so I'm here instead. Murphy's my name.' The man stood up with difficulty and stuck out his hand. 'I'm the manager at St Peters Brick Company.' He glanced out the window. 'But not for long.' An odour seemed to surround Murphy, but his clothes were clean and pressed. An illness smell, perhaps.

John shook the bony hand. This couldn't be the same burly Brian Murphy he knew? His collar looked two sizes too big for him, his skin seemed transparent and his hair was sparse.

'Didn't recognise me, did ya?' Murphy said. 'Don't blame you. Do you mind if I sit back down? I get tired these days.' He eased himself down on the chair.

John sat down opposite his visitor across the table. 'Water?'

Murphy grinned, showing a few decayed teeth. 'Please. I've changed, Mr Leary. Cancer. I've got months to live.'

John poured Murphy a glass from a pitcher on the table. 'I'm sorry,' he said.

'Yeah, well we've all got to die of something. Pity it's this quick; I could have done a lot more things.'

John looked down. What to say? 'Is it painful?'

Murphy sat back. 'Good question, that. Most people would've used platitudes but you're straight.' He sighed. 'No, there's no pain. That's something.' He pulled out two envelopes from his jacket. The thicker one he placed on the table and he handed John the thinner one. 'That's an invitation for you to attend the fiftieth anniversary of St Peters in December.'

John eyed the thicker envelope. 'Thank you, we will be there.'

'I've invited other contractors, too, the ones who've made us a quid.' He paused and drew breath. 'I hope I'll make it. I'm tidying up my loose ends before I walk out of the place next week. Started in '67, twenty years ago ... a long time.'

'You did us proud on the Imperial Hotel, Mr Murphy,' John said. 'That must be something.'

'It is. We made good money on that,' Murphy leaned closer.

'And so did Leary's.' John tilted his head and Murphy grinned. 'Don't know what I'm talking about, do you?' he said. John shook his head. 'What I mean is, your boy did all right.'

'My boy?'

'Richard. Cleaned up, he did.'

John understood and smiled. 'Yes, he can get the best price for anything.'

'He can indeed,' Murphy said and cleared his throat. 'He cleaned up for himself.'

John was startled. 'I beg your pardon?'

'I'm dying, Leary. Making all my confessions. I'm telling you that Richard had me.'

'What?'

'Leary's brick orders came with a cost.' Murphy tapped the table with his finger. 'Your son got extra money for every brick that spat out of my kilns.'

'You're not serious,' John said.

'And why shouldn't I be? I'm dying. That's why I'm telling you.' Murphy finished his drink. 'Your boy did very well from us, very well. Just check out the Imperial Beneficial Charitable Trust.'

John ran a finger between his collar and skin. What was this man talking about? Was he delusional? He could be, with his illness. Why accuse Richard of extortion? Then a coldness started to fill him. Like the one he'd felt at Catherine's hospital bedside and at the ball when he'd been about to tell her that they'd just about won the big new project and she'd told him about Richard's gambling. *Dear God, no.*

'It's true,' Murphy said. 'Oh, Richard might deny it ... doesn't matter now.' He stared at his hands. 'Nothing does.'

John stood up and had to bluff. Family was family. 'I know about it. I'm also a benefactor of that trust.'

Murphy blinked, paused then smiled. 'Are you now? Well there you go. Richard didn't tell me.' He tapped the remaining envelope on the table. 'Well, that's good.' He picked up the envelope, his hand shaking, and handed it to John. 'In this you'll find the full reconciliation of the amounts paid into it.' He grinned again. 'I'm sure you'll find that the sums will tally with ... *your* books of account?'

John took the envelope. It felt as heavy as a St Peters' brick. 'Thank you. I'm sorry about your illness, Murphy.'

Murphy's mouth went firm. 'You're like your son. Anyway, it was me who was weak. Your son ... sorry, the Trust ... made money out of that. Don't worry, the secret will die with me.'

John stood up and glanced at the door to the adjoining room. 'I have another meeting, Mr Murphy. I'll see you out.'

'Don't bother.'

John watched as the man opened and closed the office door. He then dropped back on his seat and drank a glass of water. Ripping open the envelope, he stared at the figures set down on two pages. His eyes blurred but the total figure at the bottom leaped out at him: £300. Richard had never mentioned the Trust, nor had any of his staff. He jumped up and opened the door. 'Mrs Mansfield!'

His secretary came in. 'Yes, sir?'

'Get onto the accounts department,' he said as he put on his glasses and looked down. 'And get me all the details you can on the ... Imperial Beneficial Charitable Trust.'

Mrs Mansfield jotted this down and looked up. 'Anything else, sir?'

John looked at her. 'No, not for now.'

His secretary left and John sat down. He brought a hand to his face and stared at the floor. All these months Richard must have been still gambling. He had to be. Why get money from Murphy otherwise? John couldn't understand it. Richard had outfoxed him! Was it all a ploy to get his shares back?

After a minute he rose, walked to the interconnecting office door and opened it. Brendan and Richard broke off their conversation and looked at him. 'Excuse me, Brendan,' he said, 'I have to speak to Richard.'

Brendan gave him a questioning look, but said, 'Very good. I'll keep working on the tender.'

'Richard,' John said, 'come in here.' He couldn't look at his son as he passed him. John closed the door. 'Sit down. I have fifteen minutes before my next meeting. And I want you to tell me why I shouldn't *sack you!*' His voice rose in anger.

Richard was stunned. 'What?'

John was standing by the table. He slammed his hand down on it. 'What you've done is bloody disgraceful. Murphy, the Brick Company manager?'

Richard's face was guarded. 'What about him?'

'He was just in here and he's dying, but what he told me made me sick. You've been skimming, taking money from them.'

Richard closed his eyes for a moment and opened them. 'He's right, Father, but I didn't get the money for myself. It's for a charity.'

John stared at him for a moment. 'You actually did it? You stole money for your habit? Again?'

Richard paused. 'I did and I hate myself for it.'

John ran a hand through his hair and struggled to find his voice. 'And this ... charity?' John picked up the Murphy reconciliation and flung it at his son. The two sheets fell to the floor, one disappearing under the table. 'That account's accurate?'

Richard picked up one sheet and looked at it. 'Yes. It was a genuine Trust.'

John clenched his teeth. 'Richard, I don't bloody care what you call it! Did you use that money for gambling?'

Richard kept silent for a moment. 'Up to my wedding, yes, and you know that, but not—'

John felt for a chair and sat down. 'Dear God!'

'Father, during the last two years, I did at first, yes, set up the Trust to get money for the cards. But since I've married Victoria I've been doing ... as well as I can.' Richard examined the document. 'See,' he said, 'the last entry is in October last year ... 1886.' He handed the paper to John who took it, put on his glasses and read it.

John stared at his son. All these months and he'd been fooled. 'That's the first page,' John said and bent down and picked up the second sheet under the table. 'It continues Richard, because bricks were still being delivered to site. The last entry is May this year. So what did you do with that money if, as you say, you were not gambling?'

Richard looked straight at him, his eyes clear. 'At church each Sunday, I put it in the plate.'

John was surprised at the answer and then he snorted. 'That's hard to prove isn't it?'

Richard folded his arms. 'I didn't realise I was on trial.'

John glanced out the window. 'No, you're not,' he said and looked back at his son. 'All your behaviour since your wedding has been exemplary. But—' There was a knock on the door. 'Come in.'

Mrs Mansfield stood there. 'Mr Leary we have no record of the Trust you mentioned.'

John looked at Richard. 'Thank you, Mrs Mansfield. That will be all.' She closed the door behind her.

Richard kept silent for a while, then turned to face his father. 'You don't know what it's like. You have no idea.' John was about to speak but kept silent. 'You, who have no weaknesses.'

'Wait up, Richard,' John said. 'That's not the issue. You have betrayed me. You led me along all that time, just to get your shares back.'

'No.'

John stood up, his fists clenched. A tingle went down his left arm, a familiar sign. No, he wouldn't collapse, not here. He breathed in and out, taking his time. 'I said if you failed again, I'd break you to a carpenter.' He paused. *God, this is hard.* 'And that's what's going to happen. Get out, Richard. Go home and await my instructions.'

Richard stood up and looked at him. John waited for the defence, the excuses and the lies. 'Very well,' Richard said, and turned and left.

John looked at his departing son then sat down, his fists still clenched. Well, at least he'd copped it sweet. If his son had lied again he would've hit him. His stomach tightened and bile rose in him. John drank another glass of water and took a deep breath and waited till his left arm settled.

John got into his carriage and slumped back on the seat. It was only four-thirty but Mrs Mansfield would do the right thing and tell people he'd gone home ill. He held on as Gibbs cracked the whip and the carriage lurched forward. Why had he got his hopes up? And yet ... and yet Richard's performance, if it wasn't honest, had been a masterpiece of theatre: the christening, the attention to Victoria, his affirmations of responsibility to his wife and son, Brendan's testament to Richard's humility and his willingness to work with others. All a charade. Anger rose again in him as it had festered all afternoon. His son, his heir, now cut off. Distracting himself to stave off another collapse, he brought out a file on the Melbourne project and concentrated on it until his carriage reached Point Piper.

John entered his drawing room and Catherine stood up. Her face was drawn and tired.

She managed a little smile. 'Hello, dear,' she said. 'I heard the news.'

'How?'

'Victoria's been here.'

John removed his jacket and poured himself a Jameson's. 'Yes, Richard's done it again, and he's paid the price.' He walked to the window and stared out at the warm afternoon. 'By God, I can't believe it.'

Catherine came up close to him. 'Come and sit down. I've got unpleasant things to tell you, but I'm conscious of your health.'

John took a sip, its sharpness biting, and brought the bottle to the lounge and sat down. 'What things?'

Catherine eyed the bottle and sat beside him. 'Victoria told me. Oh dear, she's so upset.'

John waved her away. 'It's Richard who's to blame.'

'Victoria knows that, John. She wanted to tell me what he'd done.'

John refilled his glass. 'Catherine, I know what he's done. It's finished.'

'Please dear,' she said. 'Just for me. Please listen.'

John sat back and loosened his tie. 'It won't change my mind.'

Catherine inhaled and seemed to gather her thoughts. 'Victoria said Richard has gambled *only once* in the last two years. That's an eternity for a gambler, I'm told, and Richard *was* seeking help.'

'Yes, he told me that.'

'And this … helper, so Victoria told me, says that a minor setback is expected.'

John paused. 'But the theft, Catherine, the skimming. That's what sticks in my craw.'

'I know it's hard. And Richard's most recent loss was large—£500.'

'My God,' John gasped. This was getting worse. 'That's a bloody fortune! Catherine … before you go on. Do you believe what Victoria is telling you? Do you? She loves our son, will do anything for him.'

'I do believe her,' she said. 'I really do. She isn't denying the facts. Let me go on … *please.*'

John wanted to leave and be on his own to think, but Catherine's look was pleading. 'Very well,' he said.

'Richard was devastated at his fall. He broke down with Victoria, he—'

'Please Catherine, spare me the emotions.'

Catherine shook her head. 'Oh very well, but they're important to this whole mess. Richard loves Victoria, John, really loves her and would do anything for her. Like he'd done before, he went to the loan sharks and paid them back and their massive interest.

Now, please listen and don't get angry.' Tears filled her eyes. 'Oh, I don't want to tell you. I don't want you in hospital again.'

'You have to tell me, Catherine. Where did he get the money to pay the loan sharks?'

Catherine dabbed at her eyes and took a deep breath. 'From his father-in-law through Victoria. He couldn't come to you.'

Hughes—not that, for God's sake, not that. John dropped his head. *Would I have helped him?* He didn't know. 'Does Joseph know why he needed the money? This is bad, if he does. I'll be a laughing stock.'

Catherine closed her eyes for a moment and John chastised himself. This wasn't about him. 'No,' she said. 'Victoria requested the money from her father and told him it was for an endowment for Mark. But Richard has his pride and would not be in debt to his father-in-law.'

'Commendable. So how did he repay *that?*' John calculated the options. Richard had little security. His house? Maybe. John felt his stomach tighten and the coldness return. No ... anything, but that. He wouldn't have had the time. John sat up. 'He didn't mortgage his shares? Tell me, Catherine, he didn't?'

Catherine looked down and straightened her dress. By God he'd been taken for a fool. She cleared her throat and looked straight at him. 'He mortgaged his house and repaid the money back into Mark's endowment fund.'

John breathed out. The shares were safe, but he had to be sure. 'You believe her?'

'I asked the same thing, dear. Victoria said she would show me the mortgage document if need be. I didn't go further.'

John closed his eyes. That was something at least, but it was small cheer.

Catherine stood up and took his hand. She said, 'That's the gist of it, my dear. Richard has made a big mistake and Victoria says he's crushed by it.' She squeezed his hand, 'and more importantly by what you think of him. I didn't bring him into this life but I've been a mother to him in my own way. I'm desperate for him, too.'

John reached for the bottle.

'Please don't have another. For my sake?' she pleaded.

John put down his empty glass.

'I know he's done the wrong thing,' Catherine said, 'and from what Victoria has told me, he's paying the price in spades for destroying your trust in him. I'm sorry, dear, I'd like to talk more but I have to see to the dinner.'

John watched her leave the room. Yes, Richard might be suffering but this was all third-hand. Sure, Victoria would defend her husband; she would do more—lie for him. How real was Richard's remorse and his resolve? Had he conned Victoria into believing him? Gamblers were a crafty bunch. Possibly, but Catherine was convinced that Victoria was telling the truth and Catherine was a shrewd judge.

Despite her warning, John poured himself another whisky, its heat now filling him, smoothing his anger's raw edge. Richard's dramatic fall from grace might just be a one-off, but how could he be certain of that? For the first time that day he laughed—bitterly. There were only two things that were certain: his faith and his death.

It was November and eleven in the morning. With the humidity ever present, Brendan and his new bride posed with their relatives for photographs in front of St Patrick's, Church Hill. A crowd had gathered: Rocks people, curious at the quality of the wedding and its trappings.

As John and Catherine walked to their carriage, he saw Richard and Victoria walking ahead. These last five weeks, he hadn't seen his elder son, and that was affecting him. 'Excuse me, dear,' he said to Catherine. 'I'd like to talk to Richard.'

Catherine touched his arm. 'Remember what we talked about last night.'

He nodded and said, 'I'll see you in the coach.' John understood what she meant. *Be tolerant, or at least try to be.* He caught up with the pair. 'My dear,' he said to Victoria, 'forgive my abruptness, but could I speak with Richard?'

Victoria glanced at her husband and Richard took her hand and squeezed it. 'Of course,' she said.

'Thank you. Will you walk with me to my coach?' John said to Richard. He felt calm. Brendan's wedding this morning and his own need to talk to Richard were helping him now. His faith had jolted his conscience: it wasn't the day to have this issue hanging over them, infecting all they did and thought. 'Catherine spoke to me. She told me everything that happened to you.'

Richard kept quiet for a time, the silence broken only by leafy branches moving in the breeze. 'Father, I had no idea Victoria would say anything to either of you. I didn't send her. I don't need her to defend me.'

John believed him. 'She must love you very much.'

'She does, Father, and I her.'

John thought about his time in church during the wedding. It seemed to send a message of hope and forgiveness and he managed a half smile. Perhaps next week in the business of his daily grind he'd feel differently. 'The last time we spoke, you said I had no weaknesses. Well, I do, many of them, and I won't judge you for what you've done.' He paused. 'I just want to understand you, if I can.'

Richard looked at him for some time. 'Do you? Do you really know what the urge is like?' He shook his head. 'It takes hold of you, Father, it drives you to do things over which you have no control.' He pulled on John's sleeve to make him stop. 'When I pass a pub, I walk quicker and sometimes lately I *run* to avoid what's inside, the pull of the bet, the lure of a win. Do you know what I'm talking about?'

John could see the intensity on his son's face. 'No, I don't.'

'No, and I can't expect that you could ever understand. I have help, but in the end it's up to me. I nearly left Victoria a widow and my son fatherless because of my craving. There, I can say it now. That's what I've got, an addiction to gambling. I've finally woken up to my stupidity in ignoring the things that matter.' Richard spread his hands. 'Look, on site you or I would tear strips off a labourer for dancing on a plank four storeys above the ground. But I was more stupid than that; I put myself at far greater risk.' He looked away. 'And you've every right, every right, to ridicule and despise me.'

Richard's frankness impressed John and he felt disquiet for an instant that he'd had spies out, monitoring his behaviour. These agents had uncovered talk about a big gambling loan being repaid, and they'd claimed his son was the debtor, but otherwise he'd had no details. As long as Richard gambled, he was sitting prey to loan sharks.

'You're my son,' John said, 'and it doesn't matter what you are or what you've done, I will still be your father.' John raised a finger. 'But by the Christ we worship, be straight with me. Always be straight with me.' He paused. 'I have to know some more. I have to be sure.'

'Go on.'

He put his arm on Richard's shoulder. 'How do you manage cash these days?'

'Like my wages?'

'Yes. I'm sorry to ask but I have to know.'

'I'm not offended. My wage goes to Victoria. She then provides me with the basics I need each day. You can check with the accounts section if you like.'

That was encouraging. 'Good,' John said. 'I hope you understand why I had to demote you, son. I made the decision based on what I knew of you at the time. The future may prove me wrong, but I had to do it then, because I'm a father and you are, too; we both have responsibilities.'

Richard bristled. 'Indeed, Father. And I've made a decision. I'm leaving Leary's.'

'What?'

'It's for the best. I still want to build, but I want the freedom to do it my own way.'

John was flabbergasted. 'But you can't leave!'

Richard smiled wryly. 'It's for the best, really.'

John's voice quavered and he hated himself for it. Thank God Brendan had agreed to stay. 'Please think about it, Richard. Leary's is your home.'

'It is, but you have to leave home at some time.'

John had to do something. He had to keep Richard in the fold. A germ of an idea came to mind and he glanced back at the newly-weds. They'd finished with the photographer and were preparing to board their coach. 'We'll talk some more. Now join that wife of yours.'

John waved to the bridal party, which was engulfed with well-wishers. He cleared his throat and called out to them, 'Come on, or we'll be late.' He then got into his coach to join Catherine.

'What did you say to Richard?' she said, her face anxious.

'I wanted to tell him something and find out something as well.'

Catherine squeezed his hand. 'Good. How is he?'

John was still taken aback by Richard's plans to leave the company. 'Contrite, it would seem, and that's a start.'

'Are you going to leave him a carpenter, for ever?'

'It doesn't matter now, dear. It seems he's leaving Leary's.'

She was shocked. 'But he wouldn't, surely?'

'I think he will.'

'What are you going to do?'

'I don't know, Catherine. Let's talk about something else, please?'

'All right.' She paused. 'It was a wonderful service, wonderful.'

John felt his spirits rise. 'It was. Julie looked grand.'

'And our son.'

'Yes.' Brendan had seemed in a happy trance all through the service. John looked behind as the four bridal coaches headed off.

'Very late in the season for a wedding,' Catherine said. 'I had a few cutting comments from guests. Things like, "Early November maybe, but the twenty-sixth ... never". Connie looked stunning as always, nearly upstaging Julie. She said that her adopted baby has changed her life and that she and Bill are closer, which is nice to hear.'

John was only half listening to her, his mind musing on other things. He'd had other plans for Richard than leaving Leary's! But he'd put them on hold while his son was serving his penance. Now Richard had forced his hand. John's vision for Leary's would have to come out in the open.

He turned to his wife, the first person entitled to be shown it. 'What would you say if I decided to spend more time with you and the family? And how would you like both of us to do some travelling together?'

Catherine smiled, her eyes glistening. 'That would be wonderful, dear.'

'Good. Then you'll be pleased to hear that next year, there'll be some big changes at Leary's Contracting.'

'What changes?'

'I'm stepping aside.'

'You're *what*?'

'I'm resigning as managing director of the company.'

Catherine looked into his eyes. 'You're serious?'

'I am. I'm going to talk to my sons when we get home, before our guests come, and make the announcement.'

'Today! Why today?'

'It's the best moment to choose, Catherine. Believe me.'

Gerry stretched forward to hug the bride, something he'd wanted to do all morning. He savoured the moment, Julie's perfume and her beauty. 'God bless you, my girl.'

Julie ended the embrace and rearranged Gerry's stiff collar, which had caught up in her lace. 'Thank you, Uncle,' she said and sat beside him, with Brendan on the other side. Gerry wiped his eyes. They'd positioned him in the shade, while they waited on the lawn for the guests to arrive.

'It's just grand to see you two finally hitched,' he said.

Brendan tapped his uncle's knee and said, 'And to have you here to celebrate. Later on we'll put you at a good table and get you a full plate, don't worry.'

'Good, and sit me next to Julie's Da, Bert. He looks like a man to share a pint.'

'He will, Uncle,' Julie said and smiled. 'Believe me.'

'Lass, you might like to know that your new husband will end up the boss of Leary's.'

Brendan glanced at Julie. 'Now, Uncle, you've been at the whisky already.'

Gerry shook his red face. 'And why not? It's not every day my favourite gets married.' Gerry slapped his thigh. 'I collared your father last night, made my case for you. I gave Richard his due but said that Brendan was the one.'

Julie looked at both men and smiled. 'If you two are going to talk business, I'll leave you to it. But only a few minutes, Brendan. It's our wedding day!'

'There,' Gerry said, 'got you hobbled already.'

Julie smiled again and left them.

Brendan watched her go, grateful for her tact. He felt uneasy, talking about Richard behind his back. 'Richard has had his troubles and he's paid his dues.'

Gerry's smile was now gone. 'He has, but he'll have to watch himself for life. Brendan, I want you to help him. I think he's got the makings of a man now.'

'I will try, Uncle. I will.'

Gerry slipped his hand into his jacket and pulled out a piece of paper. 'Here. This will pay for some furniture for your Petersham home.'

Brendan looked at the cheque. 'Fifty pounds. Oh, thank you, Uncle, thank you.'

Gerry patted Brendan's shoulder. 'And buy good stuff. Do you hear me? No rubbish.'

'I hear you. Now, I have to go, but we'll be back. Julie's mother will be over to chat,' Brendan said and looked up. 'And here's Sean coming over to keep you company. Is it true you're supervising the base for the Queen's new statue in Macquarie Street?'

'Now don't go spoiling my day talking about the English monarch. Yeah, it's true, but I only did it for the poor. My fee will go to the orphans. Be off with you.' Gerry grinned. 'Don't forget, I want a big plate.'

Bill Bucknell sat opposite Connie in their carriage as it departed the church. 'I heard from a supplier that Richard Leary might go to Melbourne to build that new pub.'

'Is that likely?'

'Well, the man said he'd seen Richard in Melbourne. What was he doing there? We'll soon know because I've got connections in the city. Cunningham makes up his mind next week, I'm told.'

Connie smiled. 'I hope we win the job. What a lovely wedding that was. Now I can't wait to get to Point Piper. I'm excited for Catherine—it's good of her to host the wedding reception on behalf of the bride's parents. I'm sure she'll make it a great event.'

John closed his study door and flung aside the curtains that had been warmed by the sun. The breeze blew in, bringing the sounds of their guests' laughter and happy conversation. Unlocking and opening his desk drawer he brought out two envelopes and placed them on his desk next to his completed model ship. Today Christine's legacy, her fifty-one per cent share of Leary's, would be settled on his sons.

There was a knock on the door.

'Come in,' he said.

Richard came in and Brendan followed.

John pointed to two armchairs on the other side of his desk. 'Sit down.' Richard looked calm and Brendan smiled at his father. 'I've made a decision. From the first of January, 1888, Leary's Contracting will have a new Managing Director and majority shareholder.'

Both sons were riveted.

'Father,' Richard said, 'this is sudden.'

'I had to come to this decision at some stage. I believe that a company can only have *one* leader if it is to survive and grow. Choosing that leader has always been difficult for me, because you two have complementary skills. Richard, you're a proven industry "gun" and a major project leader.'

Richard smiled ironically. 'But at present I'm merely a carpenter, Father.'

'Noted, Richard, noted.' There was the rub and John knew it. Had he made the right choice for Richard's future? Should he change his mind? Would Richard respect him if he did? 'Brendan, you have the intuition and drive to take this company forward. If we win the Victoria—'

'*When* we win it,' Richard said and he smiled with even greater irony.

'Sorry,' John said. '*When* we win it, we'll need a leader on the ground in Melbourne.' John paused. His next step was entirely a leap of faith. 'Richard, I want you as that man.'

Richard sat back. 'Father, I told you I'm leaving Leary's. I think that's best for all concerned.'

'You'll have to change your mind, because I'm not accepting your resignation. I'm backing you to the hilt. Please stay with us and front up Leary's in Melbourne.'

Richard swallowed, cleared his throat and exhaled. 'I still think it's best that I go.'

'Richard,' Brendan said, 'stay with us. You have the experience and this is your home.'

Richard looked at them both. He seemed torn between his fear of his demons and his emotional commitment to his family. Finally he nodded. 'You make it hard, but I'll stay.'

'Excellent,' John said, relief in his voice.

'But,' Richard said, 'what happens in the very unlikely event that we don't win the Victoria?'

'Then,' John said, 'you'll be the new head of construction for all Leary's projects.'

Richard smiled. 'Not managing director? So I take it that Brendan is your choice to lead the company?'

John looked at his elder son. That was done with deftness and honour. 'Yes, Richard, I'm sorry but—'

'There's no need to apologise, Father,' Richard said, his eyes misted. 'I prefer action to paperwork. I revel in the big jobs, and the bigger they are, the better.' He turned to his half-brother and shot out his hand. 'Congratulations, Brendan. But do the job well—bloody well.'

Brendan clasped his brother's hand.

John got up, went around and stood in front of his sons. He said, 'Richard, you will now receive half your grandmother's shares, as promised.'

'Thanks, Father. With my nine per cent holding, that gives me a total of thirty-four and a half per cent, yes?'

'Correct. Brendan, up until now I've held forty per cent of Leary's shares. From today, I'm making half of those over to you. Added to your grandmother's shares, that gives you a total of forty-five per cent.' John stretched out his hand. 'Congratulations, Managing Director-elect and major shareholder.'

Brendan shook his father's hand.

'You're in the chair from January,' John said, 'and I'll be sitting at the board to give you help.'

Brendan looked at Richard. 'I'll need you both, if we're to take Leary's to where it can be. The best contractor in New South Wales.'

'And Victoria,' Richard said.

John reached back and handed the envelopes to his sons. 'These are your new salaries, plus a bonus cheque each for your work on the Imperial.'

Brendan took his envelope and placed it in his suit jacket. 'Very good.'

Richard opened his and looked at the contents. 'If I may, Father—could you make this cheque payable to Victoria?' He paused. 'With a son and all, you know, expenses ...'

John understood and his heart swelled. This was proof that Richard eschewed all cash for his own sanity. Cash was a necessity in daily life but he didn't want too much in his pockets in case he was tempted to gamble. John felt lucky at that moment: the essentials he wanted were things like Richard's commitment and Catherine's love—and he could count on them. 'Of course. The more we can do for Mark, the better. Give it here and I'll change it on Monday.'

The study door opened and Catherine looked in at each of them.

John smiled and said, 'It's all settled, dear, and I think very well.' He looked at his sons. 'Agreed?'

'Agreed,' they said together.

'Well then, come on,' Catherine said, smiling. 'Our guests are waiting. There's a wedding to celebrate.'

Acknowledgments

Grateful thanks go to Pamela Hewitt, who was the first to review the work and shape it into a good story. Bert Hingley, my mentor, raised it to another level and his insightful, pragmatic and thoughtful input was inspirational.

Cheryl Sawyer, herself a published and respected historical fiction author, managed the myriad sequences of production in a seamless way.

Final copy-editing credit goes to Kathy Mossop, who helped me greatly in nuancing and deepening the protagonist's character as he came to terms with his age and its challenges.

The images produced on the covers of the three novels are very much worth noting. Mark Thacker from Big Cat Design has done a brilliant job in capturing the mood of the times.

The builders of the colony get my thanks and admiration. Without their passion, sweat and contribution, their legacy and the world-class quality of today's built environment would not have been possible.

Historical Note

Sydney in the 1880s was experiencing a building boom. It was the high Victorian era and the British Empire was thriving. Much of the Empire's architectural style was replicated in Sydney in its monumental commercial buildings. Government and other buildings maintained their classical lines.

The ten-storey Australia Hotel was built in Sydney on the corner of Castlereagh Street and Martin Place. Started in 1889, it was completed in 1891. It was the first 'skyscraper' which in the 1880s was any building built between 10 and 20 storeys! It was demolished in 1971 and in its place was built the current MLC 68-storey reinforced concrete building with its pre-cast concrete panelled façade. In Chicago in 1885 through to 1891, 10- to 20-storey skyscrapers in steel construction were built.

The Imperial Hotel and its cost to build is a fiction but not a fantasy, as it most probably would have been built as described. The cost of materials noted and the wages paid are consistent with those of the period. The steel technology, lifting techniques, fire suppression and fire egress were all known practices. There were design and safety limitations to the buildings constructed over

10 storeys. The principal ones were fire suppression and the protection of the occupants in the event of a fire, and safely evacuating them from the upper floors. The fire-sprinkler concept started in Great Britain and was used in America prior to the 1880s, although not universally. Mr Richard Gailey, an immigrant architect, employed the fireproofing technique of galvanised iron and concrete in his buildings, much as is described in the Imperial Hotel.

Putting a sprinkler tank in the top level of the Imperial Hotel and connecting it to a series of sprinkler pipes basically mirrors the technique used in today's buildings. Passenger elevators, patented by Elisha Otis in 1857, facilitated the concept and implementation of tall buildings. The Farmer's department store, which is now a Myer store on the corner of George and Market Streets in the city, was the first building in Sydney to use elevators.

The Cochrane Hotel did exist. However that part of Day (Union) Street no longer exists, absorbed by the spaghetti strands of the western distributor.

The front cover of the book shows the Corn Exchange on the north-western corner of Sussex and Market Streets. The building still remains. At the northern end of this site is a 16-storey hotel built in the 1980s by Civil and Civic Pty Ltd, a former Lend Lease company in which I was employed as a Project Manager.

An excellent source was J.M. Freeland's wonderfully detailed book *Architecture in Australia,* which I highly recommend to readers interested in the history of Sydney and Australia's built form.

On the social front, one fascinating reference written in the era of *Succession* was James Inglis's account of Sydney and its people. Inglis was a member of the Legislative Assembly in 1885 and lived in Strathfield, in Sydney's inner-west. He wrote a book called *Our Australian Cousins*, published by Macmillan. The following references, pertinent to the story, are taken from this source and appear below.

- York Street was the place to live, especially between Sydney Town Hall and Wynyard square. Some merchants' palaces were selling for up to £30,000.

- Shop windows were small and mean. The structure of each shop jutted out into Pitt and George streets. Horses were hitched to posts and the horses were called walers.
- The taxi cabs were elegant, light in draft, roomy and comfortable. The horses were sleek and well groomed. The drivers charged four shillings per hour, nine pence for a quarter of an hour.

And of course Sydney wouldn't be the capital we know if it weren't for the consumption of alcohol. In 1878, £3,500,000 worth of alcohol was sold in Sydney. This sum would have paid for a bridge across the harbour ...

And yes, there was a period of mourning following the Prince Consort's death.

The larrikins were ubiquitous in the city and Inglis describes them thus: 'The Sydney larrikin—as the street Arab, the anti-type of the London rough, or Liverpool loafer, or New York hoodlum, is called—is the most detestable creature on the Earth's surface. Devoid of respect for age, sex, or rank, he is an unmitigated nuisance, a hateful thing, abhorrent to every right-minded citizen. The larrikins are numerous in Sydney. They are brutal cowards, who would not hesitate to rob a sick child, or steal the letters off a gravestone. They insult women, assault unwary pedestrians, defy the police, haunt the parks at night and are up to every anti-social act and outrage.'

Lassetter's in George Street did exist: it was the biggest hardware store in Sydney.

The markets in which Catherine Leary was attacked were on the site of the present Queen Victoria Building.

Succession tells the Leary story in the 1880s. Readers of the first two volumes of The Sandstone Trilogy will know that approximately thirty years separate the second and third volumes. That period was chosen for a reason. It was my intention to occupy that period with a series of Leary stories that have as background an iconic piece of Sydney architecture. Following *Succession*, John Leary and his sons will continue to mould and influence the Sydney built environment for many years to come. So I ask readers' indulgence in permitting me to undertake that journey ...

I've become a fan of Gerry Gleeson, the stone mason, to such an extent that I want to explore the struggle of how he came to be transported to the other side of the world in 1828.

The Author

Michael Beashel is Sydney-born and his Irish forebears immigrated to New South Wales in the 1860s and settled in Millers Point. He spent his youth in Bondi, is married with adult children and lives in Sydney's inner-west.

Beashel was head of Asset Development for a global accommodation services company registered on the NYSE and has made his mark in some of Australia's iconic construction companies. In Sydney, he has restored government buildings such as the Customs House and the Town Hall, and completed commercial buildings in the private sector. In SE Asia, he managed a construction division that built apartments and hotels in Bangkok and Ho Chi Minh City.

This industry—its characters, clients, trades people, designers and bureaucrats—provides rich material for his writing. He has an eye for the emergence of Sydney's built form, from the early days of the colony to the present, and a love of construction. He says about his writing, 'It's a passion. I revel in using the building industry as a tapestry to weave a great tale seasoned with historic facts and memorable characters. Human shelter is an essential need and I suspect people have a fascination for understanding its context and construction within their societies. Australia still is a young country but there are many, many outstanding building stories.'

Beashel holds a B. App. Science (Building) from Sydney's UTS and is a member of the NSW Writers' Centre. His first novel in the The Sandstone Trilogy is *Unbound Justice*, followed by *Unshackled* and *Succession*.

www.ingramcontent.com/pod-product-compliance
Lightning Source LLC
Chambersburg PA
CBHW032031120726
47901CB00001BA/145